The Anonymous Bride

TEXAS
BOARDINGHOUSE
BRIDES
★

The Anonymous Bride

VICKIE MCDONOUGH

BARBOUR
PUBLISHING

Cover design: Faceout Studio, www.faceoutstudio.com
Cover photo: Pixelworks Studios, www.shootpw.com

Published by Barbour Publishing, Inc., P.O. Box 719, Uhrichsville, OH 44683, www.barbourbooks.com.

Our mission is to publish and distribute inspirational products offering exceptional value and biblical encouragement to the masses.

 Member of the
Evangelical Christian
Publishers Association

Printed in the United States of America.

DEDICATION/ACKNOWLEDGMENTS

This book is dedicated to my editor,
Rebecca Germany, my copyeditor, Becky Fish,
and the wonderful staff at Barbour.
Thank you for believing in me as a writer and giving me
the opportunity to tell the stories of my heart.
You all are the greatest to work with.

*Whoso findeth a wife findeth a good thing,
and obtaineth favour of the LORD.*
PROVERBS 18:22 KJV

CHAPTER 1

Lookout, Texas
April 1886

Sometimes God asked difficult things of a man, and for Luke Davis, what he was fixing to do was the hardest task ever.

Luke reined his horse to a halt atop the ridge and gazed down at the town half a mile away. Lookout, Texas—the place where his dreams had been birthed and later had died. He wasn't ready to return, to face the two people he'd tried so hard to forget.

"I'd rather face a band of Sioux warriors, Lord, than to ride into that town again." He sighed and rubbed the back of his neck.

Alamo, his black gelding, snorted, as if sensing they'd reached the end of their long journey. Luke directed his horse down the path to the small river that ran south and west of the town. A healthy dose of spring rain had filled the crater dug out by past floods where the river made a sharp turn. Local kids used it for a swimming hole, and a new rope had been added for them to swing on. Memories of afternoons spent there were some of Luke's favorite, but those carefree days were over.

He glanced heavenward at the brilliant blue sky, halfway hoping God would give him leave to ride away. When no such reprieve came, he dismounted at the water's edge and allowed his horse to drink while he rinsed three days' worth of dust off his face.

Alamo suddenly jerked his head up and flicked his ears forward. The horse backed away from the bank and turned, looking off to the right. Luke scooped up a handful of water and sipped it, watching to see what had stirred up his horse. Tall trees lined the life-giving river, and thigh-high grasses and shrubs made good hiding places. He knew that for a fact. How many times as a boy had he and his two cousins hidden there, watching the older kids swimming and sometimes spooning?

"Must have been some critter, 'Mo." He stood and patted his horse, finally ready to ride into Lookout and see up close how much the town had changed. How she'd changed.

Three heads popped up from behind a nearby bush. "Hey, mister," a skinny kid yelled, "that's our swimming hole, not a horse trough."

Rocks flew toward Luke, and he ducked, turning his back to the kids. Alamo squealed and sidestepped into Luke, sending him flying straight into the river. Hoots of laughter rose up behind him as cool water gushed into his boots and soaked his clothing. His soles slipped on the moss-covered rocks as he scrambled for a foothold.

"Foolish kids." He trudged out of the river, dripping from every inch of his clothing. His socks sloshed in his water-logged boots. Dropping to the bank, he yanked them off, dumped the water, and wrung out his socks. With his boots back on, he checked Alamo, making sure the horse wasn't injured; then he mounted, determined to find those kids and teach them a lesson. Playing childish pranks was one thing. He'd done his share of them. But throwing rocks at an animal was something else altogether.

"Heyah!" Alamo lurched forward. Luke hunkered low against the horse's neck until he cleared the tree line. He sat up, scanning the rolling hills. He didn't see any movement at first, but when he topped the closest hill, he found the rowdy trio racing for the edge of town. Luke hunched down and let his horse out in a full canter, quickly closing the distance between him and the kids.

All three glanced back, no longer ornery but scared. He'd never harm a child, but instilling a little fear for the law couldn't hurt anything.

The two tallest boys veered off to the left, outpacing the smaller kid. The boy stumbled and fell, bounced up, and shot for town. Luke aimed for that one as the older boys dashed behind the nearest house. The youngster pressed down his big floppy hat and pumped his short legs as fast as he could. The gap narrowed. Slowing Alamo, Luke leaned sideways and reached down, grabbing the youth by his overall straps. The child kicked his feet and flailed his arms, but Luke was stronger, quicker. He slung the kid across his lap.

"Let me go! I ain't done nothin'." The boy held his hat on with one hand and pushed against Luke's leg with the other hand. "You're gettin' me wet."

"Just lie still. And I wouldn't be wet if you hadn't thrown rocks at my horse." Luke held a firm hand on the kid's backside, but the boy still squirmed, trying to get free. "Don't make me tie you up."

Suddenly, he stilled. "You wouldn't."

"Whoa, 'Mo." Luke calmed his horse, fidgety from the child's activity. Alamo had carried him through all kinds of weather, fights with Indians in the Dakotas, and chasing down train robbers, but one skinny kid had him all riled up.

"My ma ain't gonna like you doin' this to me, mister."

Luke grunted, knowing the kid was probably right—but then his mama should have taught him not to throw rocks at strangers. The next man might shoot back.

Being sopping wet with a cocky kid tossed across his lap certainly wasn't the homecoming he'd planned.

Luke scanned Main Street as he rode in, noting the changes made over the past decade. Most of the buildings on this end of town, with the exception of the saloon, sported fresh coats of paint. The town hadn't grown nearly as much as he'd expected it would in the eleven years he'd been gone. With the new street that had been added after he left, the town roughly resembled a capital E: Bluebonnet Lane was the spine; and Main, Apple, and the new street served as the three arms.

Almost against his will, Luke's gaze turned toward the three-story Hamilton House that filled the end of Main Street. The house, no longer white with black accents, had been painted a soft green and trimmed with white. Rachel's influence, no doubt. If he kept going, he'd ride right up to her front door.

How much had she changed? Did she and James have a passel of children? A sharp pain stabbed his chest. They should have been his and Rachel's children, but the woman he'd loved had betrayed him. Married someone else—the town's wealthiest bachelor.

He shook his head. *Stop! You're here to put the past behind you. Once and for all.*

He couldn't allow himself to think about how Rachel had hurt him. He had to find a way to forgive her so he could move on, find a wife he could love, and start a family. Pushing thirty, he wasn't getting any younger. And why did returning home make him more nervous than he'd been the day he joined the cavalry a decade ago?

The boy he'd captured found new strength and bucked several more times. "My ma will take her broomstick to you, and I'm gonna laugh when she does."

Luke chuckled and shook his head. This kid needed his rear end tanned good, or maybe, beings as Luke was soon to be the town marshal, he should just lock the boy in jail for a few hours. That ought to scare him straight for a day or two.

A man exited the saloon, drawing Luke's attention to his right. The Wet Your Whistle had been enlarged and sported a fancy new sign in bright colors, which looked out of place against the weathered wood of the building. To his left, the livery looked to be well cared for. Was Sam still the owner? Or had his son taken over?

He rode past Polly's Café. The fragrant scents emanating out the open door reminded him that he hadn't eaten since his skimpy breakfast of coffee and a dried biscuit, leftover from dinner the night before. Maybe his cousins would join him for their noontime meal if they hadn't already eaten. 'Course, he had an issue of business to attend to before he could think of food.

Dolly, twin sister to Polly, evidently still owned the dressmaker's shop directly across from the café. The spinster had painted the small structure a ghastly pinkish-purple more suited to a saloon gal's dress. He almost felt sorry for the old building until he remembered that it sat next door to his cousins' freight office and they'd have to stare at it every day. He grinned. Served those rascals right.

He hauled the youngster up, slung him over his shoulder, then dismounted and tied Alamo to the hitching post outside of the Corbett Freight Office. A man and woman he didn't recognize approached on the boardwalk in front of the building. They gave him a quick glance, eyeing the child on his shoulder and his wet clothing. The man grinned and nodded, and they passed by, but the woman puckered up as if she'd sucked a lemon too long.

"Where do you live, kid?"

"None of your business." The boy kicked again and pounded on Luke's back. "Let me down, mister, 'fore I spew my breakfast all over your backside."

Luke chuckled and resisted smacking the boy's rear end. The kid had spunk; he'd give him that much.

"Ma! Ma! Help me!" The boy started bucking like a mule in a nest of rattlers.

A woman across the street halted and looked up, eyes wide. Her hand flew to her chest. She hiked her skirts and bounded down the boardwalk steps like a she-bear on attack. She quickly marched across the dirt street and stomped up the steps toward Luke. Her bonnet shielded her face, but for a woman with a child, she had a pleasing figure with curves in all the right places.

11

Luke lowered the kid but held on to the twisting boy's shoulders.

"Ma, he tried to kidnap me. Help me!"

Luke shook his head. "That's not the way of things, ma'am."

"Please let go of my daughter." The woman lifted her head and glared at him from under her sunbonnet.

Daughter? How had he missed that?

He glanced down at the kid again. The floppy hat hid the kid's hair and covered half her face. He yanked it off, and a matching set of auburn braids fell down against the girl's chest.

"Hey! That's my hat." She grabbed at it, but he held it high out of her reach.

What decent woman let her daughter run around dressed like a boy and playing pranks with older kids?

He clenched his jaw and stared at the woman again. Something inside him quickened.

The woman's irritated expression changed. Pale blue eyes widened, and her mouth gaped like a fish, opening and closing several times before anything spilled out. "Luke?"

A wagonload of gunpowder exploding right beside him couldn't have blindsided him more. "Rachel?"

She was older but still beautiful—still the woman he'd loved for so long. Luke straightened. No, he wouldn't give the thought a foothold. He'd known he would see Rachel when he'd decided to return to town, but this sure wasn't the meeting he'd expected. He'd faced all manner of dangers in his years in the cavalry, but as he stood there soaking wet in front of the woman who'd stolen his heart and then stomped on it, his brain plumb refused to send words to his mouth.

"You know this fellow, Ma? Make him give me my hat." The kid—the girl—stood as bold as you please with her hands on her hips, not looking the least bit repentant.

Luke captured Rachel's gaze, her light blue eyes looking big in the shadows of her navy calico bonnet. He forced himself to speak. "You should. . .uh, keep your daughter away from rocks."

Rachel's brows puckered. "What?"

Realizing how ridiculous that sounded, he tossed the hat at the girl, spun around, and stormed toward his horse. For years, he'd thought about what he'd say to Rachel if he ever saw her again, but he'd never envisioned it being something about naughty kids or rocks. He groaned and shook his head. She probably thought he'd gone plumb loco. And maybe he had.

CHAPTER 2

A horse in the street whinnied, drawing Rachel back to conscious thought. Luke Davis had returned to Lookout after eleven years. Why now?

"Ow, Ma! Let go." Jacqueline pried up the little finger of Rachel's trembling hand, and she released her death grip on her daughter's shoulder.

"Sorry, sweetie."

"Who was that man?"

The man who should have been your father—should have been my husband. Rachel watched Luke enter the livery with his horse following and forced some words through her dry throat. "Just someone I knew a long time ago."

"Well, he slung me over his saddle like I was a dead deer. Ain't you gonna do nothin' about that?"

Rachel took hold of her daughter's arm and forced her feet into action. She didn't want to be standing in the same spot if Luke suddenly exited the livery. On wobbly legs, she managed to make it two doors down, where a bench sat in front of the Lookout Bank. She plopped down, pulling Jacqueline with her.

This day had looked so promising when she'd first gotten up. Who could have dreamed that one man's return would change everything? Did he hate her for what she'd done? He didn't look happy to see her, but she understood why.

Dampness registered beneath her hand, and she glanced at her daughter. "Why are you all wet? Why are you dressed like that? And why aren't you in school?"

"I'm all wet because that yahoo was soppin' wet when he flung me across his lap."

"Why did he do that?" Rachel blinked, knowing she sounded like Jacqueline had back when she was four and asked *why* all the time. But she needed to know what had happened. What had Luke meant about her daughter and rocks? "Why was he all wet?"

"How should I know?" Jacqueline's dark blue eyes sparked, and she glanced toward the street. "Maybe he likes to take baths with his clothes on."

Pursing her lips, Rachel stared at her daughter. "Don't be crude, Jacqueline." She perused her daughter's flannel shirt, faded overalls, and boots—the clothes she was only supposed to wear when gardening. When had she changed out of her school dress? The girl was bound and determined to run with the boys of the town and skip school whenever she could. Rachel twisted her hands. If only she were a better mother, then maybe her daughter wouldn't run wild like a mustang. She sighed and stood. "Let's get home and get some dry clothes on you."

"I don't mind 'em. They'll dry soon enough." With her hands on her hips, she stared upward. "Who is that man?"

Rachel walked down the boardwalk toward Hamilton House. The big, three-story home she'd inherited when her husband died rose up at the end of the street like a monument to the Hamilton family. James wouldn't like how she'd turned the place into a boardinghouse to help support her and Jacqueline after he'd gambled away the Hamilton fortune.

"Ma—aaa. You're ignoring me."

15

No, not ignoring you. I just don't want to talk about Luke Davis.
She stiffened her spine and glanced down at her daughter. "He's someone I went to school with many years ago."

"Why'd he come back here?"

"I don't know."

"Why are you so riled up?"

Rachel clenched a fold in her skirt and took a deep breath. She had to get control of herself. Guilt could be such a heavy burden, and seeing Luke again had brought it all rushing back as if the past eleven years had never happened. "I'm just surprised to see him again."

Jacqueline pursed her lips, studying her mother as if she didn't quite believe her. "Well, he'd better never haul me up on his horse again."

Rachel stopped in her tracks. "Just what did you do to him to cause that? I know Luke, and he's not the kind of person who'd manhandle a child without good reason."

Jacqueline's eyes grew wide as if she'd just been caught sneaking cookies from the jar in the kitchen. "Nothin'. I swear I didn't do nothin' to that sidewinder."

Rachel hiked up her chin. "We do not swear or call people names, young lady."

"Well, he's got no business treating a girl like that. Made my belly ache."

Rachel's gaze swerved down to her daughter's stomach. "I'm sure he didn't mean to hurt you, but you still haven't explained yourself."

Jacqueline shrugged. "We just yelled at him for watering his horse in our swimming hole."

That didn't seem such a bad thing. Why would Luke take offense to that? Maybe he had changed in the years he'd been gone. Gotten cranky as he'd aged. Still, she couldn't help thinking there was more to the story than Jacqueline was sharing. "Let's get home and have dinner; then it's back to school for you."

Jacqueline hung her head. "Aw, do I have to? I wanted to go fishing with Jonesy and Ricky this afternoon."

"We have extra guests staying with us since the mayor's family is in town to celebrate his and his wife's twenty-fifth anniversary. I could use your help. Besides, you know how I feel about you skipping school to fish and hang around with those older boys."

"You just don't like them because they're poor." Jacqueline glared up at her.

Rachel stopped on her front porch, noting that the white wicker rockers were all aligned neatly and the greenery in the potted plants was filling out nicely. Too bad she couldn't keep her daughter so orderly. "That's not true. My family was poor. Folks who don't have much are just as good and decent as anyone else. The reason I object is that you're ten, and you have no business running around with boys who are three years older than you."

Rachel held on to her daughter's shoulder to make sure she didn't bolt. Why couldn't children come with instructions? She hated the way Jacqueline challenged her constantly and dressed like a boy every time Rachel turned her back. She dearly loved her daughter, in spite of everything, but she wished that she was more obedient and ladylike.

Two boys dashed across the road toward them. "Hey, Jack, that was a close call, wasn't it?" said Ricky Blake. The tall, towheaded youth skidded to a halt, and Jonesy almost ran into his back.

"My daughter's name is Jacqueline, not Jack, and I'll thank you to remember that." Rachel narrowed her eyes, just realizing what the boy had said. What had been a close call?

Jacqueline scowled, and her gaze roved back and forth between the boys and Rachel. Her daughter was hiding something, but for the life of her, Rachel didn't know how to get at the truth.

The boys dashed past them, and Jacqueline suddenly jerked away and chased after them.

"Jacqueline, you come back here this instant!"

The trio disappeared around the corner. Ray and Margie

Mann and Thelma Jenkins all stopped on the boardwalk outside the bank and stared. Rachel ducked her head. Everyone in town knew her daughter ran wild, despite her efforts to control her.

And now Luke was back in town. Her troubles had quadrupled in a single day.

The bell over the freight office door jangled as Luke strode in. He couldn't shake Rachel's image from his mind. She'd seemed as stunned to see him as he'd been to see her again. She'd looked good, too good for someone he was trying to forget. But she was a married woman, and he'd best remember that. She'd made her choice a long time ago.

A blond man sitting behind the desk looked up with curious blue eyes, and Luke honestly couldn't tell which cousin he was. The gangly youth he'd left years ago was now an adult. "Garrett?"

The man's brows dipped. "Can I help you?"

"Yeah, I want to know when your next gold shipment is due in so I can steal it." Luke struggled to keep a straight face and was careful to keep his hands clear of his gun. Both of his cousins were crack shots.

"Pardon?" Garrett stood and walked around his desk.

Bold move for an unarmed man. Luke grinned. Evidently the confusion ran both directions. "Don't you recognize me, cuz?"

He scowled at Luke for a second; then his brows dashed upward. "Luke? Is it really you?"

Luke nodded, and Garrett let out a war whoop that brought Mark running out from the back room, holding his rifle. Though a good two inches shorter than Luke, Garrett grabbed him in a bear hug and lifted him clear off his feet. Mark obviously didn't know whether to shoot or join the ruckus.

"Welcome home, cuz." Garrett dropped him and slapped him on the back. "How come you're all wet?"

Mark's eyes widened. He laid the rifle on Garrett's desk and

18

hurried forward, his hand outstretched. "Welcome home, Luke. It's great to see you again."

They shook hands. Luke's face hurt from grinning more than it had in a decade. Mark, too, gave him a slap on the shoulder but jumped back when he realized the state of Luke's clothing. Both brothers leaned on Garrett's desk, arms crossed. They had the same color hair—although Mark's was curlier than his older brother's—and the same robin's egg blue eyes, but that's where the similarities ended. Garrett had the chiseled jaw of his father, where Mark's features were more finely etched with the look of his mother's side of the family. Two tall, muscular men stared at him instead of the lean youths Luke had left behind.

Garrett glanced out the window and back to Luke. "It hasn't rained all week, so. . ." He waved his hand at Luke's clothing.

"Had a run-in with some of the local kids down by the swimming hole. Two adolescent boys and a girl about eight or nine." Luke chuckled, remembering what a handful Rachel's daughter was. "Spunky little thing."

The brothers exchanged a look. Luke figured it had to do with the girl being Rachel's daughter. Had one of the boys been hers, too? Mentally calculating the years, he decided they were too old. He leaned against the doorjamb, arms crossed. "I can't tell you how good it is to see you again."

"Are you home for good? Done with your wanderings?" Garrett always did get right to the point.

Luke shrugged. "I'm here for a while. I'm the new town marshal."

The brothers blinked in unison, their mouths dropping open. Luke smiled at taking them by surprise again. Twice in one day had to be a record.

"Well, that's good news." Garrett rubbed the back of his neck. "We haven't had a marshal since November, when the last one died of a heart condition."

"How'd you wrangle that job?" Mark asked.

"When I decided to leave the cavalry, I telegraphed the mayor to see if he knew of any jobs in the area, and he told me about needing a marshal and offered me the position. He figured my years in the cavalry qualified me."

"Yeah, things have gotten rowdy down at the saloon. I hope you can settle them down so us decent folks can get some sleep."

Luke bit back another smile and shook his head. "Since when are you two hooligans considered decent folk?"

Garrett stood. "Look around, cuz. We're upstanding business-men now. We have to protect our reputation."

The brothers shared another look. One of Mark's brows darted upward.

Luke shook his head and chuckled. He couldn't help wondering how many days had passed since one of them had pulled a prank on the other or on some unsuspecting citizen of Lookout. "I'm starving. How about you two"—he lifted his hand to his mouth and faked a cough— "*upstanding citizens* join me for dinner?"

"You buyin'?" Mark asked.

"Sure, why not? I've got eleven years of cavalry pay burning a hole in my pocket."

Both men's gazes dropped down to Luke's trousers. He laughed out loud. "You're so predictable. C'mon, let's go grab some grub."

They crossed the street, shoulder to shoulder, like a trio of gun-slingers looking for trouble. Luke's gaze swung toward Hamilton House. The three-story structure would have looked strangely out of place if not for the two newer mansions built to the right of it.

He imagined Rachel sitting on the inviting porch, knitting or mending at the end of the day. He hoped she'd lived a happy life with James. Her lifestyle certainly was better than it would have been if she'd married Luke. The best he could have hoped for back then was to have a small farm and a one-room shack. Yeah, Rachel had married for money, and it certainly paid off. She'd probably never given him a second thought after he left town.

So much for young love and promises of everlasting devotion. Clamping his jaw on that thought, he bounded up the steps to the boardwalk.

His heart jolted. A woman in a dark blue bonnet strode toward them, head down and looking at a list in her hand. Rachel? She glanced up, and dove gray eyes met his instead of Rachel's pale blue ones. He was both relieved and disappointed. The woman's cheeks flushed at his stare, and she looked down and walked past him.

Someone shoved him from behind, and he stumbled forward. "We ain't never gonna eat if you stand there gawking at every woman that passes by."

"Now, ease up, Garrett. He's been stuck out on the frontier with a bunch of smelly soldiers for the last eleven years."

Luke chuckled with them, not bothering to tell them that he'd seen women, but they'd all been married to officers, for the most part anyway. Besides, even though Rachel had married someone else, he'd never been able to consider starting life with another woman. That was one of his reasons for returning to Lookout—to get Rachel out of his system, once and for all.

They selected a table near the front window and placed their orders with a young man Luke didn't recognize. He stared out the window, trying to get a feel for the town and how much it had changed. How many of the folks that he knew from before still lived here?

"So, tell us what you've been doing the past eleven years."

Luke stared at his cousins. "You'd know if you read my letters."

Both men squirmed, but Garrett spoke up, "We read 'em. It's just been a long while since you wrote last."

"Been a lot longer since I've heard from you." Luke lifted his brow. Years had passed since he'd gotten a letter from either cousin, but he decided not to press the issue. Most men didn't like writing missives, and besides, his cousins had been hard at work developing their freight operation, from the looks of it. "Been busy rounding up Indians, cattle rustlers, and train robbers. Making the frontier safe for settlers."

"Sounds like you had your hands full." Mark grabbed a slice of bread from the basket in the center of the table and buttered it. "You must have spent plenty of time in the sun. You're brown as an Indian."

Luke chuckled. "Not quite." He snagged a slice of bread and slathered on butter. He closed his eyes, relishing the softness of the white center, the crispy crust, and flavorful spread. "Been a long time since I ate bread this good. It's a far cry better than hardtack."

He leaned back in his chair, enjoying the atmosphere of the small-town café. He'd missed this. Folks relaxed, not worried about Indian attacks. Silverware clinked, and in the doorway to the kitchen, he saw Polly waddling back and forth, dishing up plates of food.

"Yeah, Polly's cooking is the best. Why, if she was fifteen years younger and fifty pounds lighter, I'd marry her myself." Garrett grinned and grabbed a piece of bread.

"Why *aren't* you two married? I would have thought by now that you'd both have a ring around some pretty gal's finger."

Mark turned red. "Been busy. Starting up a freight business and delivering goods keeps us away from town for days at times. Most women want a man who's home every night."

"Speaking of women"—Garrett's eyebrows waggled up and down—"are you going to visit Rachel anytime soon?"

Luke halted the bread that was halfway to his mouth. "Now why would I do that? I don't reckon it would make James too happy."

Garrett and Mark exchanged a telling glance.

Why did they keep doing that? "What? Spit it out." Luke lowered his hand holding the bread, expecting some earth-shattering news from the looks on his cousins' faces.

"Uh. . .didn't we write and tell you about him?" Mark asked.

"About who?" All manner of thoughts skittered around Luke's mind like insects swarming a lantern at night.

"James is dead," Garrett said, looking pointedly at him. "Died three years ago. Broke his neck when he got thrown from a spirited stallion he'd won in a poker game."

Luke opened his mouth, but all the thoughts that had scurried through his mind now fled.

Chapter 3

The kitchen screen door banged shut, and Rachel jumped. She pulled in a breath and forced her voice to sound steady. "Please do not slam the door, Jacqueline."

"I caught a mess of trout and bass." She dropped the smelly fish onto Rachel's clean kitchen worktable.

Rachel pursed her lips. How could Jacqueline just waltz in and pretend nothing had happened after defiantly disobeying her? "You know if you catch fish that you're supposed to clean them before bringing them in."

Jacqueline flopped into a chair. Auburn hair sprouted loose from her braids, making her resemble an old rag doll whose hair had seen better days. "Can't you do it just this once? I'm all tuckered out. Fishin's hard work."

Shaking her head, Rachel knew she had just the right ammunition for this argument since her daughter loved fried fish. "If you want me to cook those, you'll have to clean them."

Jacqueline sighed. "But I'm starving. Can't I eat something first?"

"Supper is nearly ready." Rachel used the end of her apron to pull a pan holding two baked chickens from the oven. Fragrant scents filled the room, making her stomach rumble. "Take the fish outside, put them in some water, and wash up. You can clean them after we eat, and I'll fix them up after supper. Set the table when you come back inside."

Clad in overalls and a blue plaid shirt, her child scowled, but then she scrambled out the kitchen door with the string of fish in tow. Rachel shook her head. James had always wanted a son, but only Jacqueline had lived to reach full-term. With an aching heart, she remembered the three infant boys she'd lost. Jacqueline tried so hard to be a boy when Rachel only wanted her to be a sweet little girl.

She mashed the potatoes with more force than necessary. Thoughts of James always stirred up a swirl of resentment in her heart. At least he could no longer make her feel helpless. She rolled her neck, trying to relax. She was thankful she no longer had to tiptoe around the house, worrying that she'd set James off; yet she felt guilty for her train of thought. *Forgive me, Lord, for thinking such things about the deceased.*

She dished up the turnips and sliced the chicken into pieces. Jacqueline tromped back inside, her face shiny with moisture.

"Run and change quickly into your green dress."

"Aw, do I have to?"

"You do if you want to eat, and I'm telling you right now, you're getting no pie and you will wash the dishes alone, afterwards; and you'll pen Colossians 3:20 thirty times."

Jacqueline's eyes went wide. "But why? I took the fish outside."

"How quickly you forget." Rachel tsked then shook her head. "You deliberately disobeyed me this morning when I told you that I needed your help for dinner, and you chose to run off with those boys when you should have gone back to school."

Jacqueline crossed her arms and frowned. "But I caught a whole mess of fish. You'll have extra meat to fix for supper, so I did you a favor."

The little manipulator. "It's no favor to disobey me, and in case you didn't notice, supper is ready now. Go get changed and hurry back. I've got to get the food served for our guests."

Jacqueline stomped off. Rachel hoped she hadn't been too hard on the child. Disciplining didn't come easy to her. She despised spanking even though she'd always heard, "Spare the rod and spoil the child." But after the way James had slapped Jacqueline in anger and spanked her repeatedly with his belt, she couldn't bring herself to lay a hand on her daughter, even if it meant the girl was a bit wild. Surely she would grow out of this stage as she got older. Maybe in a few years she'd think of boys as potential beaus and she'd like wearing dresses and looking pretty. *Please, Lord, let it be so.*

After serving the mayor's guests and eating, Rachel stayed in the kitchen and tinkered while Jacqueline washed the dishes. Normally, she enjoyed doing the dishes with her daughter. It was a time that the girl often dropped her guard and talked. Rachel wiped off her worktable and the stove. "Listen, sweetie, I appreciate the fish you caught, but I don't want you going off alone with those boys."

"Why?" Jacqueline crinkled her forehead. "They're my best buddies. Ricky dug up some great worms. Found a couple of fat, white grubs." Just that fast, she grinned. "Jonesy dared him to eat one, and he did."

"Ewww. That's disgusting." Rachel crinkled her lip. "You didn't eat one, did you?"

Jacqueline's eyes twinkled. "No, but if they'd dared me to, I would have."

"Don't let those boys talk you into doing something you don't want to do." Rachel stared at her child. How could such a pretty young thing be a tomboy? Why couldn't she love dresses and hair bows instead of pants and hanging around with rascally boys? She was young and naive, and Rachel had to protect her from the wiles of men—and boys. She pulled out a kitchen chair and sat down. "Sweetie, women have to be cautious around men. They're different than us. You can't relax and let down your guard with them."

Her daughter looked over her shoulder, innocent blue eyes staring at Rachel. "Ricky and Jonesy are my friends."

"Friends sometimes. . ." How could she explain that even friends could hurt you to get what they wanted? She sighed. That was no topic for a ten-year-old.

Rachel picked up a towel and dish and started drying. As soon as they were done, she could take her mending outside and sit down for a while.

"Ricky says there's a new marshal in town."

Rachel closed her eyes and willed strength back into her bones. So, her work wasn't over for the day. The marshal always took his meals at the boardinghouse, and in return for her work, which included cleaning the little house next door and doing the marshal's laundry, the town would pay her an additional forty dollars per month. The extra money would be a blessing, but it added to her busy workload. Why hadn't the mayor let her know a new marshal was coming today? "We'll need to go over and make sure the house is ready for him."

"Now? You cleaned it two weeks ago, and nobody's been there since. What's there to do?"

"Plenty. Dust, air out the place, put clean sheets on the bed. I wonder when he'll start taking his meals here." Rachel got a bucket and put a clean cloth in it. She'd have to run over and take care of things right away. Since the marshal was already in town, he'd probably be sleeping at the little house next door tonight. Her mending would just have to wait until tomorrow.

"You sure you don't want me to stay here so I can greet new boarders if we get any?"

Rachel smiled at her wily child. "Good try, but this won't take too long."

Jacqueline moaned but left her apron on and followed Rachel out the kitchen door.

At the Sunday house, as it was called, Rachel left the front door open. "Raise a few windows to let some fresh air in. I'll make the bed. You dust and then run outside and gather some wildflowers if you can find some nearby."

Jacqueline moaned halfheartedly but perked back up. "They say the new marshal is some kind of cavalry hero."

"Well, that's good. He should be well qualified to guard our little town if he's been a soldier." Rachel snapped open a clean sheet, enjoying the fresh, sun-kissed scent, and made the bed. She topped it off with a colorful bear's paw quilt she'd made the year after James had died.

The Sunday house, with its large, single room and the roof that slanted down on the back quarter of the house, giving it a lean-to look, reminded her of the type of home that she and Luke might have had if they'd married. The kitchen area had been turned into the bedroom, since the marshal didn't need to cook. If he was a tall man, he may have to duck to avoid hitting his head where the ceiling slanted over the bed. A parlor of sorts was set up in the main area with a settee, a rocking chair, desk, and table big enough for two people to eat at. The cozy place would be much better than staying in the jailhouse as early Lookout marshals had done.

Buying the Sunday house when the German owners moved farther south to be near their kinfolk and donating it to the town had been one of the nicer things the Hamilton family had done.

Footsteps sounded outside on the porch. Rachel's gaze darted around the tidy room. Everything was in place except for the flowers. She was glad that she'd come on over rather than waiting until tomorrow.

Jacqueline swiped the window sill and looked up. She tucked the dust cloth behind her and scurried over to stand by Rachel. "I saw the mayor."

"You'll find it's quite a nice home," the mayor's voice boomed through the open door. "A German farmer built it about ten years ago. His family stayed here when they came to market on

Saturdays. They spent the night and stayed for church before going home on Sunday afternoons. It's called a Sunday house, and it's the only one in this part of Texas, but I heard tell there are lots of them in the hill country."

Rachel wrung her hands together and resisted rolling her eyes. Surely the marshal had better things to do than listen to the history of the Sunday house. She wished there was a back door so that she and Jacqueline could slip out, but she needed to meet the man anyway since he'd be taking his meals at her boardinghouse.

The door squeaked, and Mayor Burke strode in. "Well, howdy there. I was coming your way next."

The marshal seemed to hesitate just outside the door. Finally, he stepped inside. Rachel grabbed hold of the bedpost; her pulse took off like a race horse at a starting line. Luke's eyes widened, and then he schooled his expression.

"*You're* the new marshal?" Jacqueline's voice rose to an abnormal pitch.

Luke eyed her daughter and then stared at Rachel. She shifted her feet, trying not to squirm. She had longed to see him again for so many years, and here he stood.

"I don't guess any introductions are needed since you two have known each other since you were in diapers." The mayor chuckled and glanced at Luke. "Guess you noticed there's no stove here. Did I mention you'll be taking meals over at Rachel's boardinghouse?"

Luke's eyes narrowed; a muscle ticked in his jaw. "That won't be necessary, mayor. I can fend for myself."

The skin on Rachel's face tightened at the irritation in Luke's voice. Her knees gave out, and she dropped onto the bed, then realized where she sat and jolted back onto her feet, clinging to the bedpost.

Mayor Burke raised his hand. "No need, Marshal. Meals are part of the deal, and Rachel is one of the best cooks around. She'll take good care of you."

Luke's lips pursed, as if he doubted the mayor's words.

"My ma's the best cook in this whole town." Jacqueline hiked her chin as if daring him to disagree.

"We should be going." Rachel's heart fluttered like a cornered rabbit's. How could she bear seeing Luke three times a day and dining with him? Evidently he didn't favor the idea either, since he looked as if he had eaten a sugarless rhubarb pie.

Eleven years ago, she'd pleaded for his forgiveness when she told him she had married James, but he'd said then he'd never forgive her. Over the years, she'd prayed for him and hoped he'd found it in his heart to pardon her for hurting him so much, but by the glare in his eyes and his hardened jaw, she knew the truth. He hadn't forgiven her, and he never would.

Ducking her head, she took Jacqueline's hand, and they skirted past the two men. At the door, she halted and forced herself to face Luke. She cleared her throat, hoping her voice didn't warble. "Breakfast is at six thirty."

CHAPTER 4

"Howdy, cuz." Garrett gave a welcoming nod.

Luke stopped next to the Corbetts' freight wagon and eyed several crates of supplies Garrett was tying down on the buckboard. "Looks like you're off again."

"Yep. We're taking this load to Snake River Ranch. Be gone a couple of days." He tossed the end of the rope across the wood to Luke. "You'll look out for things around here while we're gone, won'tcha?"

After securing the rope, Luke pulled to make sure it was taut. He grinned. "With you two hooligans gone, the town is bound to be as quiet as a funeral."

Garrett slapped him on the back. "Just keep thinking that way, and one of these days some real outlaw is gonna get the drop on you."

Luke shook his head. "Where's that rascally brother of yours?"

His cousin jutted his chin toward the other side of the street. "Over at the café. Polly's packing up a meal for us."

Luke walked around the stout draft horses, checking the rigging. He didn't need to, since both his cousins took excellent care of their animals, but it gave him an excuse to hang around for the moment. He hated seeing the brothers leave town again. Spending time with them helped keep his mind off other things.

Garrett lifted his hat and plowed rows in his blond hair with his fingers. His blue eyes stared back without the glint of amusement they often held. "How's it going with Rachel?"

Luke's gaze darted sideways at the unexpected change of topics. He hadn't told them how difficult it was being around Rachel. "Don't see much of her."

"Aren't you taking your meals at her boardinghouse?"

He shrugged, not wanting to admit the extremes he'd taken to avoid seeing her. "I usually take my plate home or to the jail."

Garrett shook his head. "James is dead, and Rachel's available again. What are you waiting for?"

Luke narrowed his gaze and clenched his jaw. Why couldn't Garrett leave well enough alone? "You know why."

His cousin's hat lifted as his brows rose. "All that happened a long time ago. She's a beautiful, young widow, and there's no reason you two couldn't get hitched now."

"There are a wagonload of reasons." Luke straightened.

"Well, if you're interested in her at all, don't wait too long. A local rancher named Rand Kessler has been comin' calling on her regularly."

Luke flinched at the thought of another man courting Rachel, but she was a beautiful woman of marrying age. It was to be expected. So why did it bother him so much?

"Y'all have a safe trip." He strode away, not giving Garrett a chance to say more. In the two weeks that he'd been home, both cousins had tried to get him to reconcile with Rachel. But they didn't know how much he'd loved her and how deeply her betrayal had gutted him, leaving him a shell of a man. If he couldn't trust the one woman he would have died for—the woman who was supposed to be his bride—how could he trust any others?

Joining the cavalry had been the only thing he could think of to keep him away from females. And it had worked for the most part.

He forced his jaw to relax. If he kept clenching it like he had the past few weeks, he'd need to visit a dentist soon. Maybe then he'd be worth his weight in gold. He chuckled and surveyed Main Street as he walked toward the boardinghouse. He lengthened his stride as he neared it, turning right onto Bluebonnet Lane. Next door to Rachel's home rose a huge white house with tall columns supporting the porch overhang. He'd heard that the banker who'd taken over after James Hamilton died lived there, and beside it, not quite so huge but still twice as big as any other house in town was Polly and Dolly's home. He shuddered at the pale pink color. What would entice a person to insult their home by painting it the color of a little girl's Sunday dress?

He shook his head. Who was this Rand Kessler fellow? Maybe he should make the rounds of the local farms and ranches and introduce himself. Yeah, that was a grand idea.

Turning right again, he made his way down Apple Street. The houses on this street were smaller, and many were not as well cared for as those on Bluebonnet Lane. He tipped his hat to a woman whose name he didn't know as she walked toward him. He recognized her as the wife of a local rancher. She was tall but not nearly as pretty as Rachel.

He uttered a growl and clamped his jaw down again. How was he supposed to get her out of his system when he saw her every day?

Forcing his mind on other things, his gaze shifted toward the end of the street where the old shack that he'd grown up in used to be. The vacant lot now served as a garden. At least someone was getting some use from the property. Just by looking at the land, you'd never know a fire had burned down his home and killed his mother. He should have returned then, but by the time he received the news, his ma had been buried a month. Maybe if he hadn't left home, she'd still be alive. He tried not to hold on to too many regrets. They rubbed blisters on his emotions.

A mangy dog darted out between two houses and limped across the street. Someone yelled, and a rock whizzed dangerously close to the poor creature. The two youths he'd chased from the creek the day he arrived in Lookout dashed across the street after the critter. Jack charged after them, trying to keep up.

Luke pursed his lips tight and marched toward them. The boys, so focused on picking on the poor dog, didn't notice him at first, but Jack skidded to a halt. Her panicked gaze zipped toward her friends, who, seeing Luke, ran off between two houses, and back at him. Suddenly her expression softened. A stick thumped to the ground behind her.

"Why. . .afternoon, Marshal Davis. Fine day, ain't it?" Jack's wide smile and lightly freckled nose made her look sweet and innocent.

The little imp. "Not so fine a day for that dog you and your friends are harassing."

"I wasn't chasing the dog."

Luke lifted his brows. "A lawman can generally tell when someone's lying."

Jack stomped her foot. "I was chasing those boys, not that dog. He cain't help it if he's hungry and muddles things up searching for food. People oughtn't be mean to critters." She lifted her pert little nose in the air.

This coming from the kid who tossed a rock at his horse? Luke squatted, giving her the benefit of height. "That's right. The good Lord gave animals to man to help him. It's our job to take care of them, and in return, they become our companions and make our jobs easier. He doesn't like it when we mistreat them, and neither do I. Stop throwing rocks and sticks, you hear me, Jack?"

"But I wasn't gonna throw it at the dog. Honest, Marshal."

Luke studied her pleading, dark blue eyes, so different from Rachel's. They begged him to believe her. Maybe she was telling the truth. "We don't throw things at people, either. You can hurt them, too."

The girl had the sense to look ashamed and nodded. "Can I go now?"

"Yeah." He wondered if his speech had done a lick of good. How could feminine Rachel end up with a girl who dressed like a boy and even wanted to be called a boy's name? He shook his head. What did he know about raising young'uns?

Tracking the dog, he found the mongrel sniffing at the trash barrel behind the saloon. The yellow mutt's ribs showed, and his skin hung loose. Luke needed a dog about as much as he needed a pink house, but he couldn't let the poor creature starve to death or be treated cruelly by others. "C'mere, you ugly thing."

The dog hunched down then trotted ten feet away. He looked as if he'd like a friend but was afraid to trust. Luke sniffed a laugh. "I know exactly how you feel."

Luke kicked through the trash, looking for something to tie around the dog's neck. Not finding anything, he marched up the boardwalk to the freight office. His cousins kept rope for tying down their freight and wouldn't mind if he helped himself to a few feet of it. Pulling out his knife, he whacked off a ten-foot length from a large roll. Hurrying back, he hoped the dog was still there and that the boys hadn't found him. He fastened a noose on the move and had it ready when he rounded the corner.

At first he didn't see the critter, but then he found him lying under one of the few trees in town. Luke tiptoed toward him, the rope ready. The dog sniffed the air, saw him, and stood, looking ready to bolt. Luke couldn't blame him after the way those kids had treated him. He tossed the rope and caught his target on the first try. The dog yipped and shied away, pulling up the slack and causing the noose to tighten around his neck.

Luke grinned. Maybe he'd just roped a new friend.

Garret drove the team away from Snake River Ranch. Without the weight of the heavy load, the wagon jostled more, but the horses were able to move faster. They should be home to Lookout by evening.

The morning sun broke over the horizon, chasing away all shadows of night. He pulled down the brim of his hat as his mind wandered to their next shipment. Maybe it was time to hire someone to help with the deliveries so they could keep the office open all the time. But that would mean not traveling with his brother, and he'd miss that. He and Mark shared a bond that many brothers didn't.

Garrett peered sideways. How Mark could read a book while the wagon dipped in and out of ruts in the road, he'd never know.

Too bad Luke had taken the marshal's job, or they could have hired him. He'd fit right in.

"Why do you suppose Luke decided to come home after all these years?" Garrett nudged Mark in the shoulder to draw him out of his book.

"Huh?" His brother glanced up, his mind obviously still in the story. After a moment, his gaze cleared. "What did you say?"

Repeating the question, Garrett took the novel from his brother's hand, knowing he'd be distracted by it.

"Hey!" Mark grabbed for the book, but Garrett held it out of his reach.

"Answer my question, and I'll give it back."

"I don't know. Maybe he got tired of riding all over the frontier, chasing Indians and outlaws, getting shot at, sleeping on the ground, and eating beans with dust in them."

Garrett grinned. "When you say it that way, it makes perfect sense."

Mark snatched back his book, found the page, and started reading again.

Garrett didn't care much for reading, except on a winter's night when there wasn't a whole lot else he could do. "I thought maybe he came back to fix things with Rachel, but I've changed my mind."

"Why's that?"

"Well, for one, he didn't even know that James was dead."

"Yeah, that's true." Mark rubbed the back of his neck. "I'm sure I wrote and told him, but he must not have gotten the letter. I feel kind of bad about that."

"It's not your fault. Besides, it's not like he'd come riding back if he'd known. He didn't even make it home for his own mother's funeral, what with mail being so slow and all." Garrett studied the landscape that had finally awakened from winter's chill. Colorful wildflowers dotted the valleys and rolling hills, and the grass was green again. The temperature was perfect, not like the deplorable heat of summer or chilly winters. Now that he thought about it, having a wife to cuddle up with on a cold winter's night didn't sound half bad. Neither did coming home to a hot cooked meal instead of having to scrounge up something after a full day's work. Maybe it was time to start looking for wives—for him and Mark—and one for their cousin. "I think Luke needs a wife."

Mark sighed and closed his book. "Trying to read with you gabbin' is as bad as trying to get a word in between Miss Polly and Miss Dolly."

"That *is* a hard thing to do." Garrett chuckled. "Do you think Rachel would make a good wife for Luke?"

"Don't be meddlin' where you haven't been invited." Mark's expression turned testy. "You'll only cause trouble. Besides, I heard Rand Kessler had his eye on her."

"That's all the more reason to find Luke a wife." Garrett held up a hand when Mark scowled. "Now, hear me out. I talked with him about Rachel, and I can tell that whole situation still bothers him. Don'tcha think it's rather ironic that he took the marshal's job in Lookout and didn't know that Rachel was a widow or that she was the one who'd be fixing his meals?"

Mark grinned. "Yeah, that is a bit funny. Though I don't think he's been spending any time at the boardinghouse. Half the time he eats with us."

The wagon tossed them from side to side as they turned off the deeply rutted ranch trail and back onto the road to Lookout.

"Well, I don't think he'll be truly happy until he settles down and gets married. And if Rachel isn't the gal for him, then we ought to help him find the right one. He is family, after all."

"Meddlin'." Mark pursed his lips and shook his head. "Besides, who is there in town that would make a decent match for Luke?"

Garrett lifted his hat and scratched his head. He swatted away a horsefly that flew too close to his face. "There's that newspaper lady."

Mark's brows flew up. "I wouldn't wish her on my worst enemy, even if she ain't half bad lookin'."

Garrett lifted his hat and scratched his head. "Then who?"

"Luke's what? Close to thirty?"

"Yeah, pretty close, I imagine. He's about a year older than me, and I'll be twenty-nine this summer. I can think of some unmarried females, but they're all too young for him."

"I know some men marry much younger women. But personally, I think it's better to find a more mature woman, not one you have to finish raising."

Garrett held back a grin. Mark was beginning to get on the bandwagon, and he didn't even know it. Looking up, he studied the brilliant blue sky. A hawk circled high above, screeching now and then. Garrett moved in, ready for the kill. "You know how hurt Luke was when Rachel married James. We need to find him a good woman. One he can love who will help him forget Rachel once and for all."

Garrett rubbed his chin with his thumb and forefinger. "What do you think about the Widow Denison? She may be a year or two older than Luke, but she's not too bad on the eyes." He glanced at his brother.

"What about her five rowdy kids? You want to strap Luke with the job of caring for them?" Mark asked.

Probably not the greatest idea. "There's always Polly and Dolly."

Mark looked at him as if he'd gone loco then schooled his expression. "I thought they were saving themselves for us."

Garrett stared at him for a moment then saw the corner of his brother's mouth twitch. "Ha! You almost had me there for a minute."

Mark hooted and bumped his shoulder against Garrett's. "Face it, brother, there's not a decent, marrying-aged woman in all of Lookout other than Rachel."

"We could always order up a mail-order bride."

Mark's eyes widened again. "You can't be serious. You wouldn't know what you were gettin'. Pretty or ugly. Nice or cranky. Old or young. She might not even be able to cook."

"I'm not the one marrying her."

"So you want our cousin to marry some woman who arrived on the stage, sight unseen?"

Garrett shrugged. "I don't know. It was just an idea. Besides, Ray Mann ordered Margie out of a magazine, and they seem happy."

"Sometimes I wonder about you. Ma must have dropped you on your head."

Garrett focused on the road ahead. Yep, Luke definitely needed someone to help him get over Rachel, and another woman would do the trick. Maybe he could check a few magazines or newspapers and see what kind of women were offering themselves up for mail-order brides. What could it hurt?

CHAPTER 5

A knock sounded on the jailhouse's open front door, and Luke glanced up from the wanted posters he'd been perusing. Jack leaned against the jamb, looking as if this was the last place she wanted to be. "Uh...Ma wants to know if you're gonna eat with us, or should she keep your supper on the back of the stove like usual?"

For a moment, Luke wished things were different, that he didn't feel as if he had to avoid Rachel. But until his emotions were less raw, this was best. Seeing her again had opened up a gaping wound he'd thought had healed, and being around her continually reminded him of what he'd lost. Why had God urged him to return? So far, it had only made things worse.

He shook his head, forcing away his melancholy thoughts. The truth was he wouldn't mind the company of her boarders. He'd had plenty of men to talk to when he was in the cavalry and missed the camaraderie. At least he could enjoy his cousins' company. "I'll get the food later and just take it back to my house."

Off to his right, the old mutt whined. Jack's eyes widened, and she stepped inside his office. "You put that dog in jail? Why? What did he do?"

40

"Stealing and being a public nuisance." Luke forced away a grin.

Jack's cute little mouth formed an O. "What did he steal?"

"People's trash. Food. Heard tell he snatched a pie right out of Myrtle William's kitchen window."

The girl's blue eyes swung from the dog to him and back. "You're joshin'."

"Nope."

Tonight she was wearing a dress, and her auburn hair hung down in two neat braids. It looked like Rachel had won the battle to tame the incorrigible child this evening.

"What will happen to him?" Jack moved closer and leaned against Luke's desk.

This was the first time he'd had a long look at her. She favored Rachel, especially in the nose and mouth, but in her expressions, he could see a touch of her father. His gut clenched. He didn't want to think of Rachel with another man. *God, how do I let go of this? Help me, Lord.*

"Marshal? What's gonna happen to the dog? You ain't gonna hang 'im, are you?"

Luke had to grin at that. "No, kiddo, I don't reckon we can hang him for being hungry. I figure he can make restitution by helping out around town."

She turned and leaned her elbows on his desk, looking at him with wide blue eyes. "He's dumber than a horse flop. How you gonna do that?"

"I imagine he's smarter than he looks." Luke glanced at the dog. One yellow ear flopped forward, while the other hung back. Scars mottled his snout, where gray hairs had started growing. "First, I need to get him fit. I've tended his wounds and figure some good food and rest should help him get back into shape."

"Don't forget a bath. Your jail stinks like dirty dog."

"Yeah, gotta tend to that tonight before I take him home."

"So you aim to keep him?"

Luke shrugged one shoulder. "Don't see why not. There's no law against a marshal having a dog."

"But he's just a mangy, ol' mutt. Homer Henry's got some pups he's givin' away. Reckon you could have one if you wanted it."

Luke couldn't help comparing himself to the dog. Alone. Unloved. He wasn't about to turn him away. "Every living thing needs somebody to love them, even an old dog like that one."

"Oh."

Luke straightened, an idea forming in his mind. "Maybe you could help me get him back in shape."

Interest danced in her eyes, but she did a good job of trying to hide it. "Don't see how."

"Maybe you could see if your ma could spare a soup bone now and then. Bring him the table scraps sometimes."

Jack smiled for the first time. "I could do that. What'cha gonna name him?"

Luke leaned back, and his chair squeaked. He placed his hands behind his head. "Hadn't thought about it. What if I let you name him, since you're going to help care for him?"

"Truly?" Jack's dark eyes flickered like blue fire, and her smiled widened. She was a cute little thing when she wasn't being a bully and trying to act tough.

He nodded.

Jack clapped her hands, and the mutt whined and ducked under the cot. Luke chuckled. Some guard dog he'd be.

Rachel set Luke's plate of chicken and dumplings and green beans on the back of the stove, hoping he'd arrive to eat before it cooled. She shook her head and sighed. In the weeks that he'd been home, he hadn't eaten with them once. Most mornings, he arrived early for coffee and a biscuit, then dashed out the door before she could finish fixing the rest of the meal. Nights, he'd slip in after she'd retired, grab his plate, and eat at his house.

She returned to washing the dishes. Jacqueline had scurried out the door after supper with a plate of table scraps and no explanation as soon as the guests were done. She'd probably taken up the cause to help feed someone's pig.

Her thoughts turned to Luke again. Though eleven years had passed, she still remembered the crushing hurt in his eyes the evening she'd told him she had married James. When he'd asked why, she couldn't tell him the truth. The shame of it all had made her sick for weeks. She'd avoided everyone and hadn't learned that Luke had left town until nearly a week after the fact. Her stomach swirled just thinking about how she'd wounded him. All he had done was love and trust her, and she'd betrayed him in the worst possible way. But what other choice did she have back then?

She washed the dishes, dipped them in the rinse bucket, and set them on a towel to await drying. After getting over the shock of seeing Luke again, she longed to talk to him, see where he'd been the past decade. But he'd barely spoken to her. Somewhere deep inside, she hoped for a second chance—that maybe God had brought Luke home so she could right a wrong—but it wasn't to be. Luke Davis wanted nothing to do with her.

She jumped when the kitchen door slammed shut. Jacqueline stood inside the door, her face bearing a pleasant expression instead of its normal scowl. She dumped the plate that had held the scraps into the sink and picked up a towel and started drying without being asked. She hadn't washed her hands, but Rachel wasn't about to mention that and stir up trouble.

"Where did you go, sweetie?"

Jacqueline glanced up, eyes sparkling. "The marshal's got a dog, and he's letting me help care for it."

Rachel closed her eyes at the turn of events. The only man she'd ever loved had formed an alliance with her daughter to care for a dog, but he wanted nothing to do with her.

"I get to name him." Jacqueline stacked the plates as she dried them. "I was thinking of something like Rover, or maybe Tramp, since he likes to dig in the garbage."

Rachel turned to face her daughter. "You don't mean he's adopted that ol' yellow dog?"

The girl grinned wide and nodded her head. "He had him locked up in his jail, Ma! Isn't that funny?"

Rachel smiled, enjoying the lighthearted freedom from the conflict that so often flowed between the two of them. "I can't imagine."

Jacqueline dried the last dish and tossed the towel over her shoulder like Rachel so frequently did. Mimicking such a little action shouldn't mean much, but it did. Perhaps if Rachel continued to lead by example, maybe her daughter would eventually model the more important things in life. She glanced out at the setting sun, wishing their time together didn't have to end, but tomorrow was a school day. "It's time for you to wash up and get ready for bed, sweetie."

"Aw...okay." Jacqueline tossed the towel over the top of a chair instead of putting it on the hook by the stove. At the hallway, she turned. "I kind of like Prince or King for a name, except that dumb mutt sure don't look like royalty."

"Don't call God's creatures dumb, please. He loves each and every one of us, even old dogs. And keep thinking. You'll find just the right name." Rachel put the towel back on the hook. "I'll come and pray with you after I get my pie dough made. Since the temperature has been so warm lately, I thought I'd bake them tonight instead of after breakfast."

"Good idea." Jacqueline spun around and headed across the hall into the bedroom they shared.

Rachel scooped flour from the fifty-pound bag in the pantry and dumped it in her big mixing bowl. After sifting out the weevils, she added some salt and sugar and stirred it together. She mixed in the water and one-third cup of lard, stirring until everything balled together. Just as she picked up her rolling pin, a knock sounded on the back door. Rachel jumped and turned, wielding the pin like a club.

Luke opened the door and lifted his dark brows. "You're not planning to whack me with that, are you? I did knock."

Hoping to hide her galloping heartbeat, she set a smile on her face and lowered her arm, hiding the rolling pin behind her. "Good evening."

Luke nodded and glanced at his plate of food.

Rachel peeked past him out the door in the waning light, wondering if he'd brought the dog with him. She hoped he could train that pest to stay away from her trash heap. "Where's your deputy?"

He glanced at the door. "Don't have one yet."

Her lips twitched, and she couldn't resist teasing him. "That's not what I heard. Or maybe I should say, 'Where's your prisoner?'"

Luke's brows lifted, and he casually leaned against the door frame, looking manlier than any fellow had a right to. "Rachel, I have no idea what you're talking about."

All humor flew out the door. Had her daughter been lying to her about the dog? What if she'd trapped a wild creature and was feeding it? Rachel clutched her hands to her chest, knowing that some critters carried the rabies. "Jacqueline said you had a dog locked up in your jail."

"Oh, that." For the first time since returning, Luke dropped his guard, and amusement danced in his brown eyes. "I tied that ol' dog up outside, but he kept trying to get away and was gaggin' himself, so I locked him in a cell. Jack thought it was funny."

Rachel straightened, turned her back to Luke, and started rolling out her dough. "Please don't encourage her with that name. She's Jacqueline."

"I figured if I called her Jack like she wants, maybe she'd warm up to me a bit. I'd like to help her change her ways before she gets hurt or into serious trouble."

Rachel cracked the spoon against the side of her bowl and spun around so fast Luke's eyes went as wide as biscuits. She wielded the spoon like a weapon. "Just what's wrong with my daughter's behavior?"

Luke bristled at Rachel's unexpected, stormy reaction. Surely she knew her daughter was gallivanting all over town with older boys. Rachel had been a near perfect daughter—sweet, kind, helpful, rarely disobeying her mother's wishes. How could she have ended up with such a wild child?

"I asked what is wrong with Jacqueline's behavior."

Luke straightened. "She's running with older boys, and I think they're causing her to do things she probably wouldn't do on her own."

Rachel's face paled, and she latched onto the back of a kitchen chair. "What kind of things?"

"The day I arrived, she and those boys threw rocks at my horse." He omitted the part about Alamo knocking him into the river. A man had his pride, after all.

Lifting her chin, Rachel glared and pointed her spoon at him. "I know Jacqueline's been with those boys, and I'm trying to stop it, but I don't for a second believe that she would throw rocks at your horse. She doesn't have a cruel bone inside her."

He thought about how he'd found Jack in the street with that stick in her hand. The jury was still out as to her true intentions. His gut said to believe Rachel, but there was a wildness in the child that could only be driven out by a loving parent who wasn't afraid to discipline. Rachel always had a soft heart, always saw the best in others. She was a peacemaker, a nurturer, and he could see where disciplining might be hard for her. "You're gonna have to be tougher than her, Rach."

Her eyes narrowed. "Just what do you know about raising children?"

He shrugged, hoping to look nonchalant. If she'd married him instead of James, he'd know plenty about raising kids by now. "Not much. I've been a soldier for the past decade, but I've learned that people rise to what's expected of them. They need rules. Boundaries. Especially children."

"Well, I have rules for Jacqueline. It's just difficult to enforce them at times."

"Try harder. You don't want to lose Jack because you're afraid she won't like you if you spank her."

Rachel puckered up like a raisin and crossed her arms over her chest. "I am not having this conversation with you. You don't know a thing about raising a girl. There's more involved than tanning her backside whenever she does the wrong thing."

" 'Foolishness is bound in the heart of a child; but the rod of correction shall drive it far from him.' "

Her brows lifted. "So you're quoting the Bible to me now?" Suddenly her expression changed from anger to despair. "I try to make Jacqueline mind, but she bucks me at every turn. I want her to be disciplined and to act like a normal girl, but I don't know how to make that happen." She swiped at the tears streaming down her cheeks. "I'm sorry I'm such a disappointment to you, Luke." She turned and fled the room.

He stood there looking at the empty doorway. Why had she gotten upset at him? He was just trying to help Jack. To encourage Rachel to be stricter.

He'd seen plenty of kids at the forts he'd been stationed at, and the ones who followed rules rarely got hurt or in trouble. The broken, bloodied body of a nine-year-old boy flashed before him. He'd told Thomas to stay away from the mustangs fresh off the plains, but the kid was stubborn. Determined to prove he was just as good a horse breaker as his dad. A brief encounter with a wild stallion had snuffed out the boy's life.

Luke snatched his plate off the back of the stove and stormed out the door, though his appetite had faded. Rachel had changed. When had she become so stubborn? Why couldn't she see that he was just trying to help her and Jack?

CHAPTER 6

Garrett sipped his coffee and studied the Dallas newspaper that a friend had sent him. He chuckled at the comical wording of some of the mail-order bride ads. He forked more of the scrambled eggs his brother had cooked into his mouth and peered over the top of the paper at Mark. "What do you think about this one?"

" *'Christian woman, 24, 5'7", thin, dark hair, seeking a father for her five children.'* "

"Five?"

Garrett nodded.

"Does that advertisement mean she's thin, or does she have thin, dark hair?"

Garrett chuckled and continued reading. " *'Has adequate house on 60 acres and $3000 in bank. Needs man willing to relocate and run dairy farm.'* "

"Sounds like she's wanting a hired hand more than a husband." Mark pursed his lips. "I bet she'll get lots of takers, but seems a bit risky to advertise that she has all that money." He shook his head. "I hope nobody takes advantage of her and runs off with it."

"Yeah. Many men would."

Mark picked up a thick slice of bacon. "Even if we found Luke a gal to marry like that one, I doubt he would want to leave Lookout when he just returned to town after being gone so long."

Garrett leaned back in his chair and glanced out the window. The overnight thunderstorm had left droplets on the panes and puddles in the street. "Yeah, I get the idea he wants to stick around here, but I don't know if he will."

"Because of Rachel?"

"Yeah. I tried to talk to him about her again, but he's touchy."

"Well, give him time. He hasn't been back all that long and has had eleven years to stew over the fact that his gal married someone else."

Garrett smeared strawberry jam on a slice of bread then licked the knife. "That's why we need to find him another woman. I mentioned that Rachel was now available, and you should'a seen how his hackles raised. Whoo-wee!"

"I still think you're messin' with fire."

"What could it hurt to write to a couple of these ladies? You might even decide to keep one for yourself."

"Me?" Mark's eyes went so wide that Garrett laughed. "What about you? You're the oldest."

Garrett shrugged. "Might be the only way to find a bride. This town's poorly lacking in females."

"Ain't that the truth? Let me have a look."

Smiling to himself, Garrett passed the newspaper to his brother and dug into the rest of his breakfast. He glanced around the kitchen of the house they had inherited from their parents. His mother would pitch a fit if she could see the unwashed dishes in the sink and the pile of dirty clothes on the floor of their bedrooms. "We sure could use a woman around this place. Maybe we ought to try to find someone to help out here a few hours a week."

"Yeah, it's filthy in here." Mark studied the room. "What kind of gal do you favor?"

49

Garrett shrugged. "Don't matter as long as she's pretty and not sassy."

"I kind of favor redheads." Mark's gaze remained on the paper as he took another bite of his toast. "You know, the color of a sorrel horse."

"You're comparing a woman's hair to a horse?" Garrett shook his head. "How romantic."

The paper dropped down, revealing Mark's clean-shaven face and sky blue eyes. He glared at Garrett then flung his toast through the air like a weapon. It hit Garrett on the nose. He jerked back his head, and after a moment of heavy silence, they both laughed.

"Okay, seriously, how about this one?" Mark tilted the paper as if to see it better. " *Twenty-five-year-old woman seeks man to marry. Must be a godly man of high character and gentle heart. I have light brown hair, blue eyes, and no visible blemishes—*' "

Garrett looked up from his plate. "Wonder what that means? You think she's got a big mole on her back like a shooting target or something?"

Mark curled his lips. "I didn't interrupt you."

"Yes, you did."

Mark shook his head but continued reading. " *I prefer a man who lives west of the Mississippi River.*' "

Garrett leaned back with one arm dangling over the back of his chair as he sipped his coffee. "Light brown hair, blue eyes, huh? Might be a good idea to order up a bride that has different coloring than Rachel."

"Aren't her eyes light green?"

Garrett shook his head. "Blue, like I imagine ice would be if it had a color."

"Oh, yeah. That's right. Hmm. . .how about a brunette? Here's one. *Black-haired/black-eyed woman, age 18, seeks husband. Can cook and sew. Prefers to marry rancher. No soldiers.*' "

"Well, that puts Luke out of the picture." Garrett stood and took his plate to the sink and added it to the towering mess.

It wobbled but didn't fall. "A brunette is a good idea, though. Or maybe we could order him a choice: blond, brunette, and a redhead."

"You're loco, you know it? What would you do with the other brides? What if Luke didn't want any of them? Then you'd be stuck caring for a henhouse full of females. This is a bad idea, I'm telling you." Mark tossed the paper toward the middle of the table. He shoved back his chair, stood, and carried his plate to the counter. "One of us needs to do these dishes 'fore we get ants in here."

"I'll flip you for it. The winner needs to take the horses over to Dan's and get them reshod before he gets too busy."

Mark nodded, and Garrett tossed the coin in the air. It spun around, reflecting the morning sunlight coming in the kitchen window, then plunked onto the floor. It wobbled around before settling on *heads*. Garrett grinned. As oldest, he was always *heads*. "Better luck next time, brother."

Mark scowled but picked up the bucket. "Getting one of those brides for us sounds better all the time. I wouldn't mind having a woman around to cook and do the cleanin' and washin'."

"That would mean one of us would have to get married." Garrett bumped his brother's shoulder with his own. "You think you're ready?"

Mark looked up at the ceiling as if deep in thought. "Could be."

Garrett lifted his brows at his brother's confession. "I guess we aren't getting any younger, huh?"

"Not today."

The door creaked as Mark opened it, reminding Garrett he needed to grease the hinges. Things would change a lot if one of them was to marry. Would they lose the closeness they enjoyed as brothers? Still, being married did have its benefits. He glanced at the paper, formulating an advertisement for Luke in his mind as he walked toward the barn. He lifted his head, enjoying the crisp scent to the air after the overnight storms. In the barn, he fed the horses and grabbed the water bucket, stopping to lean on the fence rail. "Hmmm. . .let's see."

Town marshal wants wife who can cook, sew, and clean.

"Nah, better to not be so picky."

Town marshal wants wife who can cook.

He considered Luke's height. He was a good six feet himself, so that must have made Luke six feet two. He thought about his cousin's hair and eye color. Those things were important to women.

Town marshal, 6'2", dark brown hair and eyes, wants wife who can cook.

What else would a woman want to know? That he'd been a soldier? Thinking about that one ad, he mentally marked that off his list.

Maybe that was enough. Garrett didn't know if Luke had any money to his name after being in the cavalry for so long; and even if he did, it wasn't a cousin's place to advertise such information.

What else?

A woman's looks were important to most men, but character went a long way, too.

Town marshal, 6'2", with dark brown hair and eyes, wants pretty wife who can cook. Must be willing to move to Texas.

Garrett smiled. "That should do it."

Now he just had to decide where to place the ad.

CHAPTER 7

Southern Kansas

Carly Payton's stomach swirled so badly she thought for sure she'd retch any moment. Her mount trailed a few yards behind the two horses carrying her brother, Tyson, and Emmett, a member of her brother's outlaw gang. They slowly rode into a mid-sized Kansas town whose name she didn't even know. She scanned the rugged wooden and brick buildings for the bank and found it toward the end of the street.

She studied the town again, as Ty had taught her. Knowing the layout could well save their lives later on. Several horses stood tied to rails outside the saloon and the doctor's office, while a wagon sat in front of the only general store. Few people ambled down the boardwalks of the sleepy town in the heat of the noonday sun. Carly swiped at a trickle of sweat running down her temple.

A woman dressed in calico and wearing a straw hat held the hand of her daughter as they jogged across the dirt road in front of the riders. What would it feel like to walk so freely down the street of a town without concern that someone might recognize her brother as the leader of the Payton gang?

She shook her head. What a hoot to think she could ever be a lady. Why, she didn't even like wearing dresses anymore.

Ty swung around in the saddle and glared at her as if he thought she'd tuck tail and run. She'd tried that once, and Ty's threats to either shoot her or hand her over to the gang made her too afraid to run again. Sometimes she wondered if she'd have been better off if he hadn't come for her after Ma died. At least she didn't have an aching back from bending over a washtub all day like her ma had done—or cracked, reddened hands from hot water and lye soap, or blisters from chopping wood to heat the water.

"Quit hangin' back, Carly."

"I'm not." She kicked her horse into a trot and caught up. She wiped sweaty palms on her pants, wishing she were back at camp, cooking up a rabbit stew. If Clay hadn't gotten shot and killed last month, she might well be. But a man short, Ty expected her to take his place.

They passed the sheriff's office, and she yanked her gaze away, but not before she noticed half a dozen wanted posters tacked on the outside wall. Was there one on her yet? Or had folks even figured out that the Payton gang had a woman in it? She worked hard to disguise her feminine attributes during the two train robberies and the other bank heist Ty had forced her to participate in. From under her hat, she peeked back at the posters. She might end up famous with a bounty on her head like Jesse James or Belle Starr. How much would she be worth on her wanted poster? Fifty dollars? One hundred?

As much as she dreaded the robberies, there was a strange excitement to them. Yet afterward, guilt ate at her so badly she could hardly eat or sleep. Her brother said there weren't nothin' wrong taking from other folks that had so much. Even their pa had been an outlaw before U.S. Marshals had gunned him down.

They dismounted in unison, and Emmett held the reins. He hobbled between two of the horses and stooped down as if pretending to be checking its leg for injury. Getting shot in the foot two weeks ago made him too slow to go in the bank, so he was stuck tending the horses. "Make it fast," Emmett said. "I don't want anyone getting suspicious of me out here."

Ty glanced at her. His dark blue eyes looked cold as dusk in the heart of winter. His lips pressed together into a thin line. He was probably wondering if he'd be safe with only her at his side. He jerked his stubbled chin toward the bank. "Let's get this done."

She started toward him but stopped when he scowled. "Don't forget the bag."

Returning his glare, she snatched the burlap feed sack out of her saddle bags. Making sure her hair was stuffed up under her hat, she followed him up the bank's steps, heart pounding and stomach churning. She would do her part, but she couldn't help being nervous.

Ty had taken her in after their mother died when no one other than the saloon owner had shown any interest in her. At fourteen, most folks must have assumed she could make it on her own, or more likely, they weren't willing to help the daughter of the town's laundress. Once he found out their ma was dead, Tyson had come for her. He let her cook for his gang of outlaws, although he'd nearly sent her packing after the first meal. She smiled, remembering Will, the oldest of the outlaws and former chuck wagon cook for a ranch. If he hadn't taken her under his wing, they'd all have starved. If only he hadn't been pumped full of lead during a train robbery last year.

What would it feel like to get shot? She knew it hurt, from the moans of the gang members injured during robberies. She swallowed hard, hoping nobody got hurt today.

Her brother was a cranky sort and often griped at her; but for years, he'd protected her from his gang members and vowed to shoot anyone who laid a hand on her—at least until the day she'd decided to leave.

She shoved back her shoulders and pushed aside all thoughts but the duty at hand. Daydreaming could get them all killed. Their boots echoed on the boardwalk, spurs jingled. As they entered the dimly lit building, Carly's eyes took a moment to adjust. The fresh scent of wood polish made her stomach roil, and well-shined boards creaked beneath their feet. At the counter on the right, two female clerks stood talking to each other. Carly bit back a smile. There were no barred windows on the counter and no guard. Obviously, this bank hadn't had trouble for a long while.

Ty leaned close to her ear. "This bank is ripe for the pickin'."

An empty desk to the left probably belonged to the manager. Ty had surveyed the town for ten days, watching people come and go, and had timed their entry with the manager's lunch break. Her brother might not be honest, but he was smart.

The two clerks turned toward them, and the taller woman stepped up to the counter. She smiled, revealing pearly whites with a wide gap between her top middle teeth. "May I help you?"

"Need some information on opening an account here." Ty flashed a wide grin that generally melted the hearts of any nearby females. With his black hair, blue eyes, tanned skin, and comely features, women would battle their best friend for his attention. He sauntered up to the counter, looking as if he had all day. He leaned casually on his elbows, grinning at the unsuspecting clerks, and shook his head. "I'm surprised this bank ain't overflowing with men, considerin' how pretty you lovely ladies are."

Carly rolled her eyes at the blush on both women's cheeks. The second clerk giggled behind her hand.

"I'm Miss Holt, and this is Mrs. Springer." She batted her lashes as if she'd been in a dust storm. "I apologize, but Mr. Wattenburger, the bank manager, is the only one who can open accounts. He's currently at lunch but will return soon."

Carly eased toward the wall, fascinated by the elaborate gold brocade wallpaper that blended well with the dark wainscoting. Never having seen anything so fancy, she reached out and touched the raised surface. Ty cleared his throat, pulling her mind back to their business. If she inched to her left a few feet, she'd be behind the counter.

"I'm only in town a short while. Maybe there's someone else here who could help me?" Ty glanced toward a back room where the vault was probably kept.

"I'm sorry, but Mr. Wattenburger is the only one that can help you." Miss Holt glanced at a watch pinned to the bodice of her stiff white blouse. "He should be back in less than a half hour. Could you wait?"

"Perfect. That gives me just enough time." Ty straightened and reached for his gun.

Her Colt ready, Carly did the same and slipped behind the counter.

"I'm sorry, but you can't come back—" Mrs. Springer slammed her mouth shut and frowned at them. Miss Holt gasped and stepped back.

Carly pulled the burlap sack out from under her arm and held it out. "Just fill this up, and make it fast. We don't want nobody gettin' hurt."

With shaking hands, the two women emptied the cash and gold coins from their teller drawers into the bag. They cowered together, all visible admiration for Ty gone.

"What about the vault?" he asked.

"I–it's closed." Miss Holt hiked up her chin.

Mrs. Springer gasped and nudged her friend with her elbow. "Tell him the truth. I don't want to get shot. I have two little ones, you know."

Ty narrowed his gaze and stalked to the back room, then reappeared in the doorway. "Get back here. Both of you."

Mrs. Springer whimpered but plodded forward, arms linked with Miss Holt. "Please don't shoot us. I've got children, and I'm a widow. They don't have anyone else to care for them."

Carly's heart went out to her, knowing her mother had been in the same situation.

"Hey, kid! Get that bag in here."

She jumped and hurried to the vault, coins clinking in the

bottom of the sack. Ty dumped in handfuls of money that were banded with a paper wrapping around the middle. Carly's eyes widened at the sight of so much cash. Robbing trains never brought in anything like this, although they had ended up with some nice watches.

Ty threw the bag over his shoulder. "Let's go."

Carly scurried out of the room, and Ty stopped, waving the gun at the two women. "You keep quiet until the manager returns. I'll have a gunman watching the door, and if you call out an alarm, he'll shoot you. Understand?"

Tears rolled down Mrs. Springer's cheeks, and she nodded. Miss Holt was slower to respond.

Ty stepped up to her. "You understand, Miss Holt? I'd hate for such a pretty little thing to end up with a hole in her chest."

He pressed the barrel of his gun to her bodice, and her eyes went wide. She nodded. Ty grabbed Miss Holt suddenly and kissed her hard on the lips. Mrs. Springer squealed, wobbled, and collapsed with a thud on the ground. Miss Holt looked as if she would join her any moment.

"C'mon. We need to get outta here," Carly yelled, careful not to say her brother's name. The clerks had already seen their faces.

Grinning wide, Ty stormed past her. She followed, glancing back at the door to make sure the women stayed where they were. Outside, they vaulted onto their horses. Emmett headed one way while she and Ty went the other. Folks were so busy tending to their own business that nobody noticed a thing. Bank robbing was as easy as picking clothespins off a laundry line—and a lot more profitable.

Just outside of town, Carly pulled her horse to a stop, leaned over, and spilled her guts.

CHAPTER 8

Rachel sat on the settee in the parlor sipping tea with her good friend Martha Phillips. "So, how has Hank been? Has he been very busy doctoring folks?"

"No, not too busy. With the warmer weather, there haven't been as many people taking ill." Martha nibbled on a sugar cookie then dabbed her lips. "I suppose you've heard by now that Louise Chambers had her baby a few days ago. Hank delivered their third son."

"No, I hadn't." Rachel shook her head, thinking of the three baby boys she'd lost. Still, she mustered some excitement for the kind lady she'd met at church. "They must be delighted. How is she doing?"

"Fine, last time Hank checked." Martha let out a sigh and looked down. "I wish that I could become with child. We've been married two years now."

Rachel watched a fly creep up her floral wallpaper as she considered her response. She knew that saying it was God's will didn't help one bit. "You're still young yet. Sometimes these things take time."

"Not for you. Guessing by the age of your daughter, you must have gotten with child on your wedding night." Martha's eyes went wide and her hand lifted to her mouth. "Oh dear. I beg your pardon. Hank talks freely to me of such things, and I tend to forget that such topics are not proper conversation."

Rachel forced a smile. Martha hadn't lived in Lookout back then, didn't know the circumstances around her pregnancy with Jacqueline—but then, neither did anyone else. Once again she breathed a prayer of thanks that her daughter had been so tiny at birth. Everyone assumed she'd been born early. "Think nothing of it."

"Hank is continually telling me to think before I speak, but I confess that I find it difficult. I tend to just blurt out whatever comes to mind." She lifted her cup to her lips and gazed out the window. Her eyes suddenly went wide. She stood and set the cup and saucer on the end table. "I'm afraid it's time I was going. I need to get Hank's supper on the stove."

Rachel peered out the window to see what could have disturbed her guest. Agatha Linus and Bertha Boyd barreled down the street toward the boardinghouse like a locomotive at full steam.

"Thank you for offering to make those pies for the church bazaar." Martha tied on her bonnet and reached for the screen door. "Next time, you must come to my house for tea."

"My pleasure." Rachel waved good-bye to her friend and waited on the porch for the busybody train to arrive. Visiting with Agatha and Aunt Beebee, as Bertha was better known, was always an experience, but she needed to get supper started for her guests soon. She'd have to make the visit with the two older women short, if that was possible.

"H'lo, dearie." Aunt Beebee waved her plump arm in the air as if she was at a hallelujah service. In her other hand, she balanced a pie. As she waved, the pie leaned precariously to the left. Rachel held her breath, but Beebee righted it before it could take a tumble.

Agatha smiled, looking embarrassed by her sister's outgoing

display. Where Beebee was wide, Aggie was thin. Beebee was vibrant and gregarious, while her sister was prim, soft spoken, and proper. After losing both their husbands within a short time period, the two older women had sold their neighboring ranches and taken up living in town, much to the chagrin of the townsfolk.

"Good afternoon." Rachel smiled and held the door open to allow the two women to enter.

Beebee plopped the pie into Rachel's free hand. "That there's my prize shoofly pie." She leaned toward Rachel. "Made with our grandma's secret ingredient."

"Why, thank you." Rachel lifted the pie to smell it, wondering what it would cost her. Beebee always expected information in exchange for her treats, and Rachel doubted today would be any different.

Everyone in town knew Aunt Beebee's secret ingredient was rum, though folks never let on they knew. Rachel would love to eat pie other than her own, but she didn't partake of alcohol in any form. Her boarders would probably enjoy it though.

"Goodness me. Today must be the day to go visiting." Beebee huffed past Rachel into the house, bringing with her an overpowering scent of perfume. "I just saw the doctor's wife take her leave. Too bad she couldn't stay a bit longer."

Rachel nodded at Agatha as she came in. "Martha said she needed to get her husband's supper started. I must confess that I will need to do the same soon."

"No problem a'tall." Beebee barreled her way into the parlor, bumping the end table and rattling Rachel's hurricane lamp. "We only came for a short visit."

The hair on Rachel's neck stood on end. When Beebee and Aggie's visits were short—and they rarely were—it meant they came with a specific purpose in mind. What could they want?

Beebee backed toward the settee and dropped down. The couch creaked and groaned from her near three hundred pounds. Rachel swallowed, hoping the antique that had belonged to

James's grandmother could withstand the torture it was enduring. Beebee lifted her skirt a few inches off the floor and fanned it. "Whew! It's mighty warm for April."

Rachel glanced at Aggie, whose eyes widened at her sister's unconventional behavior. Aggie ducked her head, cheeks flaming, and stared into her lap. Sometimes Rachel wondered if the women had been adopted or had different mothers. No two sisters could be any more different.

"I'd have been here sooner but have been laid up with a sore foot. It's downright impossible to find decent shoes in this town." Beebee patted her large hairdo that resembled a hornet's nest. "I just had to come over and see how you were getting along now that Luke Davis is back in town. Seems he's been spending plenty of time with your daughter. And poor Rand Kessler. Whatever must he be thinking?"

Rachel's heart somersaulted. She'd known Beebee had had an agenda for visiting, but she hadn't considered it might be Luke. She set the pie on the parlor table and took a seat.

Aggie shook her head. "I told her to leave be, but she wouldn't listen."

Beebee frowned at her sister, and Aggie ducked her head again, fingering the fold of her matronly gray skirt. Beebee turned her gaze back toward Rachel and rested her plump hands on her skirt, the colors of a field of wildflowers.

Rachel swallowed hard, knowing whatever she said to Aunt Beebee would get around town quicker than a raging fire.

"It must be hard on you to have Luke back, I mean with you having to cook and clean for the man, what with him not even being your own husband." Beebee shook her head and swung her gaze toward her sister. "Don't you think that would be difficult, Agatha—to have the man you once thought you'd marry but didn't back in town and having to care for him? Why, James is probably rolling in his grave, bless his heart."

Aggie's gray eyes went wide. She reached up and pulled the

collar of the stark white blouse away from her throat.

"Now that James is gone, surely you and Luke are gonna get back together. For the child's sake. That little scamp certainly needs a father, and I never thought that Kessler fellow was right for you."

"Bertha, that's none of your business." Aggie fanned her face with her hand. "And Rand Kessler is a fine gentleman."

Rachel jumped to her feet. "Oh, forgive me. I forgot to ask if you'd like some tea."

"Don't mind if I do." Beebee glowered at her sister and reached for the teapot still on the table beside the settee. She pulled off the lid and peered in.

"I could heat it up if you'd like." Rachel wanted to suck back the words as soon as she said them. Heating the water would take time and cause the ladies to stay longer.

"No need. As hot as it is, cool tea will be refreshing," Beebee said.

Rachel grabbed the pie Beebee had brought and hurried to the kitchen for extra cups. She glanced around, knowing all she needed to do, and breathed a prayer for patience. Back in the parlor, she filled a cup and handed it to Beebee.

Rachel offered another cup to Aggie, but she shook her head. "Thank you, but I just had some tea a short while ago."

Beebee drank nearly the whole cup, set it down, and reached for a cookie from the platter on the table. She lifted her brow at Rachel. "Well. . ."

Rachel didn't know what to say that Beebee couldn't construe the wrong way. She rubbed her thumb back and forth on the cording of her seat cushion. "Luke and I merely have a business arrangement. As a benefit of his job as marshal, I cook for him and any prisoners he has and clean the Sunday house, and I receive some additional income for doing so. There is nothing personal about it."

Aunt Beebee snagged the final cookie, looking less than

convinced. She waved a beefy hand in the air, scattering crumbs. "All of us who were in Lookout back then know that you two young folks were as tight as a tick on a hound dog. Now that that worthless James is gone, there's nothing to keep you from marrying Luke."

Rachel and Agatha gasped in unison.

"Bertha, that's hardly any concern of yours," Agatha protested.

"It's nobody's concern." Rachel grasped the edge of her chair as if she were on a runaway wagon. "All that is in the past. I'm a widow with a daughter now."

Beebee's thick lips turned up. "That Luke Davis is a handsome man—and unmarried. If you don't snatch him up soon, someone else will, mind my words."

Agatha lurched to her feet. "Uh...thank you for your hospitality, but I'm afraid we must be going. Come along, Bertha."

"But I'm not done visiting yet." Taking up her cup, she sipped her tea and gave her sister a pinched look.

Rachel forced herself to stand. "I'm afraid I must head to the kitchen now, or I won't have supper ready on time for my guests."

"Well, if you insist." On the third attempt, Beebee managed to stand.

"Please come again sometime." The words nearly scalded Rachel's throat as she uttered them, but she refused to be inhospitable, even if her guests made her uncomfortable. "Maybe around two," she said, hoping the older ladies would be napping then. "That will give us more time."

Beebee nodded, making the rolls on her three chins jiggle like a turkey's wattle. "We'll just do that. Come along, Agatha. We best be getting out of Rachel's way so she can get her cooking done. Do enjoy the pie, Rachel, and have that girl of yours bring the plate back when you're done with it. Mind that she doesn't break it."

"Thank you," Rachel mumbled.

As Beebee lumbered out the front door, Aggie stopped beside

Rachel. "I'm terribly sorry. She means well."

Rachel nodded and stood in the open doorway, watching the two women make their way down the street. The bank president had the misfortune to step outside the bank just as the ladies approached.

"Well, how do there, Mr. Castleby." Bertha was so close the banker took a step back.

Rachel held tight to the doorjamb. Had she kept her expression clear enough when Beebee had talked about Luke and her marrying? Would everyone in town expect Luke and her to get married? What would Rand think if he heard such talk?

She thought of Luke's cold expression the first few times she'd run into him and shook her head. Luke Davis no longer had designs on her. She was the last person he would consider marrying.

CHAPTER 9

The Bennett Farm near Carthage, Missouri

Leah Bennett dumped the last of the dishwater out the kitchen door and rubbed her lower back. Only nineteen, and she felt done in already. Shaking her head, she turned back into the kitchen to see what else needed cleaning before she could start working on the huge mending pile that never seemed to have an end. Mabel and Molly, her fifteen-year-old twin sisters, dried the last of the supper dishes with their heads together, giggling and talking about which of the town's boys they hoped to see at church on Sunday. The twins were the closest sisters to Leah in age, but they'd never needed her companionship.

"You two hurry up. The laundry needs to be taken down from the line and folded."

"But we wanted to walk out to the fields and see Pa." Molly drew out her words in a whine that made Leah want to cover her ears.

Leah shoved one hand to her hip. "Pa doesn't need you gettin' in his way."

"You're bossier than Ma." Molly stuck out her tongue while Mabel looked down, quietly drying the plate in her hand.

Leah turned away, not wanting her sister to see that her pointed words had hit their target. She never wanted to be the boss, but with so many children in the family and her being the oldest, she had to take over whenever Ma was tending to young'uns or something else that constantly demanded her attention.

Ten-year-old Sally shuffled in from the eating room, carrying a bowl of water and a wet rag. She placed it in the dry sink that Leah had just emptied. "The tables and chairs have all been washed down and straightened, and Ida finished sweeping the floor. Can we go out and play now?"

Leah shook her head. "Go weed the carrots first."

Sally scrunched up her face and leaned against the doorjamb. "Do we hav'ta? All we ever do is work."

Leah adopted the pose she'd frequently seen her mother use with one hand on her hip and her index finger wagging and echoed her words. "With eleven children in this family, there's always something that needs doing."

Sally stuck out her lip, and eight-year-old Ida sidled up beside her, bearing the same expression. "Andy says you're too bossy for your britches, and I agree." Sally hiked up her chin.

Leah sighed. Was a little respect too much to hope for? "I don't wear britches, young lady. You two get outside and weed the carrots. When that's done, you can play until dark."

The girls locked arms and marched out the back door, still frowning. Why couldn't they mind her like they did their mother? Because she wasn't their ma, and she hoped she never was one. Having children just meant extra work—and heartache if something happened to them. Nope, she never wanted to be a mother.

As long as she could remember, her ma was either pregnant or nursing and sometimes both. Not even forty yet, Alice Bennett looked closer to sixty. Leah washed out the bowl Sally had used and set it in the rinse bucket. Ma had probably finished tucking the youngest of her brood into bed already, but she hadn't come back downstairs. She'd most likely fallen asleep during the children's prayers.

Leah checked the bread rising for tomorrow. She punched down the first bowl of dough and then the second one, sending a yeasty odor into the room that reminded her grumbling stomach that she was still hungry. With so many mouths to feed, she never seemed to get enough to eat. Kneading dough always helped relieve her frustrations. She placed the frayed towel back over the bread and fingered a corner. Just one more thing that needed mending.

In the parlor, she sorted through the pile of clothing and picked out everything that needed to be repaired with blue thread. She grabbed the sewing kit and went outside to sit in her favorite rocker—the only one that didn't creak.

In the field next to the barn, Allan and Andy, her younger brothers, led the two cows toward the barn where they'd be fed and milked. There was plenty of work on a farm the size of the Bennetts', but there was a soothing rhythm to it. She selected a baby gown and found the place where her youngest brother, still a crawler, had snagged it on a loose floorboard. She cut a tiny patch from some scrap material and quickly stitched it over the tear.

Giggling preceded Mabel and Molly a short while later as they bounced out the front door and flopped down on the steps. "Tell her." Molly nudged her twin.

"Tell me what?" Leah folded the mended gown and laid it in the rocker next to her. She picked up a colonial blue shirt with loose buttons that belonged to three-year-old Micah. In the fields past the barn, she saw her father walking behind the huge draft horses, plowing.

"Nooo, you do it." Mabel shook her head and wrung her hands.

Molly grinned. "Sue Anne Carter is going to be a mail-order bride. She's got a magazine with ads in it, and she's studying them for a husband."

Leah blinked, and her mending dropped to her lap. There were advertisements where one could find a husband? "Why would she do such a ridiculous thing? Sue Anne could have any man she wanted."

Mabel piped up now that Molly had brokered the subject. "Maybe she wants to get away from her strict father, or maybe she wants an adventure."

The image of Sam Braddock rose in Leah's mind, as handsome and strong as any man she'd known. He'd been the only male to ever capture her heart, and he'd returned the attraction. But he died when influenza ravished the neighboring town, killing Leah's dreams. She placed her hand over her heart. Even after a year, the pain still felt fresh. She remembered her eagerness to marry Sam as the days to their wedding had drawn closer. Instead, Sam had been buried that day.

She shook her thoughts back to her best friend. Sue Anne hadn't mentioned anything to her about being a mail-order bride. And how could she consider traveling hundreds of miles to marry a man she'd never met? Seemed like a recipe for disaster.

The twins were huddled together, whispering, but Leah could still hear them. "Tell her the rest," Molly whispered.

"Nooo, we ain't supposed to know. Remember?" Mabel crossed her arms and flipped her long brown braids behind her.

Leah looked back at Molly and leaned forward. The little busybody never could keep a secret.

Molly glanced at Mabel. Guilt marched across her face, but her eyes twinkled with mischief. She stood up and swung her faded skirt back and forth as if she were dancing. "Mr. Abernathy is buying you from Pa."

"Mo–ll–y!" Mabel jumped up, her gaze darting to the field where their father worked. "Pa is gonna be furious with you for telling."

Leah's hands dropped to her lap like lead weights. Mr. Abernathy was. . .old. And fat. And had hair growing out of his nose and ears. "Wh–what do you mean, buying me?"

Proud that she knew something her big sister didn't, Molly puffed up like a toad. "Mr. Abernathy wanted *me*." She shuddered, as if the thought repulsed her. "But Pa said I was too young to marry and that he could have you instead. Pa said he had too many mouths to feed. Am I ever glad, for once, that I ain't the oldest."

"I don't believe you." Leah glanced at Mabel. Seeing the confirmation in her sister's brown eyes, her heart jolted, Molly might lie, but Mabel couldn't. Needing to get away by herself, Leah stood. "Did you two finish the laundry?"

Evidently realizing they'd said enough, the twins fled down the stairs and around the side of the house without answering. Pa was selling her like some. . .old cow? Shock pulled Leah back down into the rocker. He wanted to be rid of her because he had too many mouths to feed. Hadn't she proven her worth by taking up the slack when Ma needed help and working from before sunup to past dusk? How would Ma manage without her?

Tears stung her eyes. Hurbert Abernathy had to be forty. More than twice her age. He was an obese, smelly man, and the whole town knew he preferred gambling to working. How could her father agree to let her marry someone like that? Even if it did help the family.

Tears trailed down her cheeks. Once Pa made up his mind, he wouldn't be swayed. What could she do? She had no money. Nowhere to go.

Maybe she should visit Sue Anne and have a look at that magazine. Could marrying a stranger be any worse than being forced to wed Hurbert Abernathy? Funny, how an idea could sound outlandish one moment but seem perfectly sane the next because of desperation.

She stood, gathered the mending, and carried it back into the parlor. A lump the size of a goose egg made it hard for her to swallow. If she wasn't appreciated for all the work she put into this family, then she would leave. Tomorrow, she'd pay Sue Anne a visit.

Lookout, Texas

Shuffling sounded outside the open door of the marshal's office, pulling Luke's gaze away from the rifle he was cleaning. The yellow dog lifted up his head, sniffed the air, lumbered up from his spot near Luke's desk, and wagged his tail. The mutt whined and stepped forward as a girl stopped in the doorway.

Jack stood just inside the jail, dressed in a dark green calico dress with her braids hanging down the front. Her lunch bucket hung from one hand while she clutched a book to her chest with the other. The dog sniffed her pail and then stuck his head under her hand. Jack set down the tin bucket and scratched his head. Luke grinned as the old dog closed his eyes, looking contented and loved.

"Well, now, don't you look pretty."

Her cheeks turned red, but then she curled her lip and twisted her mouth up on one side. "Uh huh, and this ugly, ol' dog is purty, too." She crossed her arms over her chest, and the mutt looked up longingly. After a moment, he flopped down, lying his head on Jack's shoe, probably dreaming of the tasty table scraps the girl often brought him.

Luke studied Jack. What had happened to make such a young girl so jaded? He knew Rachel was a loving mother, so that only left her father. Or maybe she acted out because she'd lost her father. He leaned forward, catching her eye. "You *are* a pretty girl. Why I've known women who'd give just about anything to have auburn hair like yours."

Jack picked up one of her braids, looked at it, then dropped it as if it had burned her. "Yeah, then why do the kids tease me for having red hair? It ain't even red. More like brownish. Sort of."

Luke leaned his rifle against the wall, wiped his hands on an old towel, and stood. "Some kids always tease. When I was your age, I was real tall and skinny, and a boy in my class took to calling me chicken legs."

Jack looked on with interest, her blue eyes intent. "What did you do?"

Oops. He couldn't exactly tell her he'd waited after school and took that bully down a few notches. He shrugged. "Best thing to do is just ignore them."

Jack's lips curled again. "That's hard. Sometimes I just want to punch them."

"And is this person bigger than you? A boy?"

She nodded.

"Want me to talk to him?"

Jack's gaze sparked but then dulled. "No, but thanks. If you do anything, it'll make things worse. You can't be around all the time, and besides, you're not my pa."

She had no idea how much that comment poured salt into past wounds.

Luke sat on the chair across from Jack. "I was sorry to hear about your father dying."

Jack scowled. "I wasn't, so why should you be?"

Taken aback by her comment, he studied her as she stooped down to pet the dog. What would cause a child not to grieve over the loss of her father? Being the only child of a wealthy couple, James had been cocky and spoiled, but never cruel—although at times, he had bordered on it. Luke wanted to ask if her father had hurt her or Rachel, but it wasn't a topic to be broached with a child. Maybe his cousins could shed some light on that subject.

"I was wondering something." Jack kept her gaze down.

"What's that?"

She glanced up, nibbled her lower lip, then looked out the door. "Would you teach me to box?"

Luke tried to keep his expression straight. Wouldn't Rachel

love that? "Uh. . .I'm not sure that's a good idea."

"Why not?" She gazed up with innocent blue eyes, making him wish he could protect her from all the pains of the world.

"Because if you get in a fight, especially with someone bigger, you could get hurt."

"I get hurt anyway."

"Jack, you let me know if anyone bothers you, and I'll take care of it. All right?"

The girl studied him as if she didn't quite trust him, but she nodded. Relief washed through Luke. Some kids were just plain mean and wouldn't have a second thought about hurting a girl. He searched his mind for a lighter topic of conversation. "Have you thought up a name for this old dog yet?"

Jack lifted her head and smiled, revealing white teeth with a tiny gap between the middle two. "Took me a while. I thought about Prince or King, but those names just don't seem to fit him. Then I thought maybe we should call him Bandit since he likes to steal stuff from trash heaps."

"He's reformed his ways after being in jail for a few days."

Jack giggled and flopped onto the floor next to the dog. "Or maybe because you and me's feeding him every day." A wicked gleam entered her eyes. "I thought about maybe calling him Stinky, because. . .well, you know how the jail smells a while after he's eaten."

Luke chuckled and rolled his eyes. "Why do you think I leave the door open so often?"

Grinning again, Jack patted the dog, whose head now rested in her lap. She glanced up, vulnerability showing in her gaze. "I decided on Max. What do you think?"

"Max, hmm. . .I like it. Not too high and mighty, and not something he'd be ashamed of. Good choice."

She looked relieved. "Well, I suppose I should get along home. Ma probably has chores for me to do, though I'd rather go fishin' with Ricky and Jonesy."

Luke leaned forward, his elbows on his knees. "Those fellows are a bit old for you to be running around with, aren't they?"

She lifted one shoulder then dropped it down. "They're fun. Besides, the girls I know only want to play school or house."

"What's wrong with that?"

Jack's eyes went wide. "It's girl stuff. I like to fish and hunt and do what the boys do."

"Uh, has anyone told you that you *are* a girl?"

Jack stood, evidently not liking the turn of conversation. "Ma tells me all the time. I just wish. . ."

She didn't finish her sentence, and he sat still, hoping to learn what motivated her to dress like a boy and to run with them. "Wish what?"

Her eyes took on a sheen, and she batted them as if she had dust in them. "That God had made me a boy instead of a girl."

Luke opened his mouth to respond, but she tore out of the jailhouse as if a colony of wasps were on her tail. He flopped back in his chair. Max whined and stared out the door before coming over to sit by him.

Why would such a cute little girl want to be a boy?

Rachel opened the windows of the library, allowing the warm May breeze to flutter the curtains and air out the room. She looked forward to Tuesday afternoons when the ladies of town would gather just after lunchtime in her library. Since the huge house also had a parlor, she had gladly offered use of this room so that the quilt frame could remain up until the product was finished. The room was so large that her guests still had plenty of space to peruse the vast number of books that James's mother had been so proud of.

She removed the towels covering the raisin bread and sugar cookies and went to the kitchen to get the coffeepot. The ladies would start arriving anytime, and she wanted to have everything ready. As she entered the kitchen, a knock sounded on the front door, sending her spinning around to answer it. She pulled the door open and smiled. "Sylvia, Margie, I'm so glad you could come today." She stood aside, holding open the screen door to allow the pastor's wife and Mrs. Mann to enter.

Sylvia's gaze wandered up the showy staircase with its spindle balusters and wide steps. "You have such a lovely home."

"That Amelia Hamilton sure did know how to fancy up a room." Margie never failed to remind people that her good friend had once owned and decorated Hamilton House.

Ignoring the jibe, Rachel forced a smiled. Though she'd redecorated the upstairs bedrooms and had the outside repainted, Margie seemed to take pleasure in reminding everyone that the older Mrs. Hamilton had first decorated the big home. "Would you care for some tea or coffee while we're waiting on the other ladies?" Rachel gestured toward the library's open french doors. Another knock sounded. Agatha stood on the other side of the screen door, fidgeting and looking over her shoulder.

"Is everything all right, Aggie?" Rachel looked past her but saw nothing except the normal activities of the peaceful town: a wagon rolling up Main Street, two cowboys talking outside the mercantile, Luke ambling along in front of the bank with Max trotting at his side. She pressed her hand to her chest where her heart had started galloping and forced her attention back to her guest.

Aggie wrung her hands and leaned forward as if preparing to share a big secret. "Bertha's down for her afternoon nap, and I slipped out. I'm hoping the door didn't wake her when the wind caught it and made it slam shut." The thin woman pressed her lips together and peered over her shoulder again.

"C'mon in. Sylvia and Margie are already here." Rachel's heart went out to the older woman. Having Aunt Beebee visit for an hour was almost more than she could cope with. She couldn't imagine how difficult it must be to live with the talkative, opinionated woman. She held her hand out toward the library. "Please find a seat while I get the coffee."

In the kitchen, Rachel removed her apron, wrapped a towel around the handle of the coffeepot, and carried it into the library. She poured three cups then set the pot on a trivet on the table in the corner where the lamp rested. "The coffee is ready, and I have some raisin bread and sugar cookies if you'd like some."

"That sounds delightful," said Sylvia, as she stood and made her way toward the table with the other two ladies following like ducklings.

Another knock pulled Rachel back into the entryway. "Martha! I'm so glad you could come today."

"Me, too. Hank didn't have any emergencies where he needed my assistance. He's just studying his medical books, so I told him I was going to the quilting bee. I brought some of Aunt Maude's oatmeal cookies."

"Thank you. It's always a treat to get to eat someone else's cooking." She stepped back to let her friend enter.

"I, for one, think you shouldn't have to provide refreshments other than coffee, which would be difficult for someone else to bring, since you host us each week and allow us to leave the quilt frame up. That makes the stitching so much easier."

Rachel hugged Martha's shoulders, grateful for a friend who was thoughtful enough to look out for her well-being. "Three ladies have arrived so far."

"That's a nice group."

Rachel set the plate of cookies beside her bread and helped herself to two of them. She took a seat on one of the chairs she'd pulled in from the dining room. Immediately, Margie Mann's gaze turned to hers, and the bite of cookie lodged in Rachel's throat. No subject was sacred with Margie around.

"So, how do you like having Luke Davis back in town?"

Aggie's eyes grew wide. Martha and Sylvia, who were fairly new to town, missed the ramifications of that question.

"I don't think that's a topic that should be broached here," Aggie said.

Margie swatted her hand through the air. "Oh, pish-posh. It's a perfectly fine subject. He seems to be doing a decent job as marshal, though we hardly need one as quiet as our town is."

Maybe Rachel could satisfy Margie's curiosity without venturing too far into deep waters. "I hardly see the man."

"Nonsense. You cook him three meals a day, clean his house, and do his laundry. How is that possible if you don't see him?"

It was hardly any of Margie's affair, but Rachel knew the woman would poke and prod until she was satisfied. "I do fix Luke's breakfast and dinner, but he prefers to eat at his house. I pack him a lunch, which he picks up at breakfast, and he eats that at the jail, as far as I know. I do my cleaning while he's away, so I only see him if I run into him walking around town."

Sylvia's gaze went back and forth between the two women, looking as if she'd missed something. "Why should Rachel care what the marshal does?"

A gleam lit Margie's eyes, and she leaned forward. "Luke and Rachel have a. . .past." She whispered the last word. "Everyone in Lookout thought for sure they'd marry up one day, but she jilted him for James Hamilton."

Sylvia glanced at Rachel, an apology in her eyes. Rachel wanted to talk to the minister's wife about Luke and her remaining feelings for him but hadn't had the chance yet.

Martha stood, helped herself to another cookie, and then stopped next to Rachel's chair. "I'm sure Rachel didn't jilt Luke. She's not capable of such an action."

"She married for money, that's what Ray's ma always said. Shucked that young Davis boy and broke his heart so badly that he left town." Margie paused to sip her coffee. "The thing is, I can't figure out why he'd come back here after so long. I bet that just irritates Rand Kessler to no end."

Aggie looked as if she were about to faint. The woman never

gossiped and had a heart as big as all of Texas. "I. . .I. . .uh. . .nice weather we've been having lately, isn't it?"

"Why, yes it is, Agatha," Sylvia rushed to pick up the new train of conversation. "Just perfect. Not too hot, not too cold, and the wildflowers are so lovely."

Margie looked as if she'd sucked on a green persimmon. Rachel stood to refresh the coffeepot, and Martha followed her into the kitchen. "The nerve of that woman," she hissed. "I'm sorry, Rachel."

Needing a moment to catch her breath and to allow her heart to slow down, she leaned back against the cabinet. "I should be used to folks' chatter by now."

Martha rubbed her hand down Rachel's arm. "I can tell Luke is still a tender spot for you. I don't know much about the situation except what I've heard around town lately." She glanced at the ground, and her cheeks reddened. "But do you think it's possible that you two might get a second chance? It is strange that he returned after being gone for eleven years."

Rachel's heart fluttered. If only Luke had come back because of her, but she knew the truth. She'd seen the disgust in his eyes, and he'd proven his feelings by the way he avoided her. He didn't even think she was a good mother. She took a moment to force the shakiness from her voice. "Honestly," she glanced at her dear friend. "I'm surprised he didn't return sooner. It's the only home he's ever had, even if the actual house is no longer there. His cousins are here, as well as many old friends. He shouldn't have to give that up just because I'm here, too."

"Well, the Lord works in mysterious ways. Maybe He's got a miracle or two up His sleeve."

Rachel stared at Martha's gleaming eyes, knowing that in Luke's case, nothing could be further from the truth.

CHAPTER 10

Carthage, Missouri
May 1886

Leah Bennett quickened her steps as the town of Carthage came into view. She was in no hurry to return home, but the sooner she'd finished her errands, the more time she'd have to spend with Sue Anne. She glanced down at her list of things to do, determined to finish them quickly. At the City Flour Mills, she entered the front office and rang the bell on the counter. A tickle in her nose made her sneeze, just as she always did whenever she entered the mill. Flour and dust motes floated in the air and coated her lips. A man she'd seen before entered from a back room, dusting off his hands.

"Good day, Miss Bennett. What can I do for you?" He wiped his hands on a dingy towel hanging from one front pocket. His tanned face was coated with white flour, as was his dark hair, making him look older than she suspected he was.

Leah refrained from grinning at him. "I need to have a fifty-pound sack of flour delivered to our farm next time you make rounds."

"I'm happy to oblige. We have a wagon heading out that way on Thursday." He smiled, wrote something down in a ledger book on the counter, and quoted her the price.

She paid him and marked that item off her list. Next stop, the apothecary. Hiking up her skirt, she crossed the dirt street, dodging horse flops. As she entered the apothecary, her nose wrinkled at the pungent scents in the small building, but the assortment of colorful bottles in different shapes and sizes never failed to intrigue her.

Mr. Speck looked up from his desk behind the counter and adjusted his wire-framed glasses. "Ah, Miss Bennett, a pleasure to see you again. I hope all is well with your family."

Leah nodded. "For the most part, but Ma has developed a cough."

"Is it a dry cough or a phlegmy one?"

"Thankfully, it's just a dry cough, but it's been persistent for half a week." She looked down, breaking his gaze. After her mother developed the cough, Leah found it hard to know how to pray. In her heart, she wanted her mother to be well, but if it took her ma a while to recover completely, Pa might realize how much he needed Leah to run the household and change his mind about forcing her to marry Mr. Abernathy. But she knew how stubborn her pa was once he made a decision. He wasn't likely to back down, especially if money was involved. He worked sunup to sundown, struggling to raise enough food for their big family, and would tell her she needed to do her part to help out, even if that meant leaving home and marrying a man she couldn't abide.

The tall, thin man moved from behind the counter and in three steps crossed the room. He picked up two huge glass containers, set them on the counter, and measured out some ginger and something she didn't recognize into two packets, then twisted them closed. After writing instructions on a paper, he handed them to her. "That should take care of your mother. Just follow the directions to make a tea that will help her cough get better, and make sure she gets plenty of rest."

She accepted the packets and put them in a cloth bag that

she'd brought to help carry things, all the while wondering how a mother of eleven was supposed to find time to rest. Leah didn't mind doing more to ease her mother's load, but she couldn't do everything, and her siblings bucked her efforts to get them to help. "Thank you, Mr. Speck."

She closed the door, feeling sorry for the homely man. With his overly large eyes, buck teeth, and thinning hair, the poor fellow had never found a woman to marry. She knew he wanted to wed, because he attended the same church as her family, but sadly, the few eligible women shied away from him, including her. Was it wrong to hope to marry a comely man? Or should a woman be satisfied with one who was a good provider and kind to her? Or was even that too much to hope for?

Leah nibbled on her bottom lip, pondering the issue. She knew that you should judge a person by what was in his heart and not his features, but if you had to look at that face first thing in the morning for the rest of your life, shouldn't it be one that pleased you? She considered living with Mr. Abernathy and shuddered.

A jingling of harnesses pulled her from her thoughts, and she stopped to allow a wagon to pass. The driver touched the edge of his hat at her and smiled. Leah nodded back then scurried across the street before another buggy passed. At the mercantile, she needed to get several colors of thread, some coffee for her pa, and a bag of salt, and she wanted to talk to Sue Anne.

At the entrance of the store, she stopped and glanced at her thin calico dress. The gray with pink rosebuds had faded so that the flowers looked more like stains than roses. She glanced inside the store and breathed a sigh of relief when she found it empty of customers. Scents of all sorts assaulted her: the tang of pickles from the barrel near the counter, spices, leather, onions. She loved the variety of the store and seeing so many new things, even though she was rarely able to purchase anything except the everyday supplies they needed.

Sue Anne's father glanced up from a ledger book he'd been

writing in and smiled. "Afternoon, Miss Bennett."

"Mr. Carter." Leah nodded. "Good to see you again. Would Sue Anne happen to be around?"

He nudged his head to the left. "She's in the supply room unpacking a new shipment. Feel free to go on back there and see her."

"Thank you." She reached in her bag, pulled out her list, and handed it to him. "Here are the things we need today."

He pushed his glasses up his nose and scanned the page. "How much coffee would you like?"

"Ma said to get two pounds."

He nodded. "I'm guessing you want to pick out your own thread."

"Certainly. I'll do that after I say hello to Sue Anne." Leah hurried toward the supply room, her insides twittering. Would her friend think her a copycat? With a wobbly hand, she pushed aside the curtain and stepped into the other room.

Sue Anne glanced up from the crate she'd been emptying, her eyes blank. Suddenly they focused, and a smile settled on her thin lips. She stood, shook off the packaging hay from her skirt, and hugged Leah. "It's so wonderful to see you." She smiled wickedly. "And I so need a break from all this work."

"I had some errands to run, which is why I'm in town. I was also hoping you might be free to talk for a few minutes."

"This is the last crate, and I'm nearly done with it. Could you wait a few minutes, or are you in a hurry to get home?"

"No hurry. All that awaits me is work." Leah offered a weak smile, knowing the truth of her comment. "I need to pick out some thread. I can do that while you finish here."

"Wonderful. That will give me an incentive to hurry." Sue Anne sat back down and rummaged through the straw for another tin cup to add to her growing stack.

Leah ambled through the crowded aisles, gazing at the stacks of ready-made clothing and shiny new shoes in various sizes.

Then her eyes landed on the stacks of colorful fabric. She fingered a navy calico with small, yellow sunflowers. If only she had money enough to buy some fabric. "How lovely."

"That just arrived this week." Mr. Carter pulled a scoop of coffee from a large bag and poured it onto his scale. "It caught Sue Anne's eye, too."

Over the years, Leah had tried hard not to envy Sue Anne, but at times it was hard, even though she was her best friend. Being an only child of the store owner, Sue Anne had first pick of the beautiful, ready-made dresses and fabrics as they arrived. She had been generous to share her castoffs with the Bennett family, but they generally went to the younger girls since Leah was so much taller than her friend. Leah rubbed her finger over the blue calico again. If she married Mr. Abernathy, would he allow her to purchase pretty things? Repulsed at her train of thought, she shook her head and moved on to the thread rack. She selected white, black, and navy thread then laid them on the counter for Mr. Carter to add to her tally. How could Sue Anne consider leaving all of this to go west and marry a rancher?

Her friend popped out of the back room, looking bright and cheerful. "I'm finished, Papa."

He smiled. "Then I suppose you'd better go spend some time with your friend while you can. Your mother will need your help with supper."

Sue Anne grabbed Leah's hand. "Let's go upstairs. Ma's gone visiting."

They tromped up the steps in the back room, entered the second story where the Carters lived, and were met with the lingering scent of baked bread. Leah loved the inviting parlor with its pretty settee, needlepoint chair, and large wooden rocker. A colorful braided rug covered all but the corners of the wood floor. A blue floral hurricane lamp rested on a round wooden table.

Sue Anne turned before going into the kitchen. "Would you like some tea?"

Leah shook her head. "Water is fine, thank you." She sat on the needlepoint chair, enjoying being off her feet and the way the chair hugged her.

Sue Anne returned with a glass of water and a small plate of cookies. She set them on the table next to Leah and flopped onto the settee, making a whoosh and sending dust motes floating in the afternoon sunlight that gleamed through the large window. She leaned toward Leah, her blue eyes shining. "Have you heard the news?"

Leah nodded. "I think so, at least if it's the same as what Molly told me."

"I just have to show you something." Sue Anne jumped up and left the room again.

A rustling sounded from somewhere in the small home, and her friend all but skipped back, a wide grin on her face as she held up a newspaper. "I keep this hidden in my room." She sat down, opened the paper, and pointed to an ad. "I haven't told my parents yet, but I'm going to be a mail-order bride. That's the man I picked."

"So, it's true then?"

Sue Anne shrugged. "I hope so. I wrote to Simon—that's his name—Simon Stephens, and he wrote back. He owns a ranch in Nevada."

Leah grasped her friend's hand. "How can you even think of traveling so far to marry a man you don't know?"

"I won't marry him until I'm sure I know him well enough. Oh, Leah, he sounds so dreamy—curly blond hair, brown eyes, and over six feet tall."

Leah's thought drifted to Mr. Abernathy. That description fit him except for the height, but there was nothing dreamy about him.

Sue Anne sobered. "Don't you dare tell my parents. Pa would be livid and probably try to marry me off fast to someone in town."

"I won't tell them, but I learned about it from Molly, and if someone as loose-lipped as she knows, don't you think your folks will find out before long?"

"I just need to get another letter or two, and then I'll know for certain that Simon is the one." She stared into her lap. "Do you think it's silly of me? It just sounds so adventurous."

Leah shook her head. She couldn't very well scold her friend when she came wanting to have a look at the advertisements herself. "I. . .uh. . .no. In fact, I was thinking about maybe trying to find a husband myself."

Sue Anne's eyes brightened again, and she squealed, grasping Leah's hands. "You're thinking about becoming a mail-order bride, too?"

Leah nodded. At least it had sounded like a good idea last night. "Mr. Abernathy made an agreement with Pa to marry me, but I just can't."

Lifting her hand to her mouth, her friend stared back at her with wide eyes. "Oh, Leah, I'm so sorry. He's so—old."

Leah crinkled her lip and leaned forward. "And he has hair in his ears."

"And hanging out his nose." Sue Anne curled her lips inward, obviously fighting a smile. She lost the battle and giggled. "We can't have that, can we? Here, let's look at my paper."

Leah nodded, still wrestling inside. How could she marry a stranger? She'd only loved one man, but she'd lost him. She'd heard of people marrying who didn't know one another, but could love grow from such a union? Yet anyone would be better than Mr. Abernathy. Scooting over, Sue Anne patted the settee, and Leah slid beside her. They leaned forward, looking at the paper spread out on the coffee table.

"Do you want to marry a rancher? Lots of them need wives."

Leah considered that and shook her head. "No, I think I'd rather live in a town and preferably someplace that's not cold."

"Hmm. . ." Sue Anne tapped her chin. "How about this one. *'Bank clerk from Kansas City, Missouri, seeks wife. Has small house and regular income, 35, 5'6", brown hair and green eyes.'* " Looking hopeful, she glanced over at Leah.

"I don't know. He's rather old, though certainly younger than Mr. Abernathy, but Kansas City isn't too far by train. I'd hate for Pa to come find me and make me come back home. He's so stubborn, he just might do that."

"That's true." Sue Anne turned back to the paper. " *'Well-to-do saloon owner needs wife. Prefers a shapely woman who sings like a songbird.'* "

Leah gasped and swatted her friend's arm. "No, thank you. Some friend you are."

Chuckling, they searched the ads again. Suddenly, Sue Anne sat up straighter. "Here's a good one. *'Town marshal, 6'2", with dark brown hair and eyes, wants pretty wife who can cook. Must be willing to move to Texas. Travel money provided.'* "

Leah's heart leaped. She hadn't considered the cost of traveling.

"The address is Lookout, Texas. I don't know where that is, but Texas is such a big state that surely the town is far away. Clear across Indian Territory. Your father would never travel that far—and oh my, six foot two inches—how wonderful."

Leah leaned back, staring at the ad. She'd read a lot about Texas and its wild beginnings, but now it was a state, and things had settled down there. At least she hoped they had. The more she thought about it, the more she liked the idea.

Sue Anne nudged her arm. "I don't think you're going to find one better than a town marshal. Surely the man is honorable and trustworthy if he's a lawman. I wonder why he wants you to write him through a solicitor."

"Maybe he doesn't want the whole town knowing he's wife shopping." Leah leaned back, took a cookie off the plate, and nibbled it. Could she do this? Would he even want her?

Bouncing on the seat, Sue Anne squealed. "Say something, Leah. He sounds perfectly wonderful."

Leah looked at her friend. "Can I borrow some paper so I can write to him?"

CHAPTER 11

Shreveport, Louisiana
Late May 1886

Shannon O'Neil pulled open the tall double windows in the gentlemen's parlor and stared out at the dreary countryside. A cool breeze blew in, clearing the room's air of the stench of cigar smoke that had lingered overnight after the men's poker game. The damp weather and cloudy sky reminded her of her homeland. Ireland. Would she ever see the brilliant green grass and rolling hills again?

No, and 'twas best she put it from her mind. She would live the rest of her days in America, and though life here wasn't easy, 'twas far better than how her family fared as poor tenant farmers. If only her parents hadn't died so soon upon their arrival in New Orleans. Perhaps things would have turned out different.

"Miss O'Neil!"

Shannon jumped and spun around. Her hand clutched the paper in her pocket as if Mrs. Melrose could see the letter and knew her thoughts. A shiver ran down her spine.

The plump woman lifted up her chin and glared at Shannon. "Mr. Wakefield does not employ you so you can spend the day lollygagging. Have you finished cleaning and dusting this room? And why is that window open?"

Shannon's gaze ran swiftly around the gentlemen's parlor where each piece of furniture gleamed. "Aye, mum, the polishing is done, and I only opened the window to clear the air in here. 'Twas heavy with smoke from last eve's socializing."

"Fine, then see to it that the chamber pots are emptied while the family is at breakfast."

Stomach curdling at the nasty chore, Shannon dipped her head. "Aye, mum."

"Make haste now, and when you've finished that task, come find me downstairs in the kitchen or laundry." The head maid turned and strode out of the room, murmuring loud enough for Shannon to hear, "I declare, if I didn't keep a watch on each and every one of these girls, nothing would get done around here."

Gathering up the crate of empty liquor and wine bottles, Shannon made her way down to the kitchen. She set the crate on the rear porch and returned upstairs to close the window and retrieve the wine glasses. Back in the kitchen, she placed the dirty goblets in the sink to be washed. She hurried to the south wing of the huge mansion, dreading the duty before her. Though she'd worked at the Wakefield Estate for nearly a year, she was the newest servant, so the worst jobs fell to her. "But not for long."

She fingered the letter burning a hole in her pocket. Had she made the right decision to respond to that advertisement in the newspaper? He'd written twice and now sent her the money to come to Texas to be his wife. But could she actually marry a man she'd never met before? A town marshal, no less.

She'd dreamed of the six-feet-two-inch man last night. Dark brown hair and eyes. A marshal would be a man used to protecting people, but would she feel safe with him? Would he treat her kindly?

She emptied and washed out the pots for the master and mistress's room and their two daughters, but she dreaded entering their son's bed chamber. He was known for sleeping late and for forcing the female servants to please his every whim; but as bad as he was, he didn't have the cruel streak that his visiting friend and college roommate, Justin Moreland, had.

Shannon knocked hard on the door, waited, then knocked again. She wiped her sweaty hands on her apron. When there was no response, she pushed open the heavy door and peered inside. Morgan Wakefield's nightshirt lay in a heap on the floor, much to Shannon's relief. She hurried inside, fetched the pot, took it downstairs to be emptied and washed, and quickly returned it to the room, lest the younger Mr. Wakefield return and find her in his chamber. In the hall, she leaned against the wall and heaved a heavy breath. Just one more, and then the horrid deed would be done for the day.

She ventured out of the family wing of the home and into the north end where the guests resided. If the younger Mr. Wakefield was awake and at breakfast, he most likely had dragged his friend out of bed and downstairs with him. Shannon shook her head. How could anyone eat breakfast when it was nearly the noon hour?

She knocked loudly then shoved the door open, greatly relieved that Mr. Moreland was not present. Fifteen minutes later, the deed was done. She pulled the door shut as she was leaving.

"Well, well, what do we have here?" Justin Moreland leaned casually against the hall wall staring at her with lecherous eyes and a cocky smile. "Trying to sneak into my room, were you?"

Shannon jumped, her hand to her chest, and stepped back. "I was only tendin' to your—your room, sir." She curtseyed and stepped around him.

The tall, lean man leaped in front of her. "I've had breakfast, but alas, there was no dessert."

Shannon scowled, thinking of the delicious pastries with creamy filling that the cooks made for the family. Often the remaining ones were thrown away or fed to the swine rather than given to the lowly servants. She forced a smile and held her hands behind her back so that he wouldn't see them trembling. Though comely with his curly brown hair and blue eyes, something about the rogue scared her more than riding in the dark, smelly steerage on the ship that had brought her to America. "I'd be happy to fetch you a pastry, sir."

He stepped closer, grabbing her upper arms. "You're the only dessert I need. Give me fifteen minutes of your time, and I'll sweeten your pocket with a coin."

Gasping, Shannon struggled to pull free. Her virtue was not for sale at any price. "Nay, I cannot. I've duties to tend to."

"Come now, those other servants won't miss you for such a short while." Taller than she by a good nine inches, young and strong, he jerked her toward the bedroom door.

Praying hard, Shannon dug her feet into the carpet runner but slid forward as he turned and pulled her against him. *Father, help me.*

She shoved at the man's solid chest. "Nay, leave me be."

"Hey, Justin. What are you doing?"

At the sound of Morgan Wakefield's voice, Mr. Moreland halted. He scowled, then grinned and looked over his shoulder. "I'm just about to have some fun with this wench of yours. She's a comely thing, with all that dark red hair, don't you think?"

Morgan's gaze ran down Shannon's length. "She's a servant, for heaven's sake, Justin. Leave her alone. Did you forget that we're supposed to go hunting?"

Justin turned but held tightly to her with one hand. A leering grin twisted his features, and he waggled his brows. "I'm on the hunt for something else."

Morgan's lips curled. "I know of far better women to please your fancy than that one. Older and more experienced."

Justin's grip loosened. "Where, pray tell, would these lovely ladies be?"

Grinning, Morgan leaned one shoulder against the wall and crossed his ankles. "Stick with me, and you'll find out. But right now, the horses are saddled, and my father is awaiting us. Come."

Justin stared down at Shannon. Suddenly, he smiled and kissed her nose. "Tonight, my sweet tart. And next time, I'll not be dissuaded."

He released her arm so quickly that she nearly stumbled. Shannon swerved around him and ran past Mr. Wakefield, flashing him what she hoped was a grateful look. He scowled at her as if she were nothing but refuse to be scraped off the bottom of his boots. No matter, she would always be thankful that he had arrived when he had.

Hurrying down the stairs to the servants' quarters, she shoved her hand in her pocket and clutched the letter in her fist. Her decision had been made. In her room, she quickly changed out of her black servant's dress and hung it and her apron on the hook on the wall alongside its mate. She threw her few belongings into a worn satchel and donned one of her two dresses, saving the nicer one for when she'd arrive in Texas to meet her future husband, Luke Davis.

Shannon all but held her breath until she was out of the mansion, and she hurried down the lane lest someone see her and try to stop her. She had needed this job—until the day the letter arrived with enough money for her to take the train to Sherman, Texas, where she could then catch a stage to Lookout.

Her steps quickened as she reached the lane that would take her into town. "Please, Lord, let this be the right choice."

But what other choice did she have? She was alone in America with no hope of ever seeing Ireland again. She could only pray she wasn't jumping off the ship and into the ocean.

Southwest Missouri
June 1886

Carly shoved the last bite of scrambled eggs into her mouth, buttered another biscuit, and slathered peach jam on it. Normally, she had trouble eating before a robbery, but the restaurant's food was so much better than she made that she couldn't pass it up. "I wish I could fix biscuits this flaky. These are so good."

Her brother grunted an agreement and sipped his coffee, staring out the window at the small town of Decker. "Finish up. The stage is due in a half hour."

"I'm nearly done." She leaned forward, the high neck of her dress clutching at her throat. She tugged at the collar, fearing it would cut off her breathing. "This dress is about to kill me. I'd much rather wear pants."

Tyson looked her direction, blue eyes narrowed. "For what we have planned, you need that dress, so get used to it."

Thankful that no one else was in the dining room since it was well past the normal breakfast hour, Carly sighed and fanned the bodice of her dress to allow in some air. She hoped the stage robbery went well so they could lie low for a while. She was sick of stealing and constantly moving from one hideout to another, but after her brother had gambled away their share of the money from the bank robbery, he'd started planning another heist. Why couldn't she have been born into a decent family?

Ty stood. "Let's go."

Carly shoved the last bite into her mouth then downed the rest of her coffee. Standing, she gave the spacious hotel dining room a final glance. Each table was covered with a white tablecloth. Fancy chandeliers lit the room at night, but now sunlight reflected on the pieces of cut glass, making dancing rainbows on the walls. She'd miss feeling like a lady and being surrounded by such finery.

Tyson took her arm. "Don't forget your handbag."

"I don't like carrying it. That gun makes it heavy," she whispered. She'd taken to wearing a holstered gun partly to protect herself from the two newest gang members, but she couldn't very well do that or the stage operators might get suspicious. Now that they were heading toward their destination, her legs began to wobble. What if there were several men on the coach? Could she hold them at bay with her gun until her brother and the gang could take over?

She lifted her heavy bag, carrying it in the crook of her arm instead of letting it dangle. What if she had to shoot another passenger?

Licking her dry lips, she allowed Ty to tug her along. When he'd proposed the plan of putting her on the stage to help with the robbery, she'd fussed and fumed, but to no avail. How could he expect her to shoot an unarmed person looking her in the eye? She doubted she could. Maybe it wouldn't come to that.

"Hurry up. We need you on that stage." Tyson yanked her arm, and she jogged to keep up.

"I'm trying to hurry, but these confounded skirts keep tripping me."

Tyson slowed his steps as they rounded the corner and saw the stage still sitting there. "You'll keep your story straight? Watch what you say to folks?"

Carly rolled her eyes. "I ain't stupid. I'll just sit down and tell them all I'm an outlaw—a member of the infamous Payton gang—and if they give me any lip about it, I'll shoot them."

A brief smiled tugged at Tyson's mouth before he sobered. "Maybe it's best if you don't talk at all."

He didn't trust her to keep up her end of the deal. She knew the stakes—that Ty had learned a large payroll was on this stage and that there weren't going to be any additional guards so that nobody would suspect anything.

Tyson stopped behind the stage and handed Carly her ticket. "You have a good trip, sis, and tell Aunt Sylvie that I hope to visit soon."

She offered him a sweet smile for the sake of anyone watching. "Oh, I will. Time will fly past, and you'll be seein' me again before you know it."

Tyson scowled at her. Another man and woman stood in front of the stage office window. She was pretty with her black hair swept up in a net thing and her blue eyes glimmering. Carly guessed her to be in her late teens.

"Are you sure about this, Ellie? You know you'll always have a home with me." A short man about the same height as the woman stared at her with somber brown eyes. By the similarity in their features and coloring, Carly assumed they must be brother and sister.

"I'm sure, John. I've corresponded several times with my intended, and he seems a perfectly nice man."

John shook his head. "It just doesn't seem right for you to go off to Texas to marry a stranger. There are men here in Decker who'd be delighted to marry you."

The woman named Ellie patted the man's chest. "Don't worry, John. You have a new wife, and she doesn't need to share her kitchen with me. I'll be fine."

A stocky man dressed in denim pants and shirt and wearing a vest stomped down the steps to the street. He carried a Winchester rifle in one hand. His thick mustache twitched. "Load up, folks. We ain't got all day."

John helped Ellie into the coach and then moved back, looking worried. Tyson handed Carly up, and she stepped on the edge of her skirt, falling to her knees on the floor of the coach.

"You all right, sis?" Ty asked, sounding disgusted.

Carly bit back a curse and managed to wrangle the skirt out from under her shoes. Stupid dress. She hadn't worn one since shortly after Ma died and had forgotten how awkward they could be. Whoever invented them sure didn't give a hoot about how a woman was supposed to get around and do everyday stuff while managing the strangling fabric. She flopped onto the seat and rearranged the despised garment.

Ellie's eyes were wide, watching her. "Are you all right?"

"Fine." Carly crossed her arms over her chest and looked to see if Tyson was still there. At least she'd managed not to curse out loud.

Her brother lifted his brows and shook his head. "Safe trip, sis."

Carly merely nodded. What point was there in pretending

when she'd just see him again in an hour or so? Too bad she wasn't really going somewhere. She let her mind wander, trying to decide where she'd go if she could travel anywhere she wanted.

In a matter of minutes, the stage pulled out of Decker with no other passengers. She had never ridden in a stagecoach before and had been excited about the prospect, but as they bumped and shimmied down the road, she wondered how she'd manage until Ty and the gang intercepted the coach, several miles out of town. She watched the landscape speed by, thankful at least she wouldn't get bugs in her teeth like she sometimes did while riding.

"Sure is bumpy, isn't it?"

Carly glanced at the woman across the seat. "Yeah, sure is."

"My name is Ellie Blackstone."

Carly felt the blood drain from her face. They'd never discussed what to do if someone asked her name. "Uh. . .Carly. . .Payton."

The woman smiled, pulled some knitting out of her satchel, and started clicking her long needles together. All the while, Carly wondered if she should have given a false name. And how could that woman knit on such a bouncy stage? If Carly tried that, she was certain she'd end up stabbing herself. She set her handbag on the seat beside her, one hand on it so it wouldn't slide off and not be handy when she needed it. She hoped she wouldn't have to shoot Ellie.

"I'm a mail-order bride on my way to Texas."

Carly blinked and stared at the young woman. "You mean you're going to marry a man you ain't never met?"

Ellie giggled. "That's right, although I have received three letters from him. He's a marshal in Lookout, Texas. I've never been to Texas before. Have you?"

Carly shook her head. "No, but I'd sure as shootin' like to go some day."

"I'm excited about the trip, although my brother is worried about me. I just couldn't stand living under the same roof as him and his new wife." Ellie stopped knitting and lowered her hands to her lap. "Don't get me wrong. Charlene was nice enough, but I could tell she didn't like sharing the house with another woman, even if I did grow up there."

"How'dja learn about the marshal?"

Ellie smiled. "I placed an advertisement in a magazine, and a month later, I got a letter from a solicitor saying the marshal in Lookout, Texas, was interested in learning more about me. I wrote him, and he wrote back several times and then asked for my hand. I agreed, and then he sent me the traveling money."

Never having heard such a story, Carly sat back in the seat. "What if. . .what if he's old—and fat?"

Ellie giggled, brown eyes sparkling. "Luke is only twenty-nine, and oh so tall."

"That's gotta be a lot older than you are."

She shrugged and renewed her knitting. "Seven years. But lots of men are that much older than their wives."

Carly leaned back, staring out the window. She couldn't afford to take a liking to Ellie when she might have to shoot her in a half hour. She tapped her hand against the hardness of the gun in her handbag. How long would her brother wait to attack the stage? They should be far enough from town so that any shots fired wouldn't be heard back in Decker, but not too close to the next town. She jiggled her foot.

What would it be like to marry a stranger? A marshal, no less. Carly shuddered. But then she sat up straighter. A marshal would know when payroll shipments would be going out on the stage. If she could get close to such a man, she could learn about them herself and might be able to score a big enough heist that she could quit being an outlaw and live a respectable life. Course, a marshal might have heard of the Payton gang, but he would have no way of connecting her to it.

But there was the issue of Ellie. "Did you send the marshal a photograph of yourself?"

Ellie shook her head and looked out the window, nibbling on

her lower lip. "No, I was afraid he might not like what he saw." She patted her dark hair. "Men often prefer blonds."

So…the marshal didn't know what Ellie looked like. Thoughts spun through Carly's mind faster than the wheels of the stage turned. If only she could take the woman's place, but there was no chance of that. Tyson would appear soon with his gang, and she'd have to leave with him whether she wanted to or not. She thought of how Emmett leered at her across the campfire most nights. He'd tried to kiss her once, and even now a shiver ran down her spine. So far, her brother had kept the man away from her, but what if something happened to Tyson?

A shot rang out behind them, and Carly jumped, along with Ellie, even though she'd been expecting her brother.

"Robbers! No, this can't be happening." Ellie clutched her knitting to her chest. "I'm not even out of Missouri yet."

Above them, shots fired back toward the outlaws. A bullet hit the window frame, sending flying splinters of wood toward them. One hit Carly in the face, and she jerked her head to the side. Didn't the gang care that she was inside the stage?

She reached for her handbag as it slid along the seat. The coach hit a dip in the road, dropped down, and then back out. Carly reached for the edge of the window to keep from being flung to the ground. *If this thing doesn't stop soon, I'll be black and blue—if I even survive.*

The stage lurched side-to-side as the horses thundered down the dirt road in their effort to flee the outlaws. The coach groaned, and harnesses jangled. Dust coated Carly's lips. Ellie clung to the window frame with one hand and pressed her other hand against the seat, her eyes wide and her knitting forgotten.

Carly reached for her handbag again, but it slid onto the ground. She leaned forward, just as Fred, a new member of the gang, pulled even with Ellie's window. His gaze sought out Carly's, and then he fired toward the other passenger. Ellie slumped sideways just as Fred was blasted out of his saddle by either the stage driver or the shotgun rider. Carly jerked to the left and ducked, as if the shot had been meant for her. Why had he shot Ellie when she wasn't even armed?

Carly dropped to the floor and fumbled with her handbag, knowing how angry her brother would be if she didn't draw her gun. The coach lurched again, and Ellie fell on top of her. Carly's heart jolted clear up into her throat. With her bag in her hand, she attempted to rise, but Ellie's weight and the constant jostling held her down. She fought the panic blurring her vision and making her heart stampede. Was Ellie dead? Or just unconscious?

Behind the stage, she heard more gunfire.

Hoofbeats pulled even with the door. "Carly, you in there?"

Unable to catch her breath, she didn't respond to her brother's question. She tried to push up, but Ellie's limp body weighted her down. The stage swayed right and left, groaning and creaking, until she feared it would tip over.

Ty cursed. "Carly's down."

More gunshots echoed behind them.

"Soldiers! Let's ride."

Ty was leaving her? She had to get out of the coach or she'd be caught. But even as she struggled to get Ellie's dead weight off her, an idea formed in her mind. Did she dare go through with it?

She heard more riders pass the stage. "Get it stopped, Chet, and see if the passengers are injured."

The stage gradually slowed, but the other riders charged on ahead, probably after her brother. Would he fight for her or just keep running like the time a gang member had fallen under gunfire? A sudden thought blasted into her mind. She had no idea where to look for her brother now that they were separated. And she had no horse. They hadn't discussed this development.

Her breath came in ragged bursts as the stage squeaked to a halt. Footsteps marched in her direction, and the door opened. Carly's heart thundered, and she lay still. Since she'd have surprise on her side, she might be able to pull her gun and shoot the man.

He muttered a soft curse. "Looks like they shot two women."

Carly felt Ellie's limp body being lifted off of her, and she sucked in a deep breath and tucked her handbag underneath her. Should she continue to play possum or try to get up?

Before she could decide, steady footsteps brought the man back, and Carly froze. She felt herself being tugged toward the door then lifted into the man's arms as her handbag dropped to the ground. He smelled of sweat, dust, and leather. He gently set her down, and she moaned. Lifting her hand to her cheek, she pretended to be coming around after passing out.

"W–what happened?" She opened her eyes and saw a man with kind hazel eyes staring back.

"Just take it easy, ma'am. You was in a holdup."

Carly gasped and splayed her hand over her chest. "Oh mercy. What about the other passenger. Is she. . ."

"Passed out cold. Might have to do with the shot that grazed her head or the sewing needle piercing her side. And she's got another bullet in her shoulder." The man shook his head. "It don't look good for her. I doubt she'll make it, especially being so far from town. Joplin's the closest, so I reckon that's where you two will end up once the rest of my team returns."

"Returns?"

The man rose and took a canteen off his saddle horn. "They went after them outlaws. Killed one back a ways, but the others rode off." He stooped down, opened the canteen, and handed it to her. "What's your name, ma'am?"

Panic sliced through Carly as she slowly sipped the water, delaying her response. Ellie may not have recognized her real name, but a lawman surely would. "Uh. . .Ellie. Ellie Blackstone."

CHAPTER 12

Lookout, Texas
June 1886

Luke scanned Main Street, crowded with people from the town and nearby farms and ranches, all come to Lookout to celebrate his thirtieth birthday. At the far end of the street, music filled the air, and five couples danced to a lively tune. Tables filled with food served by the womenfolk lined one side of Main Street. Luke scowled as Garrett approached, knowing the shindig had been his idea. Max, lying on the porch, didn't bother lifting his head but wagged his tail.

Garrett laughed and wrapped his arm around Luke's shoulder in a friendly greeting. "Just relax and enjoy the festivities, cuz. You know these folks jump at any chance to get together for a celebration, especially those who live outside of town. Farming and ranching can be a lonely life."

"Maybe so, but I don't like being the center of attention."

Mark strode toward them carrying two cups, a grin widening his face. "Nice party, isn't it?"

He handed Luke a mug of something. Luke sniffed it, ignoring his question. Apple cider. He sipped the sweet drink, watching, looking for trouble. With so many people gathered in such a small spot, it was bound to happen sooner or later.

"So, how's it feel to be thirty, ol' man?" Mark lifted his cup to his lips.

"Where's mine?" Garrett stood with his hands on his hips. "I sent you off to get us a drink, and you give mine to Luke?"

Mark grinned. "He's the birthday boy. Fetch your own refreshment."

Garrett snarled his lip at Mark and muttered a phony growl, making Luke chuckle. His cousins were all the family he had left, and Lookout had been the only town he'd ever called home. He'd prayed long and thought hard before quitting the cavalry and returning to Lookout, but in the end, family and familiarity won out—not to mention he believed it was what God wanted him to do. His gaze journeyed to where Rachel was cutting pies at a table. Tonight the town was filled with women, and he only had eyes for one. He shook his head. How pathetic he was.

"Why don't you ask her to dance?" Garrett nudged Luke in the arm.

"What?" Luke shot a glance at his cousin, realizing he'd been caught staring.

"Go ask Rachel to dance."

"It may be my birthday, but I'm still on duty."

"Someone else will ask her if you don't."

At that very moment, Rand Kessler stopped at Rachel's table. He stood close to her and said something. Rachel offered a half smile and shook her head. Rand leaned closer. Luke's hackles lifted. Rachel nodded then waved to the doctor's wife, who came and took her place at the pie table. Rand offered Rachel his arm, and she took it, allowing him to lead her toward the dancing couples.

"If you still have any interest in Rachel, don't wait too long." Garrett gave him a knowing look. "Rand Kessler's been after her to marry him for a year now."

Luke ignored the comment, though it ate at him. "How big of

102

a ranch does this Kessler have?"

"Big. He's one of the more prosperous ranchers in this area."

Great. So Rachel was after another man with money. Even if Luke *was* interested in her, she'd never give a low paid town marshal a second look. He ground down hard on his back teeth. Maybe the best thing he could do was get married; then he'd have a woman who could help take his mind off Rachel Hamil—

A blast of shots rang out. Luke flung down the tin cup and yanked out his gun. Max lurched to his feet, whimpering, and disappeared into the jail office. Luke scanned the throng of merchants, farmers, and families gathered along Main Street. Where was the shooter?

His heart galloped. A shooter in such a crowded area could be a disaster. "Did you see the gunman?"

Beside him, Garrett held the same rigid stance. "No. It didn't sound too close, but it's hard to tell with all the noise here."

Luke searched the rowdy crowd. The townsfolk square-danced, chatted, and carried on as if nothing had happened. Had the band's music muffled the gunfire so they hadn't heard it? Couldn't they sense the danger?

The rapid pop sounded again. People on the fringe of the mass spun about, turning concerned stares toward the noise. A woman screamed and grabbed her husband.

"Over there." Garrett pointed toward the bank with his gun, and then he holstered it. "Stupid kids. Don't they know they can spark a blaze with those firecrackers?"

Shaking his head at the trio of adolescents, Luke pocketed his pistol. "I'll run 'em off."

Mark stepped forward. "Let me and Garrett do it. After all, it's your party."

"Yeah, but I'm the marshal. It's what I get paid to do." He glanced at the nearby table laden with desserts, where Rachel had been serving pie. "One of you could grab me a slice of Rachel's apple pie before it's gone."

Luke loped toward the bank. Truth be told, he appreciated the town's celebration of his birthday, but he hated having everyone's attention focused on him. As the marshal, he was more used to standing back, watching everybody else. He stopped in front of the mercantile and gazed across the road, watching the spot where the youngsters had been gathered. Two of the boys were gone, but a small shape huddled near the corner of the bank. The spark of a match illuminated the child's face.

Jack.

Not again. Luke strode around the corner, gritting his teeth.

The child glanced up, eyes widening. The match fell to the ground, and Jack took off like a rabbit freed from a snare. Luke stomped the flames that flickered to life on the dry grass, sending dust over the boots he'd polished for tonight's special occasion. No point chasing Jack now. She was long gone, and besides, he knew where to find her when the dust settled. Swiping the tops of his boots on the back of his pants leg, Luke heaved a sigh. Rachel didn't need this, but they'd have to talk about Jack's latest antic. She was going to have to face the facts about her ornery child before someone got hurt.

Fifteen minutes later, after taking a spin around the outskirts of town to make sure all was in order, Luke sat with his cousins on the steps in front of his office. He cut a large bite of golden crust and tender apple, shoved it in his mouth, and licked the cinnamon and sugar from his fork. "Rachel sure does make good pie."

"Too bad she can't control that kid of hers as well as she can cook," Garrett said.

"I'm tellin' you, Luke, you ought to marry her before Rand does; then you could eat all the pie you want." Mark's brown eyes flickered with amusement.

Luke nearly choked on his final bite. "You know I can't do that."

"All that was a long time ago, cuz." Garrett sipped a cup of coffee.

"Maybe so, but after the woman you love betrays you, a man thinks long and hard before risking his heart again."

"Then maybe you should consider marrying someone else. Have you thought about that?"

Luke stared at his cousins, wishing they'd pick another topic of conversation. "Maybe you should take your own advice."

Garrett grinned wide. "Maybe I will."

Luke sobered. He was ready to marry and start a family, but so far, no woman had been able to sear Rachel from his heart. Maybe one of these days someone would. "I guess I'd marry if the right woman came along."

Finished with his own pie, Mark reached over and ran his forefinger along the edge of Luke's plate, then poked it in his mouth. "Rachel sure knows how to cook. If you're not interested in her, maybe I'll see if I can turn her head away from that Kessler guy."

"That's not funny, Mark." Luke cast a sidelong glare to his right.

"You said yourself that you're no longer interested in her. What's wrong with me pursuing her?"

Garrett straightened, flicking a beetle off his brown vest. "Rachel's free to allow any man she wants to come courting." He looked past Luke to Mark. "But why would you want to marry her? She's got that pain-in-the-neck kid."

"Jack's not so bad. She just needs some guidance," Luke offered.

"But whoever married Rachel would never have to worry about food, and she is easy on the eyes." Mark grinned, an ornery gleam in his blue gaze that set Luke on edge. "She could do lots worse than me."

Having heard enough of his cousins' foolishness, Luke stood and walked toward the table where Rachel was again serving pies. He could no longer trust her with his heart, but how could he explain this fierce need to protect her, to be near her, when he didn't understand it himself? She glanced up and smiled, making his pulse gallop.

"Care for another slice? It is your birthday, after all."

He handed her his dirty plate. "No thanks. I'm good."

"Are you enjoying your party?"

Luke shrugged. "I guess so."

"It's nice having you back in town."

He shoved his hands in his back pockets, not knowing what to say to her now that he had her to himself. "Good to be back."

"Well, I hope you have a good time tonight."

Luke nodded, and Rachel's smile dipped as he turned back toward his office. Maybe returning to Lookout hadn't been such a grand idea. Why couldn't he get his head and heart to line up together? A part of him still cared for Rachel, but he would never again trust her with his heart. He'd done that once, and she'd tromped on it. His heart wouldn't survive if she did it again.

"You need a wife," Mark said as Luke approached him.

"Quit saying that."

"Maybe we'll just have to find one for you." Garrett chuckled and bumped his brother.

"No thanks," Luke called over his shoulder as he walked past them. Max trotted out of the jail and took a place beside Luke as he strode back to the bank to make sure the fire was still out. He returned to watching his town, hoping his hooligan cousins weren't planning another one of the many practical jokes they'd pulled most of their lives. But he had a bad feeling in his gut, as though he'd drunk soured milk. Those two were up to something; he could smell it.

Mrs. Fairland sat in the corner, listening to the first and second graders read. Jack glanced back at her list of spelling words. She should be studying them, but worry plagued her like a bad case of influenza. She took a deep breath and peered over her shoulder at Butch Laird. Even from across the room, she could smell the filthy scent of the Laird's pig farm. The thirteen-year-old stood nearly six feet tall and glared back at her with squinty black eyes. He pointed his finger like a gun and pretended to shoot her.

Jack spun back around in her desk, stuck in regret as thick as Texas mud after three days of rain. She should have kept her mouth shut. Shouldn't have yelled at Butch for picking on Jonesy at lunch. Shouldn't have screamed, "If you cook Butch Lard, he turns to Butch Fat."

She swallowed hard, tightly gripping the top of her desk, remembering how he glared at her and said his name was *Laird* not *Lard*. What had possessed her to do such a thing? What would he do to her?

He was between her and the door, or she'd light out the first chance she got. Maybe she could find some way to dawdle until he headed home. Tell the teacher she needed help with her schoolwork. But that left almost as sour a taste in her mouth as the thought of fighting Butch had.

Maybe her ma was right. Maybe she should think before she spoke. But her words always came flying out before she even thought about them. She hated Butch and couldn't help taking up for her friend. She pressed down on her knees to make them quit wobbling.

Jonesy looked at her from his seat across the aisle. His eye had nearly swollen shut. Mrs. Fairland had almost sent him home for fighting, but after Ricky and Jack's explanation of how Butch had started it, she'd let him stay. Everyone knew Mrs. Fairland was afraid of Butch, which was why she didn't send him home. Too bad she hadn't, and a fat lot of help the teacher would be if Butch jumped Jack after school.

Lifting her head to peer out the window, Jack tried to gauge how far it was from the school to her home. If only the jail was closer. Luke would save her.

Mrs. Fairland stood. "Very good, children. Practice reading the next three pages at home tonight, and we'll go over them in class tomorrow."

The four youngsters from the reading group scurried back to their desks and sat down.

At the front of the class, Mrs. Fairland looked pretty in her gold calico dress, even after a full day of school. "All right, students. We've had a good day of learning."

Jack glanced at the door and scooted to the edge of her chair. If she jumped over the desk to her right, she just might make it out the door and get away.

"Make sure you study your spelling words. The test will be before lunch on Friday, as usual." Mrs. Fairland's gaze traveled around the class, a pleasant smile lighting her pretty face.

Jack slid farther off the seat until her leg was halfway across the aisle. The other kids looked at her, but she knew most were used to her odd ways.

"Class dismissed."

Like a fire had been lit under her backside, Jack blasted off the seat and crawled across the top of Amanda Moore's desk, leaving the girl wide-eyed and mouth gaping. Jack raced for the door, fumbled with the knob, and yanked it open. Thudding like a stampede of Brahma bulls echoed behind her.

She bolted down the steps, heart thundering. Just as she leapt over the last step, someone snagged the back of her dress. It ripped and gagged her throat where it pulled taut.

"You didn't think ya was gettin' away from me that easy, did ya?"

Jack sucked in air and kicked her feet. Butch tucked her under his arm and lumbered around the back of the school toward the barn. Eyes blurring and throat aching from yelling, Jack kicked hard, trying to trip the big boy.

The children shouted behind her, but she couldn't tell who they were rooting for. Suddenly, Ricky stood in front of Butch, fists lifted. "You let her go. She's just a kid. A dumb girl, no less."

Ricky thought she was just a dumb girl? The pain of her friend's words took the fight out of her, and she went limp.

"Out of my way, Peewee." Butch shoved Ricky aside like he

was nothing more than an empty gunny sack.

"Ahhh. . ." Someone who sounded like a wild Indian charged them from behind. The force of the body colliding with Butch knocked Jack free. She fell to the ground, trying hard to catch her breath, and gazed up at the clear blue sky.

Her school friends stood around them in a circle, yelling hard. "Fight! Fight!"

"Children, stop this nonsense." Mrs. Fairland stood beside the group of onlookers as if she was afraid to move closer. "Stop that fighting right this minute."

Jack sat up. Ricky, Jonesy, and the Peterson twins were punching it out with Butch. Nobody liked the big, smelly bully, and that included her. Jack jumped up, righted her dress, took a running start, and latched onto Butch's back. She wrapped her arms around his neck and held on for all she was worth, holding her breath so as not to smell him.

Butch swung sideways, shoved the twins backward, then swung the other way. Green trees blurred into the white schoolhouse. Arms flew toward Butch as the younger boys rallied. He clawed at Jack's fingers, loosening them, then suddenly a fist collided with her eye, jerking her head backward with a snap.

Jack released her hold and felt herself falling. The screaming and yelling faded as she tumbled into a pit of black.

∽

A brightness behind Jack's eyelids intruded into the black realm, pulling her from the dark pit of nothingness. She slammed into a wall of pain, radiating from her forehead over her eye and cheek. Jack froze. Moving caused pain.

She relaxed into the softness of a bed—her bed, if the delicious smells coming from the kitchen were any indication.

"This is all your fault."

The venom in her mother's voice took her by surprise. She lifted the lid of her uninjured eye and blinked to bring the room into focus. Luke stood just inside the door of the bedroom Jack shared with her mother, his arms crossed and his face scowling.

"How? What did I do to cause this?" he asked.

Her mother stepped forward. "You taught my daughter how to fight, didn't you?"

"What? No!" Luke lifted his hands as if surrendering.

Jack watched them. Whenever Luke came around, there was either a spark of light in her mother's eyes that wasn't normally there, or else the opposite—she seemed sad. How come Luke caused these reactions in her mother when no other man had? Dare she hope that maybe one day Luke could become her new pa? She'd take him any day over that rancher who didn't have the sense to stop calling on her ma. Did she even want another pa?

At least Luke wouldn't be mean like her real pa had been.

"I did not teach Jack to fight. I promise, Rachel."

That was another thing. Right from the start, they'd called each other by their first names, but whenever she asked about Luke, her mother only said he was someone she grew up with. Jack opened her eye a speck farther to see better.

Her mother scooted up close, wagging a finger in the marshal's face. "You must have done something. Just look at her! Why, she'll have a black eye for weeks."

Luke's gaze skimmed across the room to her. He looked sad and angry at the same time.

"Ah, ah, it's not nice to eavesdrop, young lady." The doctor leaned over the bed, and his face blurred as he moved in close and peered down at her. "It's good to see you coming to."

"Coming to what?" Jack asked.

Ma gasped and hurried to the other side of the bed. She sat down and clutched Jack's hand. "Jacqueline, oh, my baby, you gave me such a scare."

Jack stared up at Luke, who moved to the edge of the bed. She rolled her good eye, even though it hurt, and a smile pulled up one side of his mouth, though he still looked concerned.

"How do you feel?" Her mother laid the back of her hand over Jack's forehead. "Are you in much pain?"

"Luke didn't teach me to fight, Mama."

Her mother glanced up at the marshal but didn't seem convinced.

"Honestly." Jack squeezed her mother's hand. "I asked him to, but he said it wasn't a good idea because I might get hurt."

"Well, it's good to know he has some sense." Her ma looked as if it pained her to say those words.

"If'n he had taught me, maybe I wouldn't of gotten punched like I did."

Ma pressed her lips tight, giving Jack the look that told her a lecture was coming. "You wouldn't have gotten injured if you hadn't joined in that fight with those older boys. I told you they're nothing but trouble."

"That's not true." Jack bolted up, her head aching as if it might explode. She pressed fingertips against her temples and lowered herself back down. "B–but you don't understand. Butch—"

Dr. Phillips cleared his throat. "Perhaps the scolding could take place later? I need to examine Jacqueline now that she's awake. She was unconscious for a good fifteen minutes."

Ma looked well put in her place. "Of course. I'm sorry, Hank."

"I reckon I should go now that I know you're all right, Jack." Luke twisted the brim of his hat and watched her, making Jack squirm.

"Don't call her that," her mother growled.

"It's all right, Ma. I want him to."

Her mother crossed her arms, and her mouth looked as if it had been sewn up and the stitches pulled too tight. Jack didn't want to upset her more, knowing Ma was probably fit to be tied since her *little girl* had gotten hurt. But maybe she could twist things to her benefit. "My head sure hurts, and I'm getting hungry. Sure would like some shoofly pie after dinner tonight."

Her mother turned back toward her. "Oh, truly? Let me go check and see if I have the fixings." Looking happy to have something to do, she scurried out of the room, her blue skirts whipping behind her.

Jack looked up at Luke. A wide grin covered his tanned face, and beside her, the doctor chuckled.

Luke shook his head. "Young lady, you're a stinker. You ought to get nothing but bread and water to eat tonight."

～

Relieved that Jack seemed to be fine except for some bumps, bruises, and a black eye, Luke left the room so the doctor could check her over without distractions. He stood in the kitchen doorway and watched Rachel rummage around inside her pantry. The lingering scent of baked pies filled the air, and his gaze drifted to the pie safe as he thought of the tasty treats. What kind would she serve with supper tonight?

She held up a jug with some thick, dark liquid in it. "What happened to all my molasses?"

Luke's gaze snapped back to Rachel. Her cheeks were flushed, and her blue eyes searching. She pushed some things around on the shelf, and Luke watched her, enjoying this time of seeing her relaxed and off guard. In spite of everything between them, he had missed her. Missed holding her close and making her giggle when he kissed her ear. Missed that look of adoration in her unusual eyes. Missed seeing her carefree like she'd once been.

The pretty girl he'd left eleven years ago had blossomed into a beautiful woman with pleasant curves and a voice that still stirred his senses. Something deep inside him wanted to protect her from the troubles of this world. Too bad they could never be together again.

Jack needed a father. But as much as he'd like the job, it wouldn't be him. He straightened. Would that job go to Rand Kessler?

He looked down at the floor. If he could manage to forgive

Rachel completely, maybe they could be friends again. He'd heard a couple of sermons about forgiveness in the seven months that he'd been saved, but nobody ever mentioned *how* to do that.

Rachel turned around and gasped, splaying her hands across her chest. "Luke! I didn't hear you there."

He shrugged. "Doc needed to examine Jack, so I made myself scarce."

Rachel's face took on that pinched expression again, and she plunked the jar down hard on the table. "Why do you insist on calling my daughter by that hideous male nickname?"

"There's nothing wrong with the name Jack." He couldn't help grinning as he remembered a couple of rascally cavalry buddies with that moniker. "It's what she wants me to call her, and I figure it's a small matter if it makes her happy."

She shoved her hands to her hips. "It's not a small matter to me. She has a name. *Jac–que–line.*"

Luke chuckled at how she emphasized each syllable. "I wanted you to know that I plan on walking over to the schoolhouse each day before and after classes. Maybe I can keep something like this from happening again."

Rachel's tense expression softened. "I'd appreciate that, but are you going to do anything to the boy who hurt my daughter?"

He rubbed his jaw with his forefinger and thumb and then scratched his neck, considering what the teacher had told him. It was probably just as well that Rachel didn't know Jack had jumped back into the fight after Butch turned loose of her. "Mrs. Fairland said that several kids were throwing punches at a big kid who tends to bully the younger ones."

"You mean that Laird boy, don't you?"

He shouldn't be surprised that she knew who he was talking about since Jack had probably told her about the kid. Luke nodded.

"What do you intend to do?" She hiked her chin as if daring him to argue.

"I'm going to have a talk with him and his father. You know his mother is gone, don't you?"

Rachel nodded. "She died about six months before James did. I didn't know her too well since she lived outside of town."

Luke clenched his fist at the mention of her deceased husband. He cleared his throat. "Well, Butch's father isn't exactly the nurturing type, if you know what I mean."

Her lovely blue eyes opened wide. For the first time, he noted the dark shadows under her eyes. Was the boardinghouse too much work for Rachel, combined with the stress of her unruly daughter?

He wanted to make things easier for her. "I'll let Murphy Laird know that if his boy causes any more trouble, he won't be allowed to come back to school. I'll also mosey around the schoolhouse during the times the children are at recess."

Rachel reached out and touched Luke's arm. The heat of her fingers nearly scalded him, and he could only stare at her small hand. Why did he always turn to cornmeal mush around this woman?

"Thank you, Luke. I'd feel much better knowing that you'll be keeping an eye on Jacqueline."

He didn't want to worry her by reminding her that Jack ran all over town and the outskirts. Just because Butch wasn't at school didn't mean Jack would be safe from him. But he would do his best to protect her. "I don't think Butch was the one who hurt her—at least I can't be sure. Could have been one of the others that hit Jack. Accidentally, I mean."

"Well, at any rate, I appreciate your help and that you carried Jacqueline home. I try hard to make her toe the line, but she still runs wild." Tears swarmed in Rachel's eyes. "I don't know what more to do to make her obey me."

Luke looked at the ceiling, noticing a spider web in one corner. He wanted to tug Rachel into his arms and ease her pain, but he couldn't. "I'll pray for her more, and you need to stick to your guns and make her mind you."

Rachel's sorrow ignited into flaming anger. "What do you know about it? I tell her one thing, and she does exactly the opposite. I give her extra chores and make her write scriptures to help her see the error of her ways, but it seems to do no good. What else can I do?"

Luke shrugged. "Maybe she needs a good lickin' now and then."

Rachel sucked in a loud breath. "I will not spank my daughter."

"Why not? Spare the rod, spoil the child."

She spun around, leaning her hands on the edge of the dry sink. "I can't bring myself to spank her—not after. . ."

"After what?" Luke crossed the room and stood behind her, his hands aching to take her in his arms and drive away her anxiety.

"Nothing. Never mind."

"Tell me, Rachel."

She shook her head so hard, he thought sure the pins would fall out of her bun. "I can't. I don't want to talk about it."

Luke clamped down his jaw. What had happened to cause her to not want to discipline her child in the biblical manner? He didn't like where his train of thought was taking him. Knowing he shouldn't touch her, he reached out, placing his hands on her shoulders. As if he'd been struck by lightning, a fire surged up his arms and through his body. He closed his eyes, steeling himself against the desire to pull her close. He cleared his throat. "I'm here if you want to talk to me, Rach."

She stood stiff. Her sniffles made his heart ache. Made him want to take away her pain. *Father, help Rachel and Jack through this difficult time. Please heal Jack quickly and let there be no long-term effects from her injuries. Touch Rachel, and heal the hurting places in her heart.*

The doctor cleared his throat, and Luke stepped back. Heat swept up his neck at being caught nearly embracing Rachel. They both turned to face Dr. Phillips, and Rachel stepped in front of

Luke, drying her eyes with her apron.

"How is she, Doctor? Will she be all right?"

The doc smiled and nodded. "Yes, she will. Keep her in bed for two days, and then let her get up and do things around the house. As long as she doesn't get dizzy and fall, she should be fine."

Rachel hurried forward and took the doctor's hands. "Oh, thank you, Hank."

"Don't send her back to school until next Monday, and just feed her soup and bread today, and some apple cider if you have any."

"So she shouldn't have any pie? I was going to make her that shoofly pie she loves."

The doctor glanced past Rachel to look at Luke, and he winked. "No, let's keep her on light things today. Give her eggs and biscuits in the morning, and if her stomach handles that without problems, she can go back to eating regularly."

Rachel nodded, and Luke grinned at the wily doctor. Wouldn't Jack be disappointed her little scheme hadn't succeeded?

CHAPTER 13

Her guests wouldn't like eating burnt pie tonight, but if the stage didn't arrive soon, that just might happen. Rachel checked the watch pinned to her bodice again and tapped her toe against the boardwalk. Seventeen minutes and no more. That was all she could wait. A vision of blackened pie crusts, burnt sugar, and a kitchen filled with smoke filled her mind. She glanced down the street in the direction the stage would arrive. A telegraphed message had informed her that the new lamp she'd ordered from a specialty shop in Sherman was on today's stage.

The bright sun gleamed down on the town, buzzing with its typical Monday morning activity. People ambled in and out of stores and offices, completing business and moving on to their next item of duty. She could hear the children at school squealing during recess. She shaded her eyes and searched for Jacqueline. Her daughter had been back to school for a week, and other than some teasing about her black eye, which the girl was quite proud of, there'd been no other problems. *Please, Lord, don't let her get in trouble today.*

Rachel swiped the sweat from her temple. Noon had yet to

117

arrive, and already the day felt as hot as August. Glancing around, she pulled the fabric away from her bodice and fanned in some air. Luke strode out of his office and crossed the dirt alleyway. She lowered her hand as her heart flip-flopped.

The birthday party the town had thrown for him several weeks ago had been one she'd remember for a long time, mainly because of her disappointment. She'd hoped Lookout's marshal would ask her to dance for old time's sake, but instead, he'd seemed content just to fill up on her pie and watch the town while chatting with his cousins. Rand hadn't had any problem asking her, though. He would have danced all evening if she had been agreeable. Oh, what was she going to do about him?

Before Luke's return, she'd toyed with the idea of marrying Rand. She would have a ranch house to tend but not the huge boardinghouse. Rand was a good man, even if he was a few years younger than her. But even though she found him a pleasant man to confer with, she didn't love him. And she couldn't marry another man she didn't love. She'd been working up her nerve to tell him just that when Luke had returned to Lookout.

Luke. Now that was another subject. Her throat tightened. She could never tell him that she still cared for him. Had cared, even when she'd been married to James. No wonder her husband had been so dissatisfied. Had he sensed that she didn't love him? But how could he expect love after what he'd done to her?

Her heart ricocheted like a bullet fired inside a stone house when Luke turned in her direction. Luke and James had been friends before she married. Oh, how she wished things had been different—that she could go back and rewrite her story.

"Morning." Luke tipped his hat and slowed his pace, but that wary look that had been in his gaze ever since he returned to Lookout still lingered. "Uh...what's for supper tonight?"

Rachel sighed inwardly, wishing he'd talk to her about something other than food or his laundry, but he seemed determined to keep her at bay. He'd let his defenses down the day Jacqueline had gotten hurt, but they were back in full force. Rachel should rejoice that he'd even bothered to say good day to her when he normally tried to avoid her. *Whatever happened to forgiving those who hurt you?* "Pot roast, your favorite."

"Sounds good." Luke nodded and headed into the stage office.

Too bad it was only her cooking he loved.

She checked her watch again. If she wasn't expecting that new lamp—the one she wanted to collect before the rowdy stagehands knocked it about any more than it already had been, she would return home. The pies would be done soon. At least she only had Mr. Sampson, a traveling salesman, staying at the boardinghouse and wouldn't need to fix an overly large meal.

Her heart quickened at the rumble of horses' hooves and the jangling of harnesses. The boardwalk shook as the stage rounded the corner, looking as if it would tip over, even though it never did.

"Whoa!" the driver shouted, pulling back on the reins. The coach slowed to a halt right in front of the Barfield Stage office amid a cloud of dust and the snorting and heaving of the four sweaty horses.

The shotgun guard climbed down, dropped the steps, and opened the door. A nicely dressed, albeit dust-coated gentleman stepped down then offered his hand to a pretty blond woman dressed in a blue calico. She accepted his assistance and exited the stage. The young woman glanced around, and when she spotted Rachel, she smiled and climbed up to the boardwalk, heading straight for her, straightening her bonnet. "Good day, ma'am. I was wondering if you might point me to Luke Davis's office. I do believe he's the city marshal—at least that's what he said in his correspondence to me."

Rachel's chest tightened. "Correspondence?"

The woman knocked the dust from her skirt and looked up. "Oh yes. I'm Leah Bennett, Marshal Davis's mail-order bride."

Rachel felt the blood drain from her face. Her mouth was suddenly as dry as a Texas creek bed in midsummer, and her knees quivered as her world tilted. She grabbed a post holding up the boardwalk roof to balance herself. "Luke's getting married?"

The woman's cheeks turned strawberry red. Eyes the color of a blue jay sparkled. "Well, that's the plan. At least that's what his letter said. So could you please point me in the right direction?"

Rachel glanced at the stage office, knowing Luke would come out at any moment.

Another woman who'd just disembarked from the stage also stepped up next to Rachel. Worried green eyes flitted between Rachel and the blond woman. Her pale face stood out against the curly curtain of auburn tresses that had escaped her chignon. A deep wrinkle creased one cheek, and she had that foggy look of just having awakened. "Uh. . .pardon me, but did you say city marshal Luke Davis is the man you are to marry?"

Miss Bennett nodded and smiled. "Why yes, I told you that right after we pulled out of Sherman depot, Miss O'Neil."

"Saints preserve us." She pressed her fingertips to her forehead. "I barely remember you sayin' you were to be married, but I must have fallen asleep. I never heard who 'twas you were to wed. What a dreadful mess." The woman's gaze flittered around the town as she wrung her hands. "Whatever will I do? I've nowhere else to go."

Confused at the woman's distress and intrigued by her lilting accent, Rachel put aside her shock at Miss Bennett's declaration and rested her hand on Miss O'Neil's shoulder. "What's the matter? Maybe I can help."

The auburn beauty glanced at Miss Bennett again. "I don't know how to tell you; truly I don't."

"Whatever it is, just spit it out." Leah Bennett hiked her chin and glowered like a schoolmarm scolding her students.

"I. . .oh, how is it something like this could happen?" Sympathy edged Miss O'Neil's green eyes. Wavy wisps of hair fluttered on the warm spring breeze. "I, too, have come to marry Luke Davis."

Rachel's battered heart endured another jab. What had Luke done? How dare he send for two strangers to marry when she had been there all along!

If he was the man of God he claimed to be, wouldn't he forgive her for betraying him?

Miss Bennett's blue eyes widened. "Why, that's preposterous. There must be some mistake."

"Nay, 'tis true. I assure you. I have Marshal Davis's letter right here." Miss O'Neil opened her tattered reticule and pulled out a crinkled page. She unfolded it and handed it to Miss Bennett.

Rachel couldn't help leaning over. She scanned the words, and her dread and confusion mounted when she saw Luke's name signed at the end of the letter. There was only one way to get to the bottom of this distressing situation, and that was to confront Luke. Fortunately—or not—he exited the stage office at that moment, pausing outside the door to look at a piece of paper he held.

"But I also have a letter, and I think you'll see that mine is dated earlier than yours." Miss Bennett quickly retrieved her missive and passed it around.

Rachel pursed her lips tight. This handwriting was different from that of the other letter. Couldn't the women see that? Somebody was toying with their affections, and that was wrong. But was Luke to blame?

He stood outside the stage office door, held a piece of paper up to the sun, and studied it.

"There's Luke now," Rachel said. Both women turned to face their intended.

"Oh my, he's quite handsome—in a rugged sort of way." Miss O'Neil's cheeks flushed, giving color to her pale complexion, and she fanned her face with her gloved hand. "And so tall."

Luke turned and walked toward them, paying no special attention to the women staring at him. "Ladies." He flashed Rachel a curious look, nodded, and proceeded to walk around them.

Rachel sidestepped into his path, barely able to keep a lid on her irritation and her disappointment. "Marshal Davis, it would seem we have a bit of a dilemma here."

Luke surveyed the two women; then he turned his innocent gaze on Rachel. "What dilemma? How can I help?"

Rachel clenched her fists. How could he be so naive? If he sent for a bride—or two—wouldn't he be expecting them? She hiked her chin. "It appears both of these ladies have come to town to claim you as their future husband."

∽

"Pardon me?" Luke would have thought Rachel was joking if not for the anger in her voice and her pinched expression. He folded the payroll shipment information he'd been studying and stuffed it into his pocket, thinking he must have heard her wrong. "What are you talking about?"

"Oh dear. You tell him." The shorter, thinner woman with big green eyes and hair the color of a sorrel mare attempted to strangle the life out of the strings of her handbag.

Had they been robbed on the stage? Had some man acted inappropriately toward them? Luke gritted his teeth, ready to take action to defend them if necessary. But hadn't Rachel said something about marriage?

He cast a glance at her. Rachel's light blue eyes looked as cold as a January day in Colorado. What could have happened to turn her to ice?

The blue-eyed blond tossed her head like a mustang and narrowed her gaze. "It would seem there's been some kind of mistake, Marshal. I'm Leah Bennett. The mail-order bride you've been corresponding with."

The thinner woman sucked in a gasp. "But that simply cannot be the truth, for I have a letter right here, askin' me to m–marry you."

The Irish lilt in the woman's voice caught his attention, but his eyes widened as his mind grappled with what the women had said. "You're both here—to marry *me*?"

Rachel crossed her arms and frowned at him. "What have you done, Luke?"

"Nothing, I promise." He raised his hands, as if in surrender, and his gaze zigzagged among the three women. "I didn't write to either of these ladies."

The brides glanced at each other, apprehension evident in their eyes.

"Well, someone did. So what are you going to do about it?" Rachel crossed her arms and stared at him.

The trio of females, two steaming and one near weeping, standing side by side, created a unified barricade on the board-walk; and around them, a crowd was gathering, casting curious looks in his direction. Luke's first thought was to flee, but he held his ground like a man and scanned his baffled mind, trying to make some sense of this. He knew he hadn't written to these women, but evidently someone had, and he aimed to find out who. Dallying with a woman's affections may not be a legal issue, but in his book, it was wrong, and now these ladies were suffering and inconvenienced because someone had pretended to be him. Besides, impersonating a lawman might just be a crime.

Luke lifted his hat and raked his fingers through his hair. "I guess you'd better get the women situated at the boardinghouse. Then we'll sit down and see if we can get to the bottom of this. I can assure both of you that I did not write those letters. But I intend to find out who did."

CHAPTER 14

Rachel grasped the folds of her skirt. How could Luke expect her to take responsibility for *his* mail-order brides? It was unconscionable. She sighed, pushing away her irritation, knowing none of this was the brides' fault. There was no other place in Lookout where a decent woman could spend the night, unless with a family. Smothering her anger and breaking heart, she faced Luke. "If you'll see to their luggage, I'll show the women to the boardinghouse. Ladies, please follow me."

Thank goodness she had a large enough roast to feed the additional people. She could add more potatoes and carrots, and the two pies would be sufficient for dessert. Rachel stopped in her tracks. "Oh, no! My pies."

She hiked up her skirt and dashed for her kitchen, not caring if the brides followed or not. She raced in front of a wagon, forcing the driver to yank back on the reins.

"Hey, watch it, lady."

Everyone probably thought her to be as crazy as a rabid skunk, but if she didn't save her pies, there would be no dessert for supper tonight. And with two women in the house, that would be a disaster.

Rachel stormed in the front door, through the narrow hallway, and into the kitchen. She stopped, a hand pressed to her heaving chest. No black smoke rose from the oven door. Instead of the stench of scorched sugar, the fragrant scent of apples cooked in cinnamon filled the heated kitchen. Her gaze landed on the perfectly cooked pies cooling on the counter. What was going on?

Someone clomped out of her bedroom at a quick pace. Jacqueline rounded the corner and halted wide-eyed when she saw her mother. Gratitude to her daughter for saving the pies flowed through Rachel, but the knowledge that the girl was supposed to be at school squelched her enthusiasm. "What are you doing home?"

Jacqueline shrugged and leaned against the doorjamb. The pretty dress Rachel had insisted she wear this morning had been replaced by a faded blouse with rolled up sleeves and black trousers. The ever-present western boots covered her feet, and her daughter's hair hung in straggly braids with a sprig of grass here and there as if she'd been wrestling on the ground. The deep purple and black that had surrounded her eye had given way to yellow and green. "I got hot, and I was still hungry after dinner, so I came home to change and get something else to eat."

"You know you're not allowed to wear pants to school. They are strictly for gardening, and if you keep wearing them, I'll burn them in the trash barrel." Rachel forced her voice to sound stern. Luke would be proud of her for standing up to Jacqueline, not that it mattered now that his "brides" had come to town.

Jacqueline's eyes went wide as biscuits, but she didn't comment.

"Did you ask Mrs. Fairland if you could leave the school premises?"

The girl shrugged again. She hadn't asked permission. She never did.

"Let me fix your hair, and then you need to change into a dress and get back to school."

"Aw, Ma, it's nearly over, and me and Jonesy's goin' fishing."

Rachel gasped in spite of her determination not to let her daughter fluster her. "Fishing! You most certainly aren't going anywhere with that boy. He's far too old for you to be hanging around with, and besides, you need to go back to school."

"Ah, Jonesy's all right, and Mrs. Fairland is just testing the little kids this afternoon. There's nothing for us big kids to do but practice cipherin' or read boring books."

Jacqueline hated reading, and it didn't seem right to make her sit still all afternoon if they weren't working. But she needed to be in school. And why did she always want to play with those older boys? It wasn't as if she was interested in them in a womanly way. Her daughter just wanted to be one of the gang—something that perplexed Rachel to no end. She shook her head.

"I'll bring home some bass you can cook for supper." Jacqueline's dark blue eyes twinkled. She strode to the jar and snagged two sugar cookies, bit off a chunk of one and stuck the other in her pocket.

She'd planned to fix roast beef for supper, but fish *would* taste good and didn't cost anything, and she did have a big issue to deal with immediately. Maybe it would be better if her daughter were not around until things with the mail-order brides settled down. Still, she couldn't abide by her missing school to go fishing. A knock sounded at the front door. The brides had arrived.

Jacqueline darted past her and out the back door. "I'll be home before supper."

"No, wait." Rachel spun toward the back door. "I didn't say you could go."

"You're welcome. I saved your pies, you know." Jacqueline yanked a fishing pole off the back porch and raced toward the river. A boy Rachel recognized as Jonesy stepped in beside her as she passed behind Luke's house.

"Oh, heavenly Father, what am I going to do with this mischievous daughter You gave me?" Rachel should go after Jacqueline and insist she go back to school, but she didn't want her daughter pitching a fit in front of the new guests.

"Rachel?"

"In the kitchen." Needing a moment to calm herself, she checked the oven to make sure the pies hadn't spilled over; then she hurried to the entryway, where Luke stood with his two brides. The thought of them living under her roof, eating meals she cooked, and asking her about the man they'd come to marry made her stomach swirl. Of course, they couldn't both marry him, but the idea of even one doing so made her want to cry.

The stage line's shotgun rider stood on the porch, holding a small trunk. Rachel forced a smile at the women, both young and pretty enough to snag the eye of any man. It was easy to see how Luke could prefer them over her. Pushing away her warring thoughts, she gave her guests a true smile. They didn't know her feelings and were innocents in this awful ordeal. She owed them her kindness and hospitality. "Follow me, please."

Luke's snort erupted behind her. "You said that already, just before you hiked up your skirts and made a mad dash through town as if your dress was on fire." He chuckled, and the man outside joined him.

Heat rose to Rachel's cheeks. "Yes, well, I remembered the pies I had in the oven. I was distracted by the unusual circumstances and had lost track of the time. You'd be sorely disappointed if they'd burned and you didn't have any dessert tonight." She glared at Luke, and he had the good sense to look chagrined.

Miss O'Neil cleared her throat. "They do smell delicious. And such a lovely home you have."

"Thank you. I apologize, Miss Bennett, Miss O'Neil, for running off and leaving you standing at the depot. My name is Rachel Hamilton, by the way. Let me show you to your rooms." Both women smiled, and Rachel felt as if they'd forgiven her. She started up the steps to the second floor, holding back a sigh at the spectacle she must have made. These women probably wondered if they'd be safe in her home.

Upstairs she stopped in the wide hallway. She pointed to a

matching set of doors on the far wall. "The door to the left is a washroom where I have fresh water each morning and afternoon. The door on the right leads to the back stairs, but I always keep it locked. There are four rooms on this floor that I rent out."

She stepped forward and opened the bedroom door to the left of the main stairway. "Miss Bennett, would this suit you?"

The woman stepped past her and glanced around the cheery room decorated in a soft blue and white. "Yes, this is very nice. Just have that man place my trunk along the wall, and please take care with that. It's my hope chest."

Rachel turned to the man and waved her hand toward the wall. "If you don't mind, please put the trunk where the lady indicated."

He lugged the chest inside the room and set it down. He nodded at the women and quickly took his leave. Halfway down the stairs on the landing, he paused. "There's a crate for you at the depot, Mrs. Hamilton. I'll fetch it and bring it to you."

Rachel smiled at the dust-coated man. "Thank you. I appreciate your assistance. And please take care with that. It's my new lamp."

The man nodded and continued down the stairs. Luke stood like a statue in the hallway, longingly watching him.

"Marshal." Miss Bennett cocked her head and batted her eyes at Luke. "My satchel, if you please. It's the one tucked under your arm."

Luke looked as if he were afraid to step into her room, what with the woman batting her lashes at him as if she'd been chopping onions. Rachel ducked her head to hide her frown. Would Miss Bennett win Luke's affections with her alluring ways? Though travel worn, both of the young women were lovely and didn't have the look of a haggard boardinghouse owner and mother of a precocious child.

Luke still stood at the threshold, holding three satchels and looking as if he'd like to tuck tail and run. She'd never seen a man so uncomfortable with women. Rachel let him off the hook and took the carpetbag he held tight under his muscled upper arm and set it on Miss Bennett's bed. She slipped past Luke, relieving him of a second smaller satchel, and opened the door across the hall.

"Miss O'Neil, perhaps you'd like the green room, as we call it." Rachel stepped inside, scanning the area to make sure all was in order, even though she already knew it was. She loved the pale floral wallpaper and the spring green curtains. The flower garden quilt on the bed also had green accents, as well as a pleasing variety of pinks, violets, and blues.

Miss O'Neil gasped. "I've never stayed in a room so lovely. 'Tis charming, it is."

"Thank you for your help, Marshal. We should probably let the women freshen up a bit before we discuss the—situation." Rachel lifted her brows at Luke. His ears reddened, and he handed her the final satchel and headed toward the stairs.

"Ladies, welcome to Hamilton House. Miss O'Neil, I'll have your trunk delivered as soon as that man returns with it."

The young woman's pale cheeks turned the color of an apple. "Um. . .this is all I have, mum."

Rachel hid her surprise at the young woman's lack of belongings. Maybe she planned to send more along later, after she got settled. Only she might not be settling here once all was said and done. "All right then. Please make yourself at home."

Miss O'Neil's gaze darted across the hall at Miss Bennett's room, and she stepped forward, wringing her hands. "How much is a room for the night?" she whispered.

"Two dollars, which includes your meals, or twelve dollars for a full week."

"Oh, blessit be, I uh. . .can only afford to stay two nights. I thought I would arrive and be married right away. Perhaps you might need some assistance here? I'm used to hard work."

Compassion for the woman surged through Rachel. The girl

couldn't be more than seventeen or eighteen. Rachel couldn't afford to hire any help, but maybe someone else in Lookout could. "Don't worry about that now. Things will work out."

Rachel met Luke downstairs and motioned him to go outside. She paced the front porch, arms crossed over her chest, waiting on Luke to get his nerve up to talk to her. If her heart hadn't been split in two, she might have been tempted to feel sorry for the man.

He lifted his hat and slapped it against his leg. "Look, Rachel, I didn't write to those women. I knew nothing about them before you stopped me at the depot."

"Do you think this is some kind of sick prank? Those women have traveled who knows how far to marry you, and I've just learned that at least one of them has very little money." Rachel sighed and looked across the street. "If you're not responsible, who do you think is? Who would toy with two women like this?"

"I have my suspicions, but I want to do some investigating before I say anything."

Rachel nodded. "All right. Do you want to question the women?"

Luke shrugged. He'd probably never talk to them if he didn't have to. If Rachel wasn't so disturbed by the whole event and what it could mean to her, she might have found some humor in the situation.

"I'll try to get back before supper."

"Maybe we should talk after that. No sense in spoiling anyone's meal."

Luke nodded and walked away but suddenly stopped and turned back to her. "Oh, hey, Mrs. Fairland gave me a note earlier and asked me to pass it on to you."

Rachel puffed air into her cheeks and took the message. She knew what the schoolteacher had to say but opened the note anyway. Scanning the message, her frustration grew. That rascally child. She had been one of the children who was supposed to take the test this afternoon.

Wadding up the paper in her hand, Rachel watched Luke's long legs take him away. Somewhere in the back of her mind, she'd hoped they could have a second chance. He'd seemed truly surprised about the two brides, but was that just for her benefit? None of it made any sense. If he wanted a mail-order bride, why would he order *two* of them?

The stagehand nodded as he passed Luke, carrying a crate on his shoulder. Her lamp. In all the hubbub she'd forgotten about it.

Rachel stepped aside and allowed the man to pass in front of her. "Where do you want this, Mrs. Hamilton?"

"Just set it on the parlor floor for now, and thank you so much for your help."

"My pleasure, ma'am."

He lowered the crate to her decorated rug, and the sound of clinking glass only added to her misery. Her new lamp was broken, just like her heart.

CHAPTER 15

Rachel finished sweeping the kitchen floor and glanced outside again. The sun had set, and darkness covered the land. She swept the dirt out the back door and stood listening to the crickets. Where was Luke? Had he gotten tied up smoothing out a disturbance, or was he simply avoiding the confrontation with the brides?

She shook her head. For a lawman, he avoided females like a mouse hid from a tomcat. With his gentle ways and soft-spoken demeanor, he was far different from James. That alone made him attractive to her.

She took the stack of dried dishes from the counter and set them on the shelf near the dining room door. Glancing around the tidy kitchen, a measure of satisfaction filled her. The flickering glow of the two lanterns mounted on the wall illuminated the room. Soft yellow walls looked cheery with the light blue gingham curtains. Every utensil had a place, and each item was in its place. At least it was as long as Jacqueline wasn't in the kitchen. The girl used things and set them down, never thinking to wash them or put them away.

Rachel shook her head, still tired from her battle with Jacqueline. When she'd told her daughter that she'd get no pie after supper because she had lied and skipped out of taking that test, Jacqueline had pitched a royal fit. Both the brides had declined pie themselves and had quickly disappeared into their rooms. Mr. Sampson, one never to refuse dessert, had taken his slice and eaten it on the porch to avoid the girl's ranting. Glancing down, Rachel noticed her white-knuckled grip on the back of the chair. She released her hold and glanced at the ceiling. "Lord, help me raise this child You've given me."

Three quick knocks sounded on the kitchen door. Rachel jumped as Luke slipped in.

"About time you showed up. The brides went to bed an hour ago."

"Sorry. I got busy." He studied the floor for a moment then glanced up, the lantern light shimmering in his coffee-colored eyes. "I have my suspicions as to what happened, but I haven't been able to confirm them yet."

"Care to share?" Rachel crossed her arms and leaned back against the worktable.

"Not 'til I know for sure. I could be wrong." He captured her gaze, sending her stomach in a tizzy. How could he affect her so when she was still upset with him?

He glanced at the stove where she kept his dinner warm whenever he missed a meal. His features relaxed when he saw the meal covered with an inverted pie plate. Had he thought she wouldn't feed him because she was irritated?

"Have a seat. You must be starving by now." She retrieved his dinner and placed it on her worktable.

For once he didn't snatch his plate and disappear out the door. Luke washed his hands in the bucket of water sitting in the sink and dried them with a towel. He removed his worn Stetson, revealing a sweat ring that had darkened his brown hair, making it look black. He hung the hat on the edge of the ladder-back chair, sat, and picked up his fork.

Rachel resisted the urge to sigh. As an adolescent, she'd dreamed many nights of Luke and her sharing a meal together in their own kitchen. But all of her girlish dreams had been dashed in one horrible afternoon. Luke avoided looking at her and put away his food as if it were his last meal. If he wasn't willing to let her in on his thoughts about the brides, she might as well go to bed. Tomorrow would be a long day, and dawn came early. She walked toward the hallway. "I'm plumb tuckered out. See you in the morning."

"Rachel. . ."

She stopped but didn't turn to face him. How could he put such pleading into her name?

"Look at me, please."

She took a deep breath, gathering strength, and then spun to face him, bracing her shoulder against the doorjamb. His miserable expression made her want to wrap her arms around him and tell him things would be all right. But would they? There was only one Luke Davis, and two women had set their hearts on marrying him.

His lips pressed together so hard they turned pale. "I hope you know that I had nothing to do with this. I could never toy with a woman's affections in such a manner."

That's what her heart believed, but her mind wasn't so sure. Someone had written to the women, probably even sent money. If some man had wanted a bride for himself, why pretend to be Luke? Everyone knew the city marshal's pay wasn't that great. Why, a woman would either need to be self-sufficient or very desperate to want to marry a low-salaried lawman who put his life on the line everyday. Or be in love. She glanced at him again, sitting there, wanting her support. He'd once supported her, helped her whenever things had gone bad. His had been the shoulder she cried on for so many years—when her pa died, when things were difficult—but that was a long time ago.

She sighed heavily and tugged out a seat across from him. "I believe that you wouldn't purposely dally with a woman's affections, Luke." Heaven knew she wished he'd toy with her affections, but he no longer looked at her with love in his eyes. At least he was talking to her now.

"Thanks, Rach." A soft smile tugged at Luke's lips, sending Rachel's heart pounding. He picked up his fork and attacked the pot roast, potatoes, and carrots. It was a good thing she'd gone ahead and fixed the meal, because Jack had returned home without any fish.

"Would you like me to heat up your coffee? I was heading to bed, so I banked the fire and put the pot on the back burner."

Luke shook his head. "It's plenty warm. So. . ." He glanced up. "How are the women faring? Are they terribly upset?"

Rachel gave him a stern look. "Of course they are. Both had their hearts set on marrying you. They left their homes and traveled hundreds of miles, only to find out the man they planned to marry knew nothing about them. Oh, and did I mention there was instant competition for your attention, being as there were two brides, not one?"

"It's a fine mess, all right. When Gar—" Luke shoved another bite into his mouth, as if he'd said something he hadn't intended on saying.

"What?" Rachel's mind raced as she tried to figure out what he'd almost said.

"Never mind." For the next few minutes, he wolfed down the rest of his food; then he leaned on his elbows, staring into his coffee cup. "I have a little money. I've been saving to buy a house. I suppose I could give each of the ladies enough cash so they could get back to wherever it was they came from."

Luke was going to buy a house? Rachel's mouth dropped open. Could he have accumulated that much money on a soldier's salary? Having a house meant he'd be staying in town. How could she spend the next twenty or thirty years living in the same town as Luke, watching him one day marry another woman and then raise their children? Dread melded her to her chair. She thought of the letters from her aunt, asking her to bring Jacqueline and move to Kansas City. Maybe now was the time to finally consider her offer.

Luke glanced up, his forehead creased. "Do you think that's a good idea, Rach?"

"Hmm?" What had he said before tilting her world off its axis? "Oh, um. . .I don't know. I'm not sure either woman wishes to return where she came from. And if you weren't the one to send for them, it isn't your duty to provide for them. Why would someone impersonate you?"

Luke's guarded expression revealed nothing. "I don't want to say until I'm sure."

Rachel scanned her mind, trying to think who might be out of town that he would suspect. The Ralstons had gone to Dallas to care for her elderly mother. Garrett and Mark Corbett were on a run, delivering freight for the company they co-owned. The mayor was at a convention in Dallas.

Wait a minute! She slapped her hand on the table, receiving a curious stare from Luke.

That was it! Rachel stood so abruptly her chair fell back and banged against the floor. Luke jumped up and spun toward the door, his hand reaching for his pistol. Rachel might have smiled if not for her building anger.

He twisted back around, his diligent gaze checking the other doorways then finally settling on her. "What's wrong?"

Rachel scowled and heaved angered breaths out her nose. "It was *them*, wasn't it?"

"Who?"

"Garrett and Mark. Those two hooligans have been pulling pranks for as long as I've known them. They were the ones who ordered the brides." Rachel picked up her chair and set it aright. It was a good thing those men were out of town, because she wasn't

136

sure what she might do right now if they weren't. "I'm a little surprised at Mark doing such a thing, or maybe Garrett did it on his own. I wouldn't put it past *him*."

Luke's gaze found something interesting on the floor, his ears turning red. "I told you I'd rather not say until I can confirm it."

She marched around the table and stopped a foot from him. "So, you *do* suspect them. They've done a lot of ornery things in their lives, but this takes the cake. It would serve them right if you made *them* marry those poor girls, except I'd hate for either one to get strapped with the likes of those two yahoos."

A tiny smile tugged at Luke's lips. "It would serve them right, wouldn't it?" He chuckled.

Rachel was tempted to smack him, but a tiny giggle swelled up inside her, begging to be set free. She could imagine the pinched expressions on Mark and Garrett's faces when Luke forced them into shotgun weddings. She pressed her lips together, but a little snort erupted, making Luke laugh. Rachel joined him, feeling a release of tension for the first time that whole day.

Luke's laugh deepened, and Rachel shoved her hand over his mouth. "Shh. . .you're going to wake the whole house."

Humor still glimmered in his eyes, but he pulled her hand down, keeping quiet. "My cousins should be back tomorrow, and then we'll see what they have to say about all this." He shrugged. "Could be they aren't even involved."

"Uh-huh, and it's going to snow in July in Texas."

Luke tightened his grip on her hand, sending pleasant shivers up her arm. What he meant as a friendly gesture made her want to lean in and hug him. Pulling her hand from his, she stepped back, knowing that he wasn't aware he'd let his guard down around her for only the second time since coming back to town. "It's late, and tomorrow will be a trying day. Best we get some sleep."

Luke nodded. He claimed his hat and walked toward the door. "Sleep tight, sweet Rachel."

She watched in the moonlight as he strode toward his house,

and then she closed the back door. Had he purposely used that endearment, or had it just slipped out? Rachel scraped his plate and set it in the sink along with his cup. She turned down the lantern and ambled toward the downstairs bedroom she shared with her daughter. Her hand caught the doorknob, and she paused, thinking how warm and soft Luke's lips had felt against her fingertips when she'd covered his mouth. A sudden thought sent warm hope traveling through her being. If Luke had no intention of marrying the brides, maybe there was still hope for her.

The next morning, Luke rode Alamo back into Lookout after a brisk ride. With most of his duties in town, he'd neglected to exercise his horse. Both he and his mount had benefited from the long ride. He breathed in a deep breath when he saw his cousins' wagon parked outside the freight office. He didn't care for confrontations, and having been a cavalry officer, he'd had his share of them, but this was different. Innocent females had been given false hope—their emotions toyed with, their dreams smashed. "Help me not to lose my temper, Lord."

Luke tied his horse to the hitching post outside the freight office and stormed inside. He shoved his hands to his hips and eyed both men. Mark and Garrett looked up from their desks where they'd been working and exchanged a glance. "I reckon you heard what happened yesterday."

Both men had the audacity to grin.

"Good morning to you, too." Mark chuckled.

"This isn't a laughing matter." Luke crossed his arms and glared at the two. "I can't believe you would do such a low-down thing."

"What thing is that?" Garrett leaned back in his chair, hands crossed over his stomach, obviously trying to look innocent.

"You know good and well what I'm talking about." He paced the room, casting glares at his cousins. Too bad this wasn't a legal offense or he'd haul them both of to jail and see who had the last laugh. Then again, maybe he could arrest them for impersonating a lawman.

Mark tapped a finger on his desk, his blue eyes gleaming. "Well, you did say you'd marry if the right woman came along."

"When did I say that?"

"The evening of your birthday," Mark said.

"That's right. We just figured you needed some help finding her." Garrett nodded as he straightened a stack of papers on his desk. "We wrote to several women who had advertisements in the newspaper but sure didn't expect more than one would be willing to travel all the way to Lookout." Garrett leaned back in his chair and put his feet on his desk, crossing his hands behind his head. "We didn't know the brides had arrived until we got back in town this morning and stopped at the café for breakfast. Weren't sure any of them would show up."

Mark nodded. "Everyone was talking about it."

"Them? Just how many did you write to?"

"Five." Garrett stretched, holding up all the fingers on one hand. "But a couple weren't interested in moving to Texas." He stroked his chin with his index finger and thumb and waggled his brows. "Two did, huh? Guess you get to pick which one you like best. Are they pretty?"

Luke couldn't believe his ears. What were they thinking? Mark and Garrett had always been rascals, but they'd never been purposely hurtful. "How could you trifle with those women? Don't you realize they've left their homes and families and traveled hundreds of miles in hope of marrying me?"

"Well, you can make dreams come true for one of them at least." Mark grinned. "So, are they pretty?"

Grinding his back teeth, Luke spun toward the window and checked to make sure things were still quiet outside. It wouldn't do to let his cousins know both women were pretty enough to catch any man's eye. "They're nice enough, I suppose."

"What do they look like?" Garrett's chair squeaked.

Luke shrugged one shoulder. He might as well tell them, or they'd just hurry out the door and go see for themselves. "They're very different. One's blond with blue eyes. The other is shorter and has reddish brown hair and green eyes."

Mark chuckled. "I thought you weren't interested. Sounds like you looked them over real good. Mmm. . .I always imagined falling in love with a redhead. If you don't want her, maybe I'll try my hand at wooing her."

Luke turned back to face the two scoundrels. "These are people we're talking about, not horses or cattle. You can't play with a woman's emotions. They're not like us. They're sensitive."

Mark grinned. "I had no idea you knew that much about females. Is that why you avoid them?"

Luke studied the dirt on his boot tips. Did he avoid women? Maybe one in particular. "I see women all over town every day."

Garrett dropped his feet to the floor with a loud *thunk*. "Married women don't count. When was the last time you showed interest in a gal of marrying age?"

Luke glanced at the walls of the freight office as he contemplated Garrett's question. A large area map hung on one unpainted wall with pins stuck in it indicating the smaller towns that his cousins delivered freight to. Papers littered Garrett's desk in haphazard piles while Mark's were neatly stacked. Boxes and crates waiting to be shipped filled one wall.

His cousins didn't understand the position he was in. "If I show attention to anyone past school age, I'll have all the mamas in the county wanting me to come for dinner and court their daughters."

"Oh, to eat good food with a pretty woman. What a cross to bear." Mark folded his arms over his chest and leaned his hip on his desk. "I might believe that if there were any marriageable women in Lookout."

"We've provided the perfect solution," Garrett said. "Pick one of the brides, marry up with her, and then all the mamas will turn their eyes on someone else."

Luke smiled for the first time since entering the freight office. "Yeah, like you two yahoos."

"Hey, I don't mind a home-cooked meal and a pretty woman to share it with once in a while. It's just too bad there aren't some in this town." Garrett picked up a pencil and started shaving the end with his pocketknife. Mark scowled at the mess he was making on the floor.

"I think the best thing would be for you two to marry the brides." Luke held back his grin and tried to appear stern.

Garrett stood and pointed a finger at Luke. "Now hold on a minute. We ordered those brides for you, not us. I'm sorry that two of 'em showed up. I figured when it came right down to it, they'd back out. I never expected to get so many responses to my advertisement."

Luke stiffened. "You posted a notice about *me*?"

"It sounded like a good idea at the time," Mark said.

"What did you say? That I'm a desperate marshal who needs a wife? I don't even own a home, for Pete's sake."

Garrett shrugged and tried to keep a straight face, but it wasn't working. "Just that you were handsome, well established, friendly. Stuff like that."

"Well established? Did you also tell them that I live in a one-room cabin next to the boardinghouse where I take all my meals? I don't even own a cookstove. What woman would want to live in a cabin with no stove?"

Mark grabbed a cup off his desk and filled it from the coffeepot he picked up at the café each morning. "Want some?"

Luke scowled at him. "No, I don't want coffee. This is serious business. We need to decide what to do with those women." He fingered his pistol handle. "I'm still of a mind to march you down to the boardinghouse and make you two marry those gals."

Mark sat and took a sip from his cup. "Have you spent any

time getting to know them?"

Luke stared at the ceiling. This conversation wasn't going as planned. Perhaps he should have let Rachel join him as he confronted his cousins, but he'd told her he could handle them. Could be he'd overestimated his abilities. "No, I haven't. They just arrived yesterday while you two were conveniently out delivering freight. I got them situated at the boardinghouse while I tried to figure out what in the world was going on." He picked a paper off of Garrett's desk and examined the script, receiving a scowl from his cousin. "Once I recognized the handwriting in the letters those gals showed me, I knew pretty much what had happened."

Garrett squirmed and looked at Mark. "We were just trying to help you. Like get you a bride for your birthday."

"My birthday was weeks ago."

"Yeah, well, it takes time to communicate with a woman. You can't hurry them, and you have to answer all their nitpicky questions 'cause they're suspicious," said Mark.

"I wonder why." Luke shoved his hands to his hips and glowered at them.

"What you need to do is get to know the women. You can't be certain one of them isn't the gal for you unless you spend time with them. Why not take each one to the café for dinner or supper?" Garrett's gaze lit up as if he'd just solved the dilemma.

"And have the whole town talkin'?" Luke rolled his eyes. The town was already talking. All yesterday afternoon and evening people had stared at him and whispered as he walked along the street.

"Look, you two are the reason those women came to town. I'm going to talk to Rachel and see when's a good time, and you two are coming to the boardinghouse to apologize and make amends. Is that clear?"

His cousins shared a glance, but both men nodded. Luke stared each one in the eye, making sure they understood he was serious. "I'll let you know what time the meeting is."

He shoved open the door, and several people on the boardwalk gawked at him with curious expressions. He liked small-town life except when he was the main attraction, and he didn't want to admit that he enjoyed the time he'd spent chatting with Rachel last night. It was almost as if they were friends again, without their troubled past. He wouldn't likely get to do that again if he was with another woman. In spite of all that had happened between him and Rachel, she was the only woman he'd ever known as a close friend. A part of him longed to rekindle that relationship, but could they do that? Just remain friends?

They'd have to, because that was all he was willing to be.

CHAPTER 16

Rachel, Jacqueline, and the brides sat at one end of the dining table while Mr. Sampson ate at the other end. Rachel sighed inwardly. You'd think the middle-aged salesman wouldn't mind eating with a couple of pretty women, but he almost seemed afraid of them. Maybe he feared one of them would set her sights on him. She smiled and ducked her head.

He wolfed down the last of his eggs and stood. "Thank you for another fine breakfast, Mrs. Hamilton. See you at supper tonight." His gaze danced toward the two brides, and he nodded. "Ladies. Miss Jacqueline."

Rachel shook her head and buttered her biscuit. She hoped he did better talking to women as he hawked his wares than he'd done with the two brides.

Miss O'Neil cleared her throat and laid down her fork. "Will we be able to talk to Marshal Davis this morning? I. . .uh"—she glanced at Miss Bennett—"need to make some decisions as to what to do very soon."

"I, for one, plan to marry the marshal, so I suppose you do need to make alternative plans." Miss Bennett dabbed her lips with her napkin and eyed Miss O'Neil with disdain.

Rachel swirled more sugar into her coffee then took a sip of the hot liquid, hating that the women were fighting over Luke. How had things gotten to this point?

Jacqueline shoved another slice of bacon in her mouth. "Luke's gonna marry my ma."

Rachel choked as she swallowed. She coughed as she tried to clear her clogged throat. Tears blurred her vision. Both brides stared wide-eyed at her. Rachel turned her attention to her daughter. "Wherever did you get that idea?"

Jacqueline plowed rows with her fork lightly across the lukewarm gravy covering half of a biscuit. "It just makes sense. He nearly lives here. You feed him and do his laundry already. You need someone to take care of you. But I don't hav'ta mind him." She dabbed some peach jam onto her biscuit and took a bite.

"Saints preserve us." Miss O'Neil held her napkin to her chest and squeezed it fiercely.

"Luke does not live here. He lives next door." Rachel tried to apply salve to the wound her daughter had just inflicted.

"Same thing." Jacqueline shrugged.

Rachel closed her eyes and shook her head. "I'm not marrying Luke."

Especially now.

Desperate to change the subject, Rachel turned to Miss Bennett. "Why don't you tell us a little bit about yourself?"

The young woman took a sip of her coffee then touched her napkin to her mouth. "I have lived just outside of Carthage, Missouri, for the past twelve years, but I was born in Boston. My father got it in his system to travel west when I was a child, but Carthage was as far as Mother would go. She simply wouldn't tolerate moving to the frontier. Father owns a farm, and I'm the oldest of eleven children." Miss Bennett stared at Miss O'Neil as if saying it was her turn to share.

Eleven children! Was that why she decided to become a mail-order bride? To get away from such a large household? Rachel couldn't imagine the responsibility that must have fallen on Miss Bennett's young shoulders. Why, she doubted either woman had reached her twentieth birthday yet.

Suddenly, she felt old. She was twenty-eight and still two years younger than Luke, but maybe he was now looking for a much younger woman to marry.

Miss O'Neil cleared her throat. "I came to New Orleans from Ireland with my parents, but they both died shortly after we arrived. I uh. . .met a couple from Shreveport who took me there to work on their estate just outside of town." She fingered the handle on her coffee cup and stared at it, looking apprehensive. "I was a h–housemaid."

Rachel's heart ached for the girl. She'd lost her parents, was all alone in a foreign country, and now had to deal with competing for Luke's affections. No wonder she was so desperate. She couldn't have made much money working as a servant, which explained why she only had the funds to stay two nights.

Rachel tapped her finger against her plate, thinking. When a close friend or distant relative visited, she would often offer them a room for free, but she hesitated doing that with someone she barely knew since the boardinghouse was her sole source of income. And it would hardly be fair to give one bride free room and board and not the other bride. Still, she couldn't just toss the woman out on the streets.

Miss Bennett stood. "I'm going to my room to freshen up. I imagine the marshal will be here soon."

Rachel watched her sashay out of the room. The woman put on airs for some reason, though her clothing was faded and thin. She seemed bound and determined to become Luke's bride, but why? Had something driven her away from her home, other than her numerous siblings?

Jacqueline jumped up. She disappeared into the kitchen and

returned with a bowl filled with the contents of the scrap bucket. "I'm running this over to Max."

Rachel stood and gave her a hug. "All right, but you come right back. Just because it's Saturday, doesn't mean you can play all day. We need to weed and water the garden before it gets too hot."

Jacqueline nodded and tugged loose from the embrace, then swaggered out of the dining room, walking like a boy. She'd even requested that the brides call her Jack. Rachel couldn't understand the changes in her once sweet child. Were they because her father had died? Or just a natural part of growing older?

"Um. . .excuse me, Mrs. Hamilton, but have you by chance thought of a place I might find employment?"

Rachel turned her attention back to Miss O'Neil. Her curly auburn hair looked as rebellious as Jacqueline as it fought against the confines of its hairpins, and her green eyes looked large against her fair complexion. Her Irish accent only enhanced her beauty.

"Oh no. I haven't thought about that, but let me do so now." She took a minute to consider the establishments and then the families in the area. "Um, well, there's a family just outside of town that has a new baby. They already have two other small children. Perhaps they could use some help, or they might know of someone else who does. Why don't we start there? I've been meaning to go visit them anyway."

Miss O'Neil smiled. " 'Twould be nice, as long as it won't inconvenience you."

"No, not at all. Just let me get the dishes cleaned up." Rachel stood and placed Miss Bennett's plate on top of her own. Miss O'Neil set Mr. Sampson's plate on top of hers and followed Rachel into the kitchen, putting them on the worktable. Rachel looked at her boarder. "Thank you for bringing those in, but you go and relax."

"I don't mind helpin'. I'm used to staying busy. When I'm idle, I worry too much."

"If you're sure, I'd be happy for some help."

"I shall finish clearing the table, if 'twould be all right."

Rachel nodded. She took some hot water from the stove's reservoir, poured it into the sink, and then scraped the plates into the scrap bucket for Max. Miss O'Neil brought the salt and sugar bowls in, set them down, and then darted back into the dining room. The two women were so different. Miss O'Neil, while lovely, was quiet and seemed quite insecure. Miss Bennett's clothing indicated someone who also had little money, but she seemed sure of herself. How did they end up becoming mail-order brides?

Luke was certainly handsome, but they hadn't known that before coming to Lookout. And they knew nothing of his personality. What if he changed like James had after he married? Her husband had been charming—except for when he grew angry or drank or lost at gambling, which happened more and more often toward the end. Rachel shuddered at the memory. But Luke wasn't like James. He'd never hurt someone, no matter how angry he might become.

The chair behind her banged against the table, and she jumped. Just thinking about James had set her on edge.

"Sorry. I accidentally kicked the chair."

Rachel peered over her shoulder, her heart still thudding. "It's all right. I was just lost in thought, and the noise startled me."

Half an hour later, Rachel and Miss O'Neil headed out the front door. Miss Bennett sat in a rocker on the porch, reading a book. Rachel lifted her basket over one arm, stopped, and turned to her. "We're off to visit a friend and see her new baby. Would you care to come with us?"

Miss Bennett stuck her finger in the book to mark her place and looked up. "No, thank you. I've had my fill of babies. I believe I'll sit right here and wait for the marshal to show up."

Miss O'Neil's gaze darted up Main Street. "I'd hate to miss Marshal Davis's visit. Should I be staying, too?"

Rachel shook her head. "Luke is easy enough to find if you

want to talk with him. You need to come with me so we can attend to that other business you asked me about."

Miss O'Neil nodded. "Aye, you're right. 'Tis most important."

Rachel and her guest crossed the dirt road, walked toward the stage depot, and stayed to the north side of the street so they wouldn't have to walk past Luke's office and risk running into him. What would the brides say when they learned he wasn't the one who had contacted them? It would be better for Miss O'Neil to accept the fact that Luke wasn't likely to marry her and for her to find gainful employment. She obviously didn't have the money to return to Shreveport.

"I suppose Marshal Davis will wed Miss Bennett."

Rachel looked askance at the young woman. "Why would you think that?"

Miss O'Neil shrugged one thin shoulder. "She's quite pretty and so self-assured."

"That's true, but you're every bit as pretty as she." Rachel couldn't help wondering if the girl had been mistreated at some point in her life. She was as skittish as an abused animal and didn't like looking people in the eye. Rachel remembered acting the same way after experiencing James's outbursts when he lost at the gambling tables.

On a whim, she wrapped her arm around the young woman's shoulders. "Lookout is a nice little town. People here are friendly and treat each other with respect. Whether or not you marry the marshal, this is a place where you could start over."

" 'Twould be wonderful if I could. There's nothing for me to return to, either in Shreveport or in Erin—Ireland, as you call it."

They passed the banker's house and the Dykstra sisters' home as they ambled down the dirt street. Rachel shaded her eyes from the bright morning sun and gazed at the one-room schoolhouse, where church was also held. Was Jacqueline behaving herself? Rachel had heard tales from the church women about children reaching their adolescent years and acting out, but Jacqueline was only ten. Was she just an early bloomer, or were other issues troubling her?

A small cottage about a half mile from the schoolhouse sat nestled among a copse of pines and oaks. Diapers and children's clothing in various sizes flapped in the warm breeze on a line strung between two trees. A lazy hound lifted its snout, sniffed, and glanced at them, then dropped his head back onto his front paws.

Louise Chambers sat on the front porch rocking a squalling baby. She raised one hand in greeting and resumed patting the infant's backside so roughly Rachel wondered if that was why the infant was wailing. "Have a seat, if you can find one. Cyrus must be colicky. He's normally a good baby, but he's fussy today."

Rachel accepted a rocker next to Louise's and set her basket on the porch, while Miss O'Neil took the chair beside Rachel.

"I'm so glad you came to visit. I'd let you hold little Cy if he wasn't so cranky."

"How have you been feeling?" Rachel asked as two blond toddlers ran past them hollering like Comanches.

"Hush up, Sam. Ethan. I'm trying to get Cy to sleep." The dirty children instantly quieted and ran toward the hound dog sleeping under a persimmon tree.

Rachel wondered what the secret was to getting children to obey so swiftly and without arguing. Maybe she should return alone and talk with Louise sometime soon.

"I brought you some of my cinnamon bread." Rachel uncovered her basket and held up the loaf.

"That's right kind of you. I know we'll all enjoy it." Louise leaned forward and glanced around Rachel to Miss O'Neil. "My name's Louise Chambers. Them two youngsters over there are my two oldest boys. Cy, here, is the baby. Jarrod, my man, is out working somewhere in one of his fields."

"This is Miss O'Neil. She's staying at the boardinghouse for a while." Rachel wondered if Louise had heard what had happened yesterday. Perhaps they could simply avoid the uncomfortable topic. "Miss O'Neil is in need of employment, and I thought perhaps you could use some help or might know of someone else who needed the services of a nice young woman."

Louise looked past Rachel as she rocked forward. "It's a pleasure to meet you."

Rachel's boarder nodded, her cheeks a bright pink as she fiddled with the edge of her sleeve.

"I won't argue that I could use some help, but sadly, I cain't pay no one, and I don't have a spare foot in the house, or I'd offer room and board. I'm sorry, I wish I could help, but nothing comes to mind at the moment."

∼

Carly Payton held tightly to the window frame as the stage rounded the sharp turn into Lookout. She'd never been to Texas before this trip, which was one thing in her favor. If all went as planned, she would find the means to start over somewhere far away like Colorado or California, somewhere her brother would never find her, but first, she just might have to get married.

She pulled Ellie Blackstone's letter from her reticule and reread it. She could do this. Hadn't she done far worse?

Closing her eyes, she memorized the name that the letter had been addressed to: Ellie Blackstone. Once she arrived in town, she was to see a man named Garrett Corbett, who was the marshal's solicitor—whatever that was. Then again, maybe she'd bypass him and just go find her future husband on her own.

"Whoa!" The stage driver's loud voice echoed through the open windows, and the coach shimmied in a series of jerks as it slowed to a halt amid a cloud of dust and high-pitched creaks. The door opened, and the shotgun rider reached in with a smile to help her down. She accepted his hand as a lady should and allowed him to assist her. Once on solid ground again, she dusted her skirts with a fervent shake. The neck of the high-buttoned shirtwaist pressed

151

uncomfortably against her throat, and the long skirts threatened to trip her as the stiff breeze trapped them around her legs. Oh for a soft flannel shirt and trousers.

As she waited for her satchel to be unloaded, she scanned the town and took a deep breath to settle her nerves. What was the name of this place? She pulled the creased letter from her pocket and peeked below the signature. Lookout, Texas. She knew it was something odd, and she hoped that wasn't a warning. Lookout where you're going. Lookout, we'll catch you if you do wrong. Lookout for the law!

The town was just like so many others that she'd traveled through with her brother, but she hoped this one was far enough off the beaten track that he wouldn't find her, at least until she'd accomplished her goal in coming here.

If not for Miss Blackstone's timely injury and her bleeding all over Carly's dress, making her brother think she was dead, who knew where she might be? Still robbing banks and trains and anyone with money, most likely. Everything had worked unbelievably in her favor. Even Ellie's clothing had fit her fairly well; but would the townsfolk be able to tell she was a sham?

The shotgun rider set her satchel on the boardwalk among the crates they'd just unloaded. Carly cleared her throat, and the man glanced her way. "Pardon me, but do you know if there is a decent hotel in this town?"

"Nope." He shook his head. "No hotel a'tall. But you might find a room at Miz Hamilton's boardin'house. Don't know if she has any rooms available, though, what with all the brides that arrived the other day."

Carly didn't bother trying to make sense of his words. "Which way do I go?"

He grinned and yanked off his hat. A layer of dust cascaded down like a waterfall. "See that big green house at the end of the street?"

Carly held on to the sunbonnet that made her head sweaty and blocked her view of most everything and spun in the direction he was pointing. She tilted her head up. "Yeah. . .uh, yes, I see it."

The man chuckled. "That's it right there."

"Oh. Good." She grabbed her satchel off the pile of crates the stage had delivered and walked toward the boardinghouse. The light green, three-story house looked homey with its white shutters, wrap-around porch both downstairs and up, and numerous rocking chairs. At least she would get to sleep in a real bed, which would be much more comfortable than the hard ground she normally slept on. And she could take a bath. While traveling with her brother, she'd pretty much given up hope of ever being clean and sweet-smelling again. At the time, it was just as well that she wasn't. Helped deter any unwanted male attention.

As she approached the house, two women who sat in rockers on the porch snapping green beans looked up at her. She wiped her sweaty palms on her skirt and forced a smile. Being around normal people would tax her to her limits, but she could do this. It could mean starting over fresh instead of living with her brother and being an outlaw for the rest of her life—which might not be all that long if Tyson discovered she was alive and caught up with her.

The older of the two women smiled. Though pretty in her own right, her average brown hair and pale blue eyes made her look plain next to the younger woman with the wild, sorrel-colored hair.

The older woman set her bowl on the porch and stood, smiling. "I'm Rachel Hamilton. Can I help you?"

Carly nodded. "I'm Ellie." Oh, what was that name? "Uh. . . Blackstone. Ellie Blackstone. I need a room for a few days—just until I can make arrangements to marry Marshal Luke Davis."

CHAPTER 17

Rachel clutched the nearest porch post as her mind swirled with disbelief. Not another bride! Whatever was going on?

"Saints preserve us." Miss O'Neil muttered something in Gaelic, and she leaned forward, holding her face in her hands. Suddenly, she jumped to her feet, the bowl of beans falling to the floor and scattering all over the porch. With the back of her hand against her mouth, she dashed into the house.

Miss Blackstone's light brown eyes widened. "Goodness! Does she always react to strangers like that?"

Hating to be the one caught in the middle of all this, Rachel stooped down and gathered her thoughts along with the beans. *How could this happen? How do I tell her, Lord?*

"Well. . .you gonna answer me?" Miss Blackstone tapped her foot on the ground. "Evidently something I said flustered her, but I cain't figure out what."

Setting the beans aside, Rachel held out her palm. "Please, won't you have a seat for a moment?"

"I'm tired and would like to freshen up in my room before I meet the marshal. You do have a room available?"

"Yes." Rachel forced a smile. "That's not the problem."

"Then what is it?" Miss Blackstone flopped down, albeit reluctantly. "Spill the beans."

If the topic hadn't been so serious, Rachel would have laughed at the women's obvious effort to lighten a tense situation. Sucking in a steadying breath, she stared up at the soft blue sky. "There's been a horrible mistake."

The young woman straightened. "What do you mean? Marshal Davis ain't already married, is he?"

Rachel clenched her hands together. "No, not exactly."

"How can a body be not exactly married?"

"He's not, but two other women have recently come to town expecting to marry him."

"What!" Miss Blackstone lurched to her feet and kicked her satchel. "How is that possible? I came a long ways and won't have some namby-pamby stealing my place as the marshal's bride. He is an honorable man, ain't he?"

Rachel stood. "Oh yes, he surely is, but it seems his ornery cousins played a trick on him."

"But I've set my sights on marrying up with him."

Reaching out, Rachel touched Miss Blackstone's shoulder, but the other woman sloughed her hand away. Miss Blackstone narrowed her gaze, and her light brown eyes glinted.

"I'm terribly sorry for your inconvenience," Rachel said. "I'm hoping Luke will demand that his cousins make restitution for any expenses you've incurred and for your inconvenience."

Her visitor hiked up her chin. "I ain't come all this way just to be turned out. Where *is* the marshal? I got me a few words for him."

"Like I said, it wasn't his fault. Luke knew nothing until the other brides showed up."

Miss Blackstone studied her. "That's twice you've referenced my future husband by his given name. Just what's your stake in all of this?"

Rachel clasped her hands together and tried to hold her ground.

She was a peacemaker— didn't like conflict—and Miss Blackstone seemed more determined to acquire Luke for her husband than even Miss Bennett. "We grew up in Lookout together. I've known Luke most of my life."

The newest bride pulled off her bonnet, revealing glistening black hair, and fanned her face. With her lightly tanned complexion and snappy eyes, she was a lovely girl if one didn't take into account her pushy attitude. "That stage driver called you *Mrs.* Hamilton, so that means you're married, right?"

"Was married," Rachel said. "I'm a widow."

Rather than saying she was sorry for her loss, Miss Blackstone narrowed her gaze and stared at Rachel as if she, too, were a competitor for Luke's affection.

"Have you set your cap for him?"

Rachel thought back eleven years to when she'd been seventeen and had eagerly looked forward to marrying Luke. She'd loved him so much and never had eyes for any other man. If only. . .

Rachel shook her head. "No, that's not an option."

Miss Bennett stared down Main Street. "Could you take me to talk with the marshal?"

"Don't you want to get settled in your room first?"

She shook her head. "No. I need to know where things stand."

Rachel sighed inwardly. "Let me put these beans away and set your carpetbag inside. Would you care for a drink of water?"

"Afterwards."

Rachel hurried to the kitchen, wondering about Miss Blackstone. Her speech and manners seemed gruff, but she dressed nicely. She set the bowl of beans on the counter and thought about the other two brides upstairs. How could things have gotten so out of control? What were those Corbett brothers thinking?

"They weren't, and that is a fact," Rachel mumbled. Those two had done many foolish things in their lives, but this one took the cake.

Maybe she and the new bride should pay the Corbett brothers

a visit, since the low-down hooligans had yet to come and apologize or make restitution. Rachel reached out and clutched the doorjamb at the new thought that struck her weak-kneed. If there were three brides, could there be more to come?

Outside, Rachel crossed the street with Miss Blackstone beside her. She didn't know what else to say to calm the woman. Her new boarder was obviously upset. Who wouldn't be? How would Rachel respond if she found herself in a similar situation?

Her mind swirled with thoughts as her quick steps ate up the ground. She stomped up the boardwalk steps and ran smack into a solid body coming out of the bank. She was shoved sideways, colliding into Miss Blackstone, who grabbed a post, or she would have fallen into the street. The man grabbed Rachel's arm before she, too, fell, and righted her.

"Where's the fire, Rachel?" Luke stared down with a half grin on his handsome face.

She spun back toward him, irritated that her heart pounded from having rammed into him. Max squeezed out the door and past Luke's long legs. The mutt sniffed her hand, looked up and whined, then scurried back into the bank. Rachel's frustration burned like the heat of a flat iron and had probably scorched the poor dog's snout. She stepped forward and wagged her finger under Luke's nose. "There's no fire, but there's about to be a murder."

The humor left Luke's face, and his gaze dashed past her, probably to Miss Blackstone. Rachel noticed the bank teller and president staring at them from inside the bank, and she grabbed Luke's arm, pulling him out of the doorway. "Marshal Davis, meet Ellie Blackstone, your third bride."

Confusion wrinkled his brow. He opened his mouth but nothing came out for a moment. "What?"

"This woman has come to town to marry you. Imagine that."

Miss Blackstone smoothed her dress and squared her shoulders, eyeing Luke with a mixture of apprehension and the determination of a hungry huntress suddenly spotting an eight-point buck. Her expression softened, and she scurried up close to him, smiled, and held out her hand. "A pleasure to meet you, Marshal."

Luke, ever the gentleman, tipped his hat to her and shook her fingertips. "I'm right sorry about all this, ma'am." His gaze turned to steel as he glared at Rachel. "Lawman or not, I just may help you string up those two scoundrels. Let's go see what they have to say about this."

~

The glass in the window rattled when Luke yanked open the freight office door. His irritation nearly bounced off the wooden walls, and his cousins were lucky he hadn't jerked the door clear off its hinges. He allowed the two ladies to enter before him. The new bride—Miss What's-Her-Name—brushed up against him, stared unabashedly into his eyes, and gave him a sultry smile.

She was pretty all right, like the other two brides, but this one had a worldly quality that set the lawman in him on alert. Or maybe he was just fearful for his bachelorhood. Even though she looked no older than the other brides, this woman's expression spoke of experience—but just what kind of experience, he wasn't sure.

Luke rubbed the back of his neck and for the first time wished he'd never quit the cavalry and returned home. Life had gotten so complicated. *I could use some help here, Lord. What's to be done about all these brides?*

Max lumbered in after the ladies, and Luke shut the door. The dog flopped down near his feet. Mark stared up from his desk, where he'd been doing paperwork. The color drained from his face as his gaze landed on the stranger.

"Where's Garrett?" Luke asked.

Mark nudged his head sideways. "Out back, packing up the wagon. We're getting ready to head out on a delivery run again."

"Get him," Luke ordered.

"You're not going anywhere, Mark Corbett." Rachel pressed

her hands flat on his desk and leaned over, glaring at him. "You and that up-to-no-good brother of yours are to come over to the boardinghouse right now and discuss what you to intend to do about this disastrous situation."

"But we're just about to leave to make deliveries."

"Not until we get some answers."

Luke nearly chuckled at the stunned look in Mark's eyes as mild-natured Rachel turned into a she-bear. Luke strode into the back room, out the open rear door, and onto the porch. Garrett set a large crate onto the buckboard that already had a team hitched to it. A copse of trees shaded the area, giving it a serene setting totally at war with the fire raging within him. Did the brothers think they could make a quick escape and get out of talking with the brides?

Garrett smiled. "Come to help?"

Luke snorted. "Not hardly. You'll never guess who just showed up in town."

His cousin's eyes lifted as if he were deep in thought; then he refocused on Luke. "That pickpocket you were after?"

"No, but I've got something else that might interest you."

Garrett pulled a bandanna from his rear pocket and wiped his face and the back of his neck. "No foolin'? What is it?"

"Another bride."

His cousin's blue eyes had a blank stare for a split second before they widened. Red crept up Garrett's neck to color his cheeks and ears. "Uh. . .you don't say."

Luke rammed his hands to his hips. "I do say. Now get in here. We're going over to Rachel's to discuss this situation."

"But we've got deliveries to make."

"They can wait," Luke ground out each word, making sure Garrett realized the seriousness of the situation.

His cousin nodded and climbed the stairs. He grabbed another crate, and Luke glared at him. "I've got to at least get the wagon loaded and tied down, or I'm likely to lose all of this freight to some kids or a bum."

Luke wanted to argue, but although Lookout was a peaceful town and most folks were the decent sort, there were always a few families that were hard up and wouldn't mind stealing to put food on the table. He grabbed a crate, descended the steps, and slung it onto the buckboard.

Garrett hauled another crate off the porch, and after a few minutes of working in heated silence together, he tossed a rope across the top of the wagon to Luke. "So, is this one as pretty as the others?"

"Black hair and unusual, light brown eyes." Luke didn't mention his concerns about the woman. Maybe he was overreacting. Could be she just looked hardened because she was angry over the situation.

"That doesn't tell me much." Garrett grunted as he pulled the rope taut and tied it.

Luke dusted off his hands and rested them on his hips. "Guess you'll find out soon enough."

"Yep."

Garrett walked in front of his horses and patted each one on the head. "I'll be back soon, girls." He strode toward Luke and hopped up the steps. "You know, that means there's enough of them brides for each of us to have one."

Luke gave his cousin a playful shove but couldn't help grinning when Garrett walked into the office in front of him. He shook his head. This was no laughing matter, but his cousins had a way of seeing the up side of every situation. Why couldn't he be less serious and more like them?

Rachel glared at Garrett then Luke. "Took you long enough. Did you have to chase him down and haul him back?"

"Nope, he came of his own free will." Luke lifted his hat, swiped his hand through his hair, and glanced at the new bride. "These two yahoos are my cousins, Garrett and Mark Corbett."

"And this is Ellie Blackstone," Rachel said. "Now, let's head back to the boardinghouse and sort through this mess."

Garrett grinned at Miss Blackstone and opened the door. Mark hurried around his desk and offered her his arm. She glared at the two men then marched past them and took hold of Luke's arm. "I traveled here to marry the marshal, and that's what I aim to do."

Luke swallowed the cannonball-size lump in his throat. "But I—"

Rachel held up her palm. "Save it for the boardinghouse. You can tell all the brides at once, and that way you won't have to keep repeating yourself."

Suppressing a sigh, Luke followed Rachel to the door with Miss Blackstone attached to his arm. He held his hand out, indicating for the third bride to go first. She released her hold and, with a flounce of her head, strode out the door.

He dreaded the confrontation ahead. Why couldn't things have gone along nice and quiet like when he first arrived? Being around Rachel again had been hard enough, and they seemed to be moving toward a passable friendship, but now she was angry with him, and he didn't like how that felt. He glanced at his cousins, and his own anger simmered. How could those ornery brothers put him in a situation like this? What could they have been thinking when they wrote to so many women?

He was knee-deep in turbulent female emotions and had no clue how to get free of the muck. He moved closer to Rachel. She had a good head on her shoulders and didn't buckle during hard times. Maybe she could be the voice of reason in this trying ordeal.

Luke ran his gaze around town, making sure all was quiet. As he'd expected, several groups of people had gathered, and he knew exactly the topic of their conversations. Everyone watched Luke, his cousins, and the ladies like a group of Indians surveying a blanket full of beads and trinkets. They were the news of the day. Shoot, three brides coming to marry one man was probably the hottest news they had all year. No wonder they were curious.

Jenny Evans, the newspaper editor, exited her office door just as Luke passed by, as if to emphasize his point. She fell into step with him, albeit taking three steps to his one.

"So tell me, Marshal, how does it feel to have so many women wanting to marry you?" She held her pencil poised above a pad of paper, awaiting his response.

He grunted.

"Am I to take that to mean you're not happy with the situation?"

He kept his face straight, watching the bank president step out the door of his establishment. He nodded to the man he'd just spoken to a short while ago. "Mr. Castleby."

"Ignoring me won't change a thing, Marshal. I intend to get my story." Miss Evans hurried to keep up, her breath running short.

"There's no story here, ma'am."

"I beg to differ. What's going to happen to those brides? There are three of them now—am I correct?"

Miss Blackstone tossed a snappish look over her shoulder.

Luke shook his head. News traveled faster than a prairie fire in the small town. His footsteps stopped echoing as he stepped off the boardwalk onto the dirt street. "That's right," he finally answered.

"Did you write to all three of them, hoping one might come here?"

Luke halted, and she sped past him, slid to a stop, and turned back. He might not want to comment on the situation, but neither did he want his character defamed. "For the record, Miss Evans, I didn't write to any of the brides. I knew nothing about them before they arrived in town."

Her wide gray eyes stared up at him. "Well, someone must have. How else would they have known about you or known to come to Lookout?"

"I'm not at liberty to say just yet."

She licked the stub of her pencil. "Will you tell me when you are?"

He shrugged. "It's nobody's business." Luke eyed his cousins as they slinked around behind the journalist like two kids hiding from an irate neighbor after they'd pulled a prank. He was tempted to turn the rabid reporter loose on them, but he wanted to see how things played out first.

"It's a great story, Marshal."

He crossed the street and followed the others inside the boardinghouse, and turned, blocking the entrance. "The matter is private, ma'am."

"But—"

He stepped back, hand on the door knob. "Good day, Miss Evans."

CHAPTER 18

Rachel escorted her small group to the parlor. The scent of chicken baking in the kitchen filled the air and reminded her of all that she needed to do to get dinner ready on time. "If you men will have a seat, I'll show Miss Blackstone to her room and have the other ladies come downstairs."

Jacqueline must have heard them enter, because she ambled out of the bedroom and up the hall. "What's goin' on, Ma? Why's everybody here?"

Rachel turned to her new guest. "Miss Blackstone, this is my daughter, Jacqueline. She and I have a room downstairs, and if you ever have need of me during the night for any reason, you can find me there."

"Pleased to meet you, ma'am." Jacqueline squinted at the new boarder as if something was wrong, but thankfully, she used her manners.

"Same here." Miss Blackstone nodded. She lifted her head and sniffed. "Somethun sure smells good."

"That's baked chicken. Mom's is the best in town. Even better than at Polly's Café."

A blush heated Rachel's cheeks at her daughter's rare compliment. "Why, thank you, sweetie. That's very kind of you to say. Speaking of chickens, have you fed and watered ours today?"

Jacqueline scowled but turned and headed for the back door. Feeding the hens wouldn't take her long, and Rachel didn't want her daughter around to hear what was certainly to be a heated debate. "Wait just a minute."

Jacqueline stopped near the kitchen door, eyeing her with a suspicious gaze as if she expected her mother to give her more chores to do. Rachel looked at her guest. "Miss Blackstone, would you excuse me for a moment?"

The young woman nodded and shifted her satchel to her other hand.

Rachel motioned her daughter to follow her into their bedroom. She searched her unmentionable drawer for the little bag where she kept her cash. She pulled out two coins and handed them to Jacqueline. "After you feed the chickens, go to the mercantile and get yourself a treat."

The girl's deep blue eyes widened. "Oh boy! Thanks, Ma." Jacqueline snatched the coins as if she thought Rachel might change her mind and hurried out the back door. Its loud bang made Rachel cringe.

She forced a smile and returned to the entryway, where her newest guest waited. She pointed back to her right. "That's my kitchen back there. You've already seen the parlor, and the dining room is right next to it. The only other room downstairs that's available to guests is the library. We have a large assortment of books if you enjoy reading."

"I don't read much." The woman's gaze darted around the kitchen as if the room interested her. She looked refined in her cornflower blue and white blouse and dark blue skirt, but she tugged at the sleeves and kept pulling at the high collar as if it were too tight. She watched everyone intently.

"If you're ready, I'll show you to your room."

The woman nodded and followed her back through the hall and toward the stairs. The quiet rumble of male voices echoed from the parlor, and Rachel glanced inside as she passed the doorway, capturing Luke's gaze. Her heart flip-flopped. How could the man still move her after so many years?

She placed a hand on her chest as a thought hit her. Luke had been looking at her, not the new bride. Was he hoping to find a friendly face in the midst of such a horrendous event? As she climbed the stairs, she tried to consider how she'd feel if the situation were reversed. What if three men had come to town to marry her when she'd known nothing about them? The awkwardness of the situation would be unbearable.

At the top of the stairs, she noted that both brides' doors were shut. Had Miss O'Neil mentioned the new bride's arrival to Miss Bennett?

Rachel opened the door to the yellow room and stepped aside to allow Miss Blackstone to enter. The woman's eyes widened, and her mouth formed an O.

"I ain't—uh. . .never stayed in a place this purty." She slowly turned, as if taking in everything in the pale yellow room. The log cabin quilt, with its light yellow accents, matched the wall and added a splash of color.

Women always loved Rachel's rooms, while the men sometimes grimaced. But at least the beds were comfortable and the rooms clean. If the men didn't like the slightly feminine decor, they could stay in the community room above the saloon.

"Take a few minutes to refresh yourself, and then please join the rest of us in the parlor so we can get this mess sorted out."

Miss Blackstone nodded, her lips pursed. No doubt she dreaded confronting the men as much as Rachel. The third bride closed her door, and Rachel stood in the wide upstairs hallway. A small table covered with an embroidered cloth held the hurricane lamp that she lit each night to help her guests see in case they needed to go to the necessary. The striped, cream-colored wallpaper brightened the area and blended well with the floral carpet runner that covered the middle of the floor.

She looked at the three closed doors, knowing she couldn't put her task off any longer. How had she become the mediator of this mess?

She clutched her chest as a thought slapped her across the face. Three brides, each lovely in her own way, were now available, which meant that each man—Luke, Garrett, and Mark—could possibly marry one of them. If that happened, any hope of getting back with Luke would be dashed.

Remaining a widow and unmarried had never bothered her until Luke had come back to Lookout. Even Rand's frequent attentions hadn't swayed her to want to marry again. But with Luke's return, she'd begun to hope—hope he would forgive her and they could have a second chance. She clenched her fists. What could she do? She could hardly force Luke to forgive her for marrying another man, even though she'd been so in love with Luke. He didn't know the truth of the situation, and she could never tell him.

Heaving a sigh, she lifted a hand and knocked on Miss O'Neil's door. Rachel studied the floor. Why would Luke even consider her again—a tired, aging woman with responsibilities and a rambunctious child—when he could have his pick of these three pretty, young ladies?

Miss O'Neil opened the door a slit and peered out as if she were frightened of who might be on the other side of the door. "Oh, Mrs. Hamilton." She pulled the door open, offering a half smile.

"I wonder if I might have a word with you and Miss Bennett for a moment."

The young woman glanced across the hall and scowled. Rachel wondered if the two brides had suffered an altercation of some sort or if she was just concerned about losing Luke to Miss Bennett.

"Aye, of course you can." The younger woman straightened her skirt and stepped out of her room.

Rachel knocked on Miss Bennett's door, and after a moment, the woman flung it open, staring with curiosity at the two women in the hall. "I need to speak to you and Miss O'Neil, if I may."

Miss Bennett nodded and stepped into the hall, closing the door behind her. "What is it?"

Rachel licked her lips, wishing she could be anywhere but here. "The men are downstairs, ready to discuss the. . .uh. . .situation."

"Finally." Miss Bennett crossed her arms over her chest, but the worry in her gaze belied her tough demeanor.

"Yes, well, there's been. . .uh. . .a new development."

"What sort of development?" Miss Bennett asked, her eyes wary.

Rachel glanced at the door to the yellow room. "I'm afraid another bride has arrived."

Miss O'Neil looked down, wringing her hands, still upset over meeting Miss Blackstone earlier.

Miss Bennett's blue eyes widened, her nostrils flared. "Why, that is utterly preposterous. What kind of game does the marshal have going? I left my home and family to come all this way to marry, and I intend to do so."

The door to the yellow room slowly opened, and Miss Blackstone stepped into the hall. All eyes turned in her direction as each woman sized up the other. Rachel wondered what they were thinking. What would she think if she were in their situation?

A verse from Psalm 82:3 popped into her mind. "*Defend the poor and fatherless: do justice to the afflicted and needy.*" In spite of the possibility of losing Luke again, sympathy filled her heart. None of this was the brides' fault, and as a Christian woman, she was obligated to make things as easy for them as possible, no matter the cost.

Miss Blackstone lifted her chin and glared at the other two

brides. "Maybe I was the last to arrive, but I'll tell y'all here and now that I plan on winnin' the marshal's hand."

Jack tossed a handful of feed in the air and grinned as the chickens flapped their wings and raced to be the first to catch one of the tasty morsels. She didn't like tending the dumb, smelly birds, but she sure enjoyed eating them. She sprinkled another scoop of feed on the ground and then poured water from the bucket into two water bowls.

The two coins her mother had given her clinked in her pocket. Jack left the pen, set the bucket by the well, and fingered the coins. Ma must have really wanted to get rid of her since she'd given her so much money. Her mind raced with all the things she could buy with it. Twenty pieces of penny candy. Or maybe she could get a dime novel *and* a sweet treat. Or a dill pickle from the barrel—those never failed to make her mouth water.

She rounded the corner of the house just in time to see someone duck behind the Texas azalea bush that grew almost below the parlor window. Jack darted back against the rear of the house and then peeked around the corner. She had planned to stop and listen in that very spot before getting her treat. No bribe was going to make her miss out on hearing the hullabaloo that was sure to occur now that another bride had arrived.

Jack hunkered down and scurried around the corner of the house. Keeping low and behind the bush, she tiptoed to the edge of the shrub. Looking through the leaves, she recognized Jenny Evans, the lady newspaper owner. She must be out to get a story, and Jack knew she was about to get a good one. The brides had been the talk of the town when there were only two of them. What would people say now that another one had arrived?

Her ma's lacy curtains fluttered through the open window. If she stayed on this side of the bush, she was certain to miss out on most of the conversation that was sure to drift out. Miss Evans peeked up and through the window, then ducked back down and scribbled something on her pad of paper.

Jack scowled and bit the inside of her cheek. "Humbug."

Well, if Miss Evans could spy on the brides, so could she. As quick as a greased pig, she dashed around the bush and slid up against the house. Miss Evans gasped and covered her mouth with one hand while holding her notepad against her chest with the other. Her flaring nostrils and wide eyes reminded Jack of a spooked horse.

She leaned toward the woman and whispered, "What'cha doing?"

Miss Evans's mouth worked as if she'd swallowed a bug, but nothing came out. She patted her chest and seemed to be trying to breathe normally. Jack grinned, knowing she'd scared the woman half to death.

After taking a few moments to compose herself, Miss Evans leaned toward Jack. "I'm just trying to get a story for my paper," she whispered. "I asked to sit in on the discussion between the men and the brides, but the marshal refused. What else could I do?"

The woman's soft breath tickled the edge of Jack's ear, and she rubbed it. "Spy on them, I guess." She grinned, and Miss Evans smiled back.

"I won't tell if you won't." Miss Evans held out her hand. "Deal?"

Jack pressed her back against the side of the house and eyed the woman. "I won't tell if you give me twenty cents," she whispered.

Miss Evans's brows shot up, and her mouth twitched. Jack frowned. Was she laughing at her?

"I like enterprising people." She dug around in her skirt pocket, pulled out two dimes, and handed them to Jack. "Deal."

Luke paced the parlor, waiting for the women to come downstairs while his cousins argued over the event.

"I told you this was a bad idea when you first thought it up, didn't I?" Mark glared at his brother.

Garrett curled his lip. "If you were so all fired against it, why did you write to those two brides?"

Mark fell back against his chair and ran his hand through his curly blond hair. "I don't know. You made it sound like such a good idea that I got caught up wanting to find Luke a wife."

"I don't need any one bride shopping for me. When I'm ready to marry, I'll find my own." Luke muttered a growl and turned toward the side window, arms crossed. He stared outside. Whatever made them think he needed their help in finding a wife?

A noise outside snagged his attention. He stepped to the side of the window, pressing his back to the wall, and peered down. The bushes rustled, and then he saw the top of a head—Jack's head. He bit back a smile, knowing the girl was listening in. He probably should shoo her away, but given the same situation when he'd been a boy, he would have eavesdropped, too. Besides, she'd know everything soon enough.

Rachel cleared her throat. Garrett and Mark shot to their feet, looking like schoolboys who'd pulled a prank and were now sitting in a meeting with the teacher and their parents. Luke shifted his attention to Rachel and the three brides coming into the room. He'd always figured mail-order brides were homely women who couldn't find a husband, but that wasn't the case with the trio of females in the parlor.

His gaze was drawn to Rachel. Though she was probably close to ten years older than the other women, she was still willowy and pretty, with her pale blue eyes and soft brown hair. He couldn't help wondering why Rachel hadn't remarried. That Rand Kessler sure seemed interested in her.

He scowled at the thought. If he didn't want her, why did it bother him to think of her marrying some other man?

"Ladies, if you will please have a seat, we will get things started."

171

Rachel held out her hand, and each of the women scurried past her and sat.

Rachel introduced everyone and looked at Luke and then his cousins, as if she didn't know where to start. Maybe he should help her out. He stepped forward. "First off, let me say that I'm sorry about this mess. I knew nothing about any of this and didn't write to any of you."

Miss O'Neil sucked in a loud breath that sounded like a hiccup and held her hands in front of her mouth. "Blessit be."

Miss Bennett and Miss Blackstone exchanged glances but kept silent.

"What Garrett and Mark did was inexcusable." Rachel cut both men a scathing glance. "But I also know they meant well when they tried to find Lu—uh. . .the marshal—a wife." Rachel picked up a Bible off a nearby table and held it to her chest, as if drawing strength from it. She faced Luke's cousins again. "Do either of you have anything to say?"

Garrett glanced at his brother and then stepped to the center of the room. "We had good intentions, but we never expected to get the results we did. I'll admit that I wrote letters to two of you, but I really didn't think any woman would be willing to travel clear to Lookout to marry, and I only sent money for traveling expenses to Miss Bennett."

Mark cleared his throat, his neck and ears flaming red. "I, uh. . . sent travel money to Miss O'Neil."

"You were wrong about us not wanting to come here." Miss Bennett squared her shoulders as if daring Garrett to argue with her.

"That's right," Miss Blackstone said, lifting her chin in the air.

"Well, be that as it may," Rachel said, "the only proper thing to do would be to pay the ladies' ways back to wherever they need to go."

"No!" The three women shouted in unison.

Miss Blackstone shot to her feet. "There ain—uh. . .there's

nothing for me back in Missouri. I came here to marry the marshal, and that's what I intend to do."

Miss Bennett jumped up and faced her opponent, blue eyes flashing. "I was the first to arrive, so it only seems fair I should marry Marshal Davis. I have no intention of returning home, either."

"Oh, saints preserve us."

Luke stepped back. How could something like this have happened?

"Please, everybody, let's remain civil." The women sat down at Rachel's gentle admonishment. "Do any of you wish to return home?"

The trio of brides shook their heads.

"All right then, let's see if we can come up with a different solution." Rachel turned to face the men. "I suppose you men could pay the women's room and board until they found work or uh...someone else to marry."

"Or maybe they should just marry the brides." Luke grinned at the thought then sobered as he realized that still left one bride.

Garrett shook his head. "I'm not ready to marry."

"Me either." Mark leaned back in his chair and crossed his arms.

"Then what do you suggest we do?" Rachel stood in the parlor entryway looking like a warrior matron ready to fight for her young charges. "It would seem we have a stalemate."

Suddenly, Jenny Evans strode through the parlor doors with Jack fast on her heels. "A breech of promise is grounds for a lawsuit." Miss Evans's eyes shone bright. She held her notepad to her chest and looked at the brides. "I know a good attorney who will sue the britches off those three men for falsely luring you to town under the guise of marriage."

Luke stood stunned to silence like the rest of the group. Even the brides appeared shocked at Jenny's declaration.

"You've forced these poor women to leave the comforts of their home and travel hundreds of miles, and now you refuse to marry any of them?" Jenny glared at Luke. Why should her accusations make him feel guilty when he had no part in this loco scheme?

Rachel took a step forward. "I'm sure we can come to some sort of solution without something as drastic as a lawsuit."

"No, I think these women should sue the marshal and the Corbett brothers as accomplices. Of course, the suit could always be dropped if the marshal agreed to marry one of the women."

Miss Bennett stood and scurried over to stand beside Miss Evans. "I believe this woman has a point. Marry one of us, me preferably, or we'll sue you men. Don't you agree, ladies?"

The other two brides glanced at each other. Miss Blackstone shoved up from her seat and joined them. Miss O'Neil was slower to follow and seemed to do so only to avoid being left out.

Jenny smiled. "There you have it, gentlemen. What will it be? A wedding or a lawsuit?"

"This is ridiculous." Garrett jumped up. "A lawsuit could ruin us and put us out of business. We've worked hard to make a go of our freight line, and this town needs our services. Luke would probably lose his job as marshal, and how would he support a wife then?"

Miss Evans shrugged. "I'm sure he'd find a way to get by. He's big and strong and could do about any kind of work he put his shoulder to."

Luke wrestled with the thoughts bombarding his mind. He didn't want to be responsible for his cousins losing their business, yet none of this was his fault. How had this fiasco turned into a shotgun wedding with the sights set on him?

"Even if the marshal is agreeable, how will he be choosin' *who* to marry?" Miss O'Neil asked.

Garrett sat on the vacant settee and held his chin in one hand while he tapped his index finger against his cheekbone. "I have an idea. Why not have some type of contest? See which gal is the best cook or seamstress. Which one would make the best wife."

Mark leaned forward, steepling his fingertips together. "That's not a half bad idea."

"It's a stupid idea." Luke rolled his eyes. Would these fellows never grow up?

"That's preposterous," Rachel cried. "There's more to being a good wife than domestic abilities."

Miss Blackstone stamped her foot. "I got me a letter stating the marshal wants to marry me. I won't vie for him like some prize at a carnival."

Miss Bennett shoved her aside with her elbow. "I'm not giving up without a fight, and if we have to have a contest to find the winner, I'm game."

The young Irish woman looked as white as milk and remained silent.

"This is a bigger mess than you'd find at a stockyard." Miss Blackstone plopped back onto her chair, arms crossed.

"Well, you only made things worse when you showed up," Miss Bennett said. "Two brides wanting the same man was bad enough."

Miss Blackstone puckered her lips and glared at the young blond. Luke wondered if he might have to separate the brides to keep them from throwing punches. He could hardly blame them for being disconcerted. He certainly was.

"I really like the contest idea." Mark leaned back with his fingers laced behind his head. "It could solve our problem, and we could get the whole town involved. The women could make you dinner, maybe sew you a shirt or something—I don't know."

"And just where are they going to cook this dinner?" Luke shook his head at the absurdity of the idea.

"Rachel would probably let them use her kitchen, beings as it's for such a good cause." Mark grinned.

"What good cause? And there's not a kitchen in town big enough for three feuding women to cook in." Rachel crossed her arms over her chest, a frown marring her pretty features.

"We could charge people to sample and judge the food, and the money could go to the church." Garrett stood with his hands on his hips, grinning, as if he'd just solved everyone's problem.

"No, wait. Not a dinner. How about a pie-making contest? And we can help judge it." Mark licked his lips and raised his brows.

Luke shook his head. "I'm not about to ask these women to spend what little money they may have left cooking for me."

Mark drew his eyebrows down. "Of course you won't. You'll provide the supplies, and they'll do the work."

Luke scratched the back of his neck and half admired his cousins for their ingenuity, even though it was going to cost him more than money, he suspected. He glanced at Jenny Evans to see what she thought of the idea and found her scribbling notes as fast as she could write. Jack sat off to the side, behind her ma, watching the whole ordeal with wide-eyed excitement. His gaze swung over to the ladies. "What makes you think these ladies would even agree to such a harebrained idea?"

Garrett turned to face the women. "If you're serious about marrying the marshal, you'd be willing to fight for him, wouldn't you?"

Each bride slowly nodded but looked skeptical.

"Besides," Garrett said, "a contest would be a good way to see which of you would make the best wife for Luke, and the whole town could get involved."

"Now hold on. I didn't even say I wanted to marry one of 'em."

Jenny looked up from her pad and quirked a brow. Luke fidgeted, knowing he wanted nothing to do with a lawsuit.

Mark strode to the front window and looked out. "Well, you won't know for sure unless you spend some time with them—see how good they can cook. You just might fall head over heels in love, and then you'll be in debt to us for the rest of your life."

"Just where I've always wanted to be." Luke shook his head. All three women were comely enough that a man wouldn't tire of looking at them over the years, but was marrying one of them the right thing to do? Hadn't he asked the good Lord on occasion to send him a mate? But a stranger—a mail-order bride that he hadn't ordered? What would God have him do?

The Lord moved in mysterious ways, he knew, but this situation seemed too outlandish to be the hand of God.

"Personally, now that I've had time to ponder the idea, I think it's excellent." Miss Bennett curled her finger around a tress of loose blond hair.

"B–but what happens to the l–losers?" Miss O'Neil's eyes looked as wide as silver dollars.

Rachel glanced at Luke's cousins. "Since you and Mark caused this situation, it's only fair that you pay for the ladies' room and board until they can find employment or marry."

"What if that takes a while?" Mark straightened and crossed his arms over his chest. "Jobs aren't readily available for females."

Rachel shrugged. "You should have thought of that before writing to so many women."

"Maybe the contest will show off the ladies' talents, and the other bachelors in the area will be swarming for their attention." Garrett grinned.

"I'm not much of a cook, b–but I can sew." Miss O'Neil gazed up, a wary look engulfing her fair face.

"That's why we'd need to have several categories—to make it fair for all entrants." Garrett paced the room, his eyes dancing. "This could be the biggest thing to happen in Lookout in a decade."

Luke couldn't help wondering if the last big news story in Lookout had been Rachel's marriage to James Hamilton when the whole town had expected her to marry him.

"Yeah, I bet everyone for miles around would like to get in on the fun." Mark leaned forward in his chair, his elbows on his knees and his eyes livelier than Luke had seen them since his homecoming.

"I don't know. It seems rather. . .unconventional," said Rachel.

"But it would solve one bride's dilemma, providing the marshal was willing to marry the winner." Miss Evans looked at Luke, all but daring him to say no.

He swiped at a trickle of sweat on his temple. Was he ready to marry? Could he make a life with one of these women?

His gaze drifted to Rachel. Marrying would sure solve one problem—it would get Rachel off his mind. The Lord did work in peculiar ways at times, but was this the Lord's provision? Or just another of his cousins' crazy stunts?

He thought of the lawsuit. Jenny Evans was tenacious enough to actually sue his cousins. He couldn't stand by and watch them lose their livelihood if he had it within his power to help them. He felt his head nodding in spite of his reservations.

Rachel's eyes went wide; then something that looked like disappointment crossed her pretty face. Would she begrudge him marrying, having a family, and finding some happiness like she had?

"Was that a yes?" Jenny asked.

Luke shrugged. "Yeah, I reckon so."

Garrett and Mark let out a whoop in unison that made the brides jump. Luke wished he could be that excited instead of feeling like he'd just stuck his head into a hangman's noose.

CHAPTER 19

Luke sipped his morning coffee and studied the newest batch of wanted posters that had come in on yesterday's stage. He didn't recognize any of the men, nor had there been any illegal activity in the region since he'd arrived other than a pickpocket who seemed to have moved on to better pickings. The peaceful little town hardly needed a marshal, except maybe on Friday and Saturday nights when the cowpokes came in.

Max looked up at him with big brown eyes, and Luke realized that Jack hadn't come by with the bucket of breakfast scraps that she normally brought each morning. He gazed out the window and watched the citizens of Lookout as they went about their daily business. Maybe he and Max should wander over to Rachel's and see what the holdup was. But then he might run into one of the brides.

Rachel hurried past his window and charged through his open door with a scowl on her normally happy face. What now?

He rose and nodded. She sure was pretty when she had a bee in her bonnet.

"Have you seen this morning's paper?" She set the scrap bucket

179

down in front of Max and slapped the *Lookout Herald* on his desk before he could respond.

Luke picked up the paper and read the headline. "THREE BRIDES BATTLE FOR ONE MAN'S HEART." Grinding his back teeth, he slammed the newspaper against his desk and paced the small office. Was nothing sacred?

"What are we going to do?" Rachel stared up at him, her soft blue eyes looking vulnerable.

Luke didn't like her fretting. He wanted to fold her into his arms until her frown turned into a smile. To avoid doing just that, he picked up the paper again and started reading: *"Lookout, Texas, to host bride contest. In hopes of helping their cousin, Marshal Luke Davis, find a wife, Garrett and Mark Corbett wrote to several mail-order brides. Imagine their surprise when not one, but three women arrived in town to marry the same man."*

Luke clenched his jaw. This whole situation was getting out of hand faster than a drunken brawl at the Wet Your Whistle. He continued reading about the pie-making contest that would be held in three days and how people could participate and raise money for the church by paying five cents for a small taste of each pie. Then they could vote for their favorite. At least the newspaper lady had told the truth about the contest and hadn't added a slant to the story. Nor had she mentioned blackmailing him with threats of a lawsuit.

He laid the paper back on his desk, slid his hip onto the corner, and crossed his arms, wishing this whole thing would go away.

"Are you really going to marry one of those women?" Rachel nibbled her lower lip, and he couldn't help watching. She'd always done that when she was nervous, and it never failed to intrigue him. Her lips looked so soft. No, he *knew* they were soft.

He shook his head to steer himself away from such disastrous thoughts. Why was Rachel so anxious?

"I reckon I will get married since I said I would. A man has to keep his word."

"I can't believe that." Her nostrils flared and eyes sparked, doing odd things to his insides. He held her gaze, and after a moment, she ducked her head and seemed to be watching Max, who'd nearly finished his breakfast. The dog glanced up, licked his lips, and burped.

Luke grinned. With Max, all was good as long as he had food and someone to love him. Was *he* all that different? What more did a man need?

He tried to imagine what life would have been like if he'd been married to Rachel all this time. He'd never have been in the cavalry and probably wouldn't be the marshal now. How would he have supported a wife and family?

He'd been so young and naive when he'd lost his heart to her. Now that he was older and had hindsight, he realized how ill prepared he'd been to marry back when he was eighteen. He and Rachel would have had next to nothing, but somehow that would have been enough. All he really needed was her—and the Lord. But he hadn't known much about God back then.

Rachel peered at Luke without lifting her head. "Could you actually marry a woman you don't. . .love?"

Filled with a sudden desire to shove away his melancholy thoughts, Luke snorted a sarcastic laugh. "Loving a woman doesn't guarantee a happy marriage. It doesn't guarantee a marriage at all."

"I'm truly sorry, Luke." She reached out and laid a hand on his arm. Her eyes glistened as if she might cry. "You have no idea how much."

He shook off her hand and strode over to stand in front of the window, not wanting to see her sad expression. How could a man stay strong and determined in the face of a woman's tears? Females never played fair. He ran a finger down the window. One of these days he needed to clean the dingy glass.

"I heard that you became a Christian. Surely you've learned that God expects us to forgive one another for our misdeeds. Can't you forgive me for what I did?"

He flinched as if she'd punched him in the gut. Didn't she know that she hadn't just broken his heart but that she'd crushed it into so many pieces it would never be the same? Left it so shattered that he'd never love again? He wanted to forgive her, but he didn't know how. *Lord, help me.*

"You'll never know how sorry I am that I married James."

"Why did you?"

"I–it's not something I can talk about."

"Don't you think you owe me that much?"

"Yes." Rachel's soft whisper almost made Luke turn around, but he held himself stiff, as if at attention. He couldn't help being intrigued. Why would she regret marrying the richest man in town? Had she learned that true love meant more than money?

He'd never considered that James and Rachel's marriage might not have been a happy one. James was a charmer who most people liked. Yeah, he could be selfish, having been the only child of a wealthy couple, and he liked to gamble more than the average fellow, but he was friendly, funny, and generous with his money.

Max whined and nosed Luke's hand. Even the dog could sense the tension in the room. Luke hated causing Rachel pain, but after all he'd suffered, the least she could do was explain why she'd dropped him so suddenly and married James.

Rachel made a noise that sounded like a strangled sob, and she dashed out the door. Luke's first impulse was to run after her, but he held his ground. He was empty—had nothing to say that could ease her pain.

He thought of a verse from Mathew that he'd read last night before going to bed. *"For if ye forgive men their trespasses, your heavenly Father will also forgive you: But if ye forgive not men their trespasses, neither will your Father forgive your trespasses."*

Luke returned to his desk and dropped down onto the chair, his fingers forking through his hair. Max rested his head on Luke's thigh, and he reached out to pat the dog. "How do I excuse what she did, Max?"

But God's Word was clear: if he didn't forgive Rachel, then God couldn't forgive him.

Luke hung his head. Without God's love and pardon from sin, he would still be a lonely sinner, lost and unsaved. Somehow, he had to find a way to get over Rachel, to forgive her, and to turn loose from his pain.

But how?

The mayor appeared in the doorway and leaned on the jamb, pulling Luke from his perplexing thoughts. Mayor Burke's dark hair, slicked down and divided in the middle, gleamed like a raven's wing. Luke could smell the odor of pomade clear over at his desk. "Mrs. Hamilton sure left in a hurry. Looked like she was kind of weepy."

Luke drew a deep breath in through his nose. He wasn't in the mood to deal with the pompous mayor just now.

Titus Burke tugged on his fancy vest. "She's a fine woman, and I don't like seeing her hurt."

The man's words ignited a flame of irritation. "I don't like it, either, and honestly, Mayor, it's none of your affair."

The man sniffed and looked over the top of his wire-rimmed glasses at Luke. His eye twitched, reminding Luke of a long-lashed mule that he worked with back at the fort. "Well, this hoopla you're causing with all these boardinghouse brides *is* my concern. Lookout can't afford a lawsuit."

How had he heard about that? Luke stood, giving himself the advantage of height. "Nobody's going to sue the town."

The mayor scowled and looked up. "I certainly hope not. This bride contest is the biggest thing since James Hamilton gambled away his family's fortune. It's the kind of thing that could put Lookout on the map."

Luke blinked, stunned by the mayor's declaration. He couldn't imagine James Hamilton broke, but that explained why Rachel had turned Hamilton House into a boardinghouse. How had she taken the news of her husband's poverty when it had come? Must have been difficult to go from having next to nothing to being the richest woman in town, and then back to nothing again. But then, Rachel had always been one to roll with the punches, except where her child was concerned.

"This bride thing is big news. We could have folks from all over the county coming here to participate."

Luke hooked his thumbs into his belt. "So?"

"The point I'm trying to make is that I. . .uh. . .the town council expects you to do your part and marry up with one of those women."

Luke lifted one brow. "Or what?"

Mayor Burke pulled off his glasses and busied himself cleaning them. He took his own sweet time putting them back on and adjusting them to fit. "Or you may find yourself out of a job."

Luke straightened, hands on his hips. "That's ridiculous. A man can't be fired because he chooses to marry or not."

"You need to do the right thing by those women."

Luke leaned forward, glaring at the mayor. The man took a step back and swallowed hard. "Look, I didn't have anything to do with their coming here. That was all my cousins' doing. Maybe you should be forcing them to marry."

"You're the one in the limelight now, and the one who can make this town look bad. Folks won't want to move here if word gets out that we don't treat our women right."

Luke clamped his back teeth together and swallowed a growl. This was ridiculous. He'd be better off leaving this hole-in-the-wall town and rejoining the cavalry. *Lord, give me patience.*

"Even if I do marry one of them, that still leaves two disappointed women."

The mayor shrugged. "We'll think of something. Maybe have a contest to find grooms for them." He chuckled.

Luke rolled his eyes. "I may regret doing so, but I gave my word to marry, and I will—unless the good Lord makes it clear that He doesn't want me to."

The mayor puffed out his chest. "Good. Things should be just fine." He stared at Luke for a moment then ambled out of the office.

Luke strode to the porch and studied the town. He had a strange feeling that things would never be fine again.

❧

Jack paced alongside the river, picked up a rock, and flung it as far as she could. If only she could be rid of the brides so easily.

"What's got your dander up?" Ricky leaned back against a boulder, relaxing in the shade.

"Whatever it is, stop chuckin' them rocks in the water. You're scarin' the fish away." Jonesy cast a glare in her direction then went back to staring at the water where he'd dropped his fishing line.

Jack stomped closer to her friends. "The marshal has agreed to marry one of those brides."

"So? He's gettin' long in the tooth," Jonesy said. "If'n he wants to marry, I reckon he should do it before he gets much older."

Jack shoved Jonesy in the shoulder. "Luke's not old."

"Well, he's way too old for you to be frettin' over." Ricky yawned, crossed his arms behind his head, and closed his eyes.

Irritation welled up in Jack like steam building in a locomotive. "Oh! You two are dumber than all them grown-ups runnin' that stupid bride rodeo."

Ricky sat up and glared at her, his eyelids heavy with sleep. "Watch who you call names, or we won't let you hang out with us anymore."

"Fine, then I won't give y'all any more of my ma's cookies." Jack crossed her arms and marched back to the water's edge.

"Aw, leave her be, Ricky. You know how good her ma's baked goods are." Jonesy winked at her as their friend dropped back down on the boulder.

The water lapping against the river's edge and the whispering of the trees above as they cast dancing shadows out over the water failed to soothe her as they normally did. All she could think about was Luke marrying one of those brides instead of her ma. She'd hoped so much that Ma and Luke would fall in love and that the three of them could one day be a family. Her ma cared for Luke, Jack was certain of that, but he didn't seem to return the affection.

She kicked at a small rock, sending it sailing into the water. Oh, she'd seen Luke look at her ma on occasion as if she was the prettiest lollipop in the jar, but then his expression would sour, as if she'd done something bad to him. She dropped onto the creek bank and pulled up her knees, resting her arms and head on them. Her eyes stung as tears threatened, and a big lump in her throat made it hard to swallow. Why did all those dumb brides have to show up and ruin things? If she'd only had a bit more time, she might have figured out a way to get Luke and her ma to fall in love.

Jonesy heaved a big sigh, dragged his line through the water, and sat down beside her. "You ain't cryin', are ya?"

"No! I just got somethin' in my eyes." Maybe that was stretching the truth, but her friends would think she was a crybaby if they ever caught her weeping. She turned her face to the side and wiped the moisture from her eyes.

"Then what's got you so long-faced? You remind me of my pa's mule."

Jack gasped and punched him in the shoulder. "I don't look like a mule."

He rubbed his arm and scowled back. "I didn't say you looked like one. Why are you in such a foul mood?"

Jack turned back to stare at the water. "All those brides."

"What about 'em?"

She pressed her face into her arms. "You wouldn't understand."

"Understand what?"

Jack shook her head, heaved a sigh, and rested her head on

her arms again. "I want Marshal Davis to marry my ma, not those other women."

Jonesy gasped. "Why in the world would you want the marshal for a pa?"

She didn't look up but could imagine Jonesy's green eyes going wide, like they did when he was scared or surprised. He didn't understand any more than the chirping birds overhead. "I like Luke. I don't think he'd be mean like my other pa was."

"Aren't all fathers mean?"

Jack shook her head. "I don't think so. I've seen men at church smile, even when their kids acted up. I've seen them stroke their child's head, like Luke did mine once, and even kiss their children."

"Well, I don't think stroking heads is much of a reason to want someone to be your pa."

"It's not just that. He took Max in and gave him a home when nobody else gave a hoot about him."

Jonesy gazed out where his line was in the water. "That dog was just an old stray."

She scowled and lifted her head. "He's a good dog that just needed someone to love him."

"If you say so."

"I do." She bumped Jonesy's shoulder, a little less hard this time. "So what do I do about those brides?"

"How would I know?"

She rested her chin on her arms and stared at the water. The sun glistened in spots where it managed to break through the thick layer of leaves overhead, looking like swirling stars. She had to do something to make the brides leave before Luke could choose one to marry. But what?

"Maybe we could do something to scare them off. Like make up a story about a ghost haunting the boardinghouse," Jonesy offered.

"Yeah," Ricky bolted up, even though Jack thought he'd fallen asleep. "We could even dress in a sheet and sneak into their rooms at night and scare them."

Jack felt their excitement growing but shook her head. "We can't do anything to give the boardinghouse a bad reputation. That's how Ma makes a living for us."

"Then let's think up something else."

The boys were silent for a few moments, each lost in their own imagination, just as Jack was. Sadly, she drew a blank the one time her own future was at stake.

Jonesy snapped his fingers. "I've got it. We could sabotage the pie contest."

A wide grin pulled at Ricky's face. "Yeah, that could be funny, since the whole town seems bent on buying pieces of the pie so they can vote on them."

Jack smiled. "It wouldn't be too hard to do. Just dump some extra salt into the pies before they're cooked."

"Remind me not to sample them," Jonesy said.

The boys laughed, and Jack joined in, feeling better for the first time in days. She had a plan, and surely it would work. She just hoped her mother didn't find out.

"Hey!" Jonesy jumped up. "I got a bite!"

CHAPTER 20

Shannon ventured out of her room and made her way downstairs. For two days, she'd chewed her fingernails worrying about making a pie and had finally worked up her nerve to ask Mrs. Hamilton for help. No doubt the other brides had already decided what they'd be baking, but she'd never made a pie before.

Back home in Ireland, her mother had barely put enough food on the table for them to survive, much less made desserts. Shannon hadn't tasted her first pie until she'd started working at the Wakefield estate, and while she thoroughly enjoyed them, especially the apple pie with cinnamon added to it, she'd been a maid, not a cook.

At the foot of the stairs, she noticed Miss Bennett and Miss Blackstone in the parlor, both studying thick books. Cookbooks would be her guess. Maybe she should try that, but then she knew nothing of measuring or cooking terms.

Miss Bennett didn't acknowledge her and kept studying the page before her, but Miss Blackstone glanced up and scorched her with a glare.

Shannon lifted her skirt and dashed down the hall, away from the heat of the other bride's stare. She had hoped to make friends with the women, but both only saw her as competition, which she was, even though she doubted she stood a chance at winning the marshal's heart. If she had any other option, she'd willingly give up her chance to marry him. Not that he wasn't a fine man, but she'd prefer to be courted and wooed by a man she knew at least a wee bit. Yet who would want to court her? Other than keeping a clean home, what did she truly have to offer a man? Hadn't her da told her on many occasions how useless she was?

She walked past the dining room to the kitchen. Mrs. Hamilton stood with her back to Shannon as she reached the doorway. The pale yellow walls looked so cheery, and everything had its place, making the room tidy and organized. She'd never worked in a kitchen before. She was kept too busy at the Wakefield estate, and by bedtime, she was so tired she could almost fall asleep on her feet.

If she ever hoped to have a fair chance with the marshal, she had to learn to cook. At least to bake a pie. She cleared her throat, and Mrs. Hamilton pivoted.

Her hands were covered in flour from the dough she was working with. She held one hand to her chest, leaving white powder on her blue apron bib. "Oh, you startled me."

"Beggin' yer pardon, mum. I was wondering if I could ask for yer assistance in an important matter."

"Of course. How can I help you?"

Shannon twisted a strand of hair and stared at the ground. Why should asking such a small thing be so hard? Maybe because she'd never asked for help before? She had made her way as best she could after her parents died and had nothing to be ashamed of. She'd even gotten that job at the beautiful Wakefield estate, although little help that would be now since she left in such haste without obtaining a referral letter. Gaining employment could prove difficult. At least she didn't have to worry about paying room and board for the time being.

"Do you mind if I keep working while we talk? I want to be sure to have supper ready on time." Without waiting for a response, Mrs. Hamilton spun around and went back to cutting out biscuits with the edge of a glass dipped in flour.

Shannon moved into the overly warm room to stand next to her hostess. "Is there anything I could help you with?"

"You might peek at my pies and see if they are browned yet."

Shannon took the towel lying on the worktable and opened the stove door with it. "They're a wee bit brown, but I'm not sure if they're done yet."

Rachel looked over her shoulder. "Go ahead and take them out, if you don't mind. Then close the door so the oven can reheat. I'll have the biscuits ready to go in soon. So, what can I help you with?"

"I. . .wondered if you might. . .uh, help me to bake a pie—for the contest, I mean. A pie that would win the marshal's heart." Shannon's cheeks grew warm. "I've. . .uh. . .never learned to cook."

Rachel's grip tightened on the glass. This was too much to bear. She'd housed the brides, cooked meals for them, kept their rooms clean, and put fresh sheets on their beds, but to help them bake pies that would steal Luke's heart away from her was too much to ask.

She blinked away the surprising tears stinging her eyes. How could she respond to such a question?

Stiffening her back, she considered what the Lord would have her do. Obviously, it wasn't His will for her and Luke to marry. A pain clutched her heart, almost as if her butcher knife had slipped and stabbed her chest. She didn't deserve Luke, but she couldn't help loving him. She'd never stopped, even though she'd tried hard to squelch any thoughts or feelings for him while married. But his return had reopened a deep wound she thought had scabbed over.

Miss O'Neil still awaited her answer. Rachel took a fortifying breath, forced a smile, and looked over her shoulder. "Of course I can teach you to bake a pie."

Miss O'Neil gazed at her with uncertain eyes. "You're sure 'twouldn't be a bother?"

Rachel's chin quivered, and no amount of willpower could stop it. She spun back around to her biscuits and forced her voice to be steady. "No trouble at all. I bake pies most days, anyway. How about tomorrow after breakfast?"

"Aye, tomorrow then. Thank you ever so much, and I'd be happy to help you as repayment, if you could just let me know how."

Rachel's lips trembled, and tears blurred her eyes. "No thanks needed."

Miss O'Neil padded away, and Rachel lost her composure. She dropped the glass on top of her dough and rushed outside. Tears that she'd tried so hard to conquer spilled down her cheeks. She trotted past the woodpile, where she'd often seen Luke shirtless, his skin gleaming with sweat, his arm muscles bulging as he lifted the ax. A deep sense of loss nearly knocked her off her feet. How could she go on knowing he was married to another woman? Was this piercing pain what he'd felt when she'd married James?

She dropped to her knees behind Luke's little house and out of view of anyone looking out her back door. Gazing up at the sky, she sought God for strength. "How do I do this, Lord? How do I help these women prepare to battle for the man I love?"

Only a few weeks had passed after Luke's return before she realized the depths of her feelings for him. But what did that matter when he refused to forgive her? And enduring the ache of his rejection had opened her eyes to how he'd suffered. New tears spilled for the pain she'd caused him. If only she hadn't trusted James. Hadn't dawdled at the river when she'd learned Luke wasn't coming. Hadn't allowed herself to be alone with James that one time. She faced the truth: She didn't deserve Luke. He was a good, honest man who'd loved her with his whole being—and she had betrayed that love.

She cried until her throat ached and her nose was stuffy. Using her apron for a handkerchief, she wiped her face and sat on the warm ground, empty and barren. "Help me, Father. Give me strength."

She glanced up at the brilliant blue sky showing through the canopy of trees. The leaves swished in the light breeze, and the warmth of the sun dried her tears. "Show me what to do. *Please.*"

After a short time of sitting and praying, a calm spread through her limp limbs and peace again reigned in her heart. If she couldn't have Luke, maybe she could help him find the best bride. She wouldn't be vindictive or allow selfishness to keep her from helping them. She didn't know which woman would be the best fit for Luke, not that it was her choice, but at least she could teach Miss O'Neil to bake a pie.

Standing, she dusted the back of her dress and wiped off her face again. As she ambled back to Hamilton House, her aunt's letters came to mind. For years, her Aunt Millie, her mother's sister, had tried to get Rachel to move to Kansas City to live with her. Rachel had never seriously considered the woman's offer. Lookout had always been her home, and she had the boardinghouse to support her and Jacqueline. But if Luke married, she didn't think her heart could take seeing him happily wed to another woman and raising children. Her lip wobbled, and fresh tears stung her aching eyes, but she batted them away. At the well, she drew up a fresh bucket of cool water and rinsed her face.

The mayor had offered to purchase Hamilton House several times since James's death. Kansas City was a bigger city than Lookout and would most likely have a school that ran higher than eighth grade, giving more educational opportunities for Jacqueline and plenty of ways for Rachel to earn some income, should she need it after the sale of her home.

She heaved in a raggedy sigh. Maybe it was time to consider leaving Lookout.

Leah dipped her pen in the ink bottle, then blotted the point and continued her letter to Sue Anne:

I envy your being engaged to that rancher. I never thought when I traveled so far from home that I'd have to battle two other women for the marshal's heart. Can you even imagine such a fiasco? Now there's to be a contest to determine who will make the best bride for him. Whoever heard of such a thing? The first round is a pie-baking contest.

Leah grinned, thinking of the second place ribbon she'd won in last year's county fair for her rhubarb pie. She'd been baking since she was a young girl and would surely win this round.

Have I told you how charming Luke Davis is? Oh my. So tall, and ever so handsome with his deep brown eyes and pecan-colored hair. He walks so straight and with such authority, although I do delight in seeing him flustered. With all the brides arriving to marry him, he's been more frustrated than a man whose wife just birthed him his seventh daughter.

I intend to win. I have no other option. What is to become of me if I should fail? I can't return home. Pa surely wouldn't allow me to after I refused to marry Mr. Abernathy and ran off without so much as a good-bye.

Losing is not an alternative I can bear to think about. I simply must win.

How is Ma? The children?

Have you received any more letters from your Simon?

I want you to know that the money you gave me just before I left town was a lifesaver. You'll remember how I didn't want to accept it, but I'm thankful now that I did. I was able to pay room and board at the boardinghouse the first few days I was here. The

*marshal has ordered his cousins to foot our bills until things are
settled. I don't like that, but there's little I can do about the situation.*

*And thank your brother again for helping me with my trunk
that night I snuck away and for driving me to Joplin. I couldn't
bear to leave it behind since Sam made it for me.*

Leah finished the missive and sat back in her chair. She would
mail the letter tomorrow morning, but tonight she had to decide
which pie she would bake. It needed to be something that would
please the marshal's palate and stand out from the others. The
contest was only two days away, and she could not fail.

She unfastened her high-topped shoes and sat on the edge of
the bed, considering her competition. Miss O'Neil, looking shy
and fearful all the time, surely wouldn't turn the marshal's head;
but then again, who needed to cook and sew when she had such
an intriguing accent and such luscious auburn hair and fair skin.
Shannon really was a lovely girl.

Leah reclined on the comfortable bed. She loved the pretty
room painted a pale blue, almost the color of Mrs. Hamilton's
eyes. Leah scowled at the memory of how the woman had looked
at Luke with such longing in her gaze. She obviously knew the
marshal well. But just what their relationship was, Leah wasn't sure.
It seemed much deeper than Mrs. Hamilton simply providing his
meals. Why, she'd bet her grandmother's cameo that they had an
intertwining past of some sort.

Turning over, she stared out the window, watching the sunset. A
bird chirped in a nearby tree, trying to outdo the crickets in the grass
below. She should probably put on her nightgown. All the stress of
the contest and being around the other brides daily wore on her.
Made her tired, even though she'd done very little work that day.
Who would have thought idleness could exhaust a person?

Maybe she should ask Mrs. Hamilton if there was some work
she could do to pass the time. After working her fingers to the
nubs at home, she had enjoyed having little to do, yet that was

getting old. Maybe she didn't mind working as long as she had a choice in the matter.

The sun sank below the horizon, painting the undersides of the clouds a breath-stealing pinkish purple. A brisk wind snapped the white curtains like flags. She actually liked the wide-openness of Texas. Something about the place pulled at her, made her never want to leave. But if she lost the bride contest, she'd have to seek employment somewhere or return home—and that was something she was unwilling to do.

Forcing herself up from the bed, she unfastened the buttons on her dress and let it drop to the floor. Miss Blackstone's calculating stare entered her mind. The woman had a perpetual scowl and talked very little, yet she was quite pretty in an unfinished way. She tried to hide her roughness, but Leah saw right through her. If the lady could cook well, she would surely be her toughest competitor. Maybe it was time to look at her more closely.

CHAPTER 21

The night before the bride contest, Rachel sat in her bedroom, brushing her long hair for one hundred strokes. Jacqueline was in bed, but the girl fidgeted, unable to lie still. Something was bothering her, but she'd been tight-lipped and scarce the past few days.

Rachel reached out to set her brush on the vanity when a shrill scream broke the silence. Jacqueline bolted up in bed as Rachel vaulted to her feet. Their gazes locked. "Stay here."

She grabbed the rifle that always sat behind the door and ran up the stairs. Miss O'Neil's door opened, and bright light from her lantern flooded the hallway. Miss Bennett stood immobile at her door, her wide blue eyes gleaming in the light. Mr. Sanderson, a new guest in town with his wife for the contest, stood at the open door of the fourth bedroom, a pistol wobbling in his shaky hand. "What's going on, Mrs. Hamilton?"

"I don't know, sir, but I'll find out."

"Do you need my help?" The man lifted one brow.

Rachel glanced at Miss Blackstone's door. "Perhaps you could stay in your room and watch—just in case?"

"This is highly irregular," said Mrs. Sanderson. "Harvey, come back inside and shut the door. I'm sure Mrs. Hamilton can handle the disruption without your assistance."

He harrumphed but didn't close the door. He winked at Rachel and motioned her forward with his gun just as another squeal erupted from Miss Blackstone's room.

Rachel hurried over and knocked on the door. "Is everything all right, Miss Blackstone?"

"N—no, there's a snake in here." At the other bride's declaration, Miss O'Neil scurried back into her room and slammed the door.

Rachel opened Miss Blackstone's door and peered around the room. How in the world could a snake have gotten up to the second story? A dim light from her lamp left the room in a contrast of light and shadows. Watching her step, Rachel crossed the room and turned up the flame. "Where did you last see it?"

The woman who'd always seemed tough as overworked dough huddled in a tight ball on her bed, arms locked around her legs. "U—under the d—dresser."

"Do you know what kind of snake it is?"

Miss Blackstone shook her head; a thick curtain of black hair fell around her shoulders. Her eyes were wide, and her lips pressed tightly together.

Rachel didn't care for snakes, but she wasn't frightened of them, except for the cottonmouths that sometimes frequented the river tributaries. Growing up in Texas and working in her ma's garden, she'd seen her share of snakes. She lifted the lamp and stooped down. Sure enough, something was under the wooden chest of drawers. She used the muzzle of her rifle and flipped the intruder out onto the rug. Miss Blackstone screeched, making Rachel jump.

"It's just a harmless garden snake."

Miss Blackstone cowered on the bed. "I hate sn—snakes of all kinds. My brother used to torment me with them."

"I'm truly sorry for your discomfort. I can't imagine how it got up here unless it somehow crawled into my laundry basket while I was gathering things off the line." She picked up the harmless foot-long snake by the tail.

Miss Blackstone squealed and dove under the covers. Rachel shook her head and left the room. "Please try to relax and get some rest. Tomorrow is a busy day." Juggling the rifle and snake in one arm, she closed the door.

Rachel glanced at the Sandersons' door, and Mr. Sanderson lifted his brows. She held up the snake. "Nothing but a little intruder, sir. Nothing to be concerned with."

He nodded and closed the door.

Miss Bennett leaned against the door frame of her room, her lip curling. "That's what all the ruckus was about?"

Rachel battled her grin. "I can't imagine how it got up here."

"I didn't think Miss Blackstone was afraid of anything. I mean, she seems so tough."

Rachel nodded. "I suppose there's something that frightens each of us. Good night, Miss Bennett."

As Rachel plodded down the stairs, she considered what frightened her most—Luke marrying another woman. She tossed the snake outside and closed the front door. Suddenly, she realized that her daughter hadn't made an appearance upstairs, and that was highly uncharacteristic of her.

With suspicions mounting, Rachel hurried to their bedroom, but much to her relief, the girl was still in bed. Miracles happened after all.

∿

Jack's heart pounded like she'd run all the way to the river and back. She'd barely made it back into bed when her mother closed the front door. Did she suspect her of putting the snake in Miss Blackstone's room?

Jack worked to slow her breathing, thinking of the open door to the pie safe. She'd hoped to stir something into the pies that would ruin them before they were cooked, but there'd been no opportunity. She might not get dessert for supper tomorrow if the mice invaded the pastries, but at least Luke couldn't pick a bride if the pies weren't edible. She grinned into her pillow, just imagining the howls of the brides when they saw their ruined entries.

A tiny measure of guilt wafted through her, but she shoved it away. Luke was worth fighting for, no matter the cost or how many years she'd be punished and sent to her room if her mother learned what she'd done.

She could hear her mother moving around the room, settling the rifle behind the door, and the click of the latch as the door closed. The double bed creaked and dipped on one side as her mother sat down. A sudden thought charged into Jack's mind—if her mother married Luke, she would get a room of her own. She smiled and wondered which one she'd choose.

Her mother heaved a big sigh and relaxed against the pillow, sending the odor of lavender her way. "Don't you want to know what happened? I know you're not asleep. And thank you for obeying me and staying in the room."

Jack cringed, knowing she'd done the opposite. Why did disobeying feel so awful?

Turning onto her side, she stared at her mother's face, illuminated by the faint moonlight shining through the open window. "Do you know what folks are calling those brides?"

Her ma shook her head. "What's that?"

"Boardinghouse brides." Jack flopped onto her back and stared at the dark ceiling. "Are you gonna let Marshal Davis marry one of them without so much as a fight?"

Her mother's heavy sigh warmed the side of her face and fluttered her hair. "There's nothing I can do about the situation. Luke agreed to marry one of them."

Jack sat up, fighting back tears. "But you have to do something. I want him to be my pa."

Rachel pulled her down into her arms, and Jack reveled in her ma's softness and sweet scent. "Oh baby, I'm sorry. Why didn't you tell me how you felt?"

"It didn't matter until all those dumb brides showed up. I figured we could take our time, and eventually he'd fall in love with us."

Rachel tightened her grip. "I'm sure he loves you, honey. How could he not?"

Jack wrapped her arm around her ma's trim waist. "But I want him to love you, too."

Her ma smoothed Jack's hair from her face. "Oh sweetie, you can't force someone to love you. It has to come natural."

"But I heard that Luke used to love you—before you married my pa. Can't you make him love you again?"

Rachel winced as her daughter's words pierced her heart. If only Jacqueline knew how badly she wanted Luke to love her. But she'd done all she knew how to get him to forgive her. She had to leave it in the Lord's hands now.

Tears burned her eyes and ran down her temples into her ears. If only there was something she *could* do.

Jacqueline tugged away from her and sat up. "I have an idea."

Rachel wiped her eyes, hoping her daughter couldn't see her tears. "What's that?"

Jacqueline clutched her hand. "Why don't you enter the bride contest?"

She opened her mouth, ready to give a dozen reasons why she couldn't, but her voice refused to respond.

"Really, Ma. Why don'tcha?"

"Well, because it's a contest just between the brides."

"But don't you care for Luke?"

Rachel nodded, unable to deny the truth. Somewhere over the past few weeks, her love for him had rekindled and flamed to life like a rampant prairie fire. "Yes, I do, but—"

"No buts. You *have* to enter that contest."

"I can't. It wouldn't be fair to the brides."

Jacqueline shook her arm, her voice sounding frantic. "If you love him, you have to. Otherwise, we're going to lose him."

Rachel considered the wisdom of her daughter's words. It was true. If she passively did nothing, Luke would choose one of the brides and marry, leaving her to endure the rest of her life alone and filled with regrets. Still, if by chance he did pick her, all the brides would be left unmarried. How could she do that to them? "I don't think it's fair for me to enter. Luke already knows me, and that might sway his choice."

"Well, enter anan. . .anon—what's that called?"

"Anonymously?"

"Yeah! That."

Rachel sat up, her heart taking off like a caged bird finally set free. Could she do it? Enter the contest anonymously? At some point she'd have to admit the pie was hers, but maybe, just maybe in the meantime, Luke would realize how much she still loved him. Excitement drove away her sadness. Maybe she still had a chance. Grinning, she pulled her daughter into a warm hug. "I think that's a brilliant idea, sweetie. But it will be a secret, and we can't tell a soul."

"My lips are locked shut." In the moonlight, Jack twisted her hand in front of her mouth as if turning a key in a lock. She bounced on the bed, grabbing Rachel's shoulders. "Oh Ma, this will be such fun. The whole town will be wondering who the pie is from."

Rachel laid back down, smiling to herself. Why hadn't she thought of the idea? Maybe because she was too busy mourning her loss of Luke. *Oh, please, Lord, let this work. Help me to win back Luke's heart.*

She turned onto her side, thinking of all the pies she'd served Luke since he returned. To make things fair, she needed to bake a different pie—something he wouldn't recognize as hers. Jacqueline fidgeted for a while; then her breathing deepened as sleep claimed her. But Rachel's mind raced. She had to find a special pie to woo the man she loved.

CHAPTER 22

"Marshal, they're ready for you to come and judge the pie contest." Mayor Burke stood inside the jail door, all but bouncing. He grinned. "And there's a big surprise for you."

Luke stood, dreading the task ahead. If he chose a winner, the losers would be disappointed, but then contests were always like that. They just didn't normally have your whole future riding on them.

He followed the mayor outside, where a crowd filled the street and boardwalks. His cousins had rigged up a table in front of the freight office, and Rachel and the ladies had decorated it with a white tablecloth, ribbons, bows, and other frippery. Atop it sat not three pies, but four.

"How in the world could something like this happen?" Luke's gaze swerved toward the mayor, who stood to the left of the table.

The man grinned and shrugged. "Nobody seems to know. One minute it wasn't there, and the next it was."

Luke lifted his hat, ran his hand through his hair, and slapped the hat back down. Picking a wife by sampling three pies was enough of a chore, but now there were four—the last, a golden-colored one that looked like a custard pie, with a sign beside it reading ANONYMOUS ENTRY. The fragrant scent of the pies made Luke's mouth water. But warning bells clanged in his head. That pie could be from any unmarried woman for miles around.

"Hey, Marshal, how's it feel to have all them gals wantin' to marry up w'ya? Maybe some of us bachelors could have the leftovers." Dan Howard laughed, and the crowd filling Main Street joined in.

"Yeah, Marshal, share the wealth," someone cried.

Luke shook his head at their good-natured teasing but focused a glare on Garrett. None of this would have happened if not for him. "Are you sure no new brides have come to town?"

"Not as far as I know," Garrett answered.

Standing beside his brother and the mayor on the left side of the table, Mark also shook his head and shrugged one shoulder.

Luke scanned the crowd for Rachel. She could confirm if another bride had arrived in town, but he didn't find her. He could hardly blame her for not attending the contest, considering their past and how she'd begged him for forgiveness. He studied the ruffled edge of the tablecloth covering the pie table and sighed. He couldn't give her something he didn't have. So why did he feel guilty about the whole situation?

"This is outrageous." Miss Bennett, standing to the right of the table with the other brides, stomped her foot and hoisted her chin in the air. "That last pie ought'a be tossed out."

With her hands planted on her hips, Miss Blackstone stepped forward. "Yeah, I thought this contest was just between us three."

Miss O'Neil fiddled with her sleeve, her eyes looking as wide as dinner plates.

Luke pinned his stare on the brides. "Has someone new moved into the boardinghouse? Another bride, I mean."

All three gals shook their heads in unison—blond, brunette, and redhead. They would certainly know if another husband-seeker had come to town.

He studied the table holding the contest entries. Each one had a label made from a folded paper, and they read BRIDE #1, BRIDE #2, BRIDE #3, AND ANONYMOUS ENTRY, but the last sign was in a different handwriting than the others. The four pies sat, begging to be cut, although one of them looked a bit charred, and two had notches out of them that looked as if a varmint had feasted on them. The pie from the anonymous bride was by far the best looking. His stomach gurgled, reminding him that he'd been so nervous this morning he'd skipped breakfast.

His gaze wandered back to the fourth pie. What if it tasted the best? If he chose that one as the winner, he might well end up marrying Bertha Boyd. A shiver snaked down his spine, and he scanned the crowd to see if she was there. Sure enough, the wagon-sized woman sat on a sagging bench on the boardwalk across the street, fanning herself with one of those cardboard advertisements on a stick that a mortuary office from a neighboring town had handed out. The crowd in the street in front of the freight office, watching and waiting to help judge the event, had tripled in size from what it had been earlier.

Max crept up beside Luke and licked his hand then trotted back into the jailhouse. The dog hated crowds, probably because most of the "kindly" townsfolk had chased him away from their trash heaps at one time or another. Luke wished he could hide out like his dog, but he straightened his shoulders and turned back to the mayor. "What do you make of this additional entry?"

The mayor sucked in his overly large belly and grinned. "I haven't a clue, but it will make a great headline: ANONYMOUS BRIDE COMPETES FOR MARSHAL'S HAND IN MARRIAGE." He chuckled and shook his head then scanned the crowd. "Where's that newspaper woman? Someone get Jenny up here," he yelled, "and tell her to bring her photographic equipment."

"I'm here, Mayor." Jenny Evans peeked her head between two beefy men. "Let me through, you big belugas."

Both men turned sideways, looking as if they were trying to

figure out if she'd called them an offensive name, and Jenny shot through the opening carrying her big camera. Jack followed right on her tail with her arms filled with photographic plates. Jenny was one gutsy lady to entrust Rachel's daughter with something so fragile.

"You brides line up behind the pie you made." Jenny set down the long legs of the tripod and arranged them the way she wanted, then set the boxy camera on top. Jack handed her a film plate, and Jenny inserted it. "All right, ladies, look up here. Hold your expressions steady."

Luke was amazed the three mail-order brides did as ordered without complaint, although Miss Blackstone hung back a bit, as if she didn't like being photographed. He now knew who made which pie. Not that it mattered, because he didn't favor one gal over the other, except he maybe liked Miss O'Neil the least because she was so skittish. She was a lovely thing with that mass of copper hair and intriguing accent, but she didn't have what it took to live in Texas.

That would have left two brides to pick from if not for the anonymous entry. He searched his mind, trying to figure out who might have made it. There weren't many marriageable women in Lookout, which was why his cousins had concocted this whole scheme. But someone from another town might have read of the event and entered, or someone from a family he hadn't yet met.

"Thank you, ladies. You can move now." Jenny waved her hand, setting the brides in motion.

"Now, Marshal," Miss Evans said, "if you'd be so kind, I'd like a picture of you in front of that mystery entry."

Luke shook his head. He'd never had his photograph taken before and wasn't going to start today.

"Go on, Luke. Don't be shy." Garrett's cocky grin made Luke want to knock it off his face. "You gonna let those brides show you up?"

The crowd joined in cheering for Luke to get his photo taken.

He sighed and took his place behind the table. Holding a hooded glare on his face, he hoped he made everyone squirm. This whole shebang was getting out of hand. Whatever made him agree to marry was beyond him. Even a lawsuit sounded half good at this point.

Jenny took the photograph, and the mayor quickly stepped in front of the table, facing the crowd. Jack slipped in beside him and tugged on Luke's pants. He leaned down. "I like that surprise pie best, don't you?"

He studied her expression for a minute but decided she knew nothing about the owner of that particular entry. Either that, or she sure could keep a straight face.

"I probably should reserve judgment until I taste them." He grinned and tweaked Jack's button nose.

Mayor Burke lifted his hands, and the crowd quieted. "All right, let's get this show on the road, and maybe we'll have a wedding tonight."

A cheer rang out from the crowd at the same time a lump the size of a turkey egg formed in Luke's throat. Nobody had said anything about an immediate wedding. Weren't there other parts to this contest yet to be held? He ran his hand over his jaw. If only he hadn't given his word to marry.

"First, we'll let the marshal taste the pies. I'll go next, and then the Corbetts. After that, it will cost you five cents for one spoonful of each pie until they are all gone. There's a jelly jar in front of each pie plate. When you pay your money to my wife over there," he motioned his hand to the right, "you'll get a dried bean. Taste the confections, then drop your bean into the jar you feel is the winner. All funds received will be donated to the church, so if you feel inclined to give more than required, I'm sure the reverend would be appreciative. And of course, Luke doesn't have to marry the gal who gets the most votes. He has the final say as to which pie he thinks is the best. If he's ready to pick a bride, I reckon we could have a weddin' tonight."

The mayor glanced at Luke, as if expecting him to object, but Luke clamped his mouth shut. He just wanted to get this over with.

"All right," the mayor said. "Let's get started."

People pushed forward, as if each wanted a chance to sample the pies before they were all gone. The noise of the crowd grew louder. Many of the folks who lived around Lookout were farmers or ranchers who worked hard and lived a lonely existence. These social gatherings were few and far between, but Luke knew that each person would be encouraged just because they came to town to enjoy the fun and were able to forget their own troubles and visit with their neighbors for a short while.

"Just wait until you bite into this, Marshal Davis." Miss Bennett grinned and batted her lashes. She served him a large slice of her pie, which was the one with the bite gone. Luke was glad she cut his slice from the other side of the pie, not that he wouldn't eat it just because of that, but he'd had his share of eating food that critters had gotten into during his cavalry days. The other brides also served him generous portions of their pies. Miss Blackstone's and Miss O'Neil's were the overly cooked ones, but they still looked juicy inside. Maybe all wasn't lost for them. He stopped in front of the fourth pie, but nobody stepped up to serve it.

"I can help." Jack, her hands now empty, scurried behind the table and reached for the knife.

Miss Bennett hurried past the front of the table and held out her hand. "You'd better let an adult handle that."

Jack scowled but dropped the knife and stepped back, arms crossed. Miss Bennett deftly cut a rather thin slice and dropped it onto his plate. She grinned. "Here you go, Marshal Davis."

Eager to get away from the staring brides, Luke took his plate back into the jail and shut the door. He didn't want people gawking at him while he ate and decided which pie he liked best. His mouth watered at the scent of cinnamon, apples, and peaches, but his fork went to the custard first. It had always been a favorite of his, and he hadn't had any since he'd left the cavalry. The sweet, buttery flavor tickled his taste buds, and his eyes dropped shut as he ran the confection over his tongue. This wasn't custard at all, but something different. Something even better. And it was a chilled pie, something he'd very rarely had. Too bad he hadn't gotten a larger slice of that one.

Garrett kicked the door open and stormed into the room, carrying his plate. "Whoowee! Can you believe all the people who came to town today? Must be a couple of hundred."

Mark followed, already chewing. His blue eyes widened, and he spit out the bite of pie. His wild gaze searched the room, then he grabbed Luke's coffee cup off the desk and downed the last of the cold coffee. Garrett lifted up an edge of the apple pie as if wary of it.

Mark spun around, one hand lifted up, palm outward. "Don't try that. Something's wrong with it."

Garrett sniffed it. "Smells fine."

"By all means, if you don't believe me, go ahead and take a bite."

Garrett eyed it again. "Guess I'll try the peach one." He cut a slice with his fork and shoved it in. His eyes closed for a second but then went wide just as Mark's had. He wagged his hand in front on his mouth. "Water!"

Mark shook his head and grabbed Luke's coffeepot. Garrett downed the mug in one long gulp then glared at this brother. "I thought you said it was the apple pie that tasted bad."

"I did."

"Well, so does the peach. Miss O'Neil must have grabbed the salt instead of the sugar."

Luke stared at his plate, wondering if the nut pie would also be bad. He glanced up at his cousins. Mark dropped down onto a chair, arms crossed, and grinned at him. Garrett set his plate on the desk and watched. Luke now dreaded having to taste the last pie, but he figured it was only fair to try each one. He put a tidbit of the nut pie on his fork and licked it. Burnt sugar assaulted his senses.

"I can tell that one's just as bad." Garrett said. "What do you think happened?"

Luke swallowed hard and set the plate down. "I don't know. This one's not salty, but the inside tastes burnt. As for those other two, I can understand *one* person accidentally grabbing the salt instead of sugar since they look just the same, but for two of them to do that?"

Mark's head jerked up. "Two?"

"Yeah, that custard—or whatever it is—tastes great." As if needing to confirm it, he retrieved his plate and finished off the last of his slice while his cousins dug into theirs.

Mark's eyes rolled upward. "That was delicious."

"Yeah, it's great," Garrett said around a mouthful. "But who made it?"

Luke shrugged. "I have no idea."

"Seems strange for a woman to enter a pie-baking, husband-getting contest but not give her name."

Garrett shrugged. "Maybe she's as ugly as the backside of a mule."

Luke didn't care for his cousin's crude comment. "So, what do I do about it?"

Mark licked the section of his plate where the custard had been. "If everything she cooks tastes like this, I'll marry her myself."

The men chuckled, and Luke shook his head. The outer door opened, and the mayor stomped inside and glared at Luke.

"What a disaster. The whole town is upset. Half the people are fussing for a refund because the pies were so bad. Only one of them was edible."

Luke walked to the door and looked out. "Guess I should go see if I can soothe everybody."

"This is a nightmare. That's what." The mayor huffed and

puffed like a wild turkey trying to impress its mate.

"It's a setback, not a disaster, Mayor." Mark always was the diplomat of the group. "It will just serve to increase interest for next week's contest."

The mayor tugged his vest down and pushed his glasses up on his nose. "How so?"

Garrett flashed the grin that Luke knew would make the mayor see his side of things. "Everyone will wonder if those brides can sew better than they can cook. If Luke postpones making a decision, I reckon most folks will come back next week to see if he chooses one then. Also, everyone will be talking and trying to figure out who the mystery bride is."

"Maybe you could somehow play it up to benefit the town," Mark said. "Have a potluck and dance afterward."

Mayor Burke rubbed his chin with his index finger and thumb. "Yes, I do see your point. Perhaps this wasn't quite the disaster I thought. Although most of the men who were asking about the leftover brides took to the hills when they learned the women couldn't cook." He chuckled, and his whole belly bounced.

Luke stepped away from the door now that he was sure things were all right outside. "It's odd that three of the four pies would be so bad."

"You think someone sabotaged the contest?" Garrett asked.

Luke shrugged. "I don't know, but it is a possibility."

"But who, and why?" Mark asked.

Since the pies were cooked at Rachel's, Luke could well imagine Jack playing a prank and swapping the salt and sugar containers, but for what purpose?

Could it be the girl was jealous and thought she'd lose his friendship if he married? Maybe he needed to reassure her that such a thing wouldn't happen.

Rachel stirred the pot of potato soup then set the spoon on her worktable. The sandwiches and pumpkin pudding were ready for lunch as soon as the brides and other guests returned from the pie contest. She'd stood in her doorway, watching the crowd, but couldn't bring herself to walk down there. If Luke selected a bride today, she didn't want to be there.

It was foolish of her to have entered, and if not for Jacqueline's help, she would have been discovered. Her gaze darted toward the pie table. Had Luke liked hers the best?

A figure parted from the crowd and strode in her direction. Rand. Rachel clutched the door frame, not wanting to face him today with her emotions all in a tizzy.

"Afternoon, Rachel." Rand removed his hat and held it in front of him.

She forced a smile, almost wishing she did have feelings for the kind rancher. "Rand."

He glanced back over his shoulder. "That's some to-do they're havin'."

"Did you sample the pies?"

He shook his head. "Nah. I thought about it, but I don't like being caught up in a crowd. Been out on the open prairie too long, I reckon. Anyway, I heard none of them were any good except that mystery pie."

Rachel's heart somersaulted. "What was wrong with the others?"

"Two of them were too salty, someone said. Not sure about the third one."

Her grip on the door frame tightened. "So, the marshal didn't pick a bride?"

"Nope. There's to be a shirt-sewing contest now."

Relief that Luke hadn't chosen a wife yet made her knees weak.

"You wouldn't want to accompany me to the judgin' next Saturday, would ya?"

Rachel closed her eyes. She didn't want to hurt Rand, but he needed to know she had no interest in him.

"Never mind. I can tell by your expression that's a no." He hung his head and curled the edge of his hat.

"I'm sorry, Rand. I like you a lot. You're a good friend, but friendship is all I have to offer you."

His mouth pushed up in a resigned pucker. "I reckon I've known that for a while, but I just didn't want to accept it."

Rachel laid her hand on his arm. "You're a good man, Rand. You deserve a woman who will love you with all of her heart."

"Thank you for your honesty." He nodded and shoved his hat on. "I won't pester you anymore."

She watched him stride back toward the dispersing crowd, her heart aching. But she'd done the right thing. She wouldn't marry another man she didn't love.

She returned to the kitchen, and her hands shook as she carried the plate of sandwiches to the buffet in the dining room where she set them beside the individual bowls of pudding. She just needed to ladle up the soup, and all would be ready.

"Who would do such a thing?"

"I've never been so humiliated in all my life."

Rachel hurried into the entryway at the distressed sound of the brides' voices.

Miss O'Neil held her handkerchief in front of her red face. "Oh Mrs. Hamilton, everything was such a—" The girl lapsed into a phrase in Gaelic.

"My thoughts exactly." Miss Blackstone's face scrunched up, and she kicked at the bottom step of the inside stairway. "The whole thing was a disaster."

Miss Bennett anchored her hands to her hips. "I want to know who would trick us like that."

"Please, won't you sit down to lunch and let us sort this out?" Rachel held out her hands, hoping to calm everyone.

"I. . .I don't believe I can eat." Miss O'Neil dropped into a chair and rested her chin in her hand, elbow on the table. The poor girl looked so forlorn.

Miss Blackstone rolled her eyes, while Miss Bennett claimed her seat at the dining table.

Rachel laid her hand on the Irish girl's shoulder. "Some warm soup will make you feel better."

While the women waited, Rachel quickly ladled the soup into the tureen and placed it with the other food on the buffet. By now, the other guests had entered and also seated themselves. She stood at the head of the table, curiosity nibbling at her. She knew about the mice getting into the pie safe and damaging a couple of the pies, but how had two of them turned out too salty? "Shall we pray?"

Miss Blackstone made a snorty sound that resembled a laugh, but everyone else ducked their heads. "Heavenly Father, we thank You for Your bountiful blessings and pray that You will work out things for each of the young women seated here today. Bless my other guests, too, and keep them safe in their travels."

Conversation was kept to a minimum while her guests served themselves. Rachel walked to the front door, wondering where Jacqueline was. She rarely missed mealtimes. Just then, she saw her daughter exit the marshal's office, hike up her skirt, and make a beeline for home. Rachel pursed her lips. Would that child never learn proper manners?

Jacqueline skidded to a halt on the porch when she saw her mother watching her. "You missed all the excitement, Ma! I just gotta go wash up. Sorry I'm late for lunch, but I was talking with Luke."

Rachel stepped outside. "Jacqueline, ladies do not run—and don't refer to the marshal by his given name."

"Sure, Ma." Jacqueline waved her hand as she hurried around the side of the house toward the back where the water pump was.

Shaking her head, Rachel walked back inside, suddenly remembering the day the brides had arrived. She'd done the very thing she'd chastised her daughter for doing when she'd remembered the pies she'd left in the oven. She sighed and went to the buffet and dished up Jacqueline's soup.

When they were all seated again, Rachel looked around the table. "So, what happened? Mr. Kessler mentioned something about the pies being too salty."

The three brides looked suspiciously at one another. Miss Bennett hiked up her chin. "It seems someone must have switched your sugar for salt. My pie and Miss O'Neil's were both overly salty and inedible. We made our pies at the same time, remember?"

"Maybe you just grabbed the wrong container," Jacqueline said, helping herself to a bowl of pudding off the buffet.

Miss Bennett frowned at her. "I've been cooking all my life and have never made that mistake."

"That nut pie tasted as if the inside mixings had been burnt," Mr. Sanderson offered.

"I guess I cooked it too long." Miss Blackstone stirred her food on her plate. "I didn't normally cook on a stove, so I didn't make many pies."

Rachel wondered about her comment. Where had she lived that she had to cook without a stove?

"The fourth one was the best," Jacqueline interjected as she took her seat. "It was better than perfect."

If the other three pies had turned out bad, that meant Luke probably liked hers the best. Rachel ducked her head to hide a smile.

"You didn't by chance get the salt and sugar in the wrong containers, did you?" Miss O'Neil asked.

Rachel shook her head. "If I had, we'd have noticed. Most things I cook have either sugar or salt in them. I don't understand how such a thing could happen. I keep my containers clearly marked."

Miss Blackstone shook her head and slurped her soup. "Sure seems odd that all three of ours turned out bad. It's almost as if someone did it on purpose."

"Uh huh, like that anonymous bride," Miss Bennett muttered.

Rachel winced and stuck a spoonful of soup in her mouth. Her gaze drifted to Jacqueline. The girl didn't want Luke marrying one of the brides, but would she go so far as to ruin the other entries?

Jacqueline looked up and smiled with innocence. Wouldn't she look guilty if she'd done such an unconscionable thing?

"I'm certainly curious who that fourth entry was from," Mrs. Sanderson said.

Her husband grinned. "That sure stirred up a lot of interest. Everyone's speculating who it belongs to."

"Well," Mrs. Sanderson said, "the marshal is a handsome man. I can see why an unwed woman would want to throw her hat into that contest and win him for a mate."

Mr. Sanderson's spoon stopped in front of his mouth, and he scowled. His wife patted his arm. "Now, Harvey, don't let such a little comment spoil your dinner. The marshal is a comely man, but you're the one who's held my heart all these years." She smiled sweetly at him, and he nodded and resumed eating.

Rachel's heart ached. Would she ever know the love of a good man again? Her thoughts flashed to Rand, but she knew he wasn't the man for her. She'd only ever imagined herself married to Luke. With him out of the picture, could she love someone else?

She shook her head and stared into her soup. No, Luke was the only man she'd ever love. Oh, she'd tried to care for James after they were married, but he pushed her away with his cruel streak. And on the day he first slapped Jacqueline and knocked her down, Rachel knew she could never love him. If only she'd never married him.

Her mistake had been to allow James to comfort her that day at the river. She hadn't spent time with Luke in over two weeks because he'd been working so much. When she learned he wasn't coming, she'd gotten teary-eyed. James had hugged her. Told her he'd never neglect her like Luke had.

She shivered, remembering how he'd kissed her temple. How his hold on her had tightened. "I love you, Rachel. I have for a long time." He kissed her lips, and for the briefest of seconds, she'd felt like a princess because the most eligible bachelor in town cared for her. But then she saw Luke's face in her mind and knew where her heart belonged. She struggled—told him to stop—but James, carried away by his passion, shoved her down. She'd tried to fight him off, but he was too strong. And afterward, he'd told her that Luke would no longer want her since she was a fallen woman. James offered to marry her, but now she realized that she'd only been a pawn.

James had been spoiled as a child, and as an adult, he took what he wanted. Somewhere along the line, he'd decided he wanted her and was determined to steal her away from Luke. When he realized he couldn't overcome her love for Luke, he stole the most special gift she had to give her husband, her purity.

"Something wrong, Ma?" Jacqueline stared at her with worried eyes.

"Uh. . .no baby, I just need to get more soup." Jumping to her feet, Rachel hurried to the buffet, grabbed the tureen, and hustled into the kitchen where she slowly refilled the big bowl. She hung her head. Did Luke know what James had done? Did he know why she had to marry James?

No wonder he couldn't forgive her. She could hardly forgive herself. Tears burned her eyes, but she blinked them away lest they fall in the soup or her guests notice. Somehow she had to find it within herself to keep going until Luke chose a bride. She'd been foolish—hopeful—to enter the contest, but she wouldn't do it again.

Chapter 23

Jack hurried through her morning ablutions and dried her face with a once-blue towel, now faded to a soft gray, that smelled of sunshine and the outdoors. She always felt more awake after washing her face in the cool well water.

The house smelled of fried bacon and eggs, making her tummy squawk. She slipped the hated dress over her head and buttoned up the front. Whoever made the rule that girls had to wear dresses should have been forced to wear one himself. It was hard to run in them—not that ladies should run—but who wanted to be a lady?

Boys had all the fun. They got to work with horses, fish, even chop wood while women had to cook, clean, wash, and sew. How was that fair? She ran the brush through her hair and braided it. If her ma would let her, she'd cut it all off short; but according to Ma, a woman's glory was her hair. Men liked women to have long hair, she said.

Jack smacked the brush down on the vanity, wincing at the loud noise. If her ma heard that, she would lecture her about taking care of what they had and have Jack polishing every piece of furniture in the whole house as punishment.

She rubbed her hand over the dark wood, thankful that she hadn't scratched the vanity that her grandmother Hamilton had shipped from New York. Jack appreciated having nice things, because she knew that most of the kids at school didn't enjoy such luxuries.

She glanced at herself in the oval mirror, grimacing at how girlish she looked. Why couldn't she have been born a boy? Then she could have protected her ma from her father.

Yesterday had been Sunday, and her ma hadn't said anything about the pies, probably because it was the Lord's Day. Jack was sure she would today, and she couldn't wait to tell her again how much Luke had liked her pie. She had no idea how the salt and sugar had gotten mixed up when the brides were baking their pies, but she sure was glad it had.

Jack walked into the kitchen. Her ma bent and removed a pan of biscuits from the oven. She smiled when she saw Jack. "I was just coming to make sure you'd gotten up and that you hadn't taken ill. By the way, the Sandersons are leaving today."

Jack sighed. School had ended on Friday, and she'd hoped to go fishing today, but with the boarders leaving, she and her mother would have extra work cleaning the empty room.

"Put these on the buffet." She slid the bowl of biscuits toward Jack. "And please set the table and put out a plate of butter. I'm running a bit late myself."

Wondering if her ma had overslept, too, Jack carried the bowl to the buffet, then pulled cloth napkins from a drawer as well as silverware. She set the table, thinking how her ma had looked tired rather than rested. Maybe she was upset about Saturday's events. Jack had expected questions about the pies, but Ma had been especially quiet last night.

Shouldn't she have been happy that her pie was the only edible one?

Breakfast was a quiet affair. Miss O'Neil didn't come downstairs. Jack glanced over at Miss Bennett. The pretty blond slathered peach jam onto her biscuit and took a bite. Miss Blackstone ate with her face almost in her plate, as if she feared someone would take the food away from her. Jack's ma would never let her get away with that kind of behavior.

"I'm finished, Ma." Jack placed her silverware on her plate.

"Very well. Take your dish to the kitchen, please."

Jack looked at her ma's plate as she passed her, surprised at how little she'd eaten. Something was certainly bothering her.

She dumped her food scraps in the bucket for Max and set her plate in the sink, just as her ma entered the kitchen. Jack grabbed the partially filled scrap bucket and hurried to the door, hoping to make a quick escape.

"Wait. I need to ask you something."

Ack! Too late. "I gotta get these scraps to Max. You don't want him goin' hungry do you?"

Her ma followed her outside and grabbed her shoulder. "Just a minute, missy."

That stopped her. If her ma said "missy," she meant business. Jack swallowed the lump building in her throat.

"Did you swap the sugar and salt containers the day the brides were baking their pies? I want a truthful answer."

Jack felt her eyes widen. She'd thought about doing that very thing, and guilt wormed its way through her, even though she was innocent. Her remorse shifted to anger. Why did she always get blamed when something went wrong? "No Ma. Honestly, I didn't. I swear."

"Don't swear." Rachel crossed her arms. She lifted her eyes to the heavens as if she were praying. "Just tell me the truth. Did you do it so I might win?"

Jack flung her arms up. "I told you. I didn't do that."

"If I can't win fair and square, I don't want to win at all. Can you understand that?"

Jack shrugged. "I guess so. But if you don't win, we'll lose Luke."

Her ma closed her eyes as if the thought pained her. "Luke

was never ours to win. And I won't win by cheating, no matter what the cost."

Jack thought of a few times she'd cheated and won. It felt good to win, but afterward guilt had eaten away her joy, except for the time she'd beaten Butch Laird in a spelling contest. A light breeze lifted a lock of hair and blew it across her face, bringing with it the scent of wood smoke. Her ma reached down and tucked the wayward strand behind her ear. Jack studied her ma. Why couldn't Luke just pick her? She was every bit as pretty as the brides, although she was older than them. But didn't someone say *older was better*?

"Sweetie, I appreciate that you wanted to help me, but you were wrong to tamper with the pies."

"But I didn—"

Rachel lifted her hand. "I just wish you'd be honest. Other people were affected by your actions, and you'll have to be punished."

"But Ma—"

"I've decided not to enter the next round."

Jack's mouth fell open. Her ma still believed she was responsible, but even worse, she was giving up on the contest. "You can't quit." She tugged on her mother's sleeve. "I want Luke to be my pa, and you gotta marry him for that to happen."

Her ma looked up again, and Jack searched the sky to see what was so interesting up there.

After a while, her mother released a loud sigh. "Go feed Max, but when you get back, I'll have a list of extra chores for you to do as punishment."

Jack scowled and stomped off. Getting punished for something she'd done was bad enough because she deserved it, but knowing her mother didn't believe her made her stomach ache. Yeah, she'd opened the pie safe doors, but that's not what her ma had asked her about.

The thought of her ma quitting the contest brought tears to

her eyes. She swatted at them. She'd promised herself she'd never cry, because crying was a weakness. Boys made fun of kids who cried and picked on them.

She thought again of her ma not entering the other contests, and the idea sobered Jack. Somehow, she had to make sure her ma had an entry. She couldn't quit.

A few minutes later, she stopped at the marshal's office. Luke was gone, but Max lay sprawled on his blanket as if waiting for her. He lumbered up and wagged his tail. The old dog licked the gray whiskers around his nose and looked up eagerly. Jack set down the bucket, and Max started eating.

"I wish you could talk, old buddy." She scratched his back while he ate. "I'm sorry for being mean to you before. I didn't know what a good dog you were."

She thought of the many times the townsfolk had shouted at Max and chased him away from their trash heaps. Why should they care if a hungry dog helped himself to what they no longer wanted? Ricky and Jonesy had liked to chase Max and throw sticks at him, but she always tried to make them stop.

She knew what it was like to have someone yell at you and threaten to hurt you. She shivered just thinking about the evenings her pa would come home drunk or having lost at gambling. He'd holler at her ma like it was all her fault, shove her, and sometimes even slap or hit her. He hadn't been much of a father and never seemed to like her. Many times, he said he wished she'd been a boy.

Tears stung Jack's eyes again, and she swiped her sleeve over them. Max whined as if sensing her frustration and licked her cheek. "Oh Max, why can't Luke marry my ma and be my pa?"

Luke crossed the dusty street, waving to Simon O'Malley as he drove by with a load of hay in his wagon. The man kept Dan Howard, the livery owner, well-stocked in hay and feed. Luke could see Jack sitting on the floor, patting Max. As he neared, her words about wanting him for a father nearly made him stumble. He righted himself, looked around to see if anyone had noticed, and then stood outside his door. Luke's heart ached for the child, but he wasn't the answer to her prayers.

Jack didn't say anything else, but she suddenly jumped up. "Gotta go, boy."

She ran out the door and straight into Luke. He grabbed her shoulders to steady her, and she gasped and peered up. Her wariness changed to delight, warming his insides.

"Howdy, half bit. I just heard your ma holler for you."

She frowned and plodded back toward home.

What was wrong with her? If he wasn't mistaken, her lashes had looked damp from tears—and Jack never cried. Halfway home, she turned while walking backward and waved. "See you later."

His gaze followed her to the end of the street to make sure no one bothered her. She was a cute kid and reminded him of himself when he was young. Ornery, feisty. If only she were his child.

He scowled. Better not to think such thoughts. Spinning around, he marched back to his office, scanning the town and thinking about the wanted posters he'd looked through earlier. If he could capture one or two of those outlaws, he would get enough reward money so that he could order lumber for a house. He already had a lot picked out with a view of the river and could imagine a white clapboard house sitting on it.

He stopped and leaned against a hitching post. If he *were* to marry, he'd need a bigger house. The one the town provided was fine for him alone, but a wife would want to cook, and that Sunday house had no stove. He supposed he could build an outdoor kitchen. Lots of homes in Texas had them, usually on ranches and farms rather than in-town houses. That would be much easier, and maybe it would solve his problem for now.

The bigger problem he had was envisioning a woman other than Rachel in his home. Maybe because she cooked his meals now and did his laundry. He'd run into her a few times when she'd come over to clean or return his clothing. He shook his head. Somehow he needed to rid his mind of such images.

Forcing himself to focus on the brides, he stared across Bluebonnet Lane at the boardinghouse and tried to decide which woman would make the best wife. They were all pretty, but he wasn't attracted to any one of them in particular. He sighed and thumped the railing. That pie contest sure hadn't helped.

Who was the anonymous entry from? He'd racked his mind, trying to figure out who she was, but had no luck. He turned around and moseyed into Foster's Mercantile, nodding at Trudy Foster. "Everything all right in here?"

"Yes sir, Marshal. We're fine and dandy." Trudy smiled and continued sorting skeins of colorful thread.

Luke looked around for a few minutes, thinking about all the things he'd need to buy if he did get a house of his own. Finally, he exited the store. As he turned right, a woman's shapely body appeared in the doorway of his office. Miss Blackstone.

She looked down the street right at him and waved. "Morning, Marshal Davis. How are you this fine day?"

He'd been fine—until he saw her. Now his neck felt as tight as if he were dressed up in his church clothes. He pushed away from the hitching post and shoved his hands into his pocket as he walked toward her. Just what had she been doing in his office? And how had she gotten in there without him seeing her?

She looked pretty in her pine-colored calico, which made her brown eyes look almost hazel. Her hair was always a bit disheveled and tended to just be tied behind her with a ribbon, as if doing anything more to it was a chore. Something wild sparked in her eyes on occasion, making him wonder about her past.

He walked up to her and stopped since she blocked his doorway. "What can I do for you today?"

"I noticed that you never eat at the boardinghouse and thought you might be hungry." She stepped back into the office and motioned to something on his desk. She removed a towel from a plate, and the scent of bacon and eggs filled the room. His mouth watered.

"You made this?" he asked, walking over to look at the plate. His stomach rumbled.

She shifted her feet and looked around his office. "Well, uh. . . nope, but Mrs. Hamilton let me bring it to ya. I couldn't very well cook up somethin' else when she had all this left."

No, he didn't figure she could—and somehow didn't think she would have even if Rachel had allowed her use of the kitchen. Still, he sat down and tucked into the food since he hadn't had time to get over to the boardinghouse for breakfast this morning.

Miss Blackstone looked at a map on his wall. Luke noticed her hands trembling. Was she nervous being alone with him?

"Do you catch many outlaws in this little town?"

He shook his head. "No, but I run a tight command here and don't let things get out of control."

"Well, that makes me feel safer." She stared at him with her head cocked to one side until he looked away.

The hairs on the back of his neck lifted, and he couldn't for the life of him figure out why. A horse whinnied outside, and Miss Blackstone turned to look out the door. Luke studied her profile. Yeah, she was pretty, but something about her set him on edge.

He leaned back in his chair, holding his lukewarm coffee. Miss Blackstone pivoted back toward him and smiled. She looked softer, more approachable when she was happy. Maybe he was overreacting. Or just touchy, since she could be his wife one day soon. A shiver charged down his back.

He turned back to his food and noticed one of the two desk drawers was off kilter. He ignored it for the moment but knew it hadn't been like that when he'd left his office earlier. He took several more bites of food, hoping she hadn't noticed him looking at the drawer.

Had Miss Blackstone gone through his desk?

And if she had, what had she been looking for?

Carly resisted tapping her foot while the marshal ate. Just being in the jail office around a lawman made her itch to leave. Did she look more casual than she felt? Or could he tell she was nervous?

She cast a glance at the two cells in the shadows at the back of the room, and her throat threatened to close up and choke off her breath. One door was open, as if daring her to enter. If the law ever caught up with her, she would be locked up in such a place. A cold shiver snaked down her spine.

She forced her gaze back to the marshal. There hadn't been any information about payroll shipments in his desk. Tyson had said that town marshals always had that kind of information, and without it, she was stuck in this dinky town. Maybe she needed to come up with a better plan. Besides, how could she pull a payroll heist alone?

Trying to sway the marshal in her direction by flirting and taking him breakfast had probably been a dumb idea, but she had to do something to make herself stand out from the others. The marshal's fork scraped against his plate. He ate the last of the eggs and took another sip of his coffee.

"Could I freshen that up for you?"

He shook his head. "No thanks. I'm about done." He shoved the last third of a biscuit into his mouth.

The marshal was a fine-looking man with his lean, muscular body, handsome face, and dark hair and eyes. She had hoped he might like her nut pie better than the others, but that had hardly been the case. She had switched the salt and sugar before the other brides mixed up their pies, but she hadn't counted on burning hers.

Her gaze swerved toward the cell again, but she yanked it back. A stack of wanted posters on the side of the desk caught her eye. "Mind if I have a look at those?"

The marshal shrugged. "Suit yourself." He leaned back in his chair, holding his coffee cup and watching her.

She picked up the thick stack of posters and sat in the chair across from the marshal's desk. Slowly, she thumbed through each one. A hand-drawn picture of each outlaw looked her in the face. She didn't know most of the rough-looking men but did see two that she recognized—Wild Willy Watson and Hank Yarborough. Both men had run with her brother for a few months.

Pressing the posters to her chest, she stared at one lying in her lap and saw her brother's face. Her heart took off like an outlaw being chased by a posse.

The marshal's cup thunked as he set it down. He stared at her, brows lifted. "See someone you recognize?"

Carly forced a laugh. "Only someone who looks like someone I know."

Marshal Davis's eyes glanced toward the papers, and Carly quickly dropped the stack of posters back on top of her brother's likeness. She stood, and the whole pile slipped from her hands. "Oh goodness."

She squatted down, snatching up poster after poster, all the while her heart thudding as if she might be arrested. The marshal had noticed her reaction to Ty's poster. While she resembled her brother in some ways, she didn't look enough like him for the marshal to put two and two together. Too bad she hadn't had time to read the writing below Ty's likeness. Did it mention anything about him having a sister? If only she could get rid of Tyson's poster somehow.

The marshal stood and came toward her. "Let me get those for you, ma'am."

She forced herself up on wilting legs and handed him the stack. "If you're finished, I'll just take the plate back to the boardinghouse."

"Thank you kindly for bringing my breakfast." He nodded.

Carly picked up the plate, but the fork clattered to the floor. The marshal bent easily and handed it to her. She forced a grin and was half a block away before she could suck in a breath. Her gaze roamed over the town as she forced herself to relax. There was nothing to connect her with Tyson, but the marshal was a smart man. Could he tell she was lying? Whatever possessed her to do such a foolish thing as to visit him?

She continued on toward Hamilton House. Had it been a mistake to assume Ellie Blackstone's identity? Now that she was in Lookout and had seen the one-horse town, she doubted many payroll shipments passed through here. Yep, she needed another plan.

Maybe things would have been better if she'd never crossed paths with Ellie Blackstone.

Luke stood at his door and watched Miss Blackstone scurry away like a rat caught in a feed bag. She was hiding something. And if he wasn't mistaken, she was lying, too. But about what?

He sat down at his desk and slowly studied each poster. He was certain she'd recognized someone, but there were nearly twenty likenesses of outlaws, and he hadn't gotten a good look at the one she'd stumbled over. None of the wanted men were named Blackstone, but a name was a simple thing to change.

The hairs on the back of his neck stood on end. Did Miss Blackstone have other business in town besides landing a husband?

CHAPTER 24

Rachel stood in the backyard with her hands on her hips, staring down at her precocious daughter. The sun sprinkled through the trees, dappling Jacqueline's upturned face, casting shadows on the smattering of freckles on her nose. "I'm sorry, sweetie, but I've told you before, I'm not entering the bride contest this time around."

Jacqueline clutched Rachel's arm. "But Ma, you've gotta. You can't let Luke marry one of them brides."

Rachel closed her eyes for a moment, steeling herself against her daughter's pleas. Jacqueline was too young to understand all that had happened between her and Luke. "No. I can't enter."

Tears filled Jacqueline's blue eyes, piercing Rachel's heart. Her tough daughter rarely cried, and seeing her do so now made Rachel waver. Should she compete in the contest's next round? Even if she happened to win, there was still the issue of Luke's unwillingness to forgive her. She straightened her back and her resolve. "I can't."

"You mean you won't." Jacqueline stomped her feet. "You're ruining everything."

Rachel sighed and took her daughter's hand, pulling her over to sit in the double rocker that rested under a tall pine. She hugged the stiff girl. "Just because I enter the contest doesn't mean Luke would pick me anyway. He doesn't know my pie was the anonymous entry, and he's sure not going to agree to marry the winner if he doesn't know who she is. Besides, there are things you don't know about Luke and me."

Jacqueline rubbed her sleeve over her eyes. "What kind of things?"

Nibbling the inside of her lower lip, Rachel considered how much to tell her. "I was engaged to Luke before I married your pa."

The blue of Jacqueline's eyes intensified. "You nearly married Luke? What happened? Why didn'tcha?"

Rachel pressed her lips together. What a can of worms she'd just opened. It would have been best to keep quiet. A blue jay screeched overhead as if agreeing and letting her know she was intruding in its territory. She stroked her daughter's head. "It was a very long time ago, and I don't want to talk about it. I just thought if you knew about the engagement you'd understand why I can't enter the contest."

"No! I don't." Jacqueline shot to her feet. "If you were engaged once, why couldn't you be again?"

Smoothing out her dress, Rachel prayed for the right response. "Because it ended badly. I married your father, and Luke left town and joined the cavalry."

"So? He's back now, and you're not married anymore."

She made it sound so simple. But Rachel couldn't think of a way to explain without mentioning Luke's inability to forgive her, and she wouldn't make Luke look bad in her daughter's eyes. "That's all in the past. I'm not entering the contest, and that's final."

Jacqueline flung out her arms. "Why do you always have to ruin things? I hate you." She spun and ran toward the river, her braids flying behind her.

Rachel clutched her upper arms, her heart aching. She knew Jacqueline didn't hate her, but the words still inflicted pain, as they were meant to. She stared up at the sky. "Lord, I know You control all things, but I don't understand why You had to bring Luke back to town. Maybe things wouldn't hurt so bad if he'd forgive me, but to see him each day and to always have this past between us is so difficult. Is it my punishment to watch Luke marry one of the mail-order brides? Is that what You require from me as penance for what I did?"

She dropped her head. God didn't work that way. She knew that. But she wanted Luke for a husband as badly as Jacqueline wanted him for her pa. The truth was she still loved him. She sat for a while, praying and seeking God, but no answers came. Blinking the tears from her eyes, she saw the back door open. Miss Blackstone looked out and saw her then started forward. Rachel straightened her back. For some reason, God had sent the brides to live with her for a time. Maybe it was so she could speak His Word into their lives. *God, help me. Give me the fortitude to do what You've set before me, and please watch over Jacqueline. Comfort her and keep her safe while she's away from me.*

"Could I...uh...talk with you for a minute?" Miss Blackstone looked hesitant to interrupt her.

"Certainly." Rachel sniffed and patted the chair beside her, hoping her face wasn't red and splotchy from crying.

Miss Blackstone sat and glanced sideways. "You all right?"

Rachel forced out a little laugh. "Yes, I just had a confrontation with my daughter."

"Oh. Well, I was...uh...wonderin' if you could show me how to stitch a shirt for the next bride contest." She wrung her hands. "I mean, I can sew—some. I ain't never made a shirt before."

Part of Rachel wanted to shout no. To jump up and run away like Jacqueline. She already housed and fed the mail-order brides, but they wanted her to help them win Luke's heart. She simply couldn't do that. "Of course I'll help you."

Miss Blackstone smiled, looking younger than she normally did. "Thanks. That's right nice of ya."

Rachel fingered the long hair hanging down the young woman's back. "I don't want to offend you, but if you'd like, I could show you some ways to style your hair—so you'd look extra nice for Saturday's contest, I mean."

Surprise flashed in Miss Blackstone's eyes. "Thank you, kindly. I'd like that." She looked down and seemed to be studying the ground. "My ma died when I was young. I lived with my brother for a while, but he didn't have time or patience for things like fixin' hair."

"I'm sorry about your mother. I lost mine, too. If not for the Lord, I don't know how I would have made it without her."

Miss Blackstone gave her an odd look.

Rachel jumped up. "I have about a half hour before I need to start supper. Would you care to get started on the shirt now?"

Miss Blackstone nodded and followed Rachel through the kitchen and into her bedroom. As she reached for the dresser knobs, Rachel's hands shook. She hadn't looked at James's things since she put them away, shortly after his death. She pulled out the bottom drawer and scanned the garments. Several shirts lay next to the stack of store-bought silk handkerchiefs that James had preferred to her homemade ones. She really should get rid of all these things. Why had she kept them so long?

"These were my husband's." She laid the four shirts on the bed and rifled through them, finding the one she wanted. "This is a simple design. We'll need to choose some fabric. I. . .uh. . .have a small supply."

Miss Blackstone shook her head. "The marshal's supposed to give us money to buy cloth and supplies, so I won't need yours."

The young woman fingered the edge of the top shirt, a tan one. "Mine won't look near as nice as yours."

Rachel forced a smile as she gathered up the shirts. "But mine won't be in the contest."

Jack's heart pounded as she shut her bedroom door. Her mother was across the hall, busy with supper preparations, but if she noticed the closed door, she'd surely come to investigate. Jack had told herself that what she was doing wasn't wrong. In a way, her father's belongings were partially hers, weren't they?

Standing in front of the chest of drawers, she forced her hands to stop shaking. It only worked for a second before the trembling started again. She knelt down, slid open the bottom drawer, and scowled. Even after three years, she could still smell her pa's scent on his clothing, and it was all she could do not to retch in the drawer.

She quickly thumbed through the shirts that lay with his socks and the fancy hankies he'd liked. A soft blue one stood out among the others, and she picked it up and examined its stitching. Perfect, just like all her ma's sewing. If Jack put her mind to it, she could probably sew as well one day, but the thought of sitting in one spot long enough to make something this nice made her shiver. How did women do it? Sewing hours and hours at a time? They even seemed to have fun at quilting bees, but of course, they chatted with the other women and had food to eat.

Jack shoved the drawer shut and held the shirt in her hand. Luke liked blue. She knew that because he wore that color a lot. But would it fit him? She tried to remember how big her father was, but Luke seemed so much larger. Well, there was nothing she could do about that.

She heard a sound just outside the door and jumped. Grabbing her skirts up, she dove between the bed and the wall. The handle jiggled, and the door opened. Jack stuffed the shirt under the bed and tried to calm her shaking.

"Sweetie?" Footsteps followed her mother's voice into the room. "Hmm. . ."

Jack held her breath. The room was small, and if her ma

walked much farther, she was sure to see her hiding—and what excuse could Jack give for being on the floor? That she was asleep and fell off the bed?

Footsteps carried her mother away, and Jack waited a few minutes for her heart to stop banging before she peered over the bed. She nearly gasped out loud when she saw the door was left open.

"Jacqueline?" Her mother called, sounding as if she were yelling out the back door.

Ducking down again, Jack considered how she might get the shirt onto the table with the other brides' entries. Surely Luke would like her mother's the best. Nobody could sew like her ma. Jack looked down at her dress, and in spite of hating it, she thought of all the hours her mother had put into sewing it for her. She always had nice clothes made from pretty fabric and had never worn a scratchy flour-sack dress like several of her schoolmates.

She peered over the bed again, keeping watch, and every few minutes, she'd see her ma cross from the kitchen into the dining room, carrying bowls and trays of food. She ought to be helping instead of hiding like some thief. And it wasn't stealing to take something that belonged to your family, especially if you were going to put it back after the contest, was it?

Her legs had finally quit shaking, and she drew up her knees to stand. If she got up just as her ma went into the dining room, she'd have time to hurry out of the bedroom and into the kitchen. She started to stand when she heard a shuffling sound and dropped back down. Her heart set off like a wild mustang again.

It sounded as if someone else slid into the room, and she held her breath. Sure enough, she could hear rough breathing. The person's shoes tapped out a quiet repetition and then stopped. A drawer squeaked open. Someone muttered a curse, and then the drawer squealed shut again. The bottom drawer was the only one that made a noise like that. Who could be in it, and what was it the person wanted?

She longed to peek but was too scared to move. Her breath turned ragged, almost as if she'd run a long race. After a few minutes of not hearing anybody nearby, she peeked over the bed's quilt and saw her ma zip into the dining room. Jack jumped to her feet and hurried into the kitchen.

Her ma rushed back in the room. "Oh, there you are. Supper's finished, and I need your help. I was looking for you."

Jack ducked her head so her mother wouldn't see her guilt and grabbed the bowl of biscuits. She hurried into the dining room and set them on the table. None of the brides were there yet, and she wanted to run upstairs and look around to see if one of them had taken something from the dresser. Her mother hadn't, because she never opened that particular drawer. Jack tiptoed past the kitchen door and dashed into her bedroom. She needed another look, and she didn't like the thought worming its way into her head. She yanked the drawer open and knew right away that the tan shirt was gone. Someone staying in their home was a thief.

"Finish drying the breakfast dishes and you can go outside for a little bit." Rachel looked around her kitchen, glad that for the moment it was clean again. All too soon she'd have to start dinner.

Jacqueline wiped a dish with a towel and set it on top of the pile of clean dishes. "I'm so glad I don't hav'ta go to school for a while."

Rachel enjoyed her daughter being home more, but at times she could be trying. "I'm going out on the porch to mend the red checkered tablecloth. Make sure you come back in time to help with dinner."

Her daughter nodded, and Rachel left the kitchen, ready to sit down for a while. As she reached the parlor, she heard raised voices.

"I'm going over there right now and take his measurements. How are we supposed to make a shirt for him when we don't even know what they are?" Miss Bennett asked.

" 'Tisn't proper for an unmarried woman to measure a man." Miss O'Neil sat in one of the parlor chairs, hands clenched together.

Rachel stood in the doorway, suddenly realizing their dilemma. The women had less than a week left to fashion a shirt for the marshal, yet they didn't have his measurements. She dreaded the thought forming in her mind, but there was no other option. "I'll go take the marshal's measurements. And you're welcome to use the dining table to lay out your fabric, as long as it can be cleared by dinnertime."

Miss O'Neil smiled. "Aye, a grand idea to be certain."

Miss Bennett scowled. "I was just heading over to the jail to do that very thing."

Rachel shook her head, knowing the young woman would use the time alone to flirt with Luke. "I've been married before. I don't think it's appropriate for you to tend to such a task."

Miss Bennett harrumphed, grabbed the pile of dark blue fabric she'd purchased, and marched into the dining room.

Rachel returned to her bedroom, found her measuring tape, some paper, and a pencil, and headed to the jail. The breakfast she'd recently eaten churned in her stomach. She thought of being so near to Luke and yet so far. Maybe he wouldn't even be there, but even as the idea entered her mind, she saw him leaning against the doorjamb, watching the town as he frequently did.

The streets were quiet for a Monday morning. The shops were open, but many folks did their business on Saturday. She waved at Aggie, who walked down the other side of the street and entered the bank.

As Rachel neared the jail, her hands started trembling and her legs felt as solid as melted butter. Luke saw her coming and stood looking out from under his hat like a cougar eyeing its prey. He straightened as she drew near. In the years that he'd been gone, he'd changed from a lithe youth to a tall, broad-shouldered man. Rachel licked her lips, but her mouth felt as dry as flour.

Luke nodded at her. "Come to fetch my breakfast plate?"

"No, I've come to take your measurements so my boarders can start sewing your shirts."

He shook his head. "Don't know what I'll do with so many."

"Wear them, I guess. Although the woman you marry may not care for you to be donning the ones the other ladies made."

Luke quirked a brow. Rachel wanted nothing more than to tuck tail and run back home, but she forced herself to stand still. "Could we go inside? Or would you prefer staying out here?"

Luke stepped back and allowed her to enter in front of him. Rachel hesitated then walked into the jail with him following. She set her basket on the table, pulled out her supplies, and motioned for Luke to turn around.

"Hold out your right arm." Luke did as told, and she held the measuring tape against his shoulder, stretching it out to his wrist. The heat of his body burned her fingertips, and she longed to caress his arm. She forced her hand away and wrote down the length, then determined the width of his shoulders and the span from his collar to his hips. She ducked under his arm and stood in front of him. How many times in the past had she been this close to him? Had the right to touch his face or to hug him without giving it a second thought? Now her hand quivered, and she tried to finish her task without touching him again. She swallowed hard and dared to look up. Luke's brown eyes watched her, almost with—dare she hope?—longing.

"I. . .uh. . .need your help for this last measurement."

He nodded, and she handed him one end of the measurer. "Hold that against you chest, please."

She slipped behind him, wrapped the length around his chest, and pulled it tight, stopping again in front of him. Her breath caught in her throat. Luke smelled of leather and fresh soap and a scent all his own. If she didn't finish this task soon, she might swoon at his feet.

How bittersweet. If things had been different, she might well be preparing to sew a shirt for Luke herself, as his wife. Through stinging eyes, she noted the number and tugged on the tape, but when it didn't fall free, she looked up. Her gaze collided with Luke's.

He stared at her with an intensity she hadn't seen in years. His breath tickled her forehead.

"Rachel..."

For a fraction of a second, she thought he might kiss her. His gaze roved her face like a starving man eyeing a Sunday potluck picnic. Suddenly, he blinked, his expression hardened, and he stepped back.

Rachel caught her measuring tape as it fell free and snatched up her notes. "Um...thank you. I'm sure the brides will find this most helpful."

She spun around and hurried out the door.

"Rach—"

The jangling of a wagon passing on the road drowned out whatever Luke had said. Rachel's heart plummeted so low she thought certain she would trip on it. Those brides had no idea how much this little deed had cost her.

Carly handed the mayor her entry. The tan shirt with dark brown stitching hadn't been her first choice, but the blue one was gone from the drawer.

"Why, that's lovely stitchery, Miss Blackstone. I wouldn't be surprised if the marshal picks your shirt as the winner."

She straightened tall at the mayor's compliment, pretending his words pleasured her, but in truth, they meant little. She hadn't done the sewing, had instead stolen the shirt that had belonged to James Hamilton from Rachel's bottom dresser drawer—and filching from the kind woman had left a bad taste in her mouth. But she'd never be able to sew a shirt as nice as the ones Rachel Hamilton had made.

If only Mrs. Hamilton hadn't been so nice to her, then she wouldn't be feeling this regret. But a person did what she had to do. She needed Luke to pick her. Since her plan to find the payroll information hadn't worked, she needed some way to survive, and marryin' seemed better than stealing from decent folk. Besides, the marshal was a comely man, and being his wife wouldn't be so bad.

She stepped outside the jail and surveyed the table that had once again been set up for the contest. Four new signs indicated where the entries would be laid. She curled her lip and surveyed the growing crowd. Would there be a fourth entry today? Who could be the mystery bride?

Carly walked to the railing and stared down Main Street. She hadn't expected as large a group this Saturday since there was no food to be judged, but there looked to be about the same number of folks. Most likely, everyone was just curious as to who the marshal would pick for his bride.

A shuffling sounded behind her, and she spun around. Her hand reached for her gun, but she lowered it, remembering she was unarmed—that she was dressed as a lady and not an outlaw. She blinked and stared at the table. Somehow while her back was turned, somebody had placed a blue shirt on the table behind the ANONYMOUS BRIDE sign.

Carly stepped closer to inspect her competition. She bent down and looked more closely at the anonymous entry. It looked just like the cornflower blue one Rachel Hamilton had shown her that day she'd asked her for help. But it couldn't be. Mrs. Hamilton hadn't even attended the first competition. Carly spun around and studied the crowd. She wasn't here today, either. Pivoting, Carly looked at the blue shirt again. That one had to be Rachel's. It had been missing when she'd sneaked in to steal it.

She thought about the times she'd seen Mrs. Hamilton and the marshal together, talking or arguing—watching each other. Now all those covert looks Rachel had sent the marshal's way made sense. She was in love with him, and he had no idea that was the case.

That meant Rachel Hamilton was the anonymous bride—and she was out to win this contest.

Chapter 25

Jack's heart still pounded as she thought about how she'd walked right behind Miss Blackstone and dropped her ma's shirt on the table. She'd spun into the marshal's office, past the mayor and his wife, and slipped into the cell where Max was hiding under the cot. Her heart pounded like a Comanche's war drum, and she sat on her hands to keep them from shaking.

Why was she so nervous? She hadn't done anything wrong, unless it was taking one of her pa's old shirts that nobody ever used. Just because her ma didn't want to enter the contest didn't mean Jack couldn't enter for her.

Max crept out of his hiding place and sat up, dropping his head on her leg. She scratched him behind the ear, enjoying how he lifted his head and looked as if he were smiling. She was half surprised the dog wasn't with Luke. He must be out on rounds, because she hadn't seen him since dropping off Max's food this morning. Either that or he was hiding from the brides. That thought brought a grin to her face.

Miss Bennett and Miss O'Neil both came in and handed their entries to the mayor, but she couldn't see them from so far away.

"Are you going to allow that mystery bride to enter again?" Miss Bennett lifted her chin. "It's highly irregular."

"I don't guess it matters since she hasn't submitted an entry." Mayor Burke scratched his jaw with his thumb and forefinger. He glanced at his watch. "And the time limit to do so just expired."

"Saints preserve us." Miss O'Neil held her handbag below her chin as if she were praying.

"What's the matter?" asked Mrs. Burke.

"There's already an entry on the table."

The mayor and his wife exchanged a look and hurried outside, followed by the two brides. Jack jumped up and ran to the door.

"Oh, my, that's very fine work." Mrs. Burke fingered the collar of the medium blue shirt then slid her hand down the buttons, admiring it.

Jack's hopes shot upward like a firecracker.

Mayor Burke cleared his voice. "Did anyone notice who submitted this entry?"

Jack moved past him so she could see, but relief washed through her when the townsfolk stared back with blank looks.

"Surely, you ain't gonna allow that fourth shirt in the contest? Ain't it supposed to be between us three?" Miss Blackstone wagged her finger between her and the other brides.

"We allowed it last time, so I don't see how we can exclude it now." Mayor Burke handed the shirts the brides had made to his wife. "Please distribute those, and we'll commence this competition."

His wife accepted the entries and laid each one behind a numbered bride sign. "How can we start without the marshal?"

"He's probably hidin' out somewhere so's he don't hafta get hitched to one of them brides." The comment from a bearded man standing in the street brought hoots of laughter from the crowd.

Jack smiled, but her eyes were drawn to the second shirt. She slipped around the mayor's wife to get a closer look and nearly gasped out loud. On the table lay a tan shirt with brown stitching—the very shirt her ma had made for her pa. She glared at the brides.

One of them was a thief and a cheat.

Luke rode back into town after spending several hours in prayer down at the river. For the past few days, he'd thought about the brides, stewing over them and praying about which one to marry, but so far, God wasn't answering.

Even before he reached Lookout, he encountered dozens of buggies, wagons, and saddled horses lining the outskirts of town. Some folks had set up tents and made campfire circles, probably planning on overnighting and attending church tomorrow.

He wove his way through the mess, half dreading the shirt contest. No matter what, several of the brides would end up disappointed. He shook his head and rode into town.

People lined the streets like a cattle drive, in spite of the warm day. The sky had still been dark when he'd first ridden out this morning, but now the sun glimmered bright above the horizon with the promise of a perfect day—a complete contrast to the nervousness sending his belly in a tizzy and causing pain between his eyes.

He rubbed his fingertips in small circles on his forehead. Last week's measuring session had nearly driven him loco, with Rachel moving around him, leaving her scent, touching him like a wisp of wind. Was it possible that he still had feelings for her?

He reined Alamo to a stop. What was he going to do?

If only he hadn't given his word to marry.

His prayers seemed to have fallen on deaf ears, even though he knew that wasn't true. He'd pleaded with God to show him which bride to choose, yet here he rode back toward town, with no leading one way or the other and thoughts of Rachel filling his mind. All he knew to do was to pray more and wait until God revealed His will to him.

If only the mayor wasn't pressing him for a decision. And that newspaper lady. He halfway wondered if she wasn't the anonymous bride. Maybe she added the mystery entry just to beef up interest in the contest and to help sell her papers. Maybe there wouldn't be a fourth entry today.

"Hey, there's the marshal," a man from the crowd hollered.

All eyes turned toward Luke, and for the briefest of moments, the town was silent except for a baby's wail. Suddenly, the crowd erupted in cheers. Alamo jerked up his head at the roar and pranced beneath Luke. There was no getting out of this contest, so he'd best just get it over with.

He looped Alamo's reins around the hitching post outside the livery where three other horses had been tied and made his way toward his office.

"Who ya gonna pick?"

"I like that Irish gal. Don't choose her."

"You getting married today?"

The questions fired from all sides. Luke shook his head and pushed his way toward the mayor.

Jack stood behind the man and raced forward when she saw him. "Luke, I gotta tell you somethin'."

Mayor Burke shoved his way in front of her. "Not now, kid. We've got to get this judging started."

"But—" Jack reached for Luke as the mayor pushed her back.

Luke scowled, not liking how the mayor was treating the girl, but the man was right. Whatever she wanted to say could wait.

The boardinghouse brides huddled together at the far end of the table, each one looking as if she'd worn her Sunday best. Even Miss Blackstone's hair had been pulled up and pinned on top of her head. Just then, the woman scowled and reached up to scratch her head with her index finger. Luke smiled. For some reason, she didn't seem comfortable all gussied up.

Miss Bennett batted her lashes at Luke and smiled at him with her head cocked sideways. Miss O'Neil looked everywhere but at him. He bet if he were to pick her she'd faint dead away.

Garrett walked out of Luke's office with Mark on his heels. "'Bout time you got here."

"Yeah," Mark said, "we were just about to round up a posse to go hunt you down."

"Well, I'm here."

The mayor nodded and turned toward the crowd, beefy hands lifted. "All right, now that Marshal Davis is here, we'll get things started. I imagine Luke will want to try on each shirt before deciding on the winner." Mayor Burke gave Luke a shrewd glance that set his nerve endings tingling, then faced the crowd again. "And if he's ready to make an announcement, could be we'll have a wedding today."

Cheers erupted. Luke frowned and bit back a growl. He was getting tired of being manipulated.

"Gather 'round the table, Luke. Look at all these fine shirts." The mayor shook his head. "Don't know how you're going to pick just one as winner."

Luke gazed at the table, his heart dipping into his boots. There were four entries.

People crowded the tables, pushing and shoving. "I cain't see," an old cowboy yelled.

The brides were crowded from behind and moved toward Luke as if part of the herd.

"Hold on, hold on!" Mayor Burke held up his hands. "Y'all just back up right now 'fore I have the marshal get his rifle."

Mumbles and murmurs surrounded them, but the swarm slowly backed up.

"Now, the marshal will stand here and try on each shirt." The mayor waved him toward the railing.

Luke shook his head. "I'm not shedding my shirt in front of all these folks."

"Aw, don't be shy, cuz." Garrett nudged Luke in the back.

Enough was enough. Luke spun around and glared down at Garrett. After a few seconds, Garrett held up his hands. "Sorry."

"Maybe you should try the shirts on in the jail?" Mark offered loudly, over the buzz of conversation.

Luke nodded, snatched up the four shirts, and strode into his office. The crowd voiced their objections while the mayor tried to pacify them as if it was his idea to use the jail. "Now it isn't proper for a man to undress in front of all you pretty ladies."

Jack squeezed in between Garrett and Mark. "I gotta tell you somethin'."

Luke tossed the shirts onto his desk. "Make it fast."

She nodded her head up and down. "One of them brides is a cheat. That brown shirt belonged to my pa. Ma's the one who sewed it."

Garrett and Mark stood behind her. Both sets of eyebrows shot up at Jack's declaration.

Luke frowned and tugged out the tan shirt. "This one?"

"Yeah."

"How can you be sure?" Garrett asked.

"It was in Ma's bottom dresser drawer a few days ago. I know it by that dark stitching."

"It's possible someone else just happened to sew a similar one." Mark rubbed the back of his neck.

Jack shook her head. "I know it's my ma's."

"What's going on in here?" Mayor Burke squeezed in the crowded office and looked around. "Get along, Luke. We've got a whole town of folks waiting."

Luke bent down and looked at Jack. "Keep this to yourself for now. I'll check into it though."

Jack stared at him with her big eyes and finally nodded.

"All right, half bit. Scoot outside with the rest of the ladies."

"I ain't no lady," she called over her shoulder as she left and closed the door.

"That's the honest truth. That kid is as wild as them come." Mayor Burke shook his head. "How did Rachel end up with such a hooligan child?"

Luke narrowed his eyes, halfway ready to knock the mayor on his backside. He oughten to talk about Jack like that. She was just a little girl who needed a firm hand.

"So, which shirt do you like best?" Garrett laid each one out across the top of Luke's desk.

"Pick a shirt; pick a wife." Mark chuckled.

"This is just plain loco. How am I supposed to pick a wife by choosing the best shirt?" He shook his head. "You and your crazy schemes. I don't know how I got caught up in this one."

Garrett ignored him and sorted through the entries. "Which one you want to try on first?" He held up the blue shirt and fingered the collar. "This one's nice."

Luke shrugged and crossed his arms, wishing he was anywhere else.

"You know you've gotta do it, so get going." Garrett shoved the shirt toward Luke. "Put it on."

He heaved another sigh but shucked his shirt and pulled on the cornflower blue one. It fit like a gun sliding into a perfectly made holster. He adjusted the shoulders and buttoned it up. Holding out his arm, he eyed the sleeve. "Fits well enough, but the sleeves could be a tad longer. I do like this color."

Garrett held up the dark blue shirt and waggled his brow.

Luke removed the medium blue shirt and tried on the indigo one. It, too, fit well, and the sleeves were longer, but the seams under his arms were too small and restricted his movement.

"This one's got a little stain on it. Maybe one of them brides poked her finger while stitching it—or maybe the kid was right." Garrett rubbed at the spot and unfolded the tan shirt. "I like how it has this brown stitching on it. That's different."

"That's the one Jack claimed was stolen." Luke looked it over, but the tan garment revealed no clues as to who had made it. He tried it on, trying to imagine Rachel's hand sewing it. But if she had, she'd been making it for James, not him. He shucked it off and tossed it on the desk. Garrett held up the final entry. Luke

248

resisted rolling his eyes. What sane man tried on four shirts in a single day?

He shoved his arm in the white shirt, but when he tried to get his second arm in, he couldn't. The shoulders were too narrow. A rip sounded, and one of the sleeves tore off.

"Oops." Garrett grinned. "Guess that's not the winner."

Luke tossed the ruined shirt on the pile and pulled his comfortable chambray back on.

"So, which one did you like best?" The mayor drew in closer and leaned over the desk.

"I don't know. The stitching on the tan and the cornflower blue was the nicest, I guess, but I like the dark blue color best."

"So the dark blue is the winner?" Garrett asked, picking it up again.

Luke studied it, then shook his head. "No, it's too tight in the underarms and reminds me too much of my cavalry uniform. I wore that color for ten years."

Garrett held up the tan and medium blue shirts and wiggled them in front of Luke.

"The cornflower blue's my favorite."

"Do I hear a but coming?" Garrett lifted his brows.

Delaying his response, Luke looked out the window. Dozens of people stared in at him. Finally, he turned back to his cousin. "What if that anonymous bride made that one?"

Garrett shrugged one shoulder. "You have a three-in-four chance of it not being hers.

"Yeah, but that still bothers me." Luke snagged his hat off the back of the chair and put it on. "Seems like I have a right to know whose competing, being as I'm supposed to marry the winner of the contest."

Garrett grinned. "Now that would take all the fun out of the competition."

Luke leaned forward and glared across the desk. "This isn't a game, Garrett. This is my future, my life we're talking about."

His cousin sobered. "I know. Sorry for making light of things." Garrett stood and set his hands on his hips. "Look, Luke. Mark and I didn't know all this craziness would happen when we ordered those brides. We were honestly just tryin' to help you."

Luke pinched the bridge of his nose with his thumb and forefinger. "I know, but what you did was really dumb. You took those gals away from their homes and families. Gave them hope that they could start over here and get married. Even if I choose one, that still leaves two without husbands."

"Leave them to me and Mark. We'll figure out something."

Luke shook his head. "I don't know what, unless you plan to marry them yourselves."

Garrett made a choking sound as if his neck were in a noose.

Luke grinned. "How do you like it when the tables are turned?"

"They aren't exactly turned, are they? I didn't promise to marry anyone." Garrett's mouth cocked sideways in a teasing grin.

"I sure wish I hadn't either." He shouldn't have yielded to the pressure everyone put on him. A man should marry the woman he loved. A woman who was his friend. Rachel immediately came to mind.

Maybe he had it all wrong. Men in the West married women they'd just met all the time. The only way to truly get over Rachel would be to marry someone else. So why did that sit so badly with him?

Mayor Burke reached out and grabbed the blue shirt. "Well, let's get back out there and see who made this shirt."

"Hold on a minute. I'm going to have to figure out who stole that tan shirt."

"That kid's probably just making up that story." The mayor tugged on his vest.

"Jack didn't have any idea?" Mark asked.

"No, but I don't mind telling you that I've had suspicions about one of the brides for a while now."

"Which one?" Mayor Burke's fuzzy brows lifted.

Luke shook his head. "I'm not ready to say just yet."

Garrett looked as if he was staring out the window in deep thought. He glanced back at Luke, a worried expression on his face. "Could Jack and Rachel be in any danger?"

Luke shook his head. "Don't think so, but I'll keep a closer watch on them."

Outside, the crowd started chanting for Luke. "Marshal! Marshal!"

Holding the winning shirt, the mayor headed for the door but suddenly turned back and collected the other shirts. "If I go walking out with just one, everybody will know that's the winner."

"Makes sense." Garrett nodded.

"After I announce the winner, I'll put the shirts back on the table. Maybe one of you can keep an eye on them and see if the person who brought the tan shirt will reclaim it."

"That's not likely if it was stolen." Luke pursed his lips.

Mark straightened. "Unless they feel the need to return it so Rachel doesn't know it was ever gone."

Luke grinned and slapped his cousin on the shoulder. "If I ever need a deputy, you've got the job."

Mark's response was lost as the mayor opened the door. The crowd roared with excitement. Luke followed his cousins outside and glanced around, hoping to see Rachel. It looked like everyone in the county had shown up but her.

The mayor lifted his hands, two shirts in each one. "Quiet down. Hush up, now. We have a winner, although I want to say the competition was stiff." He looked over his shoulder at the brides. "Nice job, ladies."

His announcement sent the crowd into another frenzy. After a few moments, the noise settled, and the mayor continued. He held up his left hand again—the hand that held the tan and white shirts. "These two are not the winners."

Luke watched the brides' expressions as the mayor tossed the shirts back onto the table. Miss O'Neil ducked her head and wrung her hands. Miss Bennett's eyes gleamed, and Miss Blackstone puckered up her lips and shoved her hands to her hips. He was certain he knew who'd taken the tan shirt.

With a blue shirt in each hand, the mayor waved them around. "One of these is the winner."

The crowd silenced as if they were awaiting a life-changing announcement—and well it could be, for one woman. Mayor Burke held up the dark blue shirt. Miss Bennett's hands flew to her chest, and she leaned forward.

"This one here," the mayor said, "is not the winner."

Miss Bennett blinked and fell back against the side of the jail, disappointment dulling her countenance. Something twisted in Luke's gut. The last shirt must be from the anonymous bride. Bile churned, and thoughts of all the unmarried women in the area, from Bertha Boyd to the Widow Denison with her five kids, raced across his mind.

"Here's our winner, folks." Holding the cornflower blue shirt by the corners, the mayor peered back over his shoulder again. "Which one of you ladies does this belong to?"

No one moved, just as Luke knew they wouldn't. The mayor scowled and turned to face the brides. "This doesn't belong to one of you gals?"

All three shook their heads.

"Well." The mayor faced the crowd again. "Looks like the anonymous bride is our winner again. If you're here, ma'am, would you please step forward?"

Other than the playful shouts of some children, total silence reigned. Heads turned left and right as each person seemed to be looking for the anonymous bride.

"She's not coming. Just like last time." Miss Bennett stepped forward. "If she can't bother to show up, seems like she ought to be disqualified."

Luke knew her plan. If the winning entry was thrown out, she would be named the winner. He wasn't sure how he felt about that. The blond wasn't hard on the eyes, but he didn't care for her tendency to boss others around. He preferred a woman who was quieter—and sweeter.

Mayor Burke surveyed the crowd. "What do y'all think? Should we toss out the winner?"

*Yea*s and *nay*s sounded all around, until the mayor held up his hand. "Let's take a vote. Who all thinks the anonymous bride should be disqualified?"

"Yea!" The loud cheer filled the air.

"All right now, who's opposed?"

An even louder roar rumbled down the street. Luke's heart sunk. He'd halfway hoped the anonymous bride would be eliminated. But that would mean he'd have to marry one of the boardinghouse brides. Somewhere, deep in his heart, he was holding out for someone better suited to him. He just couldn't let his brain—or his heart—wrap around who that was.

He stared out at the many faces in the crowd. So many he knew, and others he didn't. Could the anonymous bride be standing right there in the road but not have enough nerve to step up and announce herself?

"All right, the nays have it. Here's what we're gonna do," Mayor Burke said. "I'm giving the marshal two weeks to take each of the brides to dinner one night so he can get to know them better. If the anonymous bride doesn't reveal herself in a fortnight, she'll be banned from participating further."

People swarmed Luke once the mayor dismissed them. He fielded comments and questions and an interview from Jenny Evans. When the music started, the townsfolk drifted back to their friends and families.

Luke turned around, and his gut twisted. The tan shirt was no longer on the table with the other shirts.

Monday morning, Luke strode into the freight office with Max at his side. The whole town was buzzing over the mysterious bride, and he was sick of fending off questions from folks who wanted to know if he knew who she was. He needed some advice. He was feeling more and more that he couldn't marry one of the boardinghouse brides.

Garrett looked up from his messy desk. "Well, howdy there, cuz."

Luke nodded. "Where's Mark?"

"Gone to fetch some coffee. Want some?"

"I could use a cup. Been several hours since I had some at the boardinghouse."

Garrett leaned back in his chair. "So which of them brides are you gonna ask out first?"

Luke crossed the room and leaned against Mark's tidy desk. "I don't know. I've been trying to figure a way to get out of taking them at all."

"The mayor won't like that."

"Nope, I don't guess so. But I've been praying hard about what to do, and I haven't gotten leave from the Lord to marry any of those gals."

"I reckon He'll give you guidance if you keep praying. Maybe you outta go talk to the reverend. He might could offer you some good advice." Garrett leaned his chair back against the wall and put his feet on his desk. "Then again, you could walk right out the door and marry the first bride you see."

"You might be onto something there." Luke ran his hand over his bristly jaw. He hadn't even taken time to shave before he rode out.

"Right about what?"

"Talking to Reverend Taylor." Luke should have thought of that sooner. He was still a fairly new Christian and needed the wisdom of a man more schooled in God's way. As soon as he left here, he'd pay the parson a visit.

"And here I thought you meant that you were gonna marry

the first woman you saw when you left here. But then again, it just might be Bertha Boyd."

Luke grinned and shook his head. His cousin was ornery all right, but he sure could make him chuckle.

Luke left the freight office, made his rounds through town, and headed toward the parson's house. At the end of Main Street, a motion snagged his attention, and he stopped and leaned against a post. Rachel was sweeping her front porch, but the way her hips swayed, she could be dancing.

Suddenly what Garrett had said came to mind. *Why not marry the first woman you see?*

A lump lodged in his throat. Marrying Rachel didn't sound as distasteful as it had when he'd first returned home. Had he gotten used to seeing her? Being around her? His clothes often held her scent as if she'd held them against her chest while returning them to his home. Her tasty meals had filled his belly three times a day. But he'd once trusted her completely, and she'd stabbed him in the back in the worst way possible. How could he ever trust her again?

Pushing away from the post, he walked down the street. Rachel saw him and stopped sweeping. Her gaze looked worried, apprehensive, but why should she be uneasy around him? He touched the end of his hat and dipped his head at her. She acknowledged his greeting by nodding once.

He should have kept on walking, but something drew him to her like a moth to a lantern. Maybe she could never be his, but he could be polite. Sociable. "How are you today?"

"Fine, thank you." She studied the porch floor rather than looking at him. "I thought I'd get out here and do the sweeping before the day heated up."

"It's a lovely day." She'd once been his best friend, the one person he shared his hopes and dreams with, and now they were reduced to talking about the weather.

She glanced up at the sky, avoiding his gaze. "Yes, it's near perfect, although I wouldn't mind a summer thunderstorm to blow through and cool things down."

"It would probably just dump more moisture in the air and make us all sweat." Luke winced at his dumb remark. Goodness, couldn't he even talk normal with her?

"I suppose that's true." She glanced at her front door. "I'd better get back inside and start breakfast. I imagine you're getting hungry, and my guests will be up soon, wanting to eat."

"Don't hurry on my account."

Rachel's cheeks turned a soft rose color. "I'll see you in about an hour, I guess."

Luke nodded and watched her go inside. He hadn't noticed before, but she looked as if she'd lost weight recently. Her dress hung looser and looked a bit bunched up at her waist. Was caring for the brides too much for her? But owning a boardinghouse, she was surely used to having guests much of the time.

Concern for her nagged his steps as he headed toward the parson's place.

Rachel watched Luke walk away. She hated the awkwardness that existed between them, but with him close to choosing one of the brides to marry, she had to distance herself from him, had to protect her heart.

There was no sense mooning over what could never be, even if her heart was breaking. She'd prayed for Luke's forgiveness ever since he returned, but she couldn't force him to pardon and forget what she'd done to him.

Back in the kitchen, she washed her hands and tied on her apron. She wondered who he would choose, though she'd decided Miss Bennett would be the best choice, even if she was as prickly as a cactus at times. Rachel hugged her mixing bowl to her chest. The young woman was a farm girl, surely a good cook and seamstress, and would make any man a decent wife so long as she held her attitude in check. Miss Blackstone was too rough and seemed unsettled. Rachel couldn't help feeling as if that woman was hiding something. And Miss O'Neil wasn't much of a cook and didn't seem to have the stamina needed to survive the rugged lifestyle a Texan lived, although she sure kept her room tidy.

Truth be told, none of the brides were the perfect match for the marshal. But then, was there even such a thing as a perfect match between a man and a woman?

Standing at the counter, she stared at the rounded bread dough that was ready to go in the oven. She'd once thought that she and Luke were a match made in heaven. But she had to go and ruin it. Tears burned her eyes and made her throat ache. If only she could go back and do things over—but then she wouldn't have her daughter. *Give me strength, Lord, to do the right thing.*

She reached into her pocket and touched the letter from her aunt. Millie had written again, asking her and Jacqueline to come to Kansas City and live with her and help work in Millie's mercantile. The move might be good for Jacqueline. It would get her away from those ruffian boys, but she wouldn't like moving and would most likely throw a fit at leaving Luke and Max. But once Luke had a wife and children of his own, he would no longer be interested in her daughter.

Rachel's chin wobbled. She had to get hold of herself before either Jacqueline came to help or someone else noticed. With the oven properly heated, she placed the two loaves of bread in it and cracked the eggs for breakfast.

An hour and a half later, after she'd sent Jacqueline out to weed the garden, she donned her bonnet and headed to the mayor's office. She had a hard time imagining living anywhere other than Lookout, but she knew her days in the small town were numbered. Living here with Luke married to one of the brides was out of the question. She hoped that the income from the sale of the boardinghouse would be all the money she and Jacqueline needed for a long while with her aunt providing room and board.

Before entering the mayor's office, Rachel turned and looked at Hamilton House. She loved the soft green with white trim and the wraparound porches that looked so inviting with all those rocking chairs just waiting for people to sit in them. But Hamilton House would soon be part of her past.

Sucking in a steadying breath, she opened the door and went inside. If things went as planned, she and Jacqueline could be on the train to Kansas City in a week or two.

CHAPTER 26

Luke stared into his coffee cup as Mrs. Taylor finished up the breakfast dishes. "Thanks, ma'am, for that fine meal."

The preacher's wife looked over her shoulder and smiled. "You're very welcome. We're happy to have you anytime, but it's the least we could do after all the wood you helped Thomas chop and stack. Why, we shouldn't need any for a month, I would imagine."

Luke nodded. "My pleasure."

"I helped, too, Ma."

Mrs. Taylor smiled at her son. "I know, Sam. I saw you out there stacking wood. You did a fine job."

The boy puffed up his chest and glanced between his pa and older brother.

"Boys, you head on out to the barn and muck the stalls." The pastor turned to his daughter, a cute blond around six years old. "Emily, help your ma finish cleaning up, and watch the baby when she wakes up."

"Yes, Pa."

The boys carried their dishes to the cabinet beside the dry sink and rushed outside. Emily scraped the plates and stacked them beside the basin where her ma was washing. Luke watched the activities around him. What would it be like to have a home with a mess of children?

The pastor couldn't be more than five years or so older than him, but he was way ahead of Luke as far as starting a family. Pastor Taylor downed the last of his coffee and stood. "Shall we adjourn to my study?"

Luke followed the man out of the cozy kitchen, down a short hall, and into a nook across from the parlor. The small room painted white held a desk on one wall, a bookcase filled with reference books, and a small settee. In front of the desk was a chair. Pastor Taylor motioned for Luke to have a seat on the settee and grabbed the top of the chair and swung it around to face the couch. Then he closed the door to the room and opened both windows. A light breeze fluttered the blue curtains as the pastor took a seat.

With short brown hair and wire-rimmed glasses, he looked more like a bank teller than a minister of the gospel. He crossed his hands over his light blue chambray shirt and stared at Luke. For a moment he refrained from speaking, and Luke sat still, resisting the urge to wiggle like a schoolboy in trouble. Was the man praying?

Luke cleared his throat. His nerves had settled during the hour and a half that he'd chopped wood and eaten breakfast, but they were on the rise again. He jiggled his foot and stared out the window. Why had he felt such a need to speak with the pastor?

"So. . .something on your mind today?"

Luke nodded, relieved to be starting yet unsure where to begin. The pastor wasn't a native of the town and probably didn't know about Luke's previous relationship with Rachel.

"You nervous about picking a bride?"

"Uh. . .no, well yes. But that's not the main reason I needed to talk to you."

"All right. Just take your time. I'm in no hurry."

Luke ran his fingers through his hair. Sucking in a steadying breath, he stared at the preacher. "I. . .uh. . .guess you could say I'm having trouble forgiving someone for a past offense."

"Ah, I see. And have you prayed about it?"

Luke's hand clamped onto the arm of the settee. "More than you can imagine."

"Is it something that's happened recently or a while back?"

"A long time ago—more than a decade, actually."

The pastor's brows lifted. "That's a while to carry an offense. Must have been a big one."

Luke pursed his lips and stared out the window, remembering Rachel's words. She'd looked at him, the whites of her eyes and her nose red from tears, and that alone had nearly done him in. *I've married James Hamilton.*

A gunshot point blank couldn't have hurt any worse. He'd been working for a year to make enough money for a down payment on a little house and to support Rachel. She'd been the love of his life, the only girl he'd ever had eyes for. But she dumped him to marry the richest man in town.

"Luke," the pastor's soft voice drew him out of the past. "I know you're a Christian, but how long have you been one?"

He shook his head. "Not long. Less than a year."

"I can tell you that forgiving isn't an easy thing, even for a man who's been a believer for most of his life." He leaned forward, head down for a moment. "If you've read your Bible, you know that it says in Mark, 'But if ye do not forgive, neither will your Father which is in heaven forgive your trespasses.'"

Luke faced the pastor. "I know that, but it doesn't tell me *how* to forgive. Just that I need to."

"I can tell by your expression how you've struggled with this. Forgiveness is a choice, Luke. We must choose to forgive and turn loose of our hurts. Nobody can do that for us."

"But how do you do that?" Luke leaned forward, his elbows on his knees.

"You have to make a conscious effort to do it. Say 'I choose to forgive you,' and then let go of the hurt. Give it to the Lord to carry."

Luke looked down at the pastor's boots. "I don't know if I can do that. I've carried this hurt for so long."

"And look what's it's done to you."

He glanced up. "What's that?"

"It has you all torn up inside. Jesus died to set us free from our sin. He wants us to live a victorious life, not one weighed down by sin and an unforgiving spirit. If you believe Christ died for you and have given your heart to Him, He'll help you with your struggles. But that doesn't mean He doesn't expect us to do our part."

"So I'm just supposed to turn loose of my pain, just like I turn my horse loose in a pasture?"

Pastor Taylor nodded. "Pretty much. You let it go and make the choice to forgive. When negative thoughts come back to pester you, mentally you have to chase them away and not dwell on them." He turned and grabbed his Bible off the desk and thumbed through some pages. "In James, the scriptures say, 'Submit yourselves therefore to God. Resist the devil, and he will flee from you. Draw nigh to God, and He will draw nigh to you.'"

He glanced back at Luke. "Once you've forgiven, continue to resist Satan and don't allow thoughts of bitterness or hurt to creep back in."

Luke considered all that the pastor said. He could see his problem had been continuing to dwell on the situation with Rachel when he should have given it over to God. He just had to choose to forgive her and then refuse to think about the offense again. Could he do that?

What choice did he have? If he wanted God's forgiveness—and he did more than anything—then he had to forgive Rachel.

"I understand now. I may have forgiven in the past, but I kept thinking of how much I was hurt—and that made me angry."

The pastor nodded. "You kept taking the offense off God's

shoulder and putting it back on yours. Give your burden to him, and then forget about it. Don't let the enemy talk you into shouldering it again."

Luke smiled. "You make everything sound so easy."

A melancholy look draped the pastor's face, making Luke wonder what he struggled with. Pastor Taylor shook his head. "It's not easy, but God gives us the grace to do it. And remember, refusing to forgive hurts you more than the people you're upset with."

Luke nodded, and for the first time, he felt he had the power to conquer his pain.

"Would you like me to pray with you?"

"Yep, I would."

Ten minutes later, Luke walked out of the pastor's house feeling freer than he had in years. He still wanted to get alone with God, but he knew now that he could forgive Rachel and let go of the past.

Carly followed the other brides upstairs. She'd miss Mrs. Hamilton's cooking when she left here—that was for certain. Her stomach ached from chicken and dumplings, green beans, applesauce, and rolls that the boardinghouse owner had made for supper. And then there was the peach pie. Mmm. . .

At the top of the stairs, Miss Bennett stopped suddenly and pivoted, crossing her arms over her chest. Miss O'Neil almost ran into her but sidestepped in time to move past her.

"I'm telling you both now that I'll be marrying the marshal, so you'd better decide what you're going to do." Miss Bennett lifted her chin to emphasize her point.

Carly walked up the two stairs to the landing, not wanting to give the snooty woman the benefit of looking down on her. "Just what makes you think you'll win?"

"I can cook and sew better than the both of you put together, that's why."

"Aye, 'tis true. I can't cook a'tall." Miss O'Neil backed toward her bedroom door. "But you can't know who the marshal will choose."

"That's right. I noticed he didn't pick your shirt." Carly glared at the blond, wondering why she was siding with the Irish girl. "Maybe the marshal don't even like blonds."

"Well, we shall see. I'm just giving y'all fair warning. I do not intend to lose this competition." Miss Bennett's countenance changed swiftly, and it looked as if a wave of uncertainty washed over her face. "I simply can't lose." She spun around, skirts swishing, enveloping Carly and Miss O'Neil in the scent of lilacs. She hurried into her room and slammed the door.

Miss O'Neil jumped. The paleness of her face matched the white wall trim. Her green eyes looked as big as the buttons on Bertha Boyd's dresses. Carly felt an uncharacteristic desire to comfort the girl. Though they were both competitors for the same prize, she felt an odd kinship to the other brides in spite of Miss Bennett's outburst. "Don't pay her no mind. We got ever' bit as good a chance at winnin' as her."

Miss O'Neil nodded, but the look of concern didn't leave her eyes. "Good evening."

The bedroom door shut quietly, and Carly continued down the wide hall to her room. Mrs. Hamilton had done a nice job decorating the boardinghouse, giving the place a homey feel. A hurricane lamp sat on top of a lacy tablecloth, bathing the dim hall in a soft light. The scents of the delicious meal still lingered, even upstairs, reminding her she'd eaten too much. This was the nicest home she'd ever been in. If only she never had to leave this place.

She reached for her door and paused, knowing her thoughts were foolish. This was a temporary stop. But she'd grown to like the little town and its people. If only she could somehow find a job, maybe she could stay here awhile. Grinning at the thought, she stepped into the room, and a whiff of something odd hit her in the face. Smoke?

Her gaze dashed around the room for the source. The door slammed shut behind her, and she whirled around, her heart jumping into her throat.

"Howdy, sis. You're a hard gal to track down."

She glared at her brother. How in the world had he found her? She tried to look relaxed though she felt anything but that. "What are you doing here, Ty?"

He sucked in a puff of his cigarette and then leaned casually against the wall and blew smoke rings. "Lookin' for my sister. I *am* responsible for ya."

"Not anymore. You left me for dead after that stage robbery."

He shrugged. "What was I s'posed to do if you were dead? Didn't see no reason to get caught tryin' to fetch your body."

She huffed out an angry sigh. "I can see how much I mean to you. I ain't even worth a decent burial."

Tyson gave her the charming grin that made many a naive woman swoon, but it was wasted on her. "Now, what'cha gettin' your petticoats in a twist for? You ain't dead."

She narrowed her eyes. "I'll thank you not to mention my unmentionables. And what if I had been lyin' in that stage, bleeding and in need of a doctor? You didn't bother to check."

He pushed away from the wall with a menacing glare and flicked the cigarette onto the carpet. "You ain't dead, so just hush up all this chatter before someone hears." A twisted grin pulled at his mouth. "And don't you look purty all gussied up like some schoolmarm."

Carly stomped on the cigarette butt before it could burn the carpeting that covered the center of the floor. She picked up the stub, stalked to the window, and flicked the butt outside. Marshal Davis stood on the street beside the bank, talking to two women. If only she could get his attention—but then what? She may not like her brother, but she didn't want him shot, and if the marshal jailed him, Ty would for sure rat on her. On the other hand, her brother was a keen shooter, and if the marshal got mortally wounded, it would ruin all her plans. How was she going to get rid of Ty before he spoiled everything?

"The marshal has a wanted poster with your likeness on it." She crossed her arms and pivoted back to face him. "You cain't stay here, you know."

He strode past her and flopped on her bed, making it creak under his weight. He didn't bother to remove his dirty boots from the quilt that Mrs. Hamilton had probably spent months making. "I can do anything I want."

Carly bit the inside of her cheek, battling both anger and desperation. "You're not concerned about the poster?"

He shrugged. "Those drawings ain't too good."

"How did you find me?"

"Pretty slick move of yours, pretending to be that other gal on that stage."

Carly tensed. If Ty knew she was impersonating Ellie Blackstone, who else did? "How do you know about that?"

"Read the story in the Joplin newspaper. It said Ellie Blackstone had survived and was traveling on to Lookout, Texas, to be a mail-order bride, but another unknown woman was near death. I 'membered that name from when I put you on the stage, so I snuck in the doctor's office one night to get you." A smirk tugged at his lips. "Imagine my surprise when it weren't you but that other gal. I put two and two together, and here I am."

Carly's heart jumped like a horse clearing a creek. How had the paper known where she was going? She didn't remember telling the lawman anything but her name. Then she realized what her brother had said and felt the skin on her face tighten. "Ellie Blackstone is alive?"

Ty shrugged. "Don't know. She was wounded bad. I imagine she's dead by now."

Sinking down on the vanity stool, she considered what it would mean to her if the woman wasn't dead. She could show up here any day.

"I don't know what your game is here, but I noticed this little town has a nice-sized bank—and only one lawman. We could make off with a haul."

So Ty had been scoping out the town. That didn't surprise her. He might not be the sharpest knife in the drawer, but she couldn't fault his thorough planning before a robbery. "I'm not helpin' you rob that bank."

He sat up and stared at her, brows lifted. "Don't sass me. You know I don't like it."

Carly's gaze drifted toward the door. She could probably get there before him, but then what? Ty wasn't beyond hurting anyone to get what he wanted—and that included her. He might act the caring brother, but he only had one goal: to take what he wanted. She couldn't stand the thought of something happening to Mrs. Hamilton. The woman had been kind, and Carly had begun to actually like her.

"Don't even think about crossing me, Carly. I don't like hurtin' ya, but I will if'n ya force me to."

She squeezed her eyes shut, trying to form a plan.

"Tell me what your scam is. I want in on it."

"My plan hasn't exactly succeeded." Otherwise she would have been long gone, and he'd never have found her.

Ty grinned and leaned back against her pillow with his hands behind his head. "That's because I'm the brains of the Payton gang. You need me."

"We're not a gang. At least I'm no longer part of it."

Ty pursed his lips and stared at the ceiling as if something was on his mind.

Carly walked over to the bed and leaned on the bedpost. "Did something happen to Emmett and Floyd?"

Ty sat up cross-legged on the bed. "Emmett got himself killed in that stage robbery, and Floyd found out his ma was dying and went home."

"You let him go?" Carly found that hard to believe, knowing

all that Floyd knew about her brother's shenanigans.

Ty shrugged. "I thought about shooting 'im for leavin' me, but he's the only man I trust. I reckon once his ma dies he'll come back. What else could he do? He ain't done an honest day's work his whole life."

"Well, he'll never think to look for you down here in Texas."

"Neither will them lawmen what's after me." He chuckled. "Gotta hand it to you, I never expected you was smart enough to take care of yourself."

Carly scowled at him. No, she could cook and do his gang's wash and even help in a robbery, but she wasn't smart enough to fend for herself. She'd forgotten how much she disliked being with her brother. How he continually belittled her as if she were nothing more than a maggot.

She strode to the window again and saw Jack outside, throwing a stick for that ugly yellow dog to fetch. If she could just get her attention—

"Whatever you're thinkin', don't. I've seen all the pretty gals what live here and that lady and her kid. I'd hate for any of 'em to get hurt because ya did something stupid."

"What is it you want?"

"I want to know what you had planned when ya came here."

Carly sighed. What did it matter now? Her plan had failed. "I came here pretending to be Ellie Blackstone. She told me on the stage she was comin' here to marry the town marshal. I thought if I took her place, I might weasel up close to the marshal and find out about payroll shipments."

A glimmer sparked in Ty's blue eyes. "And?"

She shrugged. "And nothin'. I even searched his office once when he was gone. Nothing. No payroll shipment information of any kind."

"That sounds a bit odd with him being the only protection in this town."

"Either he doesn't know about any, or there aren't any in this area, or. . ." She wasn't sure if she wanted to share this thought.

"Or what?" He slid off the bed and crossed the room, standing off to the side of the window.

She shrugged. "It's just a guess, but maybe he keeps them in his pocket or at his house."

"Hmm. Could be." Ty leaned against the wall and crossed his boot over his ankle. "Reckon it wouldn't be any trouble to search his house. Where's it at?"

Carly pinched her mouth shut. Hadn't she told him enough? If Ty didn't find the information in the house, he might shoot Luke to get it—and she didn't want that to happen. Sometime, somehow, she'd started liking the people of Lookout. She knew Luke was suspicious of her, but he was so kind to Jack and that dumb dog. She never should have let her defenses down, because now her brother could use them against her.

Ty suddenly grabbed her shoulders and shook her. "Where's the marshal's house?"

She glanced out the window, hoping someone had seen him. Ty must have realized the same thing, because he let go and stepped back, but his hand slid to his gun handle, letting her know he meant business.

"It's next door. That little house just west of the boardinghouse."

"I'll scout it out tomorrow." Ty pulled his gun and waved it in Carly's face. "You just keep quiet about me. If word gets out I'm here, someone's gonna get hurt. Maybe that cute little kid."

Carly glanced out the window again, and her heart jolted. Jack was staring up at her.

CHAPTER 27

Jack threw the stick and stared up at Miss Blackstone's window again. She was sure she'd seen someone in the room—a man to be exact.

But having a man in a woman's room was against her ma's rules.

Max trotted back with the stick in his mouth, looking happy. She took it from him, tossed it away again, and wiped the dog slobber on her skirt. Peering over her shoulder, she saw that Luke was still talking to Polly and Dolly Dykstra.

Max grabbed the stick and hurried back to her. He dropped it at her feet then stared up at her, looking as if he were grinning. He waited, wagging his tail, ears alert. She backed up a few feet so she could get a better look at the window and tossed the stick. A person stepped up close to Miss Blackstone and then quickly jumped back into the shadows. There *was* someone in her room, and that person wore a man's plaid shirt. That left only one possible solution—there really was a man in that room.

And currently, they didn't have any male boarders.

The front door opened, and her ma stepped out. "Time to come in, Jacqueline."

This time, Jack didn't argue. She had to find out what was going on. Max walked back, head drooping. The stick fell from his mouth, and his tail wagged. She bent down to scratch his ears. "Gotta go, boy. There's something strange goin' on at home."

The dog whined as Jack jogged toward her mother. How could she get upstairs without making her ma suspicious?

"Go wash up and get ready for bed, sweetie." Her mother stood in the doorway, looking down the street.

Jack gazed back over her shoulder. Was her ma looking at Luke? As much as she hoped so, she had a problem that needed investigating. "Don't you need me to take some fresh water upstairs to the boarders?"

Her ma's brows lifted. "Uh. . .thank you, but no. I did that before I fixed supper."

Jack searched her mind for another excuse. "Well, maybe they need some clean towels."

"What's going on?" Her mother glanced up the stairs.

Jack leaned forward to close the space between them. Maybe confessing was the best alternative. "I saw a man in Miss Blackstone's room, Ma."

"What? When?" She placed her hand over her heart like she often did when she was worried.

"Just now when I was playing fetch with Max. I saw him twice through the window. Honest, Ma."

Different expressions flitted across her mother's face until she settled on one—and Jack knew then that she didn't believe her.

"Just get inside and get ready for bed. I'm too tired to deal with your nonsense tonight."

"But—"

Rachel held up her hand. "No 'buts.' It's time for bed."

"You never believe me." Jack scowled and stomped past her mother. "Why would I lie about something like that? Even I know your number one rule for unmarried women—never have a man upstairs."

In the bedroom, she slammed the door. She'd told her ma about the stolen shirt, too, but she hadn't believed her enough to even look to see if it was missing.

Jack tore off her clothes and yanked on her nightgown, not even taking time to wash. Tomorrow she'd tell Luke about the man. She might just be a little kid, but she knew what she'd seen.

A leaf floated on the river's current as the water rippled along on its way to join the waters of the Red River. Luke stood by the river's edge, feeling as if all his troubles and worries had drifted away. The pastor had been right. Once he'd made the mental decision to forgive Rachel, his spirit had risen like a caged bird set free. He felt like a prisoner whose shackles had been removed for the last time. Free to move on. Free to admit he still loved Rachel.

But had he driven her away with his hard-nosed refusal to forgive for so many years? He ducked his head and kicked a rock. Rachel was so tenderhearted that his attitude must have broken her heart—just like she'd broken his.

No! He held up his hand as if shoving the enemy back. "I will not take up that offense again. I've forgiven her, once and for all."

He breathed in a cleansing breath through his nose. He needed to tell her—needed to ask her to forgive him for being so obstinate. And she would—in a heartbeat, because that's the kind of woman she was. Unable to hold an offense against anyone. A loving nurturer. No wonder she found it hard to discipline her daughter.

Luke mounted Alamo, knowing he'd spent enough time away from town. Not that much ever happened there. As he headed toward town, he watched the remains of the sunset. Bright pink, the same color as Rachel's Sunday dress, painted the belly of every cloud in the sky. Like a ripe peach, orange mixed with the pink to create an amazing sight that only the Creator of this world could have designed.

He thought about the final leg of the bride contest. The mayor had let him know that he was to take each bride out to eat and get to know her better—all except that anonymous bride, of course. That had been a decent idea until he'd forgiven Rachel, and then like a dam breaking, his heart was flooded with love for her again. Had he ever truly quit loving her?

God was giving them a second chance—and he was sure going to take advantage of it.

Max lay under the bench in front of his office, exhausted from chasing all the sticks Jack had thrown him earlier in the evening. The lights were off in the freight office, so Luke turned his horse between the livery and Polly's Café to Oak Street.

"Marshal, wait!" Jenny Evans jogged toward him, holding her skirt up to avoid tripping. "Might I have a word with you?"

Luke sighed and dismounted. What did she want now?

She opened her pad of paper and turned so the fading twilight illuminated it. "The mayor mentioned that you're going to be taking the boardinghouse brides out to supper separately so you can get to know each one better. Can you tell me where and when? Which bride will you invite first?"

Luke worked to keep a cap on his irritation. "No, I can't tell you. But I will say that I'll make the announcement of my choice of bride tomorrow night."

"Tomorrow?" Jenny's eyes widened. "Why, you can't do it tomorrow. That's Wednesday. I've got to have time to get the announcement out in the paper so folks around here will know about it. Everyone will want to come to town for that. It's the best fun anyone's had since those kids hauled Simon Jones's plow horse up into his hay loft."

Luke tried hard to remember the time of prayer he'd just finished. *Breathe. Don't let her get to you.* "Tomorrow night. Whoever is here is here. And that's final."

She worked her mouth as if trying to get something unstuck from her teeth. "The mayor might have something to say about this." She spun around and marched off.

Luke sighed. He probably should expect a visit from Mayor Burke before long.

He stopped in front of his cousins' house and noted only a faint light glimmered in the parlor. Maybe he should wait until morning, but he ached to share his news with someone. He dismounted, tethered Alamo to the porch, and knocked on the door.

Mark opened it and grinned. Shirtless, he scratched his belly and then waved Luke inside. "Didn't expect to see you at this hour."

"Is it too late?"

"Nah, come on in." Mark combed his curly hair with his fingers. "I'd offer you some coffee, but we've already dumped the dregs."

"I don't need anything. Just wanted to tell y'all something." Luke stepped inside and studied his cousins' home. Since he normally met with them in their office, he'd only been here a few times. Books stood in stacks on the floor beside the small settee and the table in front of it. Dust balls littered the floor like tumbleweeds, and piles of papers were everywhere. "Is this where you file your paperwork?"

Mark chuckled. "It's an organized mess. Trust me."

Luke shook his head. "You need a housekeeper—or maybe a wife."

Garrett walked into the room barefoot and dressed in his nightshirt. He yawned and scratched his chest. "What are you doin' here?"

Maybe this wasn't such a good idea. "I'll just wait till morning. I can see you're both ready for bed—unless you're accustomed to wearing dresses at home."

Garrett perked up, obviously not taking offense at Luke's joke and not wanting to wait for news. "No, you're here now, so spill the beans. What's going on?"

Mark turned up the lantern and motioned for Luke to sit down in the only empty chair. Luke obliged. Mark shoved aside a stack of papers, and he and Garrett perched on the edge of the settee.

Luke grinned, and both brothers lifted their brows. "I've finally forgiven Rachel."

Garrett smiled and slugged Mark in the shoulder.

Mark scowled and rubbed his arm. "That's great news. How'd she take it?"

Luke shook his head. "Haven't told her yet. It just happened—down by the river."

"I guess you had that talk with the pastor?"

"Yeah. Thanks for suggesting that."

"So, what are you gonna do now?" Mark asked.

"He's gonna stop the bride contest and marry Rachel, that's what." Garrett grinned and leaned back, arms crossed over his chest as if he were responsible.

Luke stared at his cousin. Was he that transparent?

"Oh, come on, we both know you're still in love with Rachel. That's the only explanation for you still being upset at her after all these years," Garrett said.

Luke stared at the floor, trying to make sense of his thoughts. A mouse ran out from under his chair, sniffed the air, and dashed back to his hiding spot. "If you knew I was still in love with Rachel, why did you order all those brides?"

Mark sat forward, elbows on his knees. "We didn't know then, and if we had, it would have saved us a lot of trouble."

"Yeah, but on the other hand, maybe it took some competition for your affections to make you realize where your heart belongs." Garrett looked so proud that he nearly beamed.

Luke leaned back, not wanting to admit there might be some truth in Garrett's comment. "I've forgiven Rachel, and I sincerely hope she still cares for me and will be willing to forgive my stubbornness."

"Let's hope it doesn't take another eleven years." Garrett chuckled. "We're all getting a bit long in the tooth."

Mark elbowed his brother. "Speak for yourself."

Luke smiled at his cousins' horseplay. "Do you think I still have a chance with her? Am I needlessly getting my hopes up?"

"Rachel has only had eyes for you. It was true back then and true today."

Luke ground his back teeth together as a fraction of the old hurt shoved its way to the surface like a boil. "Then why did she marry James?"

His cousins glanced at each other.

Luke stood and paced the small room. "What are you not telling me?"

Garrett ran his hands through his hair. "What did she tell you back then?"

Luke threw up his hands. "Nothing. Just that she couldn't marry me because she had already married him. I figured she wanted an easier life than I could have given her."

"You figured wrong," Garrett said. Both cousins stood, still casting odd glances at each other and back at Luke.

A knot twisted in Luke's gut. Had there been more to her decision than he thought?

"What are you not telling me?" He rubbed his nape, his peace fleeing.

Garrett ran his hand over his jaw. "It's not our story to tell. You need to ask Rachel about it."

Luke stopped in front of his cousins. "I tried that once, but it didn't work."

"Try again." Garrett crossed his arms.

All manner of thoughts assaulted Luke, none of them good. His cousins were right; he'd put off this discussion long enough. He said his good-byes and strode to Rachel's house. From the front, all was dark. He rounded the side of the house and was glad to see the kitchen light still on.

Because of the lateness of the hour, he knocked on the back door and waited instead of entering like he normally did. Rachel opened the door a smidgeon and peeked out. She looked tired, and he almost changed his mind. "I need to talk with you for a minute."

She hesitated a moment then nodded and opened the door. "I need to close the bedroom door so our talking doesn't disturb Jacqueline."

He touched her arm to stop her. "Could we take a walk outside?"

Rachel studied his face and must have seen something worthy, because she nodded. He held the door open, and she followed him out. His hand shook as he closed the door. They walked toward the back of her property, silencing the crickets with each step.

He needed to tell her that he forgave her, but now his bitterness seemed petty. Why had it taken him so long?

Rachel walked beside him, wringing her hands together. Did he make her nervous?

He sighed and faced her. "I want you to know I'm sorry."

She shook her head. "You have nothing to be sorry for. I'm the one at fault."

"I wish you'd explain to me what happened."

She turned away, fidgeting. "I should have told you right away, but I was afraid."

He clutched her shoulders, forcing her to face him. "Afraid of what?"

Her head hung down, and her hands refused to be still. "That I'd lose you."

"You lost me anyway. It's time you tell me what happened. It will help us both. Take a load off our shoulders."

The crickets resumed their chirping all around them, blending with the noise of the tree frogs. A full moon shone bright, illuminating Rachel. He tipped her face up. "Please tell me, Rach."

She shuddered, as if carrying the weight of the world. "I

277

married James because I was pregnant with his child."

Luke staggered, his hand going to his chest. Never once had he considered she might have been unfaithful. All these years he'd pined for her, and now he allowed his hopes to rise again, only to be dashed on the rocks once more. She'd been with another man. Before marriage.

Rachel stared up at him with tears charging down her face. "I'm so sorry, Luke."

He paced away, putting some distance between him and Rachel. *God, how could this happen?* His heart ached as if someone had plunged a sword through it. "I loved you like no man has ever loved a woman. I'd have done anything for you, and you betrayed me with another man—my friend, no less."

Tears burned Luke's eyes as Rachel's betrayal burned deep. The rage of his unforgiving spirit shot up like the force of a dark angel fleeing hell. He ground his back teeth together and clenched his fists.

"I tried to f–fight him off, but he was too strong." Rachel's voice sounded far away, as if she'd fallen in a well.

Suddenly his rage fled, and something worse wormed its way into his heart. Had he heard correctly? "What?"

"I told him no. I tried to get away, but we were alone, and h–he always took what he wanted."

Luke closed his eyes, hating the truth. James had his way with the woman Luke loved.

"If he wasn't dead, I'd be very tempted to kill him." Luke grabbed Rachel's shoulders. "Why in the world did you marry him after that? Didn't you know I'd take care of you?"

Rachel ducked her head. "I went to visit my aunt after the attack for six weeks. By the time I returned, I knew I was pregnant." Rachel's chin quivered. "You were out working on the Carney ranch by then. I saw James one day, and he convinced me that you wouldn't want me anymore. That no decent man would." She heaved in a breath that made her shudder. "He offered to do right by me, and we married the next day."

Luke stared up at the dark sky. *Why didn't You protect her?*

"I was also afraid if you knew the truth that you'd do something to James. His father would have made sure you went to prison—or worse—if you'd retaliated."

She was right. He knew that. But he felt robbed of the chance to vindicate Rachel. He would have back then if he'd known the truth, and that could well have ended in his death.

"Is Jack the child you had?"

Rachel nodded. "Garrett and Mark spread word that she was born early, since she was so small. I never liked what they did, but I know it was to protect my reputation. I'll always be grateful."

"How did they know to do that?"

"They found me at the river. They knew you and I were supposed to be there, and they came to swim, but t–they found me instead. I pleaded with them not to tell anyone, and for once, they did as asked."

Luke forked his fingers through his hair, hating himself for choosing work over Rachel that day. If only he'd gone to the river. "I appreciate your telling me this. I know it wasn't easy."

Rachel didn't respond. She wiped her eyes and fiddled with a fold in her skirt. Luke didn't know what to say. His cousins had lied to protect Rachel, and wrong as it was, he'd be eternally grateful. A woman had nothing if she didn't have her reputation.

All manner of thoughts swirled through his head. He'd blamed Rachel for wanting a better life—for marrying James because of his money—when the truth had been far different. He squeezed his eyes shut. Oh, how he must have hurt her by his refusal to forgive. He'd been stupid. Ungrateful for the changes God had made in his own life. Rachel had been a victim, but he'd blamed her for his own pain, when hers must have been unbearable.

"I want you to know that I'm sorry for everything—for not showing up that day—for what James did. For not being there when you needed me." He took hold of her and pulled her into a hug so quickly she gasped. She stood there woodenly, not responding, and he could hardly blame her. She probably hated him for how he'd treated her. "C'mon, I'll walk you back."

At the door, she stopped. "I don't blame you for any of this, I hope you know that. You were just trying to work hard to get us a start."

"I need some time to think and pray; then I'd like to talk to you again, if that's all right."

She nodded, and a faint smile tugged at her cheeks. The door clicked shut, and he leaned against the house, digesting all he'd learned. Never once had he considered such a scenario.

He allowed himself to think back, and the memory of that day came into focus. He'd been whipping through his chores at home, anxious to meet Rachel at the river as they'd prearranged. He'd been busy working for weeks and missed her terribly, and he had looked forward to sweet talking her and stealing a few kisses. She'd set aside an hour to sit and talk with him at the river before her mother expected her back home to help with supper. He'd been on his way to meet her when a local rancher had waylaid him and asked him to deliver a load of supplies he'd just bought to his ranch.

The choice had been hard. Everybody in town knew he'd do any kind of honest work to make money—and the rancher had offered him a fair amount. Luke needed only about fifty dollars more before he could put a down payment on a house for Rachel and him to live in after their wedding. The pull to spend time with her had been strong, but in the end, the chance to make money won out. After all, once they were married, they'd have all the time in the world together.

He remembered looking for his cousins as he drove out of town but finding James instead, lounging outside the bank with a friend. James had more than willingly agreed to deliver a message to Rachel that Luke had found work and wouldn't be able to meet her.

Luke's stomach swirled with sudden realization. His limbs trembled, and he leaned forward, hands on his eyes, sure that he would retch at any moment as the truth dawned.

It's my fault James took advantage of Rachel.

CHAPTER 28

Rachel leaned back on the chair in her bedroom, eyes closed, relishing the moments she'd spent with Luke. He hadn't said he forgave her, but he had said he was sorry. He'd barely reacted to all that she'd revealed, but he'd been right: she felt better for having finally told him the truth. Only time would tell how he would respond, and she was afraid to hope for too much. But she could still pray for him—pray that he wouldn't feel responsible for what James had done. Luke had always tried to protect her when they were young. Now that he knew the truth, would he blame himself for not showing up that day at the river?

She sighed. Her legs ached from standing much of the day. She loved tending the boardinghouse and her boarders, but by evening, she was exhausted. Maybe selling the place wasn't such a bad idea. She stretched and sniffed her fingers. In spite of the scrubbing with lye soap she'd given them, she still caught the faint whiff of the onions she'd cut up to go with the fried liver she'd made for supper.

Her gaze traveled across the room, and she watched the rise and fall of her daughter's chest as she slept. This was about the only time her child was peaceful and not running about or causing trouble. She blew out a heavy sigh. Why was raising children so difficult?

Jacqueline had said a man was in Miss Blackstone's room, but Rachel didn't believe her. The young woman had made it clear that she planned on marrying the marshal, so why would she risk her chances by inviting a man to her room?

She wouldn't. Besides, Rachel didn't know of a single man in town who'd lower himself to steal another man's potential wife or sneak into her boardinghouse. Most of the men in Lookout were good, decent sorts. She shook her head. If only Jacqueline wouldn't tell falsehoods. It surely made it hard for Rachel to tell when the girl was being honest.

She pulled her high-top boot up on her knee and untied the laces, thinking about her visit with Mayor Burke. Though a bit less than she'd hoped for, he had made her a fair offer for the boardinghouse, but was it enough to start over in a new town? Could she really leave her hometown and move in with her aunt?

The thud of heavy footsteps above her head drew her gaze to the ceiling. Why would Miss Blackstone be stomping around like that?

Who knew what that young woman was doing? Something about her made Rachel wary, but maybe it was just that she was competing for Luke's affections. Rachel's lip wobbled at the thought of him picking one of the boardinghouse brides, but she'd done all she could to get him to forgive her. She must have hurt him much more than she realized.

Rachel worked at the laces, stretching them apart so she could get her foot free from the boot. Overhead, a softer set of footprints walked in the same direction as the heavy ones. The floor creaked above her head, and she thought she heard voices. Rachel froze.

What if Jacqueline had been right?

Pulling her boot back on, she hurriedly tied the laces and

tiptoed to the open window. Miss Blackstone's window was right above hers, and she listened hard for the sound of people speaking. The darkness of night had wrapped the house. The lights were already out in the Castleby house next door, and only the faint glow of the lantern on the dresser held the darkness at bay. Crickets battled tree frogs, but she couldn't hear any voices.

Still, there were those footsteps.

The thought of a trespasser in her home flooded her limbs with strength. Maybe Jacqueline hadn't been lying.

Guilt needled her, but the desire to know the truth pushed her forward. She crept to the entryway and paused at the staircase, her heart thundering. Maybe she should get her rifle—or Luke.

Maybe she was making a big deal out of nothing.

With her hand shaking, she held on to the railing and climbed the stairs to the second floor, being careful to miss the squeaky steps. No light shone from under either Miss Bennett's door or Miss O'Neil's, but a faint glow illuminated the floorboards around Miss Blackstone's. Rachel tiptoed forward across the wide hall, wincing when a board creaked. At the door, she stood, her breath sounding like a locomotive chugging uphill. Was she overreacting?

She heard a thump in the room, and suddenly, the door flew open. A large stranger stood in the doorway, grabbed her wrist before she could react, and yanked her into the room. A gasp fell from her mouth as he kicked the door shut with his foot and pressed her up against the wall in one swift motion. His arm against her throat cut off Rachel's breath, and she shoved against it.

"Be still, and I'll loosen my hold." His hot breath smelled like smoke.

"Let her go, Ty." Miss Blackstone's voice sounded from behind the man, but Rachel couldn't see her.

He stared into Rachel's eyes. "You gonna cause me any trouble? I know ya got that purty little girl downstairs."

Fear she hadn't known since the day James had his way with

her flooded her whole being. Her body shivered as if it had been caught up in a tornado. *Dear Jesus, help me.* "W–what do you want?"

"Well, now, that's none of your business." He loosened his hold just enough for Rachel to catch a deep breath. "You're an unexpected development. You should've stayed downstairs."

"Just let her go, Ty. She's not part of this." Miss Blackstone grabbed the man's arm.

He shoved her back, and she lost her footing, falling to the floor. "Don't be tellin' me what to do."

Rachel's mind raced for a way of escape. If she could get away and run for Luke, this man would get to Jacqueline before she could return. But if she got loose and ran to her bedroom to get her daughter, surely the man would catch up with her. She had the other two brides to be concerned about, as well.

The man turned back to her, his leering gaze running over her face and down her body. "I'll let ya go if you promise to behave, although I'd like it even better if you chose not to." He licked his tongue across his lips.

Rachel turned her face away as a shiver wormed its way down her spine. "I won't cause any trouble. I promise."

He backed away nearly as quickly as he'd captured her and leaned against the door, resting one hand on the butt of his revolver. Rachel hurried across the room and stood next to Miss Blackstone, who'd managed to untangle her skirts and get back on her feet. "Do you know him?"

Her boarder nodded. "Unfortunately. He's my brother."

Rachel noted the resemblance in their black hair and some of their features, although their eye color was different. The man chuckled and touched the edge of his hat. "Tyson Payton, ma'am. A pleasure to meet ya."

Frowning, Rachel swung her gaze back to the young woman. "Did you have different fathers? I mean, since your last name is Blackstone." A sudden thought bolted across Rachel's mind. "Or have you been married before?"

"Wrong and wrong." Tyson chuckled and crossed his arms over his wide chest.

Truth be told, he was a handsome man, even in the pale light from the hurricane lamp. But his response confused Rachel. "What do you mean?"

"Ty, please. . ."

He snarled at Miss Blackstone. "I mean her name ain't whatever she told ya. It's Carly Payton."

Rachel gasped and clutched her bodice. "You've been lying? Why?"

"Never mind all that." Ty scratched his jaw and eyed her. "The question is, what are we gonna do with you?"

Rachel had dealt with stubborn, troublesome men before and drew in a fortifying breath. "Why don't you just leave and let the rest of us get on with our business?"

Tyson chuckled again. "I kinda like your spunk." Suddenly, his countenance changed. "But spunky or not, you've gotten in the way of my plans. I'm gonna have to do somethin' with ya."

Miss Blackstone—no, Miss Payton—crossed the room. "Ty, she's not part of this. Let's just cut our losses and leave this dumpy town."

While the brother seemed to be considering her suggestion, Rachel's mind raced. Had they come to town with some kind of nefarious scheme?

She wrung her hands together. *Heavenly Father, please help me.*

"No, I think it's best if we get rid of her."

Rachel's heart bucked in her chest. He was going to kill her? What would happen to Jacqueline? *Lord, no.*

He pulled out his pistol and pointed it at her. She took a step back. Surely he wouldn't shoot her here, not with Luke and the whole town so close by.

"You can't kill her, Ty. She's got that kid to care for." Miss Payton turned to face Rachel, worry etched in her face. "I'm so sorry. I never meant for him to find me here." She broke her gaze and looked down.

"You got a key to the door leading to those back stairs, lady?"

Rachel nodded and reached into her apron pocket. Thank the Lord she hadn't left the key in her bedroom.

"You go first. Quietly. Unlock the back door, then Carly next, and I'll follow. If you try anything, I'll shoot ya and then come back and finish off your kid and the rest of those gals."

Rachel searched her mind for a way of escape, but she didn't want her daughter or the brides to get hurt. If she followed along, maybe she could find a way to overpower the man and get free. *Please, Lord.*

"You got a scarf or bandanna, sis?"

Miss Payton scowled at her brother but nodded. She pulled a red bandanna out of a drawer and held it up.

"Gag her so she don't make no noise."

Rachel winced as the cloth cut between her teeth and pinched her cheek. Miss Payton tied a knot, pulling Rachel's hair.

"Sorry," the girl whispered.

Tyson slowly opened the door and peered out. He waved his gun at them. Rachel breathed a sigh of relief when she entered the hall and found the other doors still closed. In the light of the hall lamp, she located the right key and unlocked the back door, taking one last glimpse at the hall she'd so carefully decorated to be pleasing to her guests. Would she ever see her home again? Or her daughter? Swallowing hard and forcing back the tears burning her eyes, she hurried down the dark stairs that wrapped around the back side of the house, praying Luke would find them.

Yet a part of her hoped he wouldn't. She couldn't bear if he got mortally wounded.

At the back of her lot, two horses were tied in the trees, out of sight of anyone who'd pass by. How had she and Luke missed them earlier when they were in the yard? Ty grabbed her waist and hoisted her onto one horse. "Get on behind her, sis."

Miss Payton clawed her way up and managed to climb on behind her. "It wouldn't have killed you to help me," she hissed at her brother.

He took the reins of their horse and mounted his own. Tears she'd fought to keep at bay charged down Rachel's cheeks. The light still glimmered in her bedroom, waiting for her return. She thought of her daughter sleeping there so peacefully. Would she ever see Jacqueline again?

Jack covered her head with her pillow to drive away the cheerful chirps from the birds welcoming the new day. If only she could sleep another hour. Bad dreams had pestered her all night. Dreams of Butch pulling her hair. Of him throwing her in the lake when she had her Sunday dress on. Dreams of her marrying him.

"Ick!"

She tossed the pillow aside at the disgusting thought.

Her body let her know that she'd get no more sleep until she visited the necessary. Sighing, she stood and stretched. She turned around and froze. Her mother's side of the bed looked as if it had never been slept in. And the lamp still burned. How odd.

Now that she thought of it, no fragrant smells greeted her this morning or the familiar sound of her ma clattering in the kitchen. She glanced at the clock on the fireplace mantel. Eight o'clock?

Jack hurried out the door and into the kitchen. She struggled to make sense of what she saw. First thing every morning, her ma cooked biscuits and made coffee. The kitchen looked just as clean as it had been last night before bed, while the coffeepot was as cold as a winter's night.

She opened the back door and stuck her head out. "Ma?" When she got no response, she hurried to the necessary and ran back inside, racing from room to room downstairs but finding no sign of her mother. Where could she be? Had there been some emergency in town?

Jack raced to her bedroom and found her shirt and overalls. Once dressed, she ran upstairs and pounded on Miss Bennett's door.

The woman opened it and scowled down. "Is breakfast ready? I haven't smelled a thing this morning."

"Have you seen Ma?"

"You mean today? Uh, no I haven't. Why?"

Jack spun around and pounded on Miss O'Neil's door. It fell open but the room was empty. Could her ma be somewhere talking with the Irish lady?

"Try the washroom," Miss Bennett offered.

Jack jogged to the back of the second story, noting that Miss Blackstone's door was open and the room also empty. Suddenly remembering the pastor's sermon about being ready for the rapture, Jack halted. She thought about how much trouble she'd caused her mother. Was she such a heathen that the rapture had come and she'd been left behind?

Her heart pounded like the blacksmith's hammer. The washroom door handle jiggled, and she looked up. Miss O'Neil came out, her face looking pink and freshly scrubbed. If Miss O'Neil was still here, Jack felt certain that the rapture hadn't come. God might leave snooty Miss Bennett, but surely He'd have taken the kind Irish woman.

"Top o' the mornin' to you. Would it be breakfast time?" Miss O'Neil lifted her head and sniffed, and then her brows dipped down.

"Have you seen my ma?"

"Nay, I have not."

Jack started to turn, but the back door caught her eye. "Did one of y'all unlock that door?"

Both brides shook their heads. "We don't have the key," Miss Bennett said.

Jack spun around, worry for her mother rising like the summer temperature. "Ma's missing, and I've gotta find Luke."

CHAPTER 29

Luke scrubbed the sleep from his face in the warm river water. The whiskers on his jaw bristled as he ran his hand across his face. He hadn't planned to be out all night, but after crying out to God and praying like he never had, he'd fallen dead asleep near the riverbank just before sunrise. He yawned. A few more hours rest would be nice, but he needed to check on the town, and then he had to see Rachel again.

Now that he'd wrestled with his unforgiving spirit and his guilt over what had happened, he was eager to see what God would do. The blinders on his eyes had been removed, and he saw things clearly for the first time in years. He stood and looked toward town. Excitement battled regret. Alamo nickered to him and walked away from the patch of grass where he'd been grazing.

Luke patted his faithful horse, bridled him, and mounted. He'd have to eat a lot of crow with Rachel, but she wasn't one to hold a grudge. And if he wasn't wrong, she still had feelings for him. He'd just spent the last few weeks denying them, but in his heart, he knew she still cared just as he did.

Last night, once he'd let go of his anger at James, he'd wallowed in guilt for an hour or two. Good thing he wasn't a drinking man, because he wouldn't have been sober for a week after he realized how he'd failed Rachel. Instead, he had to face the facts. He *was* responsible for what happened to her, but his intentions had been good. He was just trying to get enough money to get them a home so they could get married.

Then why did he still feel bad?

As he drew near the town, he surveyed the serene scene before him. The business folks were opening up their shops. The clink of a hammer could be heard coming from the livery, and fragrant scents from Polly's Café filled the air, making his belly rumble.

The boardinghouse drew his gaze, and he hoped to see Rachel outside sweeping. But then at this hour, she was more likely cleaning up the breakfast mess. At least he knew there would be a plate of her fine cooking waiting for him.

The mayor walked out of Luke's office, hands on his hips, and looked around. When his gaze latched onto Luke, he strode toward him. Dismounting, Luke met the mayor in the street. What could he want at this early hour?

"Jenny tells me you're going to announce who you want to marry tonight. That right?"

Luke suppressed a chuckle. The mayor sure didn't waste words on greetings. Luke nodded, but a twinge of uncertainty wiggled its way through his composure. Was he doing the right thing by making a public announcement? What if she turned him down flat? What if *she* refused to forgive *him*?

"That's right, I am."

The mayor puffed up his chest. "What about the next contest?"

Luke searched his mind but drew a blank. "What contest? I thought the next thing was for me to have supper with each of the gals."

Mayor Burke nodded. "So you can get to know them better. I was thinking maybe we should have the brides cook you something else since the pie contest didn't turn out well." He tapped his thick mustache as if considering the idea then studied Luke's face. "How is it you already know which one you want?"

"I just do. And I need to get my announcement made so the other gals can make some plans. No sense leaving them hanging."

"True, but I think we should wait until Saturday when most of the folks come to town. A lot of folks will be disappointed if you do it midweek."

Luke shook his head. "Too late. I told Jenny yesterday to post an announcement in the paper. Knowing her, she's probably already got them made up and ready to distribute."

The mayor's mustache twitched, and he leaned forward. "So... which one is it?"

Luke should have expected this, but the mayor surprised him. "Surely you don't expect me to tell you when I haven't even told her?"

"I guess not." He looked put off but shook his head. "Well, if we're going to have the announcement tonight, I've got a lot to do. Have you seen Rachel today?"

"Not yet. I'm headed there now to get my breakfast."

Mayor Burke walked toward the café. "Tell her I need to see her right away. I'll be at Polly's for the next half hour or so."

Luke quirked his mouth. If the mayor wanted to see Rachel, he could go to her house. He tied Alamo to the hitching post outside the jail and glanced around. Few people were out this early. Birds chirped in the tree beside the jail, and the sun shone full in the cloudless sky, promising another scorching day. But this day was filled with hope. Hope for love. Hope for the future. Hope for a family. Luke couldn't help grinning.

He whistled, and Max ambled out the jail door, wagging his tail. Luke stuck his head in his office to see if Jack had brought the scrap bucket yet, but it wasn't there. Hmm. Where was that gal? She usually headed to see him first thing after breakfast.

He took Alamo to the livery, rubbed him down, and fed him

before tending to himself. A man who didn't take care of his animals first wasn't worth much. Reaching down, he scratched Max's ear. "Right, boy?"

As he neared the boardinghouse, Luke's steps quickened. He had a lot to repent for, but for the first time in over a decade, he had a clear hope for the future—and that future included a pretty brunette with blue eyes as pale as—

The front door of the boardinghouse flew open, and Jack galloped out the door. She jumped off the porch and raced toward him. "Luke, help!"

What in the world? He burst into a run, stopping as she skidded to a halt in front of him. His gaze scanned the house for signs of trouble. "What's wrong?"

"It's Ma. She's gone."

Luke's heart all but stopped. Was this just another of Jack's tales? "What do you mean?"

"She never came to bed last night, and she hasn't even started breakfast."

Luke's jaw tightened. What could have happened? She'd been fine when he last saw her. "Are there any signs of anything disturbed in the house?"

Jack shook her head, her unbound auburn hair swinging side to side. "No, except the back door upstairs was open—and Ma always keeps it locked to protect our guests."

"All right. Calm down and let me have a look inside."

"Where could she be? She never leaves without telling me where she's going." Jack's deep blue eyes carried too much concern for a child. Max whined and stuck his head under her hand.

Luke pulled her to his side. "Don't worry, half bit. I'll find her."

Of all the nights for him to be off licking his wounds.

What could have happened? Rachel was a very responsible person and mother. She'd never go off without her daughter or leave her guests to fend for themselves.

Jack pulled him through the house and into the kitchen. She

waved her hand toward the empty room. "See. No food. She hasn't even made coffee."

Luke's concerns mounted, knowing Rachel always did that first thing each morning. Jack yanked on his arm and dragged him to the bedroom. Luke stopped in the doorway, not wanting to intrude into Rachel's most private area.

"See. Her side of the bed is still made, and her nightgown is still on its peg." Jack pointed behind the door.

"Could she have made up her side of the bed and then gotten dressed?"

Jack shook her head. "No, we make it together right after breakfast most days."

The hairs on the back of his neck stood at attention. Something must have happened to Rachel after he left. But what? He hadn't had any reports of trouble. Yeah, he was down at the river, but he would have heard any gunfire, and the mayor would have said something if there'd been any trouble. He forced himself to step into the room. He didn't want to miss any evidence—if there was some.

"Miss Blackstone is gone, too."

Luke spun around and stared at Jack. "What?"

"I noticed when I was upstairs looking for Ma that Miss Blackstone's door was open and she wasn't in her room. Do you think they could have gone somewhere? Did something happen in town last night?"

Luke shrugged, not willing to admit that he'd shirked his duty. He might have seen something suspicious if he had been working. Maybe Rachel had gone out to help a friend. His conscience told him she'd never leave Jack or her guests unless forced. He placed his hand on his pistol, not liking the thoughts chasing through his mind. "Show me Miss Blackstone's room."

He followed the child upstairs and first checked the back door. "No signs of forced entry. Whoever came or went this way must have had a key."

"Ma's got the only one. Keeps it on a ribbon in her apron pocket."

Luke's thoughts raced around his mind like a bumblebee caught in a jar. Had someone broken in and taken Rachel and Miss Blackstone? But why those two? If someone had come upstairs, why not take the other brides, too? Why Rachel?

He had to find her. After he left last night, he realized he still hadn't told her he'd forgiven her. He had to tell her—had to let her know that he still loved her.

How could he go on if something happened to her?

One of the bedroom doors opened. Luke grabbed Jack and flung her behind him at the same time he drew his gun.

Miss Bennett yelped and lifted her hands, her blue eyes wide.

Luke relaxed and holstered his weapon. "Sorry to frighten you, ma'am. Did you see or hear anything unusual last night?"

She shook her head. "Not really. Maybe just a thump or two."

Miss O'Neil's door flew open, and Luke turned toward it, hand on gun. The young woman took a step back when she saw him. "I heard voices last night. It sure enough sounded as if Miss Blackstone had someone in her room, but I wasn't certain, because we often hear noises from the street. Right after that, I went to bed and fell asleep."

If someone had been in Miss Blackstone's room, he—or she—could have taken Rachel and the young woman somewhere. But why?

He was going to need some help. "Jack, could you go fetch my cousins?"

She nodded but seemed reluctant to leave his side. He squeezed her thin shoulder and bent down. "I promise I'll find your mother."

Jack's chin and lower lip wobbled, but he gave her credit for not crying. "All right."

Luke offered her a smile; then she spun and raced down the stairs. He looked at the brides. "You're sure you didn't hear anything else last night? See anything out of the ordinary?"

Miss Bennett shook her head, but at the glint in the Irish girl's eyes he lifted his brows.

" 'Twas smoke I smelled—before I heard the voices. I stuck my head out the window and looked around but didn't see anything a'tall. The scent didn't get any stronger, so I didn't worry about it."

"Thank you. I'm sure Rachel would want you to help yourselves to breakfast, if you don't mind fixing it. I could use a cup of coffee to help me think."

Both women nodded and headed downstairs. Luke studied the back door again but still found no signs of forced entry. Rachel must have unlocked the door.

Luke pushed open Miss Blackstone's bedroom door and surveyed the room. The bed was slightly rumpled but didn't look as if anyone had slept in it. He checked for signs of disrupted things, but all looked in order. He started to leave, but his gaze fell to a black spot on the rug. Squatting, he touched the spot and sniffed his finger. Ashes?

So, someone *had* been smoking, and that would most likely be a man. Someone Miss Blackstone knew, perhaps?

His gut twisted. Had Rachel smelled the smoke and come upstairs to investigate? That could explain why she was upstairs.

Down at the bottom of the back stairs, he checked the dry ground for footprints—there were several. He knew Rachel kept the door locked, so these prints had to have been made last night. There were two narrow sets and a larger set about the same size boot print as he made. He clenched his jaw. Was this a kidnapping? For ransom?

Please, Lord, keep her safe until I can find her.

"Luke!" Garrett yelled.

"Down here."

His cousins trotted down the stairs and joined him with Jack following on their heels. "What's going on? Jack just said you needed us fast." Garrett looked around the backyard; then his gaze landed on Luke again, while Mark held his rifle, waiting with a concerned expression on his face.

"Rachel and Miss Blackstone are missing. I think—" He glanced at Jack.

"What?" she asked, brows dipped as if she dared him not to tell her.

She'd know soon enough as it was. He would need the whole town's help to find Rachel. He squatted down and pointed to the prints in the dirt. "See here. There are two sets of women's prints, and a larger set. I think a man took them."

Jack gasped and covered her mouth with her hand. "I just remembered. I saw a man in Miss Blackstone's window last night. I told Ma." She ducked her head and frowned. "But she didn't believe me."

"I believe you." Luke pulled her to him. He stared at his cousins. "Gather the town outside my office—and fast."

His cousins nodded. "You take Main and Oak streets," Garrett said, "and I'll take Bluebonnet and Ap..." His voice faded as both men jogged around the side of the house.

"I want to help." Jack yanked on Luke's vest and stared up at him. Her vulnerability made his heart ache.

He shook his head. "I need you to stay here and watch over the brides."

Jack puckered her lips. "They don't need me. They don't even like me."

"Well, your ma will want to see you the moment I bring her home. You don't want her to get here and you not be here, do you?" Luke hoped she'd take the hint and stay out of trouble.

She toed the dirt with her bare feet. "I guess not."

"Good." He placed a kiss on the girl's head. "Say a prayer that we find them fast, all right?"

Jack nodded and looked on the verge of tears. He wished he had someone better than the remaining brides to entrust her care to, but he supposed they'd do. He hugged her tight then turned her away. "Go on, now."

As soon as Jack had traipsed in the back door, Luke started following the tracks. They led to the rear of Rachel's property and to hoof prints. Luke ground his teeth together.

"God, I need help here. Help me find Rachel, and soon. Keep her safe until then."

Spinning around, he headed back to his office. He needed his rifle. Needed his horse. And he had a rescue to organize.

CHAPTER 30

Jack hurried through the house and out the front door, then slipped back around the side, her heart pounding. She waited a few minutes and then peeked around the corner. Luke was at the back of their property, studying the ground. She'd seen the footsteps he'd shown his cousins. They were clearly marked in the dirt, and if Luke could follow them, so could she.

Something wet touched her hand, and she jumped and yelped at the same time. Max cowered beside her, staring up with questioning eyes. She knelt and patted his head. "You scared the dickens out of me."

She sneaked another glance at Luke and then ran to the nearest oak and hid behind its large trunk. Max followed at a jog. Jack tried to wave him away, but he didn't take the hint. She feared he would draw Luke's attention her way. Peering around the trunk, she watched Luke walk behind the Sunday house and stare off with his hands on his hips. He looked up at the sky, and she wondered if he was praying. Suddenly, he turned left and strode away.

Jack jogged to the shed that held the garden tools and watched Luke march past his house and down Main Street. A small crowd had already gathered outside his office. She waited for a few minutes as the crowd grew, debating whether to follow the tracks or do as Luke had ordered.

There was only one thing she could do to help her ma. She spun around and ran back into the house, leaving Max whining at the back door. She hurried past the two brides, who had made themselves at home in her ma's kitchen. Scowling, she scurried into the bedroom she shared with Ma. She opened the last drawer and pushed aside her pa's old shirts. A black pistol lay in the bottom, and next to it was a round tin can. She pulled out both the gun and the can of bullets. She might need them to save her ma.

"Jacqueline, where does your mother keep her bacon grease?"

Jack jumped as Miss Bennett appeared in the doorway. She slammed the drawer shut, heart pounding, and stood, keeping the gun behind her. "Uh...in that Elkay loganberry can beside the stove."

The woman eyed her with suspicion but nodded. "Thank you. Breakfast will be ready in about twenty minutes. You should get cleaned up." She turned, and Jack allowed the tension to drain from her shoulders, but then Miss Bennett spun around again. She nibbled on her lip. "I'm sure the marshal will find your ma."

Jack nodded. If she didn't find her first.

The woman left, and Jack nearly collapsed on the bed. If Miss Bennett had seen her with the gun, what would she have done?

She waited until both brides were busy then ran down the hall and out the front door. Max greeted her in the backyard, wagging his tail. She stuffed the small tin of bullets into her pocket and shoved the heavy gun between the bib of her overalls and her shirt. At the rear of the yard, she found the hoof prints and started following them. Max trailed alongside her, looking as if he had every intention of helping her. Grateful for the dog's companionship, she patted her thigh. "C'mon, Max. We have to rescue Ma before something bad happens to her."

"No, don't." Rachel tried to run, but her feet felt as if they were stuck in quicksand. She fought the swirling haze and tried to get free from James's groping hands, but the tight grip of his arm held her immobile. She'd thought him a charming and comforting friend, but in a moment, he turned on her. Tears ran down her cheeks, and her stomach churned. He stole the most precious gift that she'd had to give Luke. "No!"

She jerked awake and felt herself falling. Her head collided with the hard wooden floor, and she sucked in a breath, allowing her vision to clear. But when she tried to move her hands, the bristly rope cut into her wrists. She'd been dreaming, but the reality of her situation was just as dreadful.

Ignoring her head, she wrestled herself into a sitting position and studied the small cabin. Fingers of sunlight clawed their way through the gaps where the chinking had eroded between the logs, giving the room a striped look. Dust coated her lips, and she longed for some water.

Sitting was difficult with her hands tied behind her back and her ankles bound together. At least the bed had been slightly soft, though it was dusty and smelled like it had been used as a carpet for a privy. She shuddered and scooted sideways. Miss Blackstone was still asleep on the small bed. At least she was against the wall.

Rachel struggled with the ropes, but they wouldn't yield. She leaned her head against the side of the bed. What had Jacqueline done when she'd awakened and hadn't found her?

Had she been worried? Scared? Gone to Luke?

And where had Miss Black—no, Miss Payton's—brother gone? What did he intend to do?

She had to get free. To find her daughter and get her somewhere safe. To warn Luke about Ty Payton.

She searched the room, looking for something, anything she

could use to cut the ropes. But there was little in the cabin. It must have been abandoned years ago. Or maybe it was a line shack some rancher no longer used.

One chair lay on its side, halfway under the small, warped table. The fireplace was filled with debris—the remains of a bird's nest, charred wood, ashes, and leaves that had fallen down the opening. On the wall sat two shelves that held three cans. If she could get free, maybe she'd find one of them held something edible.

She scooted across the floor, trying hard to ignore the filth and the pain in her shoulders from having her arms pulled back for so long. Up close, she noticed one of the chair legs was broken, leaving a pointy end. Maybe she could cut her bindings with it.

She squirmed around until the chair was behind her and started sawing the rope back and forth against the point. Miss Payton rolled over onto her side, and Rachel stared at her. She'd been irate at her brother for tying her up and leaving her. At first, she'd tried to reason with him to let them go. But her brother was a hard case. He slapped her and told her to shut up. Rachel could see that the young woman's lip had swollen overnight.

Rachel's hands slipped, and the sharp point bit into the tender flesh of her wrist. She cried out, and Miss Payton's eyes flew open. The young woman looked around, and Rachel knew the moment she remembered her circumstances, because her eyes widened.

She struggled for a few minutes and managed to sit up on the bed. Rachel froze. Should she continue to try to free herself?

"I'm gonna kill Ty for doing this."

How would she go about that, trussed up like a turkey? "Why did your brother do this? What does he want in Lookout?"

Miss Payton sucked her lips in for a moment. "At first all he wanted was me. But now, I'm not so sure."

"Why would he come to get you?"

Miss Payton stared at Rachel so long she thought the girl would remain silent, but she must have found Rachel worthy, because she started talking.

302

"My brother is the leader of the Payton gang, out of Missouri. Maybe you've heard of them?"

Rachel shook her head.

"Well, that wouldn't please Ty. He wants everyone to know who he is."

"Were you part of his gang?"

"In a way. My ma died when I was fourteen, and I didn't have no pa. Nobody in town would help me, so Ty let me live with him and his gang. I cooked and did their laundry for years."

"I'm sorry about your mother. Mine is also gone."

Miss Payton nodded. "I hated the way the gang members gawked at me, especially as I got older. Gave me the shivers."

Rachel's heart ached for the young woman. She understood how hard it was for an unmarried woman with no family ties to make it alone. She turned away, watching the dust motes floating in the air. James had convinced her that Luke would no longer want her once she was sullied. He'd talked her into marrying him so her child would have a father. She shook her head. Some father he turned out to be. Once he realized she'd had a daughter instead of the son he'd longed for, he had lashed out and hit Rachel for the first time.

"I ran away the first chance I got. Came here, hopin' for a fresh start and that Texas was far enough away that my brother wouldn't find me. Guess I should have gone to Mexico."

Now that her shoulders had relaxed a bit and the pain in her wrist had eased, Rachel started sawing again. She doubted that Ty Payton would let her live. Her only chance was to get away.

Had he found Jacqueline? Had he hurt her? She had to get loose—had to protect her daughter.

"What are you doing over there?" Miss Payton scooted to the edge of the bed.

"Trying to get free. I've got to get back to my daughter."

Miss Payton gazed around the room. "There's not much here." She sniffed the air and then her shoulder, and wrinkled her nose.

"Eww, this place stinks."

Rachel suspected some varmints had used the bed as a nest a time or two. She shuddered at the thought of lying on that nasty mat. Her clothing also carried the foul stench.

"I met Ellie Blackstone on a stage my brother was plannin' on robbin'. He set me up as a passenger so I could hold a gun on the travelers while he robbed it." She bit her lip and looked away. "I didn't wanna do it."

Her anxious eyes turned to Rachel. "But I was scared if I didn't he might let the gang have me. The way they looked at me made my skin crawl as if I had fallen into a crate of spiders."

Rachel's heart went out to the girl, and she could understand her overpowering desire to get away. She'd once felt that way herself. "Miss Payton—"

"Do think maybe you could call me by my given name—Carly?"

"Yes, and you must call me Rachel."

Carly nodded.

"There's something I don't understand. Why did you assume Miss Blackstone's identity?"

"She told me about coming here to marry the marshal. She was all excited about it, but then she got shot. I thought she was dead and took her identity." Carly looked away and stared out the lone dingy window. "Wouldn't she have been in for a surprise once she got here?"

Rachel almost grinned. "That mail-order bride debacle sure got out of hand, didn't it?"

"You like him, don't you? The marshal, I mean."

Rachel's gaze collided with Carly's. Was her affection for Luke obvious to others? She tried so hard to hide it. "We were engaged a long time ago—when we were even younger than you are now."

Carly leaned forward until Rachel thought that she, too, might fall headfirst off the bed. "What happened?" she asked in a hushed voice.

Rachel grimaced. "It's a long story."

"We're not going anywhere anytime soon."

"We are if I have my way. You ought to see if you can find something sharp and try to cut your bindings. We need to get away from here before your brother returns."

Carly nodded and eased to her feet. She hopped around the room, searching, and with each bounce, Rachel thought for sure she'd get tangled in her skirts and fall. Carly's foot bumped something, and it clinked. Rachel's heart leaped as Carly looked up, eyes wide. "There's some glass here that must have fallen out of the window."

Rachel eased onto her knees. "Can you get it?"

Carly stooped down, trying to get her hands low enough to pick up the broken pane. Suddenly, she wavered and fell over backward. She winced, but as soon as she hit the floor, she scooted back toward the glass. Rachel held her breath. *Please, Lord.*

"Ouch!" She jumped and grimaced; then her gaze lit up. "I've got it!"

Hope surged through Rachel's heart. "Praise the Lord. Can you work it so you can cut the ropes?"

"It's awkward, but I think I can."

Rachel went back to sawing her ropes against the chair.

"So, are you gonna tell me why you didn't marry that handsome marshal?"

"He wasn't a marshal back then, just a poor youth who did every job he could trying to make enough money to get us a place to live so we could marry."

"Why didn't you?"

Rachel didn't want to tell her what had happened. Didn't want her to think less of her. Was it just pride? No, it was to protect her daughter. If the townsfolk knew that she was already pregnant when she married James, they would look down on Jacqueline, and the poor child had enough troubles as it was. "It just wasn't meant to be, I suppose."

"You mean you don't think it was God's will?"

Stopping her sawing, Rachel stared at the young woman. "I used to think marrying Luke was God's will."

"But if you'd married him, you wouldn't have that kid of yours." Carly flinched and cursed. "Sorry. I cut myself again. Don't know if this is such a good idea."

Rachel thought about what Carly said. "That's true. My marriage to James wasn't. . .um. . .a love match. But God did use it to give me Jacqueline. The Bible says, 'And we know that all things work together for good to them that love God, to them who are the called according to his purpose.'"

"And you believe that?"

Rachel nodded, seeing for the first time that something good had come from her marriage to James. He'd given her a daughter. She smiled at Carly. "Yes, I do believe that God can bring good from any situation."

Carly looked at her as if she'd gone loco. "How could good come from us gettin' kidnapped and tied up? You know my brother will probably kill you—and maybe even me, too."

Rachel swallowed hard. "That's why we can't be here when he returns. Luke will be looking for us by now. Jacqueline would have gone to him when she couldn't find me."

At least she hoped that had happened and that Carly's brother didn't have her child.

"How can you believe in God when so many bad things happen?"

Rachel felt her ropes give way a little, and she renewed her efforts to get free. "It's a matter of choice. I choose to believe. I know God's nature from reading the Bible and listening to the preacher. He's a God of love and wants nothing more than to have His children love and worship Him."

Carly ceased her efforts and wrestled her way into a sitting position. The side of her face that had been against the floor was coated in dust. "Who gets to be God's children?"

Rachel smiled. "God wants every person on earth to become one, including you."

The young woman's eyes widened with awe, and she sat up straighter. "Me?"

"Yes, it's true. But God gives us a choice whether to serve Him or not. Sin separates us from God."

Carly ducked her head. "I've done some bad things."

"We all have."

"Not you." Carly shook her head. "You're as good a person as I ever met."

The compliment warmed Rachel's heart. "Thank you, but I'm a sinner, too. God made a way for sinners to come back to Him, though. He sent His only Son, Jesus, to earth. Jesus lived here among us, but He was the sacrificial lamb, and His death on the cross meant that we could again be one with God."

"Truly?"

Rachel nodded. "All you have to do is believe that Jesus Christ is God's Son, and ask forgiveness for your sins."

Carly's face crumpled. "My brother and I have done too many bad things. It's too late for us."

"No, it's not. As long as you're still breathing, there's hope."

"Even for bank robbers?"

Rachel held back a gasp. She knew Carly harbored secrets but never suspected that she, too, was an outlaw. She cringed at the memory of her daughter interacting with the young woman. They'd had an outlaw living in their home.

"See, even you look at me different, now that you know. I only did it because Ty said I had to. I didn't never shoot nobody." She hung her head but continued to saw at the ropes.

"I'm sorry. You just surprised me is all. But whatever you've done, God will forgive you if you ask Him—even for bank robbery."

Carly remained silent, and they both worked to free themselves. Rachel still worried about their situation but marveled that God

could have put her here—just like Queen Esther in the Bible—
for such a time as this. And if He had, He would see her safely
returned to her daughter.

She bowed her head. *Help us, Lord. Keep Jacqueline safe. Help
Carly to understand that You love her no matter what she's done.*

CHAPTER 31

Luke walked his horse toward Lookout, feeling as if a five-hundred-pound weight was pulling him down. He'd searched for hours and found no sign of Rachel. The tracks had simply disappeared when they blended with other hoof prints on the road.

The hot July afternoon sun beat on him, sending rivulets of sweat down his temple and back. He stopped and took a drink of the lukewarm water from his canteen as he studied the countryside. Not even a bird dotted the pale blue sky that reminded him so much of Rachel's eyes. He wanted to see those eyes spark with laughter. To see them darken with love for him again.

He longed to hold her close and never let her go. Why had he been so stubborn? Why hadn't he realized sooner that he was at fault?

His gaze searched the rolling hills whose green was turning to dried yellow from the heat and lack of rain. He'd been barren like that before God entered his life. He'd wasted so many years, wallowing in self-pity and a refusal to forgive. But now he had a chance to start over, if only. . .

Where was Rachel? Did she have water at hand? Was she

somewhere sweating in a stuffy, little room? Was she still alive?

No! He couldn't allow that thought to creep into his mind. To give him doubts. God wouldn't bring him home and finally remove the shroud of resentment and bitterness from his heart only to take Rachel away before he could tell her he still loved her.

"God, please. Help me find her. Give me a chance to make things up to her. To show her how much I love her." He lifted his hat and ran his hands through his sweaty hair. "Show me where she is."

～

Rachel's shoulders ached from her efforts to get free. Hours of rubbing the rope across the wood spike had yielded little. She had more movement in her hands, but they were still lashed together. Her stomach complained of the lack of food, but what she craved most, next to her freedom, was a drink of cool water—and to know Jacqueline was safe.

The hot sun beat relentlessly on the little shack, heating it to unbearable temperatures. Her hair and clothing were soaked with sweat, and she longed to close her eyes and sleep. But she had to get free before Carly's brother returned. She couldn't let herself think what would happen if she didn't.

Carly gasped. "I broke through another thread. Just a little more and I should be able to get loose."

"Oh, thank the Lord." Rachel renewed her efforts. Even if Carly got free, she wasn't sure if the young woman would release her, too, or just take off without her.

They continued sawing in silence for a while, then Carly suddenly looked up. "So you gonna tell me what happened between you and the marshal?"

Rachel blinked. She'd hope Carly wouldn't bring him up again. "That was a long time ago."

Carly shook her head and grinned. "I don't think so. I've seen the way you look at him."

"What do you mean?"

"You look like a woman in love—at least what I'd expect a woman in love to look like. Not that I've ever known any." She blushed and looked over her shoulders as if trying to see her hands.

Rachel sat back a moment. "Was it really that obvious?"

Carly shrugged. "Maybe not to everyone, but I also saw how the marshal watched you whenever the two of you were together. Me and them other brides never stood a chance. Don't know why his crazy cousins thought Marshal Davis needed help finding a wife when he was already head over heels for you."

A warmth flooded Rachel's chest before she threw a cold bucket of reality on it. "You're wrong about Luke. He may have loved me once, but no more."

A man who couldn't forgive a woman for a past hurt certainly couldn't be in love with her. Yet he'd said he was sorry. Sorry for not forgiving her? Sorry for giving her the cold shoulder? Sorry for something she didn't yet know about?

"I ain't mistaken about him, but I wanna ask you somethin' else. Were you the anonymous bride?"

Rachel knew the color on her cheeks gave her away, and she nodded. "That was foolish of me. I just didn't want to let Luke go without at least trying to win back his favor."

"Your pie was the only one worth eating. All of ours were too salty or burnt." Carly scowled. "It was a waste of time to mess with those pies."

Rachel's head jerked up, a sick feeling of regret churning in her stomach. "What do you mean?"

Carly nibbled her lower lip. "Guess it don't matter no more. When them two brides was fixin' to make their pies, I switched the salt and sugar."

A shaft of guilt speared Rachel. She'd blamed Jacqueline for that little stunt. No wonder her daughter had gotten so mad. She'd been innocent, but Rachel thought her daughter had tried to fix the contest so that she would win. She leaned her head against the chair leg and closed her eyes. *I'm sorry, sweetie.*

"I knew it was you when I saw that blue shirt. I. . .uh, saw it when you showed me all them shirts. Later I snitched the tan one from your drawer."

Rachel's eyes popped open. "You stole one of James's shirts?"

Nodding, Carly turned back toward her. "I'm right sorry for doin' that, Rachel. I just knew I'd never be able to sew nothin' that could equal what them other brides was makin'. I'd hoped to borrow it and put it back, but after the contest, all of them was gone."

Rachel felt violated. Someone living in her home had stolen from her. Granted, the shirt held no value to her, but just the thought of Carly snooping around her room gave her the shudders. Had she noticed the gun in the bottom of the drawer?

And Jacqueline had told her that one of the shirts had been stolen—but she hadn't listened. Rachel hung her head, feeling guilty for not believing her daughter. She prayed she'd get a chance to apologize.

"I know you're probably mad at me now, but if I had to do it over, I wouldn't take it."

A part of Rachel wanted to stay angry. Angry at feeling so helpless. Angry at Luke for his stubborn refusal to forgive. And angry at Carly for violating her trust.

But she knew this could be a pivotal moment for the young woman. Shoving aside her hurt, she forced herself to smile. "It was just an old shirt, Carly. I wouldn't let that affect our friendship."

Carly sniffed. "It was more than that, and you know it."

"God has forgiven me a lot. How can I not forgive you for something so small?"

Tears made Carly's eyes glisten, and she dipped her head and tried to wipe them on her shoulder. "Oh! I'll kill my brother for this. I can't even blow my nose."

Rachel winced at the harsh words.

"No, wait. That's just a figure of speech. I've never killed anyone, and I'm not gonna start with Ty, even if he deserves to be shot for what he did to us."

Rachel just hoped he didn't return and do more to them. " 'Vengeance is mine; I will repay, saith the Lord.' "

"You really believe that?"

"Yes, I do."

"I hate to think what Ty will have to suffer if that's true. He's done lots of bad things." Carly shuddered, and her face went pale. She looked at Rachel. "What will God do to me?"

This was the moment Rachel had waited for. *Give me Your words, Lord.* "God will forgive you, if you only ask Him."

She shook her head. "I ain't never killed nobody, but I've done some real bad things."

"It doesn't matter to God. If you believe that Jesus Christ is His Son and that He died on the cross for your sins, all you have to do is ask forgiveness for those sins. And then try to live a life that's pleasing to God."

"Ma took me to church when I was a young'un. I do believe that Jesus is God's Son. I just never thought much about it."

Rachel smiled. "That's wonderful. Now all you have to do is ask God to forgive you of your sins."

The young woman scowled. "It sounds too easy. Shouldn't I have to do some kind of penance?"

"No, Carly. Just tell Him you're sorry and that you want Him to come into your heart and forgive your sins."

A myriad of expressions crossed Carly's face, and then she slowly nodded. "Will you help me?"

Rachel smiled. "Of course I will."

They bowed their heads, and in a matter of seconds, the angels were rejoicing in heaven over another lost lamb that had been returned to the fold.

Jack stood at the crossroads and looked back toward town. She was too far away to see Lookout, but she knew it was only about a mile over the last hill she crossed. She'd never been this far out of town alone, and though it was an adventure of sorts, hesitation nagged at her like a pesky gnat.

Ma had always lectured her on the dangers of wandering too far from town. Besides wild animals like coyote or even a wolf, there were outlaws, and the possibility of a renegade Comanche slipping across the Red River from their reservation in Indian Territory. Jack brushed her hair from her face. Did Comanches scalp people? She swallowed hard and looked at the road to town again. If she turned and walked back that way, the road would eventually turn into Bluebonnet Lane and lead right to her front door.

But what if her ma was out there somewhere, waiting...praying for someone to save her? She looked across the open prairie. Both Ricky and Jonesy lived out that way, though she'd never been to either's home.

She was dying for a drink of water. Why hadn't she thought to take some?

If she kept walking straight, she'd eventually come to the river, but if she turned and went to one of her friend's homes, she could get a drink and maybe discover news about her ma.

One thing was for certain: She wasn't stupid enough to venture any farther from town unarmed. She tugged the gun from the bib of her overalls and removed the tin from her pocket. She opened the can and found eight bullets. Though she'd never loaded a gun before, she'd watched Luke do it several times.

She slid open the cylinder, and with a shaky hand, dropped one of the bullets into the empty hole. One by one, she filled each slot and then snapped the cylinder in place. With the tin back in her pocket, she lifted her chin and walked away from town. The gun weighed heavy in her hand, but with it loaded, she was afraid to put it back in her overalls. Besides, if she needed the weapon, she wanted it to be handy.

Her feet ate up the dry ground, and the heat from the sun made the top of her head hot. Ma would berate her for not wearing a bonnet, but she could hardly do that when she was wearing overalls. What she needed was a decent felt hat like her friends wore.

As she topped the next rise, a small, white house rested in the distance. Two people walked her way, both carrying fishing poles. Jack's heart jumped. Ricky and Jonesy. She jogged toward them, but as she drew close, both boys' eyes widened and stared at the gun.

"Who you gonna shoot?" Ricky asked.

"Not us, I hope." Jonesy laughed, but it sounded forced.

"Am I ever glad to see you." Relief washed through Jack, giving her energy that the sun had threatened to drive away. "My ma is missing. Nobody's seen her since last night."

"Whoa! What happened to her?" Ricky's blue eyes glistened with curiosity.

"Why are you way out here?" Jonesy asked.

"Luke found some tracks behind our house. I was following them, but I lost them somehow."

"The marshal let you come clear out here alone?"

Jack shrugged. "He don't know I'm here. He told me to stay at home with those two brides, but they were cooking up a storm in Ma's kitchen. I couldn't stay. I have to find her."

Jonesy took his pole off his shoulder and leaned on it. "What makes you thinks she's out here?"

"The tracks headed out of town in this direction, but before long, they got mixed with the other prints on the road. I just kept walking, hoping I'd find her."

Ricky looked around then refocused on Jack. "Why would she be out here?"

Jack stomped her foot, and tears stung her eyes. "Aren't you listening? I told you someone took her. I saw a man last night in Miss Blackstone's room, and I told Ma, but she didn't believe me. When I got up this morning, I noticed Ma had never been to bed.

And Miss Blackstone was missing, too."

"Maybe that bride took her." Jonesy offered.

"But why?"

"Well, you said Luke liked your ma's pie best. Maybe she decided to get rid of the competition."

Jack hadn't considered that angle. "But how would she know Ma was the anonymous bride?" She narrowed her gaze and scowled at her friends. "You didn't tell anyone, did you?"

Both boys shook their heads and eyed the gun again as if they thought she might shoot them if they had. Jack nearly laughed at their comical expressions, but she wasn't in a laughing mood.

"Is that thing loaded?" Ricky lifted his hat and raked lines with his fingers in his white-blond hair.

"What good would it do me if it wasn't?" Jack wasn't about to tell them that she'd just loaded the gun.

"You even know how to shoot it?"

Jack shrugged. "Just point and pull the trigger. How hard can it be?"

Her friends glanced at each other, and their brows lifted. Ricky turned back to her and held out his hand. "Maybe you'd better give that to me. I wouldn't want you to get hurt—or uh, shoot one of us by accident."

Jack backed up two steps and held the gun against her chest. "But I need it to find Ma."

Ricky shook his head and handed his fishing pole to Jonesy. "No, you don't. Give it to me, and we'll help you search for your ma."

Tears sprouted in her eyes. "You will? Truly?"

Both of her friends nodded. Ricky stepped forward, hand held out in front of him. "C'mon. Gimme that gun. You're too young to be messing with it."

Jack glanced down at the heavy black weapon. Truth be told, the gun made her nervous. She handed it over to her friend. "But I gotta get that back and hide it before Ma finds out I took it."

Ricky quickly unloaded the gun and put the bullets in his

pocket. He shoved the revolver into the waistband of his pants and crossed his arms. "Now, start at the beginning. When did you last see your ma?"

Jack related the story to them. "I think Ma must have gone upstairs to check Miss Blackstone's room, and the man must've taken her prisoner."

"Why would he do that?" Jonesy asked.

Jack flung her arms up. "I don't know." She told them about the key and unlocked door and Luke finding the trail. "So I followed the prints."

"Hey!" Jonesy shoved Ricky in the arm, receiving a glare from the taller boy. "I just remembered something. The other evening I went out in the far pasture to bring in the cows for milking. You know that old shack we used to play in?"

Ricky nodded. "Yeah, so what?"

"I saw a stranger go into it, that's what. I meant to tell my pa but got busy milking and forgot until just now. And guess what else. He had two horses."

Ricky's eyes lit up at the same time hope sparked within Jack. "Maybe that's where he put Ma and that bride."

"Yeah, let's go check it out." Ricky spun around, his hand resting on the gun handle.

"Wait! Someone needs to go tell Luke about this," Jack said.

Ricky faced her again. "That's probably a good idea. You go."

Jack shoved her hands to her hips and glared at her friend. "I'm not going. It's my ma that's missing."

"I guess that makes sense," said Ricky. "But you'll have to be quiet and do what I tell you."

Jack nodded. Ricky was only a few years older than her, but he was bigger—and he was smart, for a boy.

"Then you need to go to town and fetch the marshal, Jonesy."

Their friend scowled. "I'm the one who saw the stranger. I should get to go."

"I'll let you have the pick of any of my commies if you'll do it." Ricky reached into his pocket and pulled out several clay marbles.

Jonesy's eyes widened. "You will?"

Ricky nodded, though his face looked pinched. His collection of marbles was his most treasured possession. Jack knew he was sacrificing one for her, and that meant a lot, considering how little money his family had.

"All right, I'll go to town and tell the marshal, but I'm coming right back, so wait on me before you do anything. And I'm not taking these fishin' poles." He dropped them to the ground and took off running toward town.

Ricky snatched up the rods. "C'mon. Let's run these back to my house, get some water, and go check out that cabin. Maybe we'll get lucky and find your ma."

Jack walked alongside her friend. Her ma had said both boys were too old for her to hang around with, but they'd always watched out for her and treated her like a sister. Maybe if the boys helped her find Ma, then her mother would allow her to spend more time with them. At least she could hope.

She followed Ricky back to his house, noting peeling paint and how it leaned to the right. A skinny brown and white hound dog lay with its nose hanging off the end of the rickety porch. She never knew Ricky had a dog. Ricky's pa was known to drink a lot and spend too much time at the saloon. Suddenly, she realized the sacrifice her friend was making for her by giving up one of his treasures. He didn't have many nice things in his life.

She hoped he didn't get hurt. Hoped they didn't have to use that gun. Her gaze darted upward at the pale blue sky.

Please, Lord, help us find my ma. Let her be all right. I'm sorry for not being a very good kid, and I promise to do better—if only You help us find her.

CHAPTER 32

Luke stared out over the town, itching to get back out there and look for Rachel. Mark had gone to Polly's to fetch them some dinner, and if it wasn't for the fact that Luke hadn't eaten since yesterday, he'd be out searching right now. Mark had talked him into taking a short break to see if any of the townsfolk had found Rachel.

They hadn't.

Luke's hand tightened around the porch railing. What was the point of being marshal if he couldn't protect the woman he loved? Where could she be? Was she injured?

He knew Rachel would be worried about Jack. His gaze flitted to the boardinghouse. Was the kid at home, or had she gone out somewhere with her friends? He was half afraid those two older boys were going to get her into serious trouble one day. Thankfully, he hadn't seen much of them since school had ended for the summer.

"You ready to eat?" Mark walked past the stage office and stopped in front of Luke, carrying two plates of steaming food.

Luke started to shake his head, thinking he couldn't eat while

Rachel was in danger, but then he caught a whiff of the beef stew and saw the golden corn bread Mark carried. His stomach let him know refusal wasn't an option. Besides, he needed to keep his strength up so he could keep searching.

Mark set the plates on Luke's desk. "What will you do if you don't find her by dark?"

Luke poured them both a cup of fresh coffee he'd just brewed. The inside of the jail was sweltering from the stove, but a man couldn't function without his coffee. "I'll keep looking."

Mark's blond brows lifted as he buttered his corn bread. "In the dark?"

Luke shrugged. "I don't know." He shoved a bite of stew in his mouth, but it tasted like paper. He shoveled in just enough food to keep him going.

"Look, you'd help Rachel better by getting some rest and being fresh in the morning. If you're overly tired, you might miss something."

Luke ran his hand across his bristly jaw and shoved the bowl toward the middle of the desk. "I know, but I can't stand the thought of her being out there, maybe hurt. Maybe alone."

"Yeah, I know."

Luke stared intently into his cousin's eyes. "No, you don't. I still love her. I want us to have a second chance."

Mark's brow rose nearly to his hairline. "Just when did you figure all that out?"

Luke fought a shy grin tugging at his mouth and lost the battle. "Last night. I realized I harbored an unforgiving spirit toward her when what happened was my own fault."

"How you figure that?" Mark shoved a corner of corn bread into his mouth.

Luke explained how he was responsible for James's attack on Rachel. Mark leaned back in his chair and shook his head. "You're not at fault for what James did."

"But I'm the one who sent him to meet her."

Mark frowned and shook his head. "Doesn't matter. Only James is responsible for what he did."

Luke slammed the desk. "No, it's my fault. I should have gone and met her myself. It would have only taken fifteen or twenty minutes. But no, I had work to do."

"You were trying to make money for a home so you and Rachel could get married."

Luke leaned his face into his hands. "None of that matters now. I need to get out and search while it's still daylight."

Quick footsteps sounded on the boardwalk, and one of Jack's friends skidded to a stop at Luke's door. He stood, and the boy leaned his hands on his thighs, head hanging down, and sucked in air like a suffocating man.

"What's going on? Did you find something?"

The boy held up his hand, chest heaving. "Water."

Luke glanced around the office then handed the boy his coffee. The kid took a big gulp and then spewed it out, all over Luke's floor. "That's hot! I said water."

Mark jumped up, rushed outside to the hitching post where his horse was tied, and yanked the canteen off his saddle. He leaped up the stairs and shoved it at the boy. The kid gulped down several swigs then drew his sleeve across his mouth. Several of the townsfolk who must have seen him running were gathering outside Luke's office.

Luke took hold of the boy's shoulders. "Take several deep breaths."

He did as ordered. "I saw a stranger. . .at an old shed. . .on our property. . .two days ago."

"So?"

"Jack told me and Ricky. . .about some man taking her ma, and they've gone. . .to see if she's there."

Luke tensed. If the man who kidnapped Rachel and Miss Blackstone was at that shack with them, Jack and her friend could be in danger. He tightened his grasp. "Where is this shed?"

"A mile or so past my house. Southwest of town. I can show you."

Luke glanced at Mark. "C'mon, this might be the break we've been waiting for."

Both men grabbed their rifles and followed the boy out the door. The crowd parted and let them pass. Luke touched the kid's shoulder. "You're that Jones boy, aren't you?"

"Clarence Jones, sir. But most folks just call me Jonesy."

Luke nodded and mounted Alamo. "Put your foot in the stirrup, and I'll pull you up."

Jonesy attempted to do as Luke ordered, but the boy was too exhausted to get his foot up high enough. Mark dismounted and boosted Jonesy up behind Luke.

"You got some news, Marshal?" Dan Howard, the broad-shouldered livery owner asked.

"Maybe. This boy thinks he knows where a stranger's been holing up."

"You want some of us to come?"

Luke shook his head. "No, I need y'all to keep searching closer to town. This might be a dead end, and I don't want all our eggs in one basket."

Dan nodded.

Luke reined Alamo around. "Hold on tight."

He kicked his horse, and in seconds, they were on a dead run down Main Street. The boy nearly swerved off as Luke turned Alamo down Bluebonnet Lane and headed out of town, his hope building for the first time that day.

Please, Lord. Let me find Rachel at that shed. And let her be safe.

Rachel felt as if she were falling down a deep well, and she jumped. The tiny cabin came into focus as she awakened. Her mouth was as dry as if she'd been sucking cotton, and her head ached. If only she could have a drink.

Carly had also fallen asleep. The heat from the cabin had wilted them both like summer flowers in a drought. Occasionally a hot breeze blew through the holes where the window panes once rested, but that did nothing to cool the room. At least the sun was no longer overhead and was making its western plunge toward sunset. Nighttime would bring cooler temperatures, but she dreaded it. How long could they survive without water?

She tried to work up enough saliva to dampen her mouth and started sawing again. "Carly. Miss Payton. Wake up." She kicked the table leg, and it screeched across the floor, making the young woman stir.

"Did I fall asleep? Oh, ow. My shoulders are killing me."

Rachel didn't voice that hers were, too. "We need to keep working. I don't know where your brother went or why he's been gone so long, but we've got to get free before he returns."

"Maybe he just left us here to die."

Rachel shook her head. "Don't think that—and even if he did, that's not going to happen."

The dullness in Carly's eyes disappeared all of a sudden, and then she winced. "I've nearly sawed through the rope. But I keep cutting my fingers and dropping the glass."

"I'm sorry. Just do your best. I'm not having much luck here. I broke off the point on the chair leg, so now there's nothing sharp to cut my bindings."

Carly looked to be sawing with renewed vigor. She worked hard for a few minutes; then she turned her head to face Rachel. Something she'd said earlier was grating on Rachel.

"Did you tell me that there was a fourth shirt entered in the bride contest?"

Carly blinked and stared at her. "You mean you didn't enter it?"

Rachel shook her head. "No. I decided that if Luke wasn't willing to forgive me for how I wronged him in the past, there was no chance he'd want me for a wife, so I didn't enter the second contest."

Carly rocked back and forth. "That's strange. There was four entries. If you didn't enter, then who else could've? I'm certain that blue shirt was the same one you kept in your drawer."

Rachel pursed her lips as the truth dawned. "It was Jacqueline. She argued up one side of the wall and down the other, wanting me to enter that contest. I told her I wouldn't, so she must have taken the shirt and entered it without anyone knowing." Rachel shook her head at her wily daughter.

Carly smiled a sad smile. "The mayor said that's the one the marshal liked best. I bet you don't get it back—oh!"

The young woman's shoulders heaved violently, and Rachel's heart jumped. Was the heat getting to her?

Suddenly, she pulled her hands in front of her and started rubbing her shoulders. "Look, my hands are free!"

After some finagling, Carly managed to untie her ankles and staggered to her feet. Rachel noticed that both of Carly's hands and wrists were covered in blood. "Oh, your poor hands."

Carly held them up and grinned as if they were a badge of honor. She turned and looked around on the floor, stooped, then plodded toward Rachel. "Now we just gotta get you untied."

"Maybe we should just get out of here and worry about that later."

"You cain't run with your ankles bound together." Carly shook her head, shoved the battered chair away, and squatted behind Rachel.

"I'm worried about your hands."

"They'll heal."

Carly worked for several minutes, and then Rachel felt the ropes loosen, and the tension in her shoulders released just a smidgeon. Suddenly, the ropes broke. Carefully, she swung her arms forward and rolled her shoulders. "My, but that feels good."

Rachel made quick work of freeing her feet and stood on wobbly legs. "We'd best get out of here while we can. Did your

324

brother leave any water?" She searched the small room as Carly headed for the door.

Suddenly, Carly froze. "I hear voices. Quick. Lie back down on the cot and pretend you're still tied up."

Her frantic gaze made Rachel's heart ricochet in her chest. Had they worked so hard only to have Ty Payton return now?

Rachel didn't take time to question her but did as ordered. The putrid scents of the thin mattress almost made her retch, but with no food or water for a full day, Rachel managed to keep from gagging. Reluctantly, she forced her hands behind her still aching shoulders and lay down. Carly seemed to be searching the room for something. She snatched up a leg that had come off the chair and squeezed in the small space behind the door with the weapon over her head.

Rachel held her breath, praying that Ty Payton hadn't returned. Tears threatened, but she blinked them back. She wanted to be ready if Carly needed her help.

A shadow passed by the window, and then a face appeared. Jacqueline?

Were her eyes playing tricks?

And there was Ricky's blessed face.

Rachel bolted up off the cot so fast, her head swam. Carly spun toward her, looking at her as if she were having a conniption.

"Ma?" Jacqueline squealed.

Carly lowered her club, and Rachel yanked the door open. Jacqueline charged in, nearly bowling her over. She grabbed her daughter and clung to her.

"Ma, I prayed we'd find you. I thought I'd never see you again."

Jacqueline's tears wet the front of Rachel's dress, and tears of her own streamed down her face. Suddenly, her relief was overpowered by the reality that her daughter was far from home. "Just what in the world are you doing out here?"

"You smell awful." Jacqueline pulled away, hurt darkening her eyes. "We were looking for you. Jonesy remembered seeing a stranger at this cabin two days ago and thought we should investigate it."

"Oh! I could just blister your backside, but I'm so happy to see you."

Ricky entered the cabin, looking shy. He held up a canteen. "Anybody need some water?"

Rachel held Jacqueline close again while Carly drank. Then the woman passed the canteen, and Rachel savored the lukewarm water, gulping it down.

"I don't wanna spoil this family reunion, but it won't be so happy if my brother returns before we get away." Carly pressed her lips together, looking like a no-nonsense schoolmarm.

"She's right. We need to leave. Now."

"Maybe it'd be better if we all went to my house," Ricky said. "There's not much cover along the road, and if'n that stranger returns, we could be in big trouble, even though I do have a gun." He pulled out James's old pistol, and Rachel gasped. She turned a stern glare on her daughter.

Jacqueline ducked her head and then smiled. "Well, you did say a woman should never go far from town unarmed. I was just obeyin' you, Ma."

Rachel grinned at her incorrigible daughter and looped her arm around her. "I'm sure that's not exactly what I said, but we'll talk about it when we get home."

Ricky led the way, keeping them in the tree line as much as possible. They passed what he said was the Jones farm and continued across a field to a farmhouse in the distance. All of a sudden, they heard horses' hooves pounding down the lane. With no trees for cover, they bunched together. Rachel shoved Jacqueline behind her, and tried to put on a brave front. It had been one thing to face an outlaw knowing her daughter was safe in her bed, but another thing altogether when her child was in danger.

"Give me that gun, boy." Carly faced Ricky, but the kid stepped back.

Ricky shook his head. "I'll protect us."

Carly stomped toward him and yanked the gun free of his grasp. She winced but held the weapon in spite of her injured hands.

"You'd shoot your own brother?" Rachel asked.

"I don't wanna, but I will if it means saving you and the kids. Get down." They squatted in the thigh-high grass.

"She's gonna have to load it if she hopes to shoot anyone." Ricky reached into his pocket and yanked out the bullets.

Carly quickly loaded the weapon and ducked down, turned toward the road, and held the gun outward.

Rachel hoped in the waning light of dusk that the riders might pass on by and not see them in the field. She held her breath and kept an arm around her daughter. "Please, Lord, make us invisible."

Two horses rounded the wide bend in the road at full-gallop. Rachel studied their silhouettes as the setting sun illuminated them. She couldn't make out their faces, but she recognized the lead rider and bolted up.

"Get down." Carly waved her hand behind her.

Rachel cupped her hand around her mouth and yelled, "Luke!"

Jacqueline jumped up and took off running, waving her hand. "Luke, over here."

Rachel jogged past Carly, half worried that she'd accidentally shoot Jacqueline. Her heart soared with relief to see Luke. He would protect them from the outlaw. *Thank You, Lord!*

Luke reined his horse to a stop so fast that it nearly sat down. Someone riding behind Luke flailed his arms and rolled off onto the ground. The second rider's horse jumped him and skidded to a halt. Luke vaulted to the ground and ran to Jacqueline.

"What are you doing out here? I told you to stay home."

Rachel could see the white of her daughter's teeth as she smiled. "I found Ma."

"Yeah, and you could have gotten hurt." Luke hugged Jacqueline and then stooped down and kissed her cheek.

Rachel slowed her steps. She was thrilled to see Luke, but he might not feel the same way. Oh, he'd be happy to find her safe—

Luke's gaze captured hers, and all thoughts ceased. He set Jacqueline aside, tweaked her nose, and strode toward Rachel, his eyes smoldering. Her heart leapt at the intensity of his gaze. He stopped and placed his hands on her shoulders, looking both sorry and relieved. "Are you hurt?"

She shook her head, barely able to breathe. Afraid to allow hope to take wing.

"I'm so sorry, Rach. Sorry for not forgiving you. It was all my fault."

"This wasn't your fault. Carly's brother is the one who kidnapped us."

"That's not what I meant." Luke's brow wrinkled. "Who's Carly?"

Rachel peered over her shoulder. Mark stood next to Carly, relieving her of the gun. Rachel heaved a sigh. "It's a long story, and we're starving and exhausted. Can it wait until we get back home?"

Luke pressed his lips together and nodded. "Rachel, there's so much I need to say. I—"

Fast approaching hoofbeats silenced whatever he'd been about to tell her. He shoved Rachel behind him. "Jack, hit the dirt!"

Rachel tried to see past Luke to find her daughter in the twilight, but all that caught her eye was a lightning bug. Her heart choked. Jacqueline was between Luke and the road.

Luke shoved Rachel down. "Stay here." He strode forward, gun in hand.

Had they been rescued, only to be caught again? Rachel shook her head and prayed hard.

A rider rounded the bend, and Luke shouted out. "Stop where you are, or I'll shoot."

The horse pulled up, snorted at the quick stop, and pranced in circles. "Luke? That you?"

Relief surrounded Rachel like the growing darkness as she recognized Garrett's voice.

"Yeah, I'm sure glad it's you, cuz," Luke said.

"Well you won't be glad when you hear my news. The bank's been robbed."

CHAPTER 33

Though anxious to get back to town and check things out, Luke rode back into Lookout at a slower pace than when he'd been searching for Rachel. He wouldn't risk injuring his horse by galloping in the dark. Besides, Garrett had explained that the outlaw was secure in Luke's jail with Dan Howard keeping watch.

He hated leaving Rachel, but his cousins would see her, Miss Blackstone, and Jack home safely. The two boys were close enough to their homes to walk, so all Luke needed to concentrate on was the robbery.

But his rebellious mind kept wandering back to Rachel. She was filthy and exhausted, but was that hope he'd seen in her eyes? Did he dare think she felt something more than friendship toward him after the way he'd treated her?

He'd been such a fool.

There was so much more he wanted to say to her, but that would have to wait.

The lights of town glimmered in the black night. He rode into Lookout a few minutes later and headed straight for the bank. The lights were on. Was Ray Castleby still there, or had he decided to go home and left a lantern burning to discourage others tempted to relieve the bank of its funds?

Luke dismounted, secured his horse, and then knocked on the bank door. "Ray, it's me, Luke. You in there?"

He heard the jingle of keys; then the lock clicked and the door opened. Ray Castleby looked more haggard than Luke had ever seen him. Luke studied the serene bank. The wood shone even in the flickering light of the lanterns, and the room smelled of beeswax with the faint hint of gunpowder. One of the floor planks contained a splintered hole where a bullet had been fired into it.

"I'm sure glad to see you, Marshal. Though all the excitement's over now, I still can't quit shaking." Ray motioned him to come in. The thin man's clothing was rumpled, and one sleeve had blood on it. Ray pushed his wire-rimmed glasses up his pointy nose.

"Did you get hurt?" Luke pointed at the banker's sleeve.

Ray glanced down and stared at the spot that blemished his snow white shirt. His hand trembled as he reached toward the stain. "Uh. . .not my blood. Belongs to that thief."

Ray was a high-strung man who looked to be on his last leg. The robbery attempt must have really shaken him up. "Let's have a seat, and then tell me what happened."

Nodding, Ray moseyed back to his office, and Luke followed. Ray owned the biggest desk in town, even larger than Mayor Burke's. The dark wood gleamed under the fancy lamp. Papers were stacked in neat piles. A picture of an English foxhunt covered a large portion of the wall behind the banker. Luke couldn't help staring. He'd never had reason to visit Ray's office and now stared at the largest painting he'd ever seen, with the exception of one he'd glimpsed in a saloon in Wyoming.

"I was closed, and Gerald, my clerk, had gone home."

Luke forced his attention away from the picture to what Ray was saying.

"I wanted to finish up some paperwork for a local rancher, so I was working late." He rambled on about the robber knocking then shoving his way in when Ray answered.

Luke's mind drifted back to Rachel. He wanted to see her again. To make certain she was all right and unharmed.

The banker chuckled and shook his head, and Luke realized he'd missed something.

"Uh. . .would you repeat that?" he asked

"I wouldn't have believed it myself if I hadn't witnessed it. Bertha Boyd came in the door right on the heels of that thief. At first, I thought she was another gang member. The robber swung around to face her, and she smacked him on the arm with that new cane she's been using, causing him to drop his gun. He picked it up, and Bertha plumb knocked him on the temple with another swipe of her walking stick. The gun fired, and I guess either the bullet or a wood splinter cut the thief's arm. The man collapsed at Bertha's feet, but she didn't pay him any mind. She just looked at me and said my clerk had short-changed her when she took out some cash earlier."

Ray leaned back in his chair, hands on his belly. "I've never been so happy to see that gabby woman in my whole life. I didn't even question her about the error but took the money right out of my own pocket and paid her. She might well have saved my life."

Luke grinned at the thought of the large woman foiling a bank robbery. Jenny Evans would sure have some news to post in her paper this week. "So you didn't lose any money?"

"No, we never got more than five feet from the door. It's nothing short of a miracle."

Luke stood, anxious to check on his prisoner. "God works in mysterious ways."

Ray let out a belly laugh. "That he does."

As he entered the jailhouse moments later, Luke nodded at Dan Howard sitting behind the desk, reading an old Dallas newspaper. Max lay on his blanket in the corner and didn't even lift his head.

Luke walked past the livery owner to the two cells at the back of the jailhouse and stood eye-to-eye with the prisoner. Something seemed vaguely familiar about the man leaning against the cell wall. His dark hair was greasy, and several days' whiskers covered his square jaw. Piercing blue eyes studied Luke, as if taking his measure. Cleaned up, Luke suspected most women would find him handsome. He glanced at the man's bandaged arm. "Guess the doc took care of that, huh?"

The prisoner shrugged one shoulder. Luke spun around and marched back to his desk. Dan stood and stepped away, as if he felt guilty for sitting in Luke's chair.

"Thanks for jailing the robber and watching him for me."

Luke bent and tugged on the middle drawer as a thought raced through his mind. He yanked out his stack of wanted posters and thumbed through them. He looked at a half dozen before he found the one he wanted. A slow grin tugged at his mouth as he stared at the likeness of his prisoner. Ty Payton, leader of the Payton Gang that had terrorized southwestern Missouri. He handed the poster to Dan.

He took it and then let out a low whistle. "That's him all right. Imagine, a real wanted outlaw in our little town." He shook his head. "What's this world comin' to?"

Luke peeked at the man he suspected was Ty Payton again. The prisoner had slumped down on the small cot and placed one arm over his eyes. Luke stared at him. What had brought the man from his normal hunting grounds in Missouri to Texas? And where was the rest of his gang? "Payton?"

The man lifted his arm and glanced at Luke.

"You Tyson Payton?"

"Maybe." He lowered his head and turned to face the wall, but not before Luke saw a smirk tug at the corner of his mouth.

He was Payton, all right. Luke read the information about the gang on the poster. Payton normally traveled with two other men and sometimes a woman. It was suspected that the woman was

Carly Payton, Tyson's sister.

The hairs on the back of Luke's neck stood on end, and his gut swirled with uneasiness. Where had he heard that name before?

Dan stood beside Luke's desk with his hat in his hand. "Marshal, there's a woman at the boardinghouse who came in on the evening stage while you were gone. You're gonna wanna talk to her."

Exhaustion made Luke's brain foggy. He needed to head to bed, but instead, he had a long night ahead sleeping in his jail and keeping watch on his prisoner. Part of the man's gang might still be around and plan to break him out of jail. "Can't it wait?"

Shaking his head, Dan rolled up the edge of his felt hat. "I don't think so. You probably should head on down there while I'm still here."

Luke sighed and strode out the door. He couldn't imagine what could be so important that it couldn't wait until morning. But at least he'd get to see Rachel again.

He thought about the outlaw's sister—Carly Payton. Suddenly, he stopped in the middle of the road. Rachel had said something about someone named Carly. As unusual as that name was, she had to be Payton's sister.

Luke broke into a run and charged toward the boardinghouse. His heart thundered. Was Rachel in danger again?

❧

Rachel thanked the Corbett brothers for helping them to get home and entered the house. She glanced around as if seeing everything for the first time. It looked so wonderful. Miss Bennett and Miss O'Neil both sat in the parlor and jumped up as they entered.

" 'Tis wonderful to have you all home again." Miss O'Neil hugged Rachel, then Carly and Jacqueline.

"Yes, we were so worried about you." Miss Bennett cast an odd look at Carly. "We. . .uh. . .kept some food warm for you, if you're hungry, that is."

"We're starving!" Jacqueline squeezed past them and made a beeline for the kitchen.

"Don't forget to wash up first." Rachel said.

Jacqueline tossed a scowl over her shoulder, but suddenly her expression changed. "Yes Ma."

Rachel looked into the surprised eyes of the other women. Maybe her being kidnapped had made her daughter thankful enough for her return that she'd be more obedient. She could hope so, at least.

"I'm so happy that you're all right." Miss Bennett hurried forward and hugged Rachel. She released her and looked at the floor, her hands wringing in front of her. "I owe you and the other ladies an apology. I've been so worried about what would happen to me if I lost the competition that I haven't been very nice." She looked up at Rachel and then glanced at Shannon and Carly. "I'm sorry. I would like for us to be friends, no matter how the contest ends."

Shannon's green eyes lit up. "Aye, I would like that. I have felt the same way, and I, too, want to apologize."

"I'm sorry, too, if I was mean to ya." Carly pressed her lips together.

Rachel stepped forward and embraced all three women. "Everything's forgiven, and maybe we could drop the formalities and call each other by our given names."

The women nodded and wiped their damp eyes. Everyone smiled, and the tension that had been there earlier left the room. Rachel muttered a silent prayer of thanks to the Lord.

A door opened upstairs, setting Rachel's heart pounding. Garrett had said they'd captured the bank robber, but she didn't know if he was the same man who'd kidnapped her. A young woman with her arm in a sling appeared at the top of the stairs, followed by a man. Rachel saw the woman's gaze move past her and her expression change to a scowl. Turning slightly to look behind her, Rachel realized the woman was staring at Carly.

"Um. . .I hope you don't mind that I gave these folks two of your rooms. They came in on the late stage today. I didn't want to turn them away since there's no other decent place for them to stay in this town." Leah Bennett wrung her hands as if fearing Rachel would be upset. "I didn't take any money, but I told them they could square things with you when you returned."

Rachel smiled to ease the young woman's discomfort. "Thank you. I appreciate that."

Leah smiled and nodded, looking relieved. "If you don't mind, I think I'll head on to bed."

"Good night, then, and thank you for saving us some food."

"I shall go also. We did feed the new guests." Shannon brushed past Rachel and stepped up the stairs.

After the two women ascended the stairs, the man helped the injured woman down. They looked enough alike to be siblings, with their dark hair and matching blue eyes. Carly shuffled beside Rachel, seeming restless. Did she know the new boarders?

Stepping forward, she smiled. "I'm Rachel Hamilton, owner of Hamilton House. Welcome, and I hope you will forgive my appearance. We've just been through a trying ordeal."

The man nodded. "I'm John Blackstone, and this is my sister, Ellie Blackstone."

Rachel felt her eyes widen and turned to face Carly. She stood with her head down, but she saw Rachel looking at her and gave a slight nod.

So this was the woman Carly had impersonated. "I'm glad to see you're doing so well, Miss Blackstone."

The man's eyes narrowed. "What do you know of her troubles?"

"Not much, I can assure you, and what I do know, I just learned about today. I'm sure the two women who just went upstairs told you what happened to us."

When he shook his head, Rachel sighed. "Could we all sit down in the parlor, please? We've had an extraordinary day."

"Does this have something to do with that blond woman asking me if we had family staying here already?"

Rachel offered him a smile. "It's complicated."

Miss Blackstone shook her head. "I'm not getting any closer to *her*." She pointed at Carly. "What's she doing here anyway? And why is she wearing *my* dress?"

Carly stepped forward, looking twice her age. Her shoulders were slumped and her head hung down. "I came here pretending to be you."

The real Miss Blackstone gasped and moved back. "See, John, I bet she's the one who stole my satchel."

"I'm sorry for that. I thought you were dead."

The front door flew open, banging against the wall, and everybody in the entryway jumped. Rachel's heart stampeded as Luke charged inside. His gaze pinned on Carly, and he pulled his gun. Carly shrank back.

Jacqueline raced in from the kitchen, her napkin tucked into the neck of her shirt. "What's goin' on?"

"Carly Payton, you're under arrest."

Rachel gasped, as did the Blackstones. Carly's eyes looked like a trapped mustang's. "Luke, surely this isn't necessary."

His gaze darted to her and back to Carly. "Did you know you were harboring a criminal?"

Rachel shook her head. "Not until today. Carly told me everything while we were. . ." She glanced at the Blackstones. "While we were tied up. And she gave her heart to God."

"She's still a wanted outlaw. I can't ignore that, Rachel."

She stepped forward and laid her hand on his arm, pushing slightly, until he lowered the gun. "She's not going anywhere. Let us get cleaned up and eat something. Neither of us has eaten since last night's supper."

Carly stepped forward, twisting her hands. "I'll go with you peacefully, Marshal. But I would appreciate the chance to clean up and eat first."

A myriad of expressions crossed Luke's face before he finally relaxed. "All right. But you're not leaving my sight."

Rachel sucked in a breath. "That's hardly appropriate, Luke. I'll stay with her while she cleans up, and you can wait for us in the kitchen."

A muscle in Luke's jaw ticked. "I don't want you or anyone else getting hurt, Rach."

"Carly is a believer now. She's not going to hurt anyone."

John Blackstone stepped forward. "This woman has been impersonating my sister. She stole from her and left her for dead after a stage robbery. I demand justice."

"I thought she *was* dead. If I'd known she was still alive, I'd have done different." Carly ducked her head again under John Blackstone's glare. "Her belongings are upstairs."

Luke studied the group then turned to the Blackstones. "I can assure you that Miss Payton is under arrest. She and Mrs. Hamilton have been through an ordeal today, and I'm going to let them do as they requested. Then Miss Payton will be taken to jail."

Mr. Blackstone observed them for a moment then nodded his head. He turned and motioned for his sister to go back upstairs.

"I'll need to get a statement from you both tomorrow. I can come here if you'd rather not come to the jail."

Mr. Blackstone nodded. "Here would be good. As you can see, my sister is still convalescing."

"I'll come by tomorrow morning, then, after breakfast." Luke turned to face Rachel. "Do your cleaning and eating quickly. Dan Howard's watching the jail for me, and I need to get back."

Jacqueline stepped forward and grabbed Luke's hand. "C'mon in the kitchen with me. There's food and hot coffee."

Rachel marveled at how Luke allowed her daughter to boss him around. He followed Jacqueline into the kitchen, and chairs scraped across the floor. She escorted Carly to the washroom downstairs, her heart aching for the young woman. "I'm sorry about all this."

"It ain't your fault. I only pretended to be Miss Blackstone 'cause I truly thought she was dead. I thought if'n I got away from my brother, I might could start a new life."

Rachel cringed at the thought of Luke marrying an outlaw, even though she didn't think Carly was hardened like her brother. She feared what would become of Carly and her fledgling faith. The young woman had admitted taking part in several bank and train robberies. Rachel hated the thought of the young woman locked up in jail, but she would have to pay for her crimes. Though that was the right thing, Rachel wanted mercy for her. Hadn't Carly repented of her sins? She was a new person now and needed to grow in the Lord and put her old life behind her, but how would she do that in prison? *I'll do whatever I can to help her, Lord. Protect Carly, and help her through the difficult days ahead. And help me to be a better mother to Jacqueline.*

One thing she'd decided while being held captive, if Jacqueline didn't have better guidance and more consequences for her bad behavior, she could well turn out like Carly had. As much as she disliked disciplining her child, Rachel knew it was God's will.

Give me the strength I need, Lord, to be a good mother.

CHAPTER 34

Saturday afternoon, Luke paced from the parlor of his small house to the foot of his bed. Was he doing the right thing?

If everything went as he hoped, he would be making the most creative marriage proposal he could imagine; but if things went the other way...

A hard knock sounded on his front door. He crossed the small room and yanked the door open.

"It's time," said Mayor Burke. "You ready?"

Luke shrugged, making the mayor scowl.

"Half the county has come to town. Women are selling food, baked goods, and lemonade, coffee, and tea to make money for the church. You're not thinking of backing out, are you?" The mayor shoved his hand to his hips and glared at Luke. "Why, this bride contest has been the biggest thing to hit this town in months. Everyone's speculating on which of the remaining two boardinghouse brides you'll pick." Mayor Burke chuckled. "There's even a few folks holding out for you to marry that outlaw bride you hauled off to Dallas."

Luke sighed and shook his head. "I can assure you that won't happen."

Why had he ever agreed to marry like he had? He didn't normally allow people to ramrod him into doing things. Romancing and wedding proposals were supposed to be done in private between two people in love and not made some public spectacle. But he'd given his word. And he'd prayed and prayed and still felt his plan was God's will. He only hoped Jack followed through on her end, or he'd be in big trouble.

He grabbed his hat from the peg near the door. "All right. I'm ready."

"Good. I'm glad to see you've come to your senses."

Luke shook his head and closed the door. If anything, he'd taken total leave of his senses.

❧

"I'm not going." Rachel sat on the end of her bed, wringing the edge of her apron in one hand.

Jacqueline tugged on her arm. "But you hav'ta go, Ma."

She shook her head, trying hard to fight the tears threatening at the thought of Luke marrying Leah or Shannon. Yes, things seemed better between her and Luke, but she hadn't seen him for three days, not since the evening he arrested Carly. She didn't even get to tell the young woman good-bye.

No, she couldn't attend today's activities. She still had boarders to care for, although there might be one less by evening. Her chin wobbled. She had no idea which woman he'd choose, and she could not watch.

"But Ma, I think the brides need you to be there."

Rachel winced. One of her guests would be the loser today, and she would need comforting and encouragement. Both brides had everything riding on their hopes to marry Luke. The one not chosen would be devastated. Sighing, Rachel untied her apron and stood. Attending the bride announcement would be one of the hardest things she'd ever done, but she owed it to her guests. And she needed to be a good example to Jacqueline. She would congratulate Luke and his chosen bride and comfort the loser. But who would comfort her?

Jacqueline yanked on her arm. "Hurry, Ma. We don't want to miss the announcement."

Rachel grabbed her bonnet and tied it on her head. "Fine, I'm ready."

Jacqueline ran to the front door, flung it open, and started outside, then stopped and looked back as if to make sure Rachel was coming. She hurried out and closed the door, surprised to see Main Street filled with people. Buggies and horses lined Bluebonnet Lane in both directions as far as she could see.

Jacqueline bounced. "Hurry, Ma. Looks like we're the only ones in the whole state who aren't there."

Rachel couldn't understand why her daughter was so excited. Didn't Jacqueline realize things would be different between her and Luke once he married? She saw Luke mount the boardwalk and stride straight and tall toward his office, where he was to make the announcement. She watched him go, her heart in her throat. How did one quit loving someone?

Her eyes stung, but she lifted her head high. God orchestrated the path she was to walk. He would give her the strength to face the future without Luke.

She glanced at the bank as she walked down Main Street. On Monday morning, she'd meet with Mr. Castleby and the mayor to finalize the sale of the boardinghouse. She hated leaving the only town she'd ever lived in, but Kansas City offered more for her daughter and a fresh start for them both.

Pressing her lips tight, she walked on, fortifying herself for the next few minutes. She stopped at the back edge of the crowd and stood on tiptoes, trying to find Leah and Shannon, but the crowd was too thick.

Jacqueline jumped up and down. "I can't see."

"Well, go stand over there on the boardwalk in front of the mercantile."

Jacqueline eyed her suspiciously. "You won't leave?"

Rachel was tempted to roll her eyes, feeling as if she were the child. "Not until it's over."

"All right then." Jacqueline dashed around the back of the crowd and up the steps to the boardwalk, squeezing past people, making her way toward Luke.

With so many taller men in front of Rachel, almost all wearing hats, she decided to take her own advice and crossed the street to the boardwalk opposite Luke's side of the road. Though the area was jam-packed with people, she squeezed her way up to the top step in front of the newspaper office. The jail was directly across from her, and she could see that Shannon and Leah stood on the ground in front of Luke's office.

The noise of the crowd was deafening, and so many people in one place made the summer afternoon seem even hotter. Rachel fanned her face with her hand. If this thing lasted very long, some of the women would be swooning. From the higher viewpoint, she could see that tables lined either side of Main Street farther down where women were selling refreshments. She'd opted not to do that at this event. Everything was far too festive for her mood. All she wanted was to go home and mourn the loss of the only man she'd ever loved. *Oh God, why did You have to bring him back if You were going to give him to someone else?*

The mayor shoved his way through the crowd in front of Luke, and both men stopped in front of the jail. Mayor Burke raised his hands and mouthed something she couldn't hear. The crowd suddenly quieted.

"Thank y'all for coming out on such a warm day, but it's a day of celebration. Our marshal is going to pick his bride today."

The crowd cheered in unison, and Rachel watched three tossed hats drop back down. She was probably the only person in the whole crowd not excited. Well, maybe except for the two brides. They knew only one of them would come up the winner today. Rachel was determined to do all she could to help the loser, whether the woman wanted to move on to another town or stay in Lookout and try to find employment, hard as that was in such a small town.

The mayor lifted his hands again, and the crowd quieted. "After the bride announcement, we'll have square dancing in the street, and don't forget all the marvelous confections the ladies of Lookout have created for y'all to enjoy."

He waited for the cheers to die down again. "And now for what we've all been waiting for, I'll turn things over to our marshal, Luke Davis."

Rachel swallowed hard as Luke stepped up to the porch railing. He was nearly a head taller than the mayor, and he was so strong, so capable—until she peered at his face. She'd seen him look nervous only a handful of times, and this was one of them. Was he unsure of his decision?

She clutched the porch railing to her left, afraid that she might just swoon herself.

Luke straightened, though his gaze roamed the crowd. When it collided with hers, he smiled and started talking. "I threatened to throw my cousins in jail once I learned they'd ordered three brides for me."

The crowd chuckled, but Rachel's heart had tripped over itself. How could Luke look at her like that? Was he counting on her friendship to make things easier for him?

Irritation worked its way through her body like a bad case of influenza. But then she snuffed it out. He was her friend, her oldest friend, and it was her Christian duty to help him. She would swallow her pride and disappointment and do what she could. In another week, she'd be on her way to Kansas City, and she'd no longer have to look at Luke and his bride, anyway.

"But God has a way of using strange circumstances to get our attention," Luke continued. "I gave my heart to the Lord less than a year ago. Though I've read my Bible a lot, I know there's still a lot I need to learn about walking the straight and narrow path God has set before me. Through this whole bride contest, the thing I've discovered is that God doesn't want me to walk it alone."

Luke's gaze captured Rachel's again as he stared across the street over the heads of the townsfolk. Why did he keep looking at her?

Now that she knew where the brides were, she no longer needed to see so well and made her way off the steps to the ground. Luke disappeared among a mass of heads and hats.

"It's true that no matter what I face or what any of y'all face, God will be there to help us through, if we'll only turn to Him."

Rachel figured Mayor Burke was most likely scowling at Luke's preaching, but she was proud that he would stand before such a large group and proclaim his faith. He'd changed a lot from the determined youth she'd first fallen in love with.

"I need to make a big apology to Miss Bennett and Miss O'Neil. I'm sorry, but I can't marry either of you. My heart—"

Many in the crowd gasped, and Rachel missed the last part of what he said. Suddenly, heads were turning and people were looking at her. Though tempted to back away, she held her ground. The crowd parted in front of her like the line in the middle of Mayor Burke's hair.

Someone nudged her in the back. "Go on up there, Rachel. He's asking for you."

Rachel's head swam, and she held her ground. Just coming here at all had been hard enough, but to go up front? Suddenly, Luke's words soaked in. He couldn't marry either bride? But he gave his word.

"Rachel, will you please come up here?"

Hands all around her gently shoved her. She either had to move forward or fall down. Heaving a heavy sigh, she ambled toward Luke. Why did he need her up there? Wasn't she mortified enough with half the town knowing their history?

All too soon, she stood in front of the crowd next to Luke,

though she couldn't say how she'd arrived at that place. Jacqueline peered around behind him, grinning as if it were Christmas. What was going on?

Luke took her hands, drawing her gaze to his. "Rachel, I loved you when we were ignorant youths, unaware of the hardships life could throw our way. I promised to marry, but I never said that I'd marry one of the boardinghouse brides. How could I, when my heart has always belonged to you?" He cocked his head, love making his dark eyes shine.

Rachel gasped, unable to believe what she was hearing. "You still love me?"

Luke grinned, taking her breath away. "Yeah, but my love was hidden under a quagmire of bitterness and unwillingness to forgive. It took nearly losing you to realize that I still cared. I'm so sorry for not forgiving you sooner."

She stepped closer, placing her fingers on his lips. "Shh…none of that. We're both forgiven. Let's not go backward."

Luke pulled her into his arms and leaned his head against hers. "Could you find it in your heart to marry me?"

Rachel closed her eyes as the words she never expected to hear filled her whole being. The tears that had threatened all day broke forth like a flash flood. She nodded. "Oh yes. There's nothing I'd like more in this world."

"Hey, we can't hear. What'd you say to her, Marshal?" Bertha Boyd shouted and shook her cane at them.

Jacqueline squeezed in between Rachel and Luke. "Did you ask her? What did she say?" She yanked on Rachel's skirts. "Say yes, Ma. Please say yes."

Luke raised a hand in the air, and the crowd quieted. "It's no secret that Rachel and I have a long history. Most of y'all know that. Well, I've asked her to marry me, and she has agreed."

The whole town erupted in cheers, hoots, and hollers. Jacqueline squealed and jumped up and down, wrapping her arms around them both. Luke bent and whispered something in the girl's ear, and she nodded and stepped back, grinning wide.

Luke pulled Rachel into his arms. "When will you marry me? Today?"

Rachel smiled through her tears, knowing now she'd most likely never live in Kansas City. "Not today, but very soon. A gal needs time to prepare for a wedding."

"Two weeks. That's all you get." Luke tugged her closer and lowered his mouth to hers, wiping away any lingering doubts of his devotion. All too soon he pulled away.

"One week," she said. "That's all I can bear to wait."

Love for her illuminated his eyes. He no longer looked at her with hurt or bitterness. God had forgiven them both and given them a future neither one could have anticipated.

Oh, thank You, Lord.

"There's just one thing." Luke pulled back and gazed at her. "Earlier, I told both Misses Bennett and O'Neil that I couldn't marry them, but what do we do about them?"

"I suppose we'll help them however we can, but it's best we leave the boardinghouse brides to God. Maybe He brought them to Lookout for another purpose."

Luke nodded and pulled Jacqueline into their embrace. Rachel marveled at how God could take a relationship that was torn to shreds and patch it, repair it, and make it into something wonderful, something stronger than it had originally been. Never again would she doubt God's hand at work in her life.

ABOUT THE AUTHOR

Award-winning author Vickie McDonough believes God is the ultimate designer of romance. She loves writing stories in which her characters find true love and grow in their faith. Vickie has published eighteen books. She is an active member of American Christian Fiction Writers and is currently serving as ACFW treasurer. Vickie has been a book reviewer for nine years as well. She is a wife of thirty-five years, mother of four sons, and grandmother to a feisty three-year-old girl. When not writing, she enjoys reading, watching movies, and traveling. Visit Vickie's Web site at www.vickiemcdonough.com.

Coming soon from

Vickie McDonough

Second Chance
Brides

Book 2 in the
Texas Broardinghouse Brides series

Available Fall 2010